Praise

"A decades-old mystery. A budding romance. Danger at every turn. Patricia Bradley delivers all this and more in *Fatal Witness*—an intense and entertaining journey from start to finish."

Reading Is My Superpower

"Smart, high action inspirational romantic suspense."

Booklist

Praise for *Counter Attack*

"Balancing a slow-burning romance with a twisty mystery, this will keep Bradley's fans hooked till the final page."

Publishers Weekly

"Patricia Bradley introduces her new Pearl River series with a bang with *Counter Attack*."

Life Is Story

"Buckle up, because *Counter Attack* by Patricia Bradley takes you on an intense ride!"

Reading Is My Superpower

"*Counter Attack* practically oozes with mesmerizing word flow, fascinating scene changes, and likable characters."

Interviews and Review

DEADLY REVENGE

BOOKS BY PATRICIA BRADLEY

LOGAN POINT SERIES

Shadows of the Past

A Promise to Protect

Gone Without a Trace

Silence in the Dark

MEMPHIS COLD CASE NOVELS

Justice Delayed

Justice Buried

Justice Betrayed

Justice Delivered

NATCHEZ TRACE PARK RANGERS

Standoff

Obsession

Crosshairs

Deception

PEARL RIVER

Counter Attack

Fatal Witness

Deadly Revenge

PEARL RIVER • 3

DEADLY REVENGE

PATRICIA BRADLEY

Revell

a division of Baker Publishing Group
Grand Rapids, Michigan

Published by Revell
a division of Baker Publishing Group
Grand Rapids, Michigan
RevellBooks.com

Printed in the United States of America

Library of Congress Cataloging-in-Publication Data
Names: Bradley, Patricia, 1945– author.
Title: Deadly revenge / Patricia Bradley.
Description: Grand Rapids, Michigan : Revell, a division of Baker Publishing Group, 2024. | Series: Pearl River ; #3
Identifiers: LCCN 2024005996 | ISBN 9780800741648 (paper) | ISBN 9780800746322 (casebound) | ISBN 9781493447107 (ebook)
Subjects: LCGFT: Thrillers (Fiction) | Detective and mystery fiction. | Christian fiction. | Novels.
Classification: LCC PS3602.R34275 D39 2024 | DDC 813/.6—dc23/eng/20240213
LC record available at https://lccn.loc.gov/2024005996

Cover design and images by Kirk DouPonce.

Baker Publishing Group publications use paper produced from sustainable forestry practices and postconsumer waste whenever possible.

24   25   26   27   28   29   30   7   6   5   4   3   2   1

To my Lord and Savior

"Let the words of my mouth,
and the meditation of my heart,
be acceptable in thy sight, O Lord,
my strength, and my redeemer."

Psalm 19:14

PROLOGUE

Chattanooga Detective Jenna Hart backed her ten-year-old unmarked Chevy into the church parking lot beside an even older Ford. If things went south, she could make a quick getaway. Not that she was expecting anything to go wrong.

Her confidential informant had indicated the Scorpions were meeting at the James A. Henry School tonight, and Rick Sebastian would be there. This was a first. Sebastian was slippery, and up until now, the Chattanooga Gang Unit had no hard evidence linking him to the Scorpions.

Captain Billingsley's instructions were only to gather intel and take photos. Jenna adjusted the camera on her shoulder and doused the car lights, plunging the area into darkness.

The moonless night and absence of streetlights hid her from prying eyes, but it also hid the drug dealers she'd come to monitor. Evil always preferred the darkness to light.

She climbed out of the Chevy and flinched at the screech of tires two streets over, barely relaxing when there was no follow-up crash. She scanned the area for a marked patrol car, noting a couple of working streetlights between her and the school a block away. Where was Officer Creasy? He should already be set up in case there was an opportunity for him to make an arrest.

The gang unit used two types of surveillance, passive and active, and her captain had made it plain she was only to observe and take photos, not to arrest anyone. If Jenna observed anything illegal, she was to alert Creasy, who was supposed to be in a marked patrol car two blocks away, and he could make the arrest without compromising her position.

She quickly called his cell number, and it went straight to voicemail. Jenna left him a message. "I'm here. Where are you?"

Maybe he wasn't coming. Creasy had made it plain when she'd worked in patrol that female officers should be relegated to handing out parking tickets. Jenna frowned. When she talked to him earlier, he *had* blown off her CI, saying he wasn't reliable. While she didn't think he would ignore the assignment, he could always plead that he got tied up in traffic or with another investigation.

For all she knew, Creasy could be hanging out with Phillip, her now ex-fiancé. They were buddies. Jenna had heard from one of the few friends she had at the precinct that her ex-fiancé and his cronies liked to gather at the bar, downing a few beers and coming up with new ways to make her look bad as a detective. Apparently it wasn't enough that Phillip had publicly blamed her for their breakup, even though she wasn't the one who broke off the engagement.

She clenched her jaw. Phillip wasn't going to win. She'd worked hard to become a detective, and she wasn't giving it up without a fight. She could understand if he wanted out of the relationship since they had been drifting apart, something she blamed on the long hours they both worked—her with the gang unit, and Phillip with homicide. She didn't understand why he was attacking her professionally. It was like a puzzle with pieces missing.

Where is Creasy? She didn't think the patrol officer would actually bail on her, but he was like a lot of other officers whose attitude toward the gangs was "Let 'em kill each other off."

Not that any of them ever said the words out loud. Jenna's concern was for the innocent people who got in the way.

She froze as a man in a hoodie materialized out of the darkness and jogged toward the empty school, throwing an occasional look over his shoulder. It was impossible to tell if it was Sebastian, but the jogger's lean frame was about right . . . except there was something familiar in the way the man moved.

She checked her phone again for a message from Creasy. Nothing. The meeting was going down, and if she waited, she would lose the opportunity to get intel.

Jenna was on her own, not that she actually needed the officer for backup—the whole point was to see who came to the meeting and get photos. She had no plans to do anything that would give her location away.

With a quick prayer and a deep breath, Jenna moved away from her car, rubbing her wet palm on her dark workout pants before checking her pistol. She hadn't taken time to change other than to buckle on a vest and her duty belt. She should blend in well with the dark area.

It wasn't that she had no fear of Sebastian—she did. It was rumored the drug dealer was a cold-blooded killer and responsible for the deaths of at least ten rival gang members. Jenna wanted to send him away for longer than the five years he faced if convicted on the current drug charges of cocaine possession, but rumors were all they had. Sebastian was careful, and without hard evidence and witnesses willing to testify, she had no proof of the murders, or that he even had a connection to the Scorpions.

Without that hard evidence, the DA couldn't bring up the deaths in court, not even for an indictment from a grand jury. While Jenna didn't expect to get evidence pointing to any murders tonight, she would get photographs of him with known Scorpion members. Perhaps one of them could be persuaded to turn state's evidence. And any intel she captured could be used at trial to put Sebastian away for a lot longer than five years.

Jenna took a second to text Creasy again.

> Where are you?

> Getting off 27. U?

> James A. Henry. If I observe anything of interest I'll radio you and you can intercept.

She blew tension from her lungs. Creasy was five minutes away. At least he was coming and should be ready by the time Jenna was in place.

She jogged toward the building, following the path of hoodie guy. Jenna turned a corner, and smack talk drew her attention. Sounded like it was coming from the apartments facing the school. She hugged the shadows of the school building and eased to where she could see what was going on.

A problem. That's what was going on. Five or six teenage boys were playing basketball under the security lights at the apartments. Jenna checked her watch. It was after midnight. Shouldn't they be in bed? Jenna didn't know why she was surprised they weren't.

After working the gang unit for two years, she shouldn't be surprised at anything. Besides, summer heat kept kids indoors during the day, and this was a way to let off steam.

Still, it complicated matters. Jenna couldn't help but worry that the teens might get caught in the crossfire if something went wrong in the meeting.

The hoodie guy stood off to one side, watching the game. Probably waiting for the drugs, so he wasn't Sebastian, but again, something about him seemed familiar. One of the boys broke away from the game and approached him. Jenna inched closer and hid in the dark shadow of the large trash receptacle.

"Hey, Ross!" The teen high-fived the man in the hoodie. "What's up?"

Ross? She blinked and stared at the man in the hoodie. It couldn't be.

"Not much, my man." He turned, and his face came into full view as he scanned the empty James A. Henry parking lot.

Phillip? Jenna's stomach plunged to her feet. *No.* She blinked, praying that she had seen wrong. But no amount of blinking would change the fact that the man was Phillip.

Maybe he was working undercover. No, Phillip headed up Chattanooga PD's homicide division. He'd never worked undercover.

Like a bolt from the clouds lighting up the sky, clarity exploded in her brain and the puzzle pieces fell into place. Suddenly all the times that Phillip had cancelled their dates made sense. And all the times he'd pumped her for information about the gangs . . . and Sebastian. The last time she'd asked him why he wanted to know. Now she understood—he'd been keeping tabs on how close she was to arresting his partner.

What a fool she'd been.

Jenna held her breath and pressed deeper into the shadows as Phillip's gaze swept past her hiding place before he turned back to the teenager.

"Meeting a friend," he said, dropping his voice.

Jenna caught that part, but once Phillip turned to face the teenager, she couldn't hear their conversation. They talked for a few minutes before the teen gave Phillip another high five.

My man. That's what he'd called the teenager. Her legs turned to rubber, and she braced against the wall. The boy was one of Phillip's dealers.

How had love blinded her so? Jenna hated what the gangs and drug dealers were doing to this neighborhood—just last week, two teens died in this very apartment complex from overdoses.

It was a never-ending problem that wouldn't go away until thugs like Sebastian were put in jail for good.

And Phillip was part of it. How much of what she'd passed on to him had benefited Sebastian?

Nausea hit her stomach so hard, she almost doubled over. Jenna clapped her hand over her mouth, swallowing the bile back down her throat. She had to get a grip. Sebastian would be here any minute. Jenna checked the time on her phone. Creasy should have texted he was in place by now too. No message from him, either.

Phillip turned toward her, and Jenna quickly snapped his photo with the digital single-reflex lens Canon, zooming in on his face. She was far enough away that he couldn't hear the sound the camera made. As a precaution, she used her phone to snap several and checked them. Grainy, but Phillip was identifiable.

Jenna emailed them to herself, wishing she had the same capability to send the photos on the camera. They would be clearer, which would be better for admission in court. She stayed in the shadows as the boy returned to the game and her ex remained on the sidelines.

Where was Sebastian? Minutes ago, she couldn't wait to photograph him. Now all she could think about was the fact that Phillip was somehow involved.

No wonder he'd been upset when she talked about bringing Sebastian in for questioning about the murder of a rival gang member.

"You'll never get evidence he was involved in the murder, and he'll accuse you of harassing him."

They'd argued, and he insisted it was because he was looking out for her career. She'd actually bought that when the DA agreed with him. But at least the arrest a couple of weeks ago for possession of two hundred grams of cocaine had stuck, even if he had made bail and was back on the streets within two hours. When

Sebastian was convicted—and he would be since there was no way he could wiggle out of those charges—he'd be looking at five years in a state penitentiary.

She wanted him gone for good, had been trying to nail him ever since transferring to Chattanooga's gang unit two years ago. He was like Teflon. Nothing stuck because no one had been able to get the goods on him. The message from her CI made her think that might change tonight. Jenna had to focus on that and deal with arresting Phillip when this was over.

Her heart stilled when a fancy Range Rover wheeled onto the school property and parked out of her line of sight. Three doors slammed. Probably two people in the front and one in the rear.

Jenna held her breath as Phillip jogged past her hiding place. Out of habit, she almost called out to him, thinking he would surely back her up. Evidently her mind hadn't processed the fact that her ex was a dirty cop. Once his footsteps faded, she slipped out of her hiding place and crept toward the corner of the building, then skirted what looked like a storage shed before she eased around it. Low murmuring reached her as she rounded another corner, and the Range Rover came into sight.

Instead of being near the back entrance, it was parked at the edge of the old school's parking lot in the shadows of an apartment building. The last unit with every light blazing caught her attention. *Lord, keep those people inside!*

A garbage dumpster sat near the Range Rover, and she wrinkled her nose as she caught a whiff of the sour odor emanating from it. If she could ignore the odor and reach the dumpster, she would be close enough to overhear their conversation.

Jenna hesitated. If she tried to reach it, she might give her position away, and that would blow the whole operation. Her current location would have to do. She raised the camera and framed the three men standing beside the SUV with Phillip facing them, his back to her. She zoomed in with the Canon for a good look at their faces. One was Sebastian, one she didn't recognize, but the other was Viper, a known Scorpion member.

No one had ever been able to put Sebastian in the company of the gang. Jenna quickly snapped half a dozen shots as an ambulance wailed its way to one of the nearby hospitals, covering the sound of her camera. To be on the safe side, she took a couple of shots with her phone.

She needed a photo of Phillip and Sebastian together. She quietly shifted her position, and using her phone again, she zoomed in on Sebastian just as Phillip turned and looked over his shoulder. Bingo! Captured both of them. Jenna took a second to check the photos. Way too grainy, and Sebastian was in the shadows. Maybe a video editing program could pull out the details. Again she sent the photos to her computer before she switched back to the Canon. One man turned toward the Range Rover, opened the hatch, and took out a package.

Showtime. Suddenly a dark Grand Cherokee wheeled into the parking area on two wheels. She ducked back behind the shed as three men spilled out of the Jeep with guns blazing. The man she hadn't recognized with Sebastian dropped to the ground.

Sebastian and Viper returned fire, quickly dispatching two of the men from the other SUV as Phillip took off running. The apartment door on the last unit opened, and a small boy darted out.

"Daddy!" he yelled, running to a fallen man who lay on the ground as bullets pinged the ground in front of the boy.

No! This kid wasn't dying tonight, even if it blew her operation.

"Chattanooga PD," she yelled, stepping away from the shed. She wanted to run to the kid, but that would only draw fire his way. "Drop your weapons and get on the ground!"

The remaining gang member from the Grand Cherokee wheeled and fired at her. Jenna barely felt the sting in her arm as she returned fire. The shooter fell to the ground. Silence filled the air. She quickly scanned the area for Phillip but didn't see him. She turned toward Sebastian and Viper.

Sebastian grabbed the boy and held a gun to his head. "Put your gun down," he ordered.

If Jenna did, she and the boy would die. Nothing like this should've happened tonight. This was supposed to be nothing more than gathering intel on Sebastian.

The boy squirmed against the drug dealer's hold.

Her surroundings fell away as she lasered in on the two. "No. Let the kid go. Put your gun down."

He shook his head. "Ain't happening."

Jenna kept her gun trained on Sebastian, but he used the boy like a shield. She couldn't take a chance on hitting the kid.

"Don't make matters worse for yourself by killing a kid and a cop." When he hesitated, she added, "Give yourself up."

A sneer formed on his lips as he turned toward her and barely shifted the gun away from the boy's head. Almost on cue, the boy screamed and flailed his arms and legs against Sebastian's body. "You killed my daddy!"

The boy wriggled out of his grip, and Jenna fired, hitting Sebastian in the chest. Instead of falling, he fired the automatic at her.

Her ears rang from gunfire. The last thing she remembered before blackness claimed her was the boy running for the apartment.

1

A little before midnight the man pulled his vehicle off the blacktop onto an abandoned logging road in the Cumberland Plateau in Russell County, Tennessee. Seconds later he climbed out and shot a glance toward thick clouds that smothered the full moon. A gust of wind brought with it the promise of a storm. Hurriedly he slipped on the night goggles, adjusted the strap, and set out for his target.

Fifteen minutes later he emerged from the woods that abutted the property belonging to former Pearl Springs city councilman Joe Slater. He couldn't see the back of the house, but darkened windows along the front indicated no one was up. The garage was connected to the house with a covered breezeway, and he crept toward a side door. Once inside, he found Slater's fancy SUV parked beside his wife's Escalade. The GMC Hummer was the only vehicle Slater drove.

He slid under the SUV and found the nut assembly that held the tie-rod in place. Using tools he'd brought with him, he pulled the cotter pin locking the castle nut in place and let it fall to the floor while he tackled the nut. Once it was off, he wrapped it in a handkerchief.

He crawled out from under the Hummer, and his heart almost stopped at the opening click of a door. He wriggled back and snapped his flashlight off a split second before the door opened. Overhead fluorescents lit up the room. He barely breathed while he slipped his hand in his pocket, where he carried a Glock sub-compact semiautomatic.

Footsteps approached the passenger side of the Hummer. Plaid pajamas and leather house slippers came into view and stopped so close, he could grab Slater's legs if he wanted to. The man muttered something under his breath about an insurance card as he opened the truck door and fumbled in the glove box.

"Told her it was there . . ." Slater grumbled and slammed the door. "Don't know why she couldn't wait till morning."

Less than a minute later, Slater killed the lights, plunging the garage into pitch darkness. Tension eased from the man's body, and he took a shaky breath. *That was close.*

He checked his watch and forced himself to wait thirty minutes before easing out of the garage with the castle nut in his pocket. As tempting as it was to keep it for a souvenir, it might be better to toss the nut on the shoulder of the road for the cops to find— that way they would think it simply came loose and fell off.

He was halfway across the front yard when a dog yapped. An ankle biter—it figured that Slater would have the kind of dog that sneaked up behind a person and sank its teeth into their ankle when they weren't looking.

The front porch light flickered on, revealing a large "Harrison Carter for Senate" sign in the yard. He stepped back into the shadow of the garage, his jaw clenched so tight that pain shot down his neck. After a few seconds, the dog quieted and the light went dark.

A whip-poor-will's lonely call filled the June night as he entered the woods. Legend said that the bird was an omen of death.

Thunder rumbled, and he turned and stared at the dark house. Slater had lined his pocket with taxpayers' money for the last time.

2

Jenna Hart sighed. The second week of June should smell like sunshine and honeysuckle, not gas fumes and death.

"What do you think happened?"

Jenna turned to Wayne Porter, the grizzled deputy assigned to work the accident with her. "Good question."

It was one Jenna intended to answer.

Wayne pulled a handkerchief from his back pocket and wiped his brow. "Has to be driver error—Slater took better care of that Hummer than he did his wife."

Jenna wished she was carrying a handkerchief. After four hours in the heat, several strands of wilted hair stuck to the back of her neck. While they waited for the wrecker attendant to attach the winch to the Hummer at the bottom of the gorge, Jenna removed her ball cap identifying her with the Russell County Sheriff's Office and fanned herself with it. "What if it wasn't an accident?"

He snorted. "Don't try making more of it than it is—this isn't Chattanooga."

Jenna swallowed the defensive words on the tip of her tongue. She was still the newbie here, and Wayne had been her field supervisor after Alex Stone, Russell County's chief deputy, hired her.

Instead she gathered her hair, redid her ponytail, and returned the cap to her head. The visor didn't offer much protection from the sun, but maybe it would be enough to keep more freckles from peppering her nose. Not that she had many—freckles were a rare combination with black hair. The black hair came from her dad and the freckles and her blue eyes from her mother. The mother Jenna lost when she was six.

"Rained last night." Wayne pointed toward the road. "But I don't think that had anything to do with what happened."

She didn't either. According to the victim's sister who'd just left the scene, the roads were dry when Joe Slater and his wife Katherine left for the airport in Chattanooga around seven.

The blacktop showed no sign he'd braked, only a scrape where the Hummer plunged off the road. What sent the sixtysomething Slater over the side of the mountain? Heart attack, maybe?

They should know soon enough if it was medical since the local coroner had sent the bodies of Slater and his wife to the Hamilton County Medical Examiner in Chattanooga for autopsy. Jenna turned as Chief Deputy Alexis Stone approached accompanied by . . .

Her heart froze. No. It couldn't be . . . Maxwell Anderson?

"What's the Tennessee Bureau of Investigation doing here?" she muttered.

"I think he's friends with the chief deputy," Wayne replied.

She barely had time to collect her thoughts before the two reached them.

"Jenna, you remember Max, don't you?" Alex asked.

She put her game face on, even as the memory of their one shared kiss sent heat to her cheeks. "Sure. Good to see you again."

That was the way to keep it. Cool and professional. She just hoped he did the same.

Max's lopsided smile didn't fool her. He wasn't happy to see her either, not with the way red was creeping up his neck—that'd always been the sign he was unhappy when someone messed up in their robbery division.

"Good to see you too." He turned to Alex. "Jenna was one of the best detectives I worked with in Chattanooga."

Ha! She certainly hadn't gotten that impression. If anyone had asked Jenna, which they never did, she would've told them he'd been harder on her than anyone else in the department. And if he thought that much of her, why had he kissed her at his going-away party and then ghosted her?

"So why do you think Slater tried to straighten a curve?" Alex asked. "Mechanical problem or driver error?"

Jenna shook her head. "Given this is a late-model Hummer, I doubt it was mechanical."

"Yeah," Wayne agreed. "Like I told Jenna, he babied that thing."

The whine of the winch made conversation impossible. They all turned toward the gorge as the front of the SUV came into sight, the right front wheel jutted at an odd angle.

Beside her, Max whistled and nodded toward the vehicle. "I think that's your answer. It appears the tie-rod came loose."

Jenna's eye twitched. It looked like Max hadn't changed—still Mr. Know-It-All. "That could've happened when the car went down the gorge."

"But if it happened before the accident, when Slater entered the curve, he wouldn't have had any control over the wheels," Max said.

Was he still a know-it-all if he turned out to be right? "Maybe someone loosened the nut assembly?"

"That's a big jump," he said.

Jenna cringed. She hadn't meant to say that out loud. "The vehicle is less than two years old. Why else would a castle nut come off?"

Max didn't say anything, just raised his eyebrows, a gesture she'd seen a hundred times while he waited for one of his detectives to remove their foot from their mouth. Well, she wasn't backing off her opinion, at least not until she heard from Alex.

Max looked toward the road. "If the nut that holds the tie-rod assembly in place came off before the accident, it should be around here somewhere."

"That sounds reasonable." Alex nodded to Jenna. "See if you and Wayne can find it."

The chief deputy's phone beeped, and Jenna waited while Alex glanced at the screen. Jenna wanted to be lead deputy in this case—*if* someone tampered with the car. It would be her first real case since joining the Russell County Sheriff's Office.

Alex looked up at Max. "Nathan is waiting for us." Then she turned to Jenna. "Max is here regarding threats made to Harrison Carter and the political rally he's holding at the Founders Day picnic on Saturday. There'll be a briefing at one. We'll go over anything you find here then."

Jenna nodded. "If it turns out to be more than an accident—"

"We'll talk about that if it happens." Alex turned, and she and Max strode to an SUV similar to the one Jenna had been assigned.

She'd wanted to ask about being assigned lead in the case if it turned out to be foul play, but now wasn't the time. "You ready?" she asked Wayne, tamping down the urge to give Max one last glance.

"Give me a minute to grab my hat."

"Sure." She felt someone watching her and glanced over her shoulder, her gaze colliding with Max's. He lifted his hand in a jaunty half salute. She gave him a nod and then turned and quickly walked to the wrecked Hummer as the tow truck operator prepared to lift it onto the flatbed truck.

"Hold up a sec." Sweat dripped from her brow, and she knuckled it away, then knelt beside the right tire and examined the tie-rod. Intact, and even with the dirt and debris the two-year-old vehicle picked up when it went down the gorge, everything about it was new looking—Slater must've hosed the SUV off every time he took it out, even the undercarriage.

She walked to the other side and checked it. Since only the left tie-rod assembly had broken away from the steering rack on the wheel, they were searching for one castle nut.

A quick check of the threads on the bolt showed the threads were clean rather than damaged. If the nut had worked its way off over a period of time, wear and tear would show on the threads . . . on the other hand, if someone removed the nut—

"You ready?" Wayne asked.

Jenna jumped. She hadn't heard him come up. "Let me grab a couple of waters first."

She opened the cooler in her SUV, pulled out the water, and tossed him a bottle as they backtracked on the path the Hummer had taken. The deputy didn't look good—probably the heat. "Look, you don't have to help. I can look for the nut by myself."

Wayne hesitated then shook his head. "No, I'll help. That way we can get through quicker."

"You sure?"

"I'm sure. You take the right and I'll take the left. And pray we find it soon so we don't have to walk all the way to the house."

Jenna laughed. She'd liked Wayne Porter from the start. He had a work ethic like her dad's—do your job so someone else doesn't have to do it. He would never shirk his duty, even if it killed him.

She noted several potholes on the road as she walked toward the Slater house—it'd been a bad winter and the county hadn't gotten around to repairing the lesser-traveled roads. Jenna kept her gaze glued to the blacktop and shoulder.

When they were halfway to the house, they stopped under the shade of an oak on the side of the road. It was a welcome relief from the sun, and she uncapped the bottle of water and tipped it to her lips. "What can you tell me about the Slaters? I don't remember much about them."

He took a deep draw from his bottle and put the cap back on. "Well, they're good people. Katherine is always doing something with the Garden Club—my wife's a member." He shook his head. "She's going to be awful upset when she hears about this. And Joe . . . everybody likes him, at least most everybody."

She noticed Wayne talked as though they were still alive. "Why do you say 'most'?"

"Joe was on the city council when the dam project went through. Almost everyone in town either had kin or knew somebody who had their land taken by the state to build it. A lot of hard feelings at the time."

She vaguely remembered something about the dam. "Do you know anyone who is still unhappy with him about what happened?"

"Could be anyone—this is a small county, and people tend to view everyone as family. But that doesn't mean they don't hold grudges."

Jenna agreed with him. It'd been that way when she was a kid, and evidently it was still that way. Could someone who'd had their land taken have sabotaged Slater's SUV? It was something to keep in mind. "You ready to look some more?"

"Sure." Wayne took off his cap and used his handkerchief to wipe his brow again. "It's hot for June."

Jenna started walking again, and Wayne followed suit, but they didn't find a castle nut. When they reached the drive, she walked toward the attached garage and found it locked. "I wonder if there's a key hidden outside somewhere?"

She approached the back of the two-story house and felt along the top of the door. Nothing. Maybe the Slaters had hidden one under a rock or—she glanced around the flower bed—a brick.

"What are you doing?" Wayne called.

"Looking for a key."

"We don't have a search warrant," he said.

"Why do we need one? The people who live here are dead."

Wayne eyed her like she should know why they needed one. "But they didn't die here, so we have no right to poke around in their private property," he said patiently.

How had she forgotten that? Maybe because she already viewed the accident as a crime, and somehow the legal ramifications had slipped her mind. "Let me text Alex and see what she wants us to do."

She quickly sent her boss a text, explaining they needed a warrant to get inside the garage.

The chief deputy's response was a quick text back. *"Not if Slater's sister will let us in. She lives up the road. I'll call and see if she'll meet you there, although it might be a minute."*

Jenna pocketed her phone. "Alex is getting in touch with the sister to let us in. You want to wait here or walk back to the accident site?"

Wayne glanced toward the road. "Let's go back and sit in air-conditioning."

Jenna grinned at him and followed him down the hill to the road. Sweat ran down the side of her face as she continued to search the road and shoulder. After half a mile, they reached the oak tree again. She glanced at Wayne. His uniform shirt stuck to his body. "We need to cool off a minute," she said.

"I thought you'd never suggest it."

"You know, you could've said something."

"And have you think I can't take the heat? No way."

That was exactly what she was thinking, but instead of saying anything, she took a swig of water. "Look, there's no need for both of us to look for the nut. When we reach our vehicles, why don't you sit in the air-conditioning and write up the report for the accident? And I'll keep looking."

"You sure?"

"I am. I'd rather do just about anything than paperwork." Plus she could look around Slater's garage to her heart's content.

27

Max climbed into Alex's SUV. Jenna looked great. Maybe not happy to see him, but that was his fault—he should have called her right after he left Chattanooga. Once again he felt his neck heating up. Talk about bad mistakes . . .

He brushed the memory aside and focused on his reason for being in Pearl Springs. He turned to the chief deputy. "How many people usually attend the Founders Day picnic?"

She flipped her signal on and turned onto the highway. "A couple thousand normally. With Harrison Carter here, maybe double."

That was more than enough for a killer to blend in with. If there was a killer.

"How serious is the threat to Carter here in Pearl Springs?" Alex asked.

"My superiors are taking it very seriously after they learned someone tried to run him off the road between here and Chattanooga last week. Carter chalked it up to an impatient driver until he received a threatening letter two days ago. That was Saturday, and I got the case Sunday."

"So it could be someone he upset while he was the Pearl Springs's mayor," she said and briefly glanced toward him. "But why wait this long? He hasn't been mayor for several years."

"Good question," he replied as Alex turned into the parking lot at the sheriff's office.

When they reached the chief deputy's office, Nathan Landry was waiting for them. Alex took a seat behind her desk, and Max extended his hand to the Pearl Springs police chief. "Good to see you again."

"You too." Nathan Landry grasped Max's hand firmly. "Sorry about having to delay our meeting."

"No problem. Riding to the accident scene gave Alex time to fill me in on the security measures you have planned for this Saturday's Founders Day picnic." And gave him an opportunity to see Jenna Hart again.

Nathan sat in one of the wingback chairs across from Alex's desk. "I'm not sure they're adequate after reading your email. Are you certain someone's going to try and take out Harrison Carter at the rally? Or could this be one of Carter's stunts to get publicity?"

Max settled in the other chair. "We discussed that possibility, but Carter doesn't want the fact that he's been threatened to get out—he wants a big crowd at the rally. As for being certain whoever it is will try Saturday, there's no way to know. The picnic seems like it could be a likely target—small police force. No offense intended."

"None taken, plus the park where the picnic takes place is easily accessed," Nathan added.

Alex nodded. "If I were going after our former mayor, it would be here—I'm two deputies short, and one of my best detectives is just past her introductory period. She's still new to the job."

His heart kicked up at the reference to Jenna. *Focus.* "How about your K-9 officer?" Alex had pulled him into a rescue operation for the K-9 officer and his dog a couple of months ago. What was the girl's name who was involved . . . "And the lovely Dani—how is she?"

"They're great. Mark and Gem are in Kentucky at the dog trials along with my grandparents, and Dani and her grandmother are with them. She even took her dog. Something about seeing if Lizi might be trained as a rescue dog."

"I heard Chattanooga PD used Dani's drawing skills to help find a robbery suspect," Max said as he took out a notepad and pen.

"They did," Alex said. "She's looking into taking a class on facial reconstruction, and with her sculpting talent, she'll be good."

"I'm glad she's settling in."

"What's your plan, Max?" Nathan asked.

"As soon as we finish here, I'll go to the park and see what we need," Max replied.

"I'll let the park director know you're coming." The police chief made himself a note.

Alex pulled out a pad. "Can you tell me how many officers we'll need for Saturday? I'd like to assign positions."

"I won't know until I see the park and draw the layout," Max said. "Then I'll email it to the logistics team to identify points of weakness and where we might need more manpower. Once I hear back, I'll email everything to you."

"Sounds good," Alex said. "I've called a briefing for this afternoon to discuss security at the picnic and go over what we know about the Slaters' accident."

"Do I need to be here?"

"Not necessarily. At this point I'll only be advising my deputies that we are beefing up security. Once you have your report, I'd appreciate you filling everyone in."

"Sounds good to me." Alex and Nathan were easy to work with, something he didn't always find to be true when working with local law enforcement. Sometimes a sheriff or chief of police resented it when TBI stepped into a case. He made a few notes and then looked up, smiling. "Didn't I hear you two set your wedding date?"

Nathan grinned. "Yep. Two weeks and Alex Stone will be Alexis Landry."

Alex grinned. "It was supposed to be this Sunday, but after Carter decided to hold his political rally, we postponed it a week."

"Postponed it? Wasn't that a lot of trouble?" Max had been involved with part of the wedding planning with his ex-fiancée, and doing something like moving the date would have been a logistical nightmare.

"Not so much," Alex said. "It's going to be really casual. We're having the ceremony at a friend's place on Eagle Ridge—Mae Richmond—and she and Gram are taking care of the food."

When things were simple to start with, he guessed making changes wasn't too hard. Max shifted in his chair. Talk of their wedding brought his ex-fiancée to mind. Shannon would've had a hard time rolling with the change. She liked events to be executed with precision. He straightened his shoulders and stood.

"In case I haven't told you, congratulations."

"Thank you." Both spoke at the same time.

"There you go—you're already on the same page." They all chuckled, and then Max added, "Thanks for working with me. I'll text you both when I finish at the park."

After the meeting with Nathan Landry and Alex, Max spent the next two hours wandering around the Pearl Springs Park, making notes and sketching the layout. It was a nice place with kids playing on the swings and slides.

He stopped at the steps leading up to a treehouse. For a second, he was tempted to climb up in it. On the other side, a spiral slide served as the exit. Today two young boys used the slide to climb up to the treehouse. He waved and smiled when they caught him watching them.

He wished he had kids. He was a good uncle to his brother's kids. But uncle wasn't all he wanted to be. He wanted to be a dad. And husband . . .

And why did Jenna pop into his mind?

Maybe because kissing her the night of his farewell party from the Chattanooga Police Department hadn't been a mistake. The mistake had been in not calling her afterward. He didn't blame her for being mad.

Either way, she wasn't over it. Or maybe she just wasn't interested. She was definitely different from the Jenna he remembered. He couldn't quite pin it down . . . sadder, maybe. Definitely softer than the brash detective he remembered.

Probably because of Phillip Ross. The homicide detective had been one reason he hadn't called Jenna once he was in Nashville—he'd heard from some of his former coworkers that she'd gotten engaged to Phillip.

Later the same coworkers had told him Phillip had broken the engagement, and Max should have called her then. But it'd been about that time that he'd been thrust into the middle of a hot murder case in the eastern corner of Tennessee. Working day and night, he hadn't even learned she'd been shot until weeks later. Max sighed. He wasn't proud of the way he'd buried himself in his work, but he was trying to do better.

Someone called his name, and he looked around. Two men approached, both wearing city park uniforms. Good. Nathan had said he would have the park director meet him.

"Maxwell Anderson?" the taller of the men asked.

"That's me."

"I'm Dave Martin, the director of Pearl Springs Parks and Recreation, and this is my assistant, Derrick Holliday. The police chief said you were here."

"Thanks for finding me." He held up his drawings. "I've been sketching the layout. Maybe you can tell me if I've missed anything." He nodded to a concrete picnic table a few feet away. "How about over there?"

He brushed off the table and showed them what he'd drawn.

32

"I've marked where each security person will be. What do you think? Have I left anything out other than the roads?"

Both men studied the maps and nodded. "Looks good to me," Martin said. His phone chimed, and he looked at it. "Excuse me a minute."

He turned away from them, and Max snapped photos of the drawings while he waited for Martin to finish his conversation. He looked over and caught Holliday studying him with a question on his face. "Yeah?"

"I can't understand why the TBI is interested in our little picnic," Holliday said. "Unless someone's made a threat against our illustrious former mayor."

Information about the threat against Carter was on a need-to-know basis, and neither of the men qualified. Still, Max didn't miss the sarcasm in the assistant director's voice. "You don't like Harrison Carter?"

"Didn't like him when he was mayor, and he certainly won't get my vote for senator."

"Why don't you like him?"

"He's crooked for one thing, and another . . ." His face turned red. "Let's just leave it at he's crooked."

Nothing Max had read in the background report said anything about Harrison Carter doing anything illegal. The report hadn't given any details of his tenure as mayor of Pearl Springs, only that he'd resigned from the office to run for the state senate four years ago. And now he was running for the US Senate. "Why do you say that?"

Holliday's face hardened. "The state took my grandparents' farm when Carter rammed that dam project through. He told everyone it would bring industry to this area, which was a lie." He crossed his arms. "And my grandparents didn't get near what the place was worth. You'll find quite a few people around here still upset about the dam and reservoir."

Max could understand people being upset about losing their land, but that didn't make Carter crooked. Still, it raised the idea that maybe the person who sent the letter to Carter was home-grown.

"How long ago are you talking about?"

"Depends on when you're talking about. Not many people know this, but our former mayor applied for a grant to build the dam while he was the city engineer. I know this because my aunt was his secretary, and that'd be . . ."—Holliday rubbed his temple—"at least twenty-seven, twenty-eight years ago. But if you're talking about the actual surveying and taking of the land, you're looking at around fifteen to twenty years ago."

Max dismissed what he'd been thinking. It was too long ago to have any bearing on the threats to Carter now. He was rolling up the maps to leave when Martin turned around, pocketing his phone. The man looked like he'd been sucker punched.

Martin blinked. "I can't believe it."

"What's wrong?" Holliday asked.

"That was my wife—she was really upset." He shook his head. "Joe Slater and his wife are dead. Killed this morning when his car went over a cliff just below their house." He turned to Max. "Do you happen to know anything about the wreck?"

Max nodded. "I rode to the accident site with Alex Stone, but I don't know any of the details, only that the bodies were sent to Chattanooga for autopsy."

Stunned silence followed, then Holliday shrugged. "That's really odd."

"What's that?" Martin said.

"We have a TBI agent interested in our little picnic where Carter is speaking, and now one of the men on the city council when he was mayor is dead . . ." Holliday scratched his head. "And there's Paul Nelson too."

"Who's Paul Nelson?" Max asked.

"He was a member of the city council same time Carter was mayor," Martin said.

"I don't understand."

"He comes to Pete's for morning coffee just like clockwork, sits in a corner by himself, and he didn't show up today," Holliday said. "Wonder if his car went off a cliff too?"

4

The sun beat down even hotter as Jenna trudged back up the hill toward the house. She was second-guessing her offer to Wayne as she searched for the nut that may or may not have come off of the Hummer and landed on the side of the road.

She was also second-guessing her instincts. The accident was probably just that—an accident. She straightened up and stretched her back. Second-guessing wasn't her only problem. Without Wayne as a distraction, her thoughts kept wandering to Max.

He'd looked hot today. And she wasn't thinking about the temperature.

Where had that come from? She quickly squashed the thought and couldn't believe she'd even had it. Not after the way he'd kissed her and then never called.

She focused on the side of the road, but her thoughts were soon back to Max. Next to Alex, he was the best boss she'd ever had. Even if he had expected more of her than others in their department. At the time she'd appreciated it, since she was on a fast track to make lieutenant.

And if Jenna was honest with herself, she would admit she'd

been attracted to Max, and she'd trusted him . . . until he didn't call her. *Just stop it!* Max was in her past, a past she'd vowed to never repeat, especially after the disaster with her ex-fiancé, Phillip Ross.

She would be crazy to ever trust a man again. *Just do your job. Find the castle nut if it's here.* Jenna renewed her search, and a few minutes later the sun glinted off something silver. She bent down for a closer look.

Yes! She'd found it! Jenna pulled on a pair of nitrile gloves and picked it up by the edges. She shaded her eyes and examined the nut. It didn't look wallowed out and certainly not stripped, but she couldn't tell if it'd been tampered with. They would have to send it off to a forensic lab to find that out.

She dropped it in a small evidence bag and turned to survey the road. When she worked with her dad on his old cars, sometimes they had to take a hammer to the tie-rod to get it loose. If the nut belonged to the Hummer, and this was where it worked loose, the tie-rod wouldn't necessarily have come out of the wheel joint at this point. Her gaze landed on a pothole ten feet from where the vehicle veered off the road. That hole would do it.

"Okay," she muttered out loud. The cotter pin would've come out first, so it should be between where she found the nut and the house.

She inched toward the house with renewed energy, scouring the limestone rock on the side of the road for metal. Her gaze landed on a thin piece of metal, and she stooped closer to the ground.

Just a nail. Jenna sighed. The pin could be anywhere . . . or nowhere.

No. Her instincts whispered that the bolt on the tie-rod would've been stripped if the nut came off when the vehicle went over the cliff. She kept walking and searching.

A good eighth of a mile farther, she blinked and looked again.

This time it wasn't a nail. A dull gray pin lay on top of the gravel. She picked it up and examined it. It was a cotter pin all right, but it wasn't shiny like the castle nut.

Red flags waved crazy in her head. Finding the pin and nut was too easy—it was like someone wanted them found. To cover up what actually happened? From the get-go the tie-rod coming loose on a practically new vehicle never made sense.

She turned and stared toward the house. Jenna had overheard one of the other deputies say he'd seen Slater in town yesterday. What if someone tampered with Joe Slater's Hummer last night?

A car pulled into the Slaters' drive. Alex had said the sister was coming to let her in the garage—maybe it was her. Jenna quickly texted Wayne, suggesting he return to the sheriff's office, that she would see him there. That done, she picked up her pace. Jenna didn't want the sister to leave before she got into the garage. What had Alex said her name was? Freeman. Emma Freeman.

She received a thumbs-up from Wayne just as she reached the drive. Good. As she approached, the woman stepped out of a white Lexus and stood, staring at the house. She turned as Jenna approached.

"Ms. Freeman. I'm Deputy Jenna Hart." She pulled off the sweaty gloves.

The older woman dipped her head. "Call me Emma."

"Thank you," Jenna said. "I didn't know your brother and sister-in-law, but I'm so sorry for your loss."

Emma Freeman dabbed a tissue at her red eyes, smearing mascara on her cheek. "I still can't believe they're gone." She took a deep breath and lifted her chin. "The wreck was an accident . . . I don't understand why you need to get into the house."

"Actually, I need access to the garage as well."

"The garage . . . why?"

"In a case like this, it's standard procedure."

"Oh."

When she didn't move, Jenna said gently, "I know this is hard for you, but would you mind letting me into the garage so I can look around?"

"Oh, of course." She fished a key from her purse. "This has just been such a shock."

A steady stream of information about the Slaters poured from the sister as they walked to the garage. Nerves, Jenna surmised, but she learned that Katherine Slater had been an avid member of the Garden Club and Joe had been on the city council until a few years ago.

Emma took her to a side door, and Jenna waited while she entered the code for the alarm and unlocked the door.

"The garage is attached to the house by a breezeway," Emma said, pointing to what looked like a long hallway to Jenna.

"Yes, ma'am."

"Please, call me Emma." She pushed open the door. "You make me feel old saying ma'am."

"Yes, ma—Emma. Thank you." Jenna pulled on a new pair of nitrile gloves. "I'll take it from here."

"There's a light switch just inside. While you look around, I'll unlock the house."

"Thank you," Jenna said. "Do you want me to lock the garage when I leave?"

"I'll take care of that."

Jenna nodded and entered the garage. Light flooded the building when she flipped the light switch. She did a double take. She'd never seen a garage so organized.

What few items the building contained were grouped according to their use—gardening tools on a pegboard on the back wall, carpenter tools mounted over a wooden bench with power tools beside them, and the other wall contained a cabinet.

Not that Jenna's garage looked like it was owned by a hoarder, but like most people she knew, if she didn't know what to do with something, she tended to stick it in her garage. Which was the reason she rarely parked in it. Jenna noted the empty spot next to a black Escalade.

"That's where he parked that monstrosity he owned, right next to Katherine's Escalade."

Jenna jumped. She thought Emma had gone to the house.

"Sorry. I didn't mean to startle you, but I just had to ask you something."

"Oh?" Jenna had been scanning the floor for the cotter pin and she looked up. She couldn't read the look on Emma's face, only that something wasn't sitting well with her.

"Driving over here, I kept wondering how something like this could happen. Joe is a very careful driver, and he knew that curve was there. There's no way he would have missed it." Her voice broke, and she covered her mouth with her hand.

The poor woman was hurting. She wished . . . Granna would know what to say . . . but Jenna didn't figure anything she said would help. So she waited.

After a minute Emma drew in a breath and released it. "He was so proud of that SUV—kept it in tiptop shape."

"I know this has to be hard . . ." Jenna always felt like she said the wrong thing—of course it was hard. But she really did mean it.

Emma wiped her eyes. "It is, and I guess I should let you get to whatever you need to do."

The sister didn't want to be alone. Not that Jenna blamed her, and there was really no need at this point to ask her to leave. Of course that would change if she found the cotter pin, but she would deal with that if and when.

"You can stay."

"Thank you. I won't bother you, I promise."

Jenna used the light on her phone to sweep back and forth over the area.

"What are you looking for?"

Already Jenna regretted her decision to let Emma stay. "Just looking."

There was nothing on the floor where Slater parked the Hummer. She tilted her head. If the pin came out here in the garage, it could've bounced.

She knelt and swept the light under the Cadillac. Jenna caught her breath when the light picked up a tiny object.

"Is something wrong?"

For a second she'd forgotten Emma. "No, but I'm going to crawl under the Cadillac."

She dropped to her stomach and scooted under the Escalade. Seconds later she carefully picked up a familiar piece of steel and scooted out. Jenna held the pin by the ends with her finger and thumb, careful not to touch the rest of it.

It wasn't broken. That meant someone pulled it out.

She'd been right all along!

"What did you find?" Emma asked.

Proof that someone murdered Joe Slater and his wife. Jenna raised her gaze to the hurting woman, and her elation dimmed. "Just something I need to show my boss."

5

From his hiding place above the accident scene, he scanned the area with his binoculars, recognizing each deputy at the site. Earlier his heart had almost stopped when there'd been another officer. White short-sleeve shirt, dark slacks—didn't look like a Russell County deputy. TBI, maybe, but why would Slater's accident attract the interest of a Bureau investigator? His nerves settled a little when the man left with the chief deputy.

Shifting the binoculars away from the accident scene, he found Jenna and watched as she walked toward the house. She had almost reached where he dropped the castle nut. *Don't miss it.* A smile thinned his lips as she knelt beside the road. He zoomed in the field glasses so he could see what she held in her hand.

Yes. She'd found the castle nut. *Good girl.*

Now that she'd found it, she would look harder for the pin. Earlier she and the other deputy had missed it. He watched as she examined the nut, then started walking toward the house. She knelt to pick up something. Too close to be the pin. She tossed whatever it was to the ground and walked on toward the house. Jenna stopped again right where he'd dropped the pin. After picking it up and examining it, she put it in a small bag.

He'd seen all he needed to see. Time to go.

Last night's events looped through his mind while he hiked through the woods to his truck. It had been a dumb mistake not picking up the cotter pin, but when Slater came into the garage, it'd startled him. He'd forgotten dropping it . . . until he woke this morning. He'd rushed over to search the garage, arriving just in time to see Slater deadbolt the door and set an alarm before they left.

Picking a lock, no big deal, but the alarm was a different matter. Slater hadn't set it the night before when he got in, and there hadn't been time to figure it out today. He'd rummaged around in the toolbox on the back of his pickup until he found a cotter pin and then planted it along the road.

Killing someone was the easy part. Manipulating the evidence was another matter.

6

Jenna tapped her hand on her leg, waiting for Emma to lock up, the cotter pin practically burning a hole in her pocket. Then she walked with Emma to her Lexus. "Thanks for letting me in."

"You're welcome." She glanced around. "Where's your car?"

"It's—" She'd almost said at the crime scene. "Down the hill."

"Oh." Emma glanced toward the road. "Uh . . . do you want me to drop you off?"

Jenna shook her head. She would not ask the woman to revisit the site of her brother's death. "It won't take me a minute to jog down there, but thanks."

"I-I hate for you—"

They shifted their attention as a pickup with a flashing yellow light on top came into view at the bottom of the hill. Her dad, delivering the mail. She groaned silently. He would also want to know what was going on. She might as well tell him since it would be all over the county by afternoon, anyway. If it wasn't already. "That's my dad. He'll give me a ride."

"I'll walk to the mailbox with you—I need to get their mail."

It was probably a good idea for someone to be with her. That way her dad would be hesitant to try and pry information from Jenna.

"So your dad's our mailman? He's such a nice man."

"Thank you." She'd never thought about the way other people viewed him. "He raised me after my mom died and can be somewhat of a micromanager . . . bless his heart."

Emma laughed. "That's family for you. Joe is like . . ." Her voice faltered. "My brother was like that as well."

They arrived at the mailbox at the same time as her dad.

"I thought you might be here." He turned his attention to Emma. "Mrs. Freeman, I'm so sorry about Joe and Katherine."

He'd heard already? Cell phones must be buzzing in Russell County this morning.

Emma paled slightly. "Thank you," she murmured and turned to Jenna. "If you don't need me, I need to leave . . . there's so much to take care of."

"Would you like their mail?" her dad asked.

"Oh yes, of course."

He handed her a bundle of letters and advertisements. "If you'd like, I'll leave their mail at your house until you decide what you want to do about it."

"You're so kind." She turned to Jenna. "And you have been as well."

A lump formed at the back of her throat, and she cleared it. "Thanks again for letting me into the garage. Someone will let you know if we need in again."

Jenna waited until Emma was out of earshot before turning back to her dad. "How did you know?"

"Got a text that Joe Slater had a wreck. I didn't know they'd died until I met the wrecker at the turnoff. The driver was making sure the SUV was tied down good. He told me, but I would've known anyway as bad as the Hummer looks." A wince flashed across his face. "That's a terrible way to go."

"Yeah." She started to ask him to run her down to her SUV, but his seats were full. Walking was good exercise, anyway. "How well did you know the Slaters?"

"Didn't really know her, but I always thought Slater was a pretty good old boy when we coon hunted together. Of course, that was after we got past him voting for the dam project."

"So you knew him pretty well?"

Her dad dipped his head. "I wouldn't say well since it's been a while. He quit hunting a couple of years ago and sold his dog. I would've bought the dog if I'd known he was for sale." He shook his head. "He was a good dog."

Her dad ought to know. Between him and his brother, Sam, they had the finest hunting dogs in the county and probably the state.

Her dad turned to Jenna. "Speaking of coon dogs, Sam and I have a young dog we're training. Planning to run him up on Eagle Ridge tonight, if you want to tag along. There'll be a couple of other dogs too."

It'd been years since she'd gone with her dad and uncle to work their dogs. It'd been fun as a teenager, but now? Jenna wasn't sure she wanted to trek through the woods half the night. Still, she might hear something about Joe Slater she wouldn't learn knocking on doors. If it was like it used to be, gossip was one thing her dad and his hunting buddies excelled at. "What time?"

"Since we're not hunting, we don't have to wait all that late. We'll leave the house about nine. Want me to drop by your place and pick you up?"

"No, I'll drive to your place and follow you in my SUV," she said. That way she wouldn't be dependent on him for a ride home if the young dog didn't come when called. She'd known of her dad staying out until daybreak tracking a dog in training.

Her dad nodded toward the house. "Can't say I'm surprised to see you here."

Jenna stilled. "Why's that?"

Her dad shrugged. "I heard someone tried to run Harrison Carter off the road last week, and now this. Paul Nelson might want to watch his back."

She frowned. "I don't understand."

"You wouldn't remember, but the three of them did mighty well when that dam and reservoir went in." He put his truck in gear. "Not everybody's forgotten that."

7

Max left the men talking about the Slaters and texted Alex that he was coming by. The information he'd learned about Slater, Carter, and Nelson piqued his interest even if it was from twenty years ago. He wanted to talk to Alex and anyone else who might have more information.

But mainly he wanted to see Jenna. He owed her a long overdue apology for that public kiss. The thought had gnawed at him ever since he'd seen her earlier today. But because he'd never tried to make it right, she might not accept his apology.

Max had regretted kissing her the minute he'd done it. He shifted in his seat as his conscience lobbed a dart at his heart. Okay, maybe he hadn't totally regretted it—it'd been an amazing kiss, one that she had returned.

He turned into the parking lot at the sheriff's office. Max parked and grabbed his satchel with the maps and walked to the visitor's access. Inside, he told the deputy on guard duty that he was there to see the sheriff. After a quick phone call, he was ushered through the doors.

The guard started to direct him to Alex's office, and he remembered to smile when he let the guard know he knew where it was. "Is Jenna Hart here as well?"

"I believe they're all in the conference room."

"Thanks." He'd seen the conference room earlier and strode down the hall. The door was closed, and he rapped on it. His heart kicked up a notch when Jenna opened it. From the way her eyes widened, she was just as startled.

"We have a meeting just starting," she said.

"I know. Alex is expecting me."

"Oh, sorry." She opened the door wider to let him pass and returned to her seat.

He stepped inside and scanned the room, looking for a place to sit. He noticed there was an empty seat beside Jenna in the back row. Perfect.

"Do you mind?" He mouthed the words to Jenna as he sat in the adjacent chair.

She shot him a cool glance. "Of course not."

Alex cleared her throat. "As you all know, Harrison Carter has made our Founders Day picnic one of his campaign stops. What you don't know, and this isn't for public knowledge, is that Carter has received threats on his life. It's why TBI Agent Maxwell Anderson is here. Max, introduce yourself so everyone will know who you are."

Max stood and gave a wave. "I emailed the park layout to the logistics team and will have more information in the morning on where everyone will be assigned."

"Thank you." Alex discussed the estimated crowd and Carter's schedule before asking for questions. When there were none, she turned to Jenna. "Now for the Slater accident. Jenna is responsible for an interesting development that may make us rule this a homicide rather than an accident."

A murmur went around the room, and everyone turned to look at Jenna.

"You want to come up and explain what you found?" Alex motioned her forward.

She stiffened. "Me? I thought you would—"

"No. It's your case."

Jenna's breath hitched, not loud enough for anyone except him to hear, but it told him Jenna hadn't known she would be lead on the case.

She stood and strode to the metal lectern. "Thank you," she said to the chief deputy then turned to face the others.

"When the wrecker service winched the Hummer to the road, it revealed the tie-rod had come loose. With the vehicle being so new, it didn't make sense, especially since the bolt holding it together wasn't stripped, so I looked for the missing castle nut."

Max listened as she detailed how she found the cotter pin. She had good instincts—it was one of the things he'd admired about her when she worked robbery. That, and she could think like a criminal. Chattanooga lost a good detective when she left.

"While this isn't conclusive proof of a crime, we'll follow what we have and see if it leads to homicide." Jenna scanned the room. "I would appreciate it if you let me know if you hear anything that might help us to decide one way or the other. Any questions?"

Max raised his hand. "I don't know how pertinent it is, but I understand Joe Slater was a former city council member. I'd like to talk with anyone who remembers anything unusual happening during that time . . . anything that would connect his death to Harrison Carter."

"You think the threats against Carter are connected to this accident?"

"I don't know, but I heard that some people still hold a grudge against the mayor and city council for pushing through the dam project."

Jenna frowned. "Most people don't wait twenty-odd years to get revenge."

"Just a thought," he said. "Oh, can anyone tell me if they've seen someone named Paul Nelson today?"

Jenna crossed her arms. "What does he have to do with this?"

Alex approached the lectern. "There's no need to hold everyone else up. Why don't we discuss this in my office after the meeting?"

8

A few minutes later they gathered in Alex's office. Jenna sat by the window, as far as she could get from him. This wasn't going quite how he'd envisioned.

"Okay," Alex said. "Why don't you tell me about Paul Nelson? He's on my list of people to contact about Joe Slater."

"I don't know much more than I said in the meeting. It seems there are several men who drink coffee at Pete's every morning, and Derrick Holliday said Paul didn't show up, and he thought it was strange, particularly after Joe Slater was killed. I thought you ought to know."

"I appreciate it." She turned to Jenna. "I want to apologize for springing it on you that you're the lead investigator in the Slater case, but I didn't get a chance to tell you before the meeting."

"Don't apologize. I'm just happy you think I'm qualified."

"I figure you're more than qualified," Alex said dryly.

Jenna pulled two evidence bags from her pocket. "You want me to give these to Dylan? He can examine them and see if there are any wrench marks on the castle nut."

Alex shook her head. "We better use a lab."

"Why don't you let me take them to our lab in Nashville?" Max offered.

Jenna crossed her arms. "I heard they were way behind."

"They are, but I know someone who'll put the castle nut under the microscope ASAP and tell you if it was tampered with."

"Think we'll know something by tomorrow?" Alex asked.

"No later than Wednesday."

The chief deputy nodded to Jenna. "Give him the evidence." She stood and shifted her attention to Max. "Nathan and I are going to drive out to Nelson's place and talk to him . . . would you like to ride along?"

"Normally I would, but I think I'll stay here and write up my report and make copies of the maps. I'll write up a request for the lab on the castle nut while I'm at it."

"You can use my office if you'd like." She turned to Jenna. "Max needs to give you background information on Harrison Carter. This is a good time to do that."

Even though Jenna didn't make a sound, Max could imagine the groan she suppressed. Instead she nodded.

When Alex walked out the door, dead silence followed.

Jenna spoke first. She placed the evidence from the scene on the desk. "I suppose you need these."

She was using her calm-under-fire voice. He stood and walked across the room and placed the bags in his briefcase.

"The forensic tech I'm taking these to should be able to tell if there are any scratches on it. I don't think she can do anything with the cotter pin, though."

"Thank you for doing this." At least her voice was a tiny bit warmer.

"It's not a problem. Oh, and we need to exchange phone numbers—in case one of us has a need." He rattled his number off. Seconds later his phone rang.

"Now you have mine," Jenna said.

Silence fell between them again, but it wasn't as cold. This was his one shot to apologize—after today, it would be even more awkward to bring the problem up. If only he could get the words out of his mouth . . . it felt like someone had stuffed it with cotton. "Any bottles of water around here?"

"In the break room." Her mouth twitched. "I'll get you one."

Way to go, Anderson. He'd just given her an opportunity to walk out of the room and keep walking. But she returned and handed him a bottle. He uncapped it and tipped it to his lips. *Just do it.*

"You're looking good," he said. "Being a Russell County deputy must agree with you."

A blush rose in her cheeks. "I guess."

"So, how do you like it?"

"Fine."

She wasn't giving him anything to build a conversation on. "Look, I need to clear the air. I never should have kissed you . . . and . . . and I'm sorry I didn't call. I'm not going to offer any excuses, but I'd like a chance to make amends."

She stared at him like he was a bug under a microscope, then she nodded. "Apology accepted. Now can we discuss Harrison Carter?"

She'd accepted his apology? He frowned. So why didn't it feel like she had? He looked up to see her staring expectantly at him.

"Yeah. Carter." Max had made a total mess out of it—he should've asked her out to a nice restaurant to apologize. Things like that went better with food. No, that would have made it worse. Like she'd even go on a date with him.

"Does the TBI check out every political rally when a candidate gets threats?" she asked. "Isn't that pretty common now?"

"Common enough, but someone tried to run Carter off the road a week ago."

"My dad mentioned that when he delivered the Slaters' mail."

Max frowned. "That hasn't been released to the public. How did he hear about it?"

"You'll have to ask him—he didn't say."

He nodded. "Carter passed it off as an impatient driver until he received a threatening letter. Let me get my tablet."

He opened it to his notes and focused on bringing her up to speed on Carter's case.

When he finished, she said, "You're cutting it awfully close. The political rally is Saturday."

"Tell me about it, but we didn't know we needed extra security measures until yesterday when they advised us about the letter."

Jenna wrote something on her tablet. "What did the letter say?"

He took out his phone. "I photographed it."

Max held out his phone with the picture. Instead of typed words, someone had cut letters from newspapers and magazines to write the message. *You've lined your last pocket.*

"Okay. Definitely a threat," she said.

"Coupled with the near accident that other agents are investigating, we're not taking any chances."

She looked over her notes. "What time is he arriving in Pearl Springs Saturday?"

"According to his campaign manager, around four that afternoon. He'll make his speech around six then mingle with the crowd before the fireworks begin at dark."

"That means he'll be here at least six hours," Jenna said. "If someone really is threatening him, the time around the fireworks display will be a perfect opportunity to take him out. Any chance of getting him to leave right after his speech?"

Max shook his head. "Already asked. He has family here—he sees it as a photo op."

"It won't be if someone carries through on their threat," she said dryly. "Since you seem to be in the know, have Nathan and Alex said how many officers are available?"

At least Jenna was warming up to the idea of them working together. "Ten total. The city is providing one for the platform—

the others will be busy with traffic control. Russell County is providing the rest."

"And from TBI?"

He shrugged. "You're looking at him . . . unless the threat level goes up. Right now, it's a four on a scale of one to ten."

Jenna's eyes widened. "But there'll be at least three thousand people at the picnic! Ninety-nine percent of those will stay for the fireworks."

"Everyone is short-staffed," Max said. "Carter's campaign is providing four bodyguards for him."

"I guess that's better than nothing. We'll have to work with what we have." She tapped her pen on the tablet. "How long will you be in town?"

"Until after Saturday."

She nodded and checked her watch, then slid her tablet in a backpack and stood.

"I have to leave. Thanks for filling me in. If I learn anything I think will help you with your case, I'll pass it along."

"I'd appreciate it," he said. "I guess I'll see you tomorrow?"

"Sure."

Okay, it was now or never. "Jenna," he said when she reached the door.

She stopped and looked back at him.

"Be okay if I call you later tonight? That is, if I hear anything from my logistics team?"

For the first time she gave him a familiar smile.

"Sorry. I'm going coon hunting with my dad."

9

Jenna stopped at Wayne's desk on her way out. "Thanks for doing the report."

He looked up and grinned, deepening the wrinkles in his face. "Thank you for not making me stay out in that heat. And good job on finding that pin."

She took a satisfying breath, expanding her lungs. "It feels good to be right for once."

"I know what you mean."

He stood, and she caught a whiff of his cologne. It was similar to whatever Max wore. Not that she'd noticed.

"What's the name of your cologne?" The scent was familiar, but she couldn't quite place it. "My dad's birthday is coming up, and I hate the harsh stuff he's using now."

Wayne shrugged. "You'll have to ask my wife—she always gives it to me at Christmas. You on your way out?"

She nodded.

"Me too—Sylvia wants me home early tonight. I'll walk out with you."

She waited while he grabbed a briefcase. "More paperwork?"

"Research. Alex pretty well let me know I'd be on the platform with Carter Saturday, so I pulled a few articles about him I found on the internet."

Wayne was thorough, for sure. "Pass along anything you think I need to know for this case."

"Will do. What do you think of our TBI agent?"

Jenna hesitated a half beat then said, "Max is a good investigator."

"But?"

"No buts. Any negative feelings I have toward him has nothing to do with how he does his job."

"So, you two were an item—bad breakup."

"No." How could she explain? Jenna rubbed the back of her neck.

"Professional jealousy?"

"It's not like that either." If she hadn't worked so closely with the older detective since becoming a Russell County deputy, she would've been offended. But Wayne called things as he saw them. With everyone. "It's complicated."

"Well, you might want to get it uncomplicated since it looks like Alex will probably have you working with him."

She sincerely hoped not.

They approached their vehicles, and Wayne opened his car door. "She's like her grandfather, Sheriff Stone—she'll do whatever it takes to solve a case." He nodded. "See you tomorrow."

With the thought of being paired with Max hanging over her, she climbed into her SUV and pulled out of the parking lot, pointing the vehicle toward the road out of town. She quickly dismissed any negative thoughts and focused on Alex's approval. Approval had been sorely lacking at her job in Chattanooga.

Memories of those last months with the police department dimmed her enthusiasm. She shook off the dark thoughts. She was lead investigator on this case. Mark and his K-9 partner, Gem, had been lead on the case in April. Would Alex have given her this case if Mark and Gem were here? Maybe so. Jenna had found the critical clue.

She rubbed the scar on her shoulder that would always remind her of the bullet that got past the body armor. She'd never second-guessed herself before the shooting in Chattanooga. It wasn't so much because of the shooting itself—every time she strapped on a gun, she knew there was a possibility of getting shot. Jenna also knew from experience that body armor didn't cover everything, but the vest had protected her from five of the six shots Sebastian fired.

It was afterward that destroyed her confidence—the rumors that she was a dirty cop and then the way her superiors had consigned Jenna to a desk job even after the department psychologist released her to return to work. She blamed part of that on the fiasco with Phillip.

If only she'd known her camera and phone had been stolen before she reported to Billingsley that Phillip had been at the school, but Phillip denied it. And a cop buddy backed him up. Said he was watching a Braves game with them. Then, Phillip had painted a picture of her being a scorned and vindictive woman to anyone in the department who would listen.

There hadn't been a thing she could do about it with the camera and her phone gone. If it weren't for the blurry images she'd emailed to her computer, she couldn't even prove to herself Phillip was there. Unfortunately, the phone photos didn't have a time stamp or even the school on them, so she never showed them to anyone—Phillip would only use them to further his vindictive woman image.

He'd betrayed her, and not just her, but every honest cop out there. The inability to bring him to justice still gnawed at her.

But Jenna believed justice was important to God, and one day Phillip's crimes would catch up with him. Until then, she had to take each day as it came. She'd been doing okay until Max showed up today and brought everything flooding back.

The shock of seeing Phillip with the drug dealer. The betrayal. The rumors she couldn't prove started with him. Rumors that had no basis in truth—rumors like she'd set up a drug deal with Sebastian.

Jenna had been there for surveillance. But because it'd been last minute, and the information about Sebastian's meeting with the Scorpions came from her CI, and because some officers tended to believe the worst, there'd been no way to defend herself against the rumors. People either believed her or the lies.

Since Max never reached out to her, she'd assumed that he'd landed on the side of the lies. But what if he hadn't heard the rumors? He hadn't been in Chattanooga when it happened . . .

She grunted. *He'd heard*. Max still had buddies at Chat PD, and they would have been sure to let him know one of his former detectives was suspected of being a dirty cop.

Ten minutes later, Jenna turned into the barn where she boarded her dressage horse. The barn was her safe place. The place she could leave the job, her past, everything behind, and lose herself in another world for an hour.

She grabbed a change of clothes and strode into the barn, glad it had a place for her to change.

"Hey, Kirk." She ruffled the tween's hair. Did you even call a twelve-year-old boy a tween, or was that reserved only for girls? "How's it going?"

"It'll be better when I get these stalls clean," the boy grumbled. "Granddad said I could ride my four-wheeler then."

She glanced around at the stalls. "Looks like you're doing a good job."

"Granddad won't think so."

Jenna turned so he wouldn't see her smile. Bryan Bishop and

his wife were doing a good job of raising Kirk after his parents died. "You'll be thankful one day he cared enough to make you do it right."

She ought to know—her dad had been the same way. If he'd just stay out of her business now.

Ace nickered, and she hurried to his stall. "Hey, big boy." Jenna rubbed his nose. Since she was going hunting with her dad, she didn't have time to ride today. She turned back to Kirk.

"Okay if I turn him out in the paddock?"

"I guess—no one's coming to ride today."

She put a halter on the black gelding and led him to the paddock, where she turned him loose. Ace pranced around the enclosed area bucking and jumping. Jenna chuckled at his antics. She loved watching him run free.

The horse knelt and laid in the soft dirt, rolling from one side to the other, then clambered to his feet and shook himself before he took off running again, only to abruptly stop. He snorted and stared toward the wooded area that bounded the small river at the back of the property.

Ace stamped his foot and tossed his head. She followed his gaze to the woods. A flash of light had her spidey-sense tingling. Jenna blinked, and the light was gone. Had she imagined it? She certainly hadn't imagined Ace's behavior. But why would anyone be watching her?

She shook the thought off, hating the paranoia she'd had since getting shot. Jenna scanned the woods again, seeing no sign of anyone. Ace trotted over, and she patted his neck. "I'll be back in a minute."

She halfway considered bringing him back to his stall and working around him as she cleaned it. Once again, she glanced toward the trees, seeing nothing unusual, and forced herself to return to the barn.

Jenna set to work cleaning the stall. The psychologist she'd seen after the shooting said most of the symptoms of her PTSD would leave, and they had. She no longer fainted at the sight of blood, which had been extremely embarrassing for a cop. And she didn't freeze when she heard the sound of gunfire.

She hadn't complained in the beginning when her superiors assigned her to a desk job. It was for the best, but once the psychologist cleared her, she didn't understand why they hadn't allowed her to resume her normal job. In the end, the desk job was the reason she'd moved home to Pearl Springs to create a new life for herself. Away from everything to do with her old life in Chattanooga.

Alex had believed in her when no one else did, and Jenna would do whatever it took to live up to the chief deputy's expectations. She smiled to herself. Alex had been impressed when she found the pin, and she would be even more impressed when Jenna solved the case. Some of the excitement of getting the lead in the investigation returned, energizing her.

When she finished mucking the stall, she filled Ace's water bucket and added feed and hay to the trough. The horse was waiting for her when she went to the paddock after him, and she whistled for him to come. He trotted to her while Jenna checked the woods again, feeling just a little foolish when everything looked normal.

Thirty minutes later she pulled into her driveway and parked in front of the garage she used more for storage than for her SUV. Her house wasn't large, but it fit her. She liked to think it was cozy. Jenna climbed out of the SUV and entered her house through the kitchen, automatically checking to see if everything was the way she'd left it this morning.

Clearing her house each time she returned was another by-product of the shooting, a habit Jenna hadn't been able to break yet. Tonight everything looked okay, but a lingering doubt troubled her even after she checked the almost invisible strip of tape on the fake electrical outlet.

The overhead light flickered, and in her mind's eye, she saw the flash of light in the woods from earlier. That explained her unease. She was still on edge.

Jenna turned to go back to the kitchen to make supper when she caught a faint whiff of . . . She sniffed the air. An expensive men's cologne, the same one she'd asked Wayne about.

Cold sweat popped out on her face. Now she remembered why it had seemed familiar. It was the same distinctive cologne she'd noticed Rick Sebastian wore the few times she'd been around him.

But that was impossible . . . wasn't it? Maybe not impossible, but Sebastian was in prison. He couldn't be in Russell County and certainly not in her house. Wayne's cologne must've transferred to her clothing someway.

A twinge shot through Jenna's shoulder, and she rubbed the scar again. She hated the paranoia that sometimes controlled her emotions.

A text chimed, and she grabbed her phone, glad to focus on something besides her past.

Her eyes widened. Max. She'd known giving him her phone number was a bad idea. But it wasn't like she'd had any choice. She opened the message.

It's Max, in case you don't recognize the number. Just trying to get my foot out of my mouth again. I shouldn't have asked you if I could call tonight—any call could've waited until morning. It won't happen a second time.

Three dots. He was typing something else.

It was great seeing you today.

63

Jenna stared at the message. How was she supposed to respond to that? She needed something to drink first. After laying her phone on the counter, she opened her cabinet to grab a glass.

Good grief. Reorganizing her cabinets had been on her weekend to-do list . . . maybe next weekend. She wasn't quite sure how she'd let her goblets and mugs get stuck on the same shelf with the plates . . . or how she'd let the over-the-counter drugs get scattered on every shelf. If Granna saw this mess, she would scold her for sure.

Jenna grabbed a glass. Right now she needed tea so she could answer Max's text and then change to go with her dad. She'd deal with her cabinets tomorrow . . . Procrastination seemed to be her middle name lately and probably why the cabinets needed straightening.

She filled the glass with crushed ice and grabbed the pitcher of tea she'd made this morning, making it a point not to check out how bad her fridge looked. Jenna padded to her sofa and curled up at the end and took a long sip of the sugary drink. Everyone talked about comfort food, but there was nothing like sweet tea to make the world right.

She read the text again. Max was trying. Now Jenna felt kind of bad about blowing him off earlier.

He wasn't going away anytime soon, at least not until after the political rally. She would be seeing him every day.

Why did that make her heart speed up?

She hesitated before she started typing.

> No need to apologize. It was appreciated that you asked.

Jenna deleted the last sentence.

> It was nice that you asked. And it was business.

That wasn't quite as stiff. Her finger hovered over the send button, then she began typing again.

> If you need help with the park security, let me know.

Jenna hit send.

She hadn't added that last because she wanted to spend more time with him. It was just common courtesy.

10

Twilight cast a shadowy light as he rounded a curve and turned off the blacktop onto an old logging road. His lights bounced as he wrestled with the steering wheel to keep his truck out of the deeper ruts in the narrow lane. Couldn't afford to get stuck, not with his cargo.

He pulled to a stop at the location he'd picked out earlier and climbed out of the truck. Mosquitos buzzed his head as the muggy night wrapped around him. Waving them off, he lowered the tailgate and pulled the body wrapped in a tarp to the end of the bed and eased it to the ground. Humidity thick enough to swim in soon had him panting from the exertion of pulling the tarp with the dead man in it over the terrain.

Sweat drenched his shirt by the time he reached the spot he'd picked out. He rolled the body into a shallow trench hollowed out by spring rains and pulled the tarp off, then covered the body with branches he'd cut earlier. With the heat, it shouldn't take more than a month for the body to become skeletonized.

He folded the tarp until it was a neat square and carried it back to his pickup. A check of his watch indicated it was a little after nine.

11

Jenna slapped at a head-diving mosquito, then stilled. At least the temps in the deep woods had cooled from earlier in the day. Much better than in the field where they'd waited for everyone to gather.

She rolled her tight shoulders. Jenna had almost called her dad and cancelled, but a nudge in her spirit changed her mind. Now at an hour before midnight, she wondered if the nudge had been indigestion from the barbecue she'd eaten, because so far the men had been strangely quiet about Joe Slater's accident, and she hadn't been able to steer the conversation in that direction. They only wanted to talk about dogs.

A lantern sat beside her, and Jenna moved it a few feet away, hoping it would draw the mosquitos. It and the other lanterns the men had set around lit the area in a soft glow. Later, if they had to trek through the woods, headlamps would provide a light for their path. She glanced enviously across the circle where her dad squatted on his haunches talking to his brother. Even after years of Pilates, she couldn't squat like that. She couldn't hear what they were talking about, but there was no mystery as to what he and Sam were discussing—the coon dogs they'd turned loose. And identifying each one by their bark.

She rested against the trunk of a huge oak and breathed in the woodsy scent of Eagle Ridge. Even though she hadn't heard anything pertaining to Joe Slater, Jenna was glad she'd come. It was an opportunity to try to get her relationship with her dad and uncle back on track, and it was long overdue. At least they were trying to let her live her life on her terms, and not bossing her like she was a ten-year-old.

It wasn't like she didn't understand where they were coming from. After her mother died, they along with her grandmother had raised her. Sam and her dad had been her heroes, but they didn't want to let go. Sure, they were trying to protect her from her mistakes, but her mistakes were hers to make. And one of those mistakes had been to keep them at a distance. She knew that now, driven home by the unexpected deaths of the Slaters today.

Bugle-like barking echoed through the ridge, jerking her from her memories. A rush of excitement coursed through her, just like when she'd been a kid and heard the telltale bark that meant the hounds were tracking their prey.

Her dad shot to a standing position. "They're on the scent!"

Sam, her uncle, slapped him on the back, and the other men stood as well and nodded in agreement. The bark was different when they had the scent and were trailing a raccoon. Once they had it treed, the bark would become more of a long howl, and if it were hunting season, the men would be traipsing through the woods to the spot where their dogs had the raccoon treed.

But it was June, training time, not hunting time, so tonight Jenna shouldn't have to hike through the woods even though she'd worn her lace-up Redwings.

When the barking grew fainter, her dad found a log and sat on it while Sam picked up a stick and scratched in the dirt. Her dad looked around. "Todd, why didn't you bring your dog?"

"She wasn't feeling too perky, so I left her at home." Todd Donelson hooked his thumbs in his overalls.

It was hard to believe the man who had reminded her of Ichabod Crane when she was a girl was vice president of the only bank in town.

"Todd, you busy later this week?" Junior Bledsoe asked. He'd been quiet until now, but from what she remembered, the mechanic was usually pretty chatty.

"Depends on what day," the banker said.

"How about Thursday? I got a beaver dam I need to get rid of, and I know how much you like that kind of stuff."

"Thursday sounds good."

Once again Jenna fanned the mosquitos away with her hand as Junior bumped fists with the man. The difference in the two men was almost comical—Donelson still looked like a scarecrow and Junior . . . well, he'd been well-fed.

It appeared the men weren't going to call their dogs in, and Jenna settled back again, recalling other long-ago nights that she'd spent in the woods with her dad, his friends, and their dogs.

"Been a while, Jenna."

She peered through the silvery moonlight at the speaker, Gordon Marsden, another of her dad's longtime hunting friends. He was an avid hunter and fisherman, and his love of the outdoors showed in the leathery wrinkles in his face. Earlier, he'd been the first to arrive with his dogs at the field where everyone was supposed to meet. She still hadn't gotten used to the retired postal worker looking like an aging hippie or the fact that he had a ponytail longer than hers.

"Yeah, it has," she said. Like twenty years at least. Suddenly she missed those tomboy years when she'd roamed the hills with this group and their dogs. Jenna had always preferred the training to the actual hunt, even though it was important to control the raccoon population.

"So, what's the word on the Slaters' deaths?" her uncle asked.

Jenna turned toward Sam. "You know I can't share anything about the investigation."

"Then what's the use of having a Russell County deputy in the family?" he snapped. "Come on, Jen, you can give us *something*."

"Leave it alone, Sam," her dad said. "She's not going to tell you anything."

"You trying to tell me what to do, Randy?" Her uncle glowered at her dad.

And that was why sometimes she wanted to shy away from Sam—he was always so testy. It was almost like he was looking for ways to start a quarrel.

"Come on, Sam." Gordon pulled a silver flask from his overalls, uncapped it, and took a generous sip before handing it off to her uncle. "She's as stubborn as you are, so you might as well leave her be."

Jenna frowned. Sam was drinking again? Hadn't it cost him enough? And she never remembered her dad's friends drinking on a run before. Russell County wasn't dry, and they were on private property, so it wasn't illegal, but still . . .

It didn't matter that it was off-season and none of the men carried their rifles—she had no doubt that every one of them had a pistol of some sort in their front pocket or maybe even an ankle holster.

The drinking made her uneasy—alcohol and hunting were two things that didn't mix. Especially when it included her hotheaded uncle—add a rifle, and that spelled even more trouble.

Sam took a swig from the bottle and handed it to the man beside him before he leaned against a broad oak tree. "Sure do miss huntin' in the valley."

At least his tone held a wistful note now instead of anger.

"Yeah," Todd murmured. "Haven't seen any good come from what they did, either. Wasn't that dam supposed to bring in industry?"

Finally, maybe they would talk about Joe Slater and any enemies he might have.

"Bring in industry?" A harsh laugh broke the silence. "You're joking, right?"

Jenna turned toward Junior. There was still talk in the county about how Sheriff Stone disarmed the then-farmer and took him to jail for threatening the surveyors when they crossed his family's land.

Junior turned the flask up, then coughed as he wiped his mouth with the back of his hand. "That's stuff's strong." He screwed the cap back on the flask. "Y'all know with *cost overruns* there wasn't no money left to fix up anything."

"What are you talking about?" Jenna asked. Her uncle had opened the door for her to ask about something besides dogs without it sounding like she was interrogating them. The way Junior had emphasized cost overruns sounded like he'd meant kickbacks.

Junior stilled. Across from him, Sam snorted. "Forgot you had a dep-u-ty here, didn't you?"

12

In the minutes following Junior's outbursts, it was like everyone was waiting for the other shoe to drop. The big man uncapped the bottle and took another sip. "Wasn't talking about anything. Just repeating some rumors I heard."

Jenna tried to recall the details of the dam project, but she'd been in middle school the first time she'd heard of a possible dam and then away from Pearl Springs at college when they started condemning the land, although she had been home for the summer when the men came through the county surveying land for the dam.

That year she'd skipped the summer session at Maryville to rest after a hard first year. By the time the dam was finished, she was a detective with the Chattanooga Police Department and rarely came home.

Jenna leaned forward. "I get you don't like Carter, but if you thought Joe Slater was his partner, why'd you hang out with him?"

Junior gave her a slow smile. "Joe was one of those folks you couldn't help but like—he just had a way about him. He was always helping people out, like Widow Thompson. Don't know how many times he took her groceries and paid her utility bill."

"And she wasn't the only one he helped," Todd said. "He—"

A long howl interrupted him, followed by more howls.

"That's Thunder!" Her dad jumped to his feet. Every coon hunter knew their dog's bark, and her dad was no exception. "He's got him one treed."

Suddenly a different kind of bark came from one of the dogs, a bark Jenna had never heard before.

"That's my Blue," Gordon said. "But something's wrong."

"Maybe they've treed a bear," her uncle said.

Junior grunted. "If it's a bear, more likely they've backed one in a corner."

They were all standing now, and her dad had his GPS tracker out. His dog, Thunder, wore a tracking collar to make it easier to find him once he treed a coon.

"According to this . . ."—he tapped the handheld unit— "Thunder's close to an old logging road. We ought to be able to drive right to the dogs."

More frantic barking echoed over the ridge. "Sounds like we need to get to them pretty quick," Junior said.

Jenna sighed. Just when the men had started talking, this had to happen. She should've tried harder to steer the conversation to Joe Slater's accident earlier.

Everyone trekked out of the woods to their pickups. Since her dad had the tracking unit, he took point and the others followed.

Jenna opted to ride with her dad, and he'd given her the tracker to follow. "This says there's a narrow road up ahead—turn there."

"Probably an old log road."

When they reached what looked like a driveway, he turned into it. She frowned as limbs brushed against the window. If the trees got any closer to the edge of the lane, they would have to get out and walk. "What do you think the dogs have cornered?"

"Not a clue. I just hope it's not a bear. Last time Thunder tangled with one, he lost half an ear."

"Are there bears around here?" She didn't remember any being in the area when she was a kid.

"They tend to stay closer to the Smokies, but every once in a while, one will make his way over here." He was quiet a minute, tapping his fingers on the steering wheel. "I'm glad you came tonight. I've missed our time together."

"I'm glad I came too," she said. "And thank you for taking up for me with Sam."

"Don't pay him any attention."

"I didn't know he was drinking again."

"Yeah," he said. "There's nothing I can do about it. He's the one who has to make the change."

"What made him start again?"

"Your guess is as good as mine . . . although he got really upset about a month ago when he ran into Harrison Carter."

"Why?"

"He blames Carter for losing our family farm when the dam was built."

"Didn't they go to school together?" She didn't know why she remembered that . . . unless it was because Sam liked to talk about important people he knew. He would've put their former mayor in that category.

"Yeah, they were good friends at one time—Harrison came around quite a bit when you were little. That was before he be-came mayor."

Maybe that's why she'd known about the school bit. The front tire hit a rut, and Jenna grunted as she grabbed the armrest. Her dad stopped the truck and nodded his head toward the window. The barks were much louder.

"How close are we?" he asked.

She glanced down at the tracker in her hand. "Looks like we're about even with them." Jenna pointed to the left. "They're that way."

He killed the motor, and they climbed out. The others soon joined them, and her dad cocked his head. "Doesn't sound like they're that far or like they've found a bear . . ."

"Doesn't smell like they've spooked a skunk either," Junior said. "I say go to them rather than call and have them not come."

"And I say let's call 'em in and go home," Todd said. "I gotta get up early in the morning."

Her dad eyed the banker. "Why'd you even come then? I'm going. I want to see what's got their attention."

The others agreed albeit Todd still grumbled. She fell in behind her dad as they trekked through the woods toward the barking dogs, the light from their headlamps bouncing across the rough terrain. There was no air stirring, and her long-sleeve shirt soon clung to her back. Jenna wiped sweat from her face with her sleeve.

The dogs were farther than they sounded, and their strange barking sent chills down her back in spite of the heat. Thunder was the first to come into view. He sat on his haunches, baying at . . . Jenna couldn't see anything other than a pile of brush. And that shouldn't make the dog howl like that.

He wasn't the only dog acting weird. Gordon's dog was doing the same thing.

Her dad scratched his head. "Why would someone cut a bunch of brush and pile it here?"

The hairs on the back of Jenna's neck rose. There was only one reason she could think of. "Don't get any closer until I can check it out," she said.

Sam brushed past her. "I'll check it out."

Before she could stop him, he grabbed a branch and pulled it back, bringing several others with it. Suddenly he dropped it. "Not good," he muttered.

Jenna stepped around him and shined her flashlight at the pile of branches. She blinked and looked again. A shoe with a leg attached to it lay at an odd angle. Brush covered the rest of the body.

"Don't touch anything." She pulled out her phone and dialed Alex's number.

The chief deputy answered on the second ring. "What's wrong?"

"We have another body," Jenna said calmly, though she felt anything but calm. "Judging from the leg I can see, it looks like a male."

"Where are you?"

She gave her the directions to the log road. "Let me know when you get here, and I'll send someone out to bring you in."

"Do you think the death was from an accident?"

Jenna turned toward the pile of brush, her headlamp illuminating the green leaves. "No."

13

Max flipped over in the hard hotel bed again and punched his pillow. It'd probably been a mistake to return to Pearl Springs from Nashville last night, but normally he didn't have trouble sleeping when he was away from his own bed. The problem was more than likely due to a certain Russell County deputy.

Not that she was the reason he drove back from Nashville after leaving the castle nut with the TBI forensic tech. *Yeah, right.* He told Alex when they talked that he'd returned so he wouldn't have to get up so early.

At least driving back had given him thinking time on the Carter case. From what Martin and Holliday said, Carter had made a lot of people mad in his tenure as mayor. Or at least at the beginning of it.

He dismissed the problems stemming from taxes and regulations—Max doubted anyone affected would hold a grudge for twenty years over a zoning issue. But the dam and reservoir were a different matter. People had lost land that had been in their families for generations.

And then there was the Slater accident—Joe Slater had served on the city council the same time Carter was mayor. That gave

Max another reason to focus on Russell County and Pearl Springs for the person responsible for the threats against Carter.

Max flipped over on his other side again. He'd almost drifted off to sleep when his phone jerked him awake. He grabbed it and stared at the screen. Alex? "Anderson," he answered.

"Just got a call from Jenna. She's found a body, and since you're here, I thought you might want to ride to the crime scene."

A body? He shook his head to clear it. "Could it be the Nelson guy I told you about?"

"Don't know. Apparently the body is covered by brush. Jenna is waiting for us to arrive before moving anything," she said. "Nathan's picking me up in ten minutes if you want to ride with us."

"Text me your address."

Seconds later he heard a message come in on his phone.

"Oh," Alex said. "Wear high-top boots if you have them. The body is in the woods, and we might encounter copperheads and rattlesnakes."

"Gotcha."

Max quickly dressed in jeans and a pullover and slid his feet into sneakers since his boots were in his truck. He would change shoes on the way to the site.

The police chief's truck sat idling in Alex's drive when he arrived. Max parked to the side and grabbed his boots just as Alex jogged by.

Nathan opened the passenger door, and Max couldn't help overhearing their conversation.

"Your carriage awaits," Nathan's voice teased.

"Thank you, kind knight. Sorry to get you out this time of night."

"No problem."

Max felt like an intruder and quickly looked away when it was obvious Nathan was going to kiss Alex. Their banter created a yearning in his chest. He didn't want to think he was envious, and he wasn't—it wasn't Alex that Max wanted.

"Coming?" Alex called and climbed into the passenger seat.

"Yeah," Max mumbled and climbed in the back seat of the truck.

Once they buckled up, Nathan pulled away from the drive. "Which way?"

"Razorback Ridge. I tagged her location in my GPS, and it should give us directions."

Max laced the boots he'd pulled on. "How did she manage to find a body?"

Alex looked over her shoulder at him. "I don't know. I thought I'd call her on the way."

A few minutes later, he leaned forward and listened as Jenna filled them in on the details of finding the body.

"How many hunters are with you?" Alex asked.

"Six counting me. I'm afraid we trampled all over the crime scene, but we had no idea the dogs were barking at a body."

"What's done is done. Can you tell who it is?"

"No. Brush covers most of his torso. The only reason I'm pretty sure it's a man is from the shoe and slacks on the victim. I'll send you the photo I took."

Seconds later a text chimed on Alex's phone. She opened the app and held her phone where Max could see it. The photo showed a pile of brush, and at the bottom he barely made out the sole of a man's shoe. No socks. White skin exposed between the shoe and pants leg.

Jenna sent another photo. It looked like she'd zoomed in with a closer view of the shoe. Nathan stopped at the only traffic light in town, and Alex showed them both the photos.

"That's a Crockett & Jones logo," Nathan said.

The company name rang a bell with Max. He whistled when he remembered why. "When I was head of Robbery and Burglary in Chattanooga, one of our cases involved the burglary of a shoe store, and that was one of the brands the owner reported stolen. I remember it because it's an expensive shoe, like over five hundred dollars back then."

Nathan turned off the highway onto a two-lane road. "I can't think of anyone in Pearl Springs who spends that kind of money on shoes."

"I can," Alex said softly. "And we drove out to his house today to talk to him about Joe Slater's death—Paul Nelson. He wasn't home."

Max's brain went into overdrive. What were the odds of two city councilmen who served together dying on the same day? Especially with one murdered and the other dying in a supposed accident that was looking less and less like an accident by the minute?

"If it turns out to be Nelson," Nathan said, "that puts a whole new light on the Slater deaths and the note Carter received."

Max agreed. "So who did the mayor and city council make mad enough to kill?"

Nathan grunted. "Depends on how far back you want to go. Carter was gone by the time I became chief, but he was mayor while I was Sheriff Stone's deputy, so I'm familiar with part of his tenure. I've heard the sheriff say more than once that Harrison Carter came into office and made changes too fast. Some people don't like change even when it's good for them."

"Especially if it's crammed down their throat," Alex said. "I wasn't in Pearl Springs as an adult much when Carter was mayor and don't remember those changes."

Nathan chuckled. "Count yourself fortunate. I remember the chief before me butting heads with him—Carter was frugal with the city treasury to put it nicely."

A clearer picture of Harrison Carter was forming in Max's head. "Anything that would warrant the three deaths and Carter receiving threats?"

"I'm not sure which one to start with." Nathan tapped the steering wheel. "I guess the first thing he did was raise taxes to spruce up the city park. I thought that was a good move, but some people were furious because it was the same year we had a recession. Then he placed restrictive regulations on businesses and created controversial zoning rules. But the kicker was probably building the dam on the Pearl River."

"I've heard about that," Max said. "But would the people involved still carry a grudge?"

"Around here?" Alex said. "Yep. Even I remember that no one involved liked having their property taken for the project, even though it supposedly meant attracting industry to the area."

"Which really hasn't happened so far," Nathan added.

"But all of these things are far in the past. Why now?"

"That's a good question." Alex rubbed the back of her neck. "Maybe the cases aren't connected, and the body isn't anyone we know."

Max had a feeling the chief deputy was wrong. He looked out the window as dark shadows flew by in the gray moonlight. They wouldn't be completely in the dark. "I'm glad Jenna was there when they found the body and was able to secure the scene."

"We got lucky there." Nathan made another turn, then he glanced toward Alex. "I'm glad Jenna is working out. Any signs of lingering PTSD?"

"Haven't been any problems."

"PTSD?" Max said.

Alex turned to where she could see Max. "You didn't know?"

"No." He should've checked on her, but he'd been so wrapped up in his work.

Alex hesitated, indecision playing on her face, then she nodded. "It's nothing she's tried to hide—before I hired her, Jenna was up-front about the shooting in Chattanooga that put her in the hospital and left her with PTSD. An internal investigation had found no fault with her actions in the death of a small-time drug dealer . . . other than she was on a passive surveillance and not supposed to engage her targets."

Then the chief deputy shrugged. "If it'd been me, I would've done the same thing. If Jenna had waited, a five-year-old boy would probably be dead. She's still upset the head of the gang, Rick Sebastian, slipped through her fingers."

He should've dug into the rumors more . . . Jenna probably thought he'd heard and believed them. "So, she's working out?"

"Absolutely. Chattanooga PD made a huge mistake relegating her to a desk after she was cleared by the department psychologist. I haven't regretted hiring her for one minute."

"She really was one of my best detectives," Max said.

"What do you think about her working with you on security for Saturday . . . and you maybe helping out with the Slater investigation?"

His heart jumped. "No objections at all."

"Good. I'm sure she'll tell you about her PTSD since you two will be working together—but don't mention the part about you helping with her case until I have a chance to broach the subject with her."

"Don't worry—I won't." He doubted Jenna would be happy to learn they'd be working together.

Alex laughed. "She'll be fine with it, once she has time to think about it." The GPS beeped. "There's a logging road just ahead. Turn there."

Nathan turned where Alex indicated, and Max gripped the armrest as the SUV bumped over the ruts. Headlights flashed in the side mirror.

"That's probably my CSI tech, Dylan," she said before he could ask. About a mile in, a man stood at the edge of a clearing, holding a battery-powered lantern. Several trucks were parked in the small area, and they pulled in beside a gray Chevy. Max stepped out into the damp night as Dylan pulled in behind them.

"Alex, Chief," the man holding the lantern said, nodding at them. He questioned Max's presence with his eyebrows.

Alex nodded toward Max. "This is TBI agent Maxwell Anderson. Max, Jenna's dad, Randy Hart." She turned back to Randy. "Where's the body?"

"It's about half a mile from here. Jenna sent me to show you the way."

Alex turned to the CSI tech. "Need help with your equipment?"

Dylan pushed his glasses up on his nose. "It would help if someone could carry one of the portable lights."

"I got it." Max took the folded tripod with two lamps attached and followed the others. He thought he was in good shape, but tramping through brush was a lot different than running on a treadmill.

By the time they reached the crime scene, his heart was doing a hundred plus when he set the lamps down, but he wasn't certain that could be blamed on the hike. More likely because Jenna's hand had closed over his when she grabbed the lamp pole.

"What are you doing here? I thought you were in Nashville."

At least she sounded more curious than angry to see him. He grinned. "Couldn't stay away, not with all this excitement."

She shook her head and helped Dylan set up the lamps. An hour later, he removed the last branch covering the body.

"It's Paul Nelson," Alex said.

Max was glad he'd returned. Harrison Carter's case just moved up from a four to a ten because, dollars to donuts, Joe Slater's accident hadn't been an accident at all.

He figured Carter was next.

14

Tuesday morning, Jenna poured a cup of black sludge that passed for coffee at the sheriff's office and took a sip. Her eyes widened and she shuddered at the bitter taste. If that didn't wake her up, nothing would.

She hadn't gotten into bed until four, but she should be more awake than this after going by the barn and feeding Ace and then turning him out. Jenna had even tracked Kirk down and arranged for him to feed and water her horse until this case was solved and the political rally was over. But she'd had trouble getting to sleep, and all too soon the alarm she'd set for eight had gone off.

"Is that as strong as it looks?"

Max's voice sent electricity charging through her. That was one way to wake up, but not exactly what she had in mind, especially since he was one reason she hadn't slept well. "Afraid so," she said without turning around.

"Good." He stepped past her, grabbed the carafe, and filled a Styrofoam cup.

His musky cologne sent another charge through her, triggering the memory of that one kiss. She'd definitely spent too much time thinking about Max before she fell off to sleep. Why else would she be having this response to him this morning?

Jenna turned around just as he took one sip and shuddered. It looked as though he'd skipped shaving, and he had the day-old beard going on. She swallowed hard. Max looked way too good for this time of the morning.

"This is stronger than what passes for coffee at the TBI." He took another sip. "Good job on finding the body last night."

Jenna held up her finger. She needed more octane before she dealt with the handsome TBI agent this morning. She took a bigger sip and then another, and the caffeine hit her system. *Yes!* Once Jenna finished the cup, she refilled it and then turned to Max. "Actually the dogs found it. I just happened to be nearby. Sorry you got dragged out of bed."

Heat set her face on fire. Jenna did not need that image in her brain. She quickly checked her watch. "Oops. Alex's briefing starts in thirty seconds, and she doesn't like for us to be late—I'm assuming that's why you're here?"

"She called me at seven and said I might want to come."

Jenna nodded, avoiding his gaze—she'd always been a sucker for dark brown eyes, and if she looked up, she'd get lost in his.

"That means she's had less sleep than I have." Then what he'd said sank in. Why had Alex called him at all? He wasn't investigating Russell County's crimes.

What if he planned to take over her case? No, Alex wouldn't do that to her. She pointed her cup down the hall. "We're meeting in the conference room where we were yesterday."

They were the last ones to arrive, and there were only two empty chairs in the back row. Wayne stood to let them in, and they barely were seated before Alex stepped up to the podium.

"Good morning." Alex's gaze rested on each deputy briefly as she scanned the room. "Preliminary results indicate Paul Nelson was killed with a bullet to the heart—caliber not determined yet. No tattooing, so the gun wasn't against his chest. He wasn't killed where he was found, and no report of trace evidence on the body, but it's early."

Jenna raised her hand. "How about Joe Slater and his wife? Has the report on the castle nut come in?"

"Not yet." Alex shifted her attention to Max.

"I turned it in late yesterday, and the tech said she would expedite it," he said.

"Good," Alex said. "At any rate, we're treating the accident as a possible homicide now."

"How about anyone else who served on the city council with Slater and Nelson?" Wayne asked.

"We're looking at their early years on the council, and the other two men who served with them were older and died of natural causes."

Max held his hand up, and Alex acknowledged him. "Was there a note of any kind on Nelson's body?"

"I'm getting to that." Alex shifted her notes. "When Dylan examined Nelson's clothes, he discovered the pockets in his slacks had been cut out, probably with a knife. While it's not a note saying he'd lined his last pocket like Harrison Carter received, removing the pockets indicates the same message, linking the cases."

"Is there anything in the Slater case that links it to Nelson's murder?" Jenna asked.

"Not yet," Alex said. "We may find something at Slater's house. Judge Cornelius signed off on a search warrant, and Dylan and Taylor are currently on their way to the house. Jenna, I'd like you to join them once we finish here."

Max looked up from the notes he'd been writing. "Joe's sister wouldn't let you in?"

"Just dotting my i's and crossing my t's for when the case goes to court." Alex smiled at him. "And I'd appreciate it if you would help out as well—we can use your expertise."

A band squeezed Jenna's chest. Alex was about to let Max highjack her case. "Russell County deputies are perfectly capable of looking for evidence at the Slaters'. We don't need TBI's help."

Alex stiffened, and the room seemed to hold a collective breath. Wayne nudged her. "Jenna . . ."

Don't contradict your commanding officer in public. If Jenna could hit the rewind button, she would. "I'm sorry," she blurted. "I spoke out of turn."

She probably didn't sound very sorry, but confound it, Dylan and Taylor were good, and she was no slouch when it came to finding evidence, either.

Alex fingered her notes. "I wasn't saying Russell County deputies couldn't handle it, but if these two deaths are related to Harrison Carter and the rally Saturday, we're short on time and need all the help we can get."

Jenna released the breath she was holding.

"In fact," the chief deputy continued, "I want you to work closely with Max on this, which includes planning and implementing security for the political rally Saturday."

Work *closely* with Max? This time Jenna managed to close her mouth on the protest bursting to get out.

The chief deputy shifted her attention to the other deputies. "Moving on. I want the rest of you scouring the county for any information you can find on Paul Nelson."

Jenna barely heard the rest of Alex's assignments. She was trying to figure out how she was going to work with Max and stay immune to him.

The man in question leaned toward Jenna. "Want to ride with me to the Slaters'?"

She frowned at him. "No. But you're welcome to ride with me if you don't care how long you have to stay."

Why did she say that? Because he wouldn't accept, that's why.

"Not a problem." He chuckled softly. "While we drive there,

we can go over some of the security measures for the Founders Day rally."

As usual, the man had an answer for everything. She turned toward Alex as she approached.

"I have one more job for you," her boss said. "It's too coincidental that all three of these men were involved in Pearl Springs politics at the same time. I talked to my grandfather, and he said to check the newspaper archives for the years they served together and see if you can find a motive for someone wanting to exact revenge on them."

"I'll do that as soon as we finish at the Slaters'." Jenna added the request to her list and drew a star beside it. The conversation last night among the coon hunters had crossed her mind a couple of times since finding Paul Nelson's body. Did she want to bring up the dam project just yet? Or wait and present it with a list of any other controversial projects the mayor and city council pushed through?

Jenna picked up her folder and turned to Max. "You sure you want to ride with me? You might get stuck at Slater's house or the newspaper office and be late getting away from here."

"I'm good. I'm set up at the hotel across from the hospital for the rest of the week, so I don't have to worry about driving back to Nashville."

That was just peachy.

"Jenna," someone called out to her. She turned as Alex's administrative assistant and sometimes dispatcher, Marge, bore down on her. "Your dad has been trying to reach you."

Jenna felt her pocket for her phone and groaned. It wasn't there—she must've left it at home. "Tell him I forgot my phone and I'll call him back as soon as I'm able."

"Gotcha!" Marge's thumbs-up was accompanied with a look of concern. "You okay?"

Evidently she wasn't, but Jenna wasn't about to admit it. She gave Marge a slow nod, then chuckled. "I must be getting old—late nights like last night never bothered me before."

"I know what you mean," Marge said with a wry grin.

Jenna turned to Max just as his phone rang. He held up a finger. "I need to get this."

"Why don't you meet me at my house?"

"That sounds good. Text me the address," he said and punched the answer button.

She would as soon as she got her phone. Instead she wrote it on a sticky note and handed it to him.

Ten minutes later, Jenna parked her SUV in her drive and climbed out. She glanced up the road, figuring Max would be right behind her, but he wasn't. Hopefully he would arrive by the time she grabbed her phone. Jenna jogged to her front porch and skidded to a stop, her heart flying to her throat.

The front door was cracked a couple of inches. Sweat formed on her palms, and she swiped them down her pants. Jenna could've sworn she shut the front door and locked it.

She unsnapped the strap over her gun and hesitated. Backup. The last time she hadn't waited for backup, she'd almost died. But her phone was inside the house, and this wasn't Chattanooga where break-ins happened every day. Pearl Springs was relatively safe.

Tell that to the two men who died yesterday.

Footsteps inside the house kicked her into action. She yanked her gun from the holster and kicked the door wide open as she entered. "Police!"

Jenna whipped to the side and swept the gun around the living room. Empty. The back door slammed.

She raced down the hall through the small dining area and burst into the kitchen, her nerve endings screaming something was off.

The back door was open. *No!* She'd heard it slam.

The intruder was in the kitchen. It was a trap.

She turned, and pain to the base of her neck sent Jenna crumpling to the floor and fighting to stay conscious.

A voice penetrated the haze, the words garbled. The voice . . . she'd heard it before . . . Sebastian? Her world turned dark as unconsciousness claimed her.

15

Max followed the GPS out of Pearl Springs to the county road in the address Jenna had given him. The conversation with the assistant director in Nashville had taken longer than he expected. She'd wanted to discuss with him that someone had leaked the information that Harrison Carter had received a threatening letter to the press. From her questions, he judged she was trying to make sure he hadn't been the one to leak the information.

He hadn't. The bureau would probably start receiving messages from some of the loonies out there confessing they were responsible. Crazy or not, someone would have to investigate every tip, but thankfully it wouldn't be him.

Max glanced at the numbers on the mailboxes. Jenna's house should be coming up soon. He spotted her SUV before the voice coming from his GPS told him he'd reached his destination and pulled in behind it.

He frowned at the open front door as he climbed the steps to the porch. Even though she knew he was coming, he hadn't expected the door to be open. Max pulled his Glock and stepped inside. He cocked his head, listening. No sound anywhere. Methodically, he cleared the house room by room until he came to the kitchen. Jenna lay face down on the floor. His heart stuttered.

Max dialed 911 while he made sure no one hid in the pantry, then he checked the back door. Shut and locked. Once he was assured an ambulance was on the way, he holstered his gun and texted Alex before he knelt beside Jenna.

The small rise and fall of her back assured him she was alive. Max gently turned her over. She didn't appear to have been shot, but he didn't like how pale she was. "Jenna! Can you hear me?"

No response. He felt her wrist for a pulse. A little fast, but strong. Gently he probed her head. Only a slight bump on her forehead where she'd hit the floor. Had she just fainted?

Her eyes fluttered open, and he'd never been so happy to see those blue eyes. Especially since both pupils were the same size, although slightly dilated. Her gaze connected with his, and she stiffened.

"You're okay," he said. "What happened?"

"Max?" She blinked a couple of times, and color returned to her face.

"Yep. Do you remember what happened?" Jenna struggled to get up, and he put his hand on her shoulder. "Be still—an ambulance is on the way."

She pushed his hand away. "I don't need an ambulance. I'm fine."

As if to prove it, she pushed herself up to a sitting position. "Ohhh." She swayed and grabbed her head as she turned pale again with a greenish tint. "Not a good idea, but give me a minute."

"Told you. Do you need a pan in case you throw up?"

Jenna sucked in a few deep breaths and released them. "I think I'll be all right. At least I will be when I figure out what happened."

"What do you remember?"

Jenna pinched the bridge of her nose. "I remember the door

was open, and I wasn't going to go in because I didn't have backup. But then I heard someone inside the house . . . guess I thought I could catch them. Next thing I know, I'm looking up into your eyes."

She winced as sirens announced the arrival of emergency vehicles. Minutes later paramedics rushed into the kitchen, and Max stepped out of the way and explained how he found Jenna.

The lead paramedic, Terry Conner, turned to her. "Were you hit over the head?"

Jenna shook her head. "No. I remember coming into the kitchen and then nothing until Max was bending over me."

"So, you fainted?"

"No." She crossed her arms. "Whenever I've fainted before, I was lightheaded and knew I was going out—that didn't happen this time."

"Mind if I examine you?"

"I'm fine, but go ahead."

After examining her, Terry said, "Good. Pupils are the same. How do you feel? Any double vision?"

"No. Just a little achy—not really pain, but my head doesn't feel quite right, probably from smacking the floor."

"Can you stand?"

"Let's see." She climbed to her feet without assistance. "I'm good."

"Sit down and let me ask you a few questions," Terry said. "Can you give me the date?"

Jenna sat in a kitchen chair and quickly rattled off the date.

"What day is it?"

"Tuesday."

"How about counting to ten backwards."

When Jenna did that successfully, he added, "And the months in reverse order."

She frowned. "Really?"

He grinned and nodded. "Unless you want to go to the ER."

Jenna started with December and ended with January. "Is that enough?"

"Yeah, but if anything changes, and I mean anything, get to the ER."

"I'll see to it that she does," Max said.

"See to it that she does what?" Alex's firm voice came from the doorway as she entered the kitchen.

The paramedic explained the circumstances. "I don't think she needs a CT scan—she doesn't exhibit any signs of a concussion. I think she simply fainted."

"Hey, guys, don't talk about me like I'm not here."

Alex laughed. "She sounds normal."

"Ha-ha." Jenna made a face. "There was someone in the house. I heard them walking, then the back door slammed."

Her hair had fallen loose around her shoulders, and she finger combed it. Max liked it down, with her black hair softly curling toward her face, framing it.

Alex took out a notepad. "Tell me what happened."

Jenna repeated what she'd told him, and he added what he'd found when he arrived. "The back door was shut and deadbolted."

Jenna jerked her head toward the door. "That doesn't make sense. I know I heard someone . . . and I heard the back door slam . . . but how could the door be deadbolted? It takes a key like this one to open both the front and back doors." She pulled a house key from her pocket.

"You said you didn't remember coming in here, but evidently you did," Alex said gently. "So maybe you locked the door and don't remember."

"Maybe . . ." She didn't sound at all convinced.

Alex frowned. "What I want to know is why you didn't call for backup when the door was open?"

"I didn't have my phone."

"You had your radio . . ."

Jenna groaned. "I didn't think of that."

Neither had Max.

"When I heard someone running, I rushed in," Jenna said, "and that's the last thing I remember. It's like my mind won't lock on to anything."

"It'll come back to you," Alex said. "And maybe you simply fainted—last night was traumatic, and you were up really late."

"I'm feeling fine now."

"Your color is better," Max said. "It's not green."

"I turned green?"

He waved his right hand, indicating so-so.

Alex tapped the pad. "I'll get Dylan or Taylor over here to dust for prints—just in case someone broke in, but if that's what happened, it'll probably be like the other break-ins we've had lately. Nada."

"Someone was in the house when I got here," Jenna insisted.

"You've had other break-ins in broad daylight?" Max asked.

"Five or six in the last couple of months," Jenna said. "Same MO. The perps seem to know when the owners leave and how long they'll be gone. I must have surprised them by returning home before I was supposed to. I need to check and see if they got my phone."

"Where is it?" Max asked. "I'll grab it for you."

"It's probably on my night table, but I'll get it."

While Jenna went to retrieve her phone, Alex put away her notebook. "Did you see anyone when you arrived?"

"No. And the house didn't look as though anyone had searched through it—everything looked neat . . ."

Worry crossed her face. "I'll get Wayne and a couple of deputies to knock on a few doors around here, see if anyone saw anything."

"There aren't many houses around here," Max said. "*If* there was anyone here, a person would have to be driving by at just the right time to see anything."

Alex cocked her head. "So, you're thinking Jenna may have experienced some type of PTSD?"

He shrugged. "All I'm saying is that I didn't see any signs that anyone had been here."

They both turned as Jenna's footsteps neared.

"I found it," Jenna said joining them. "And I'm ready to go to Joe Slater's house if you are."

Max eyed her. "You sure you're up to it?"

"Why don't you stay here?" Alex said. "I'll pull Dylan and Taylor to process your house. That'll give you time to recover, and then you can help with the Slater house."

"I'm good. They're slammed with two crime scenes to work. I can process my own house."

"I have a kit and can help as well," Max said.

"If you're sure." Alex glanced around the kitchen. "Are you planning on staying here tonight?"

Jenna nodded. "There's no reason not to—so far the break-ins haven't happened at night. Besides, I'm a deputy—I can take care of myself."

"I don't think staying here by yourself is a good idea," Max said. While he hadn't seen evidence of anyone being in the house, that didn't mean there hadn't been an intruder. "I'm sticking around a few days. I can stay here as easily as the hotel."

"I can't ask you to do that . . ."

Before he could tell her that she wasn't asking, Alex said, "That would be a great solution. I'd offer for you to stay at our house if Gram hadn't hired someone to redo their bathroom while they're in Kentucky with Dani Collins and Mark and Gem."

"I don't know . . ." Jenna shook her head.

"Look, I won't be able to sleep anyway, worrying about you." Max held up his hand. "I know, you're a deputy and can handle yourself, but two is better than one, and you have two bed-rooms."

"No" was still written all over her face.

"It would work," Alex said. "At least for the time being."

"We'll see," Jenna said.

Which sounded like a no. Max didn't remember her being so independent when they worked together.

Once everyone cleared the kitchen, she gave him a grateful smile. "Thanks for offering to stay tonight, but it won't be necessary."

"We'll see," he said mimicking her. "Are you sure you're up to going to the Slater house?"

"Yes, but can you give me a second to freshen up a bit?"

"Sure."

After five minutes passed, Max frowned. "Jenna?" he called. "You okay?"

When she didn't answer, he eased down the hall and checked the bathroom. It was empty. "Jenna?"

A slight noise came from the bedroom next to it, and he looked inside. At first he thought it was empty as well, then he saw movement reflected in the mirror. He looked closer. Jenna knelt between the bed and the wall with a screwdriver in her hand.

Max stepped inside the room, his footsteps sounding on the hardwood floor. She gave an audible gasp and jerked upright.

"I called and you didn't answer."

She shrugged. "I didn't hear you."

"What are you doing with a screwdriver?"

Jenna looked down at her hand and back up at him. "I, ah, dropped it, and it rolled under the bed."

He leveled a hard gaze at her, and her cheeks flamed. "Don't ever play poker."

Jenna's shoulders sagged. "I was checking on something."

"And . . . ?"

"Everything seems fine." Relief sounded in her voice.

He eyed her with raised eyebrows, waiting for her to explain. When she didn't respond, he said, "You can trust me, Jenna."

"I'm ready to leave," she said.

She ought to know evasive tactics never worked with him.

"Have I ever let you down?" When she still hesitated, he said, "Come on, tell me when did I ever not have your back?"

16

D id you find them?" Anxiety laced the cop's voice. Good.

"No." Rick Sebastian turned on the road that led to the remote cabin he'd rented. He'd been listening to the conversation from the bugging devices he'd planted in the kitchen and Hart's office when Ross's call came in. Her boss and probably the man who'd burst into the house seemed to think she had fainted. Good. "Are you certain she has photos of us together?"

"Yes," Ross said.

"You've seen them?"

"Yes. I deleted them from her phone, but something she said the last time we talked makes me believe she has copies somewhere. I searched her apartment before she moved but never found them."

"Maybe because she doesn't have any." He hadn't heard her mention any photos.

"Oh, she has them all right. She practically bragged about it."

"Then why hasn't she used them?"

Heavy breathing came through the phone. "I don't know. Maybe to torment me for ending our engagement."

Give me a break. But it was plain the narcissistic cop believed what he said. "I still don't understand why you can't claim you were working undercover that night."

"It's not that simple. I've never worked undercover, and to claim it would look suspicious. It's better if the photos never show up. For both of us."

Sebastian smiled. It was no skin off his nose—he'd paid his so-called debt to society—but if Phillip Ross wanted to think it was, so be it. Then his smile faded. While he was in prison, his lieutenant had taken over the Scorpions, and Viper had made it plain he wasn't giving up the position.

He narrowed his eyes. Jenna Hart was to blame for all of this— prison, the loss of his organization . . . maybe his hatred of the cop bordered on obsession. But it was what had gotten him through the long nights in the noisy cell block.

Getting his position back was his main priority . . . and taking her out was a close second. Unfortunately Ross had other ideas for the former Chattanooga cop, but Ross's determination to find the photographs fit in his plans. Sebastian could keep the detective happy while making Jenna Hart's life miserable.

"She interrupted me, so I'll go back and search again." Sebastian turned into the gravel drive and parked. It would be an opportunity to make sure she knew someone had been in her house.

"Did she see you?"

"No." And she wouldn't see him the next time, either. He fingered the key he'd taken from her kitchen cabinet after he'd picked the lock to her door. He would have a copy made at a nearby town and then return this one where he found it.

"Did you plant the drugs?"

"I didn't have time—I wasn't expecting Hart to come back." Not that he intended to, anyway. If he'd been caught and the cops found drugs on him, it would have been his ticket back to prison. He wasn't taking that chance.

"Well, did you at least find something you can leave at the farmhouse implicating her in the drug operation?"

He pulled a gold chain with a cross on it from his pocket. "I did, but I don't know why you think we'll need it." Hart wouldn't live long enough to reap the repercussion of being framed, anyway.

"You never can tell in this business. It'll be insurance. I want those photos, or short of that, to make sure no one will believe her if they do surface."

"Gotcha. I have things to do, and I'll call you once I have the photos."

"Hey—this conversation isn't over until I say it's over. *I'm* the reason you're out of prison."

Sebastian clenched his jaw then forced himself to relax. For now, he'd let Ross believe whatever he wanted to believe. "What do you want me to do?"

"Find a way to make everyone lose confidence in her."

"Seems like you did that in Chattanooga when you spread those rumors that she set up a meeting with me that night. You never said how you got that other cop to alibi you."

"I didn't, did I?"

Sebastian waited, knowing Ross wasn't going to explain.

"I need her discredited in Pearl Springs, and I can't come to Pearl Springs—she'd recognize me. No one will recognize you since you don't look anything like your old photos, even the one at Pikeville."

Sebastian would give him that. Gone was his close-cropped hair and the rail-thin body. He'd beefed up and filled out, including his face. "Any suggestions?"

Not that he needed any—he already had her boss second-guessing Jenna Hart's mental stability. But he needed to let Ross *think* he was in charge.

"You're smart—you'll think of something. How is the drug shipment coming along?"

"Should be ready by the middle of next week."

"Go to the farm today and make sure they're on schedule."

Sebastian bit back the retort on the tip of his tongue. A few more days and he'd let Ross know who was really in charge. "Sure, boss. Do you have a particular time in mind?"

When there was no answer, he checked his phone. Ross had hung up. Just as well. Ross wouldn't have liked his sarcastic tone. Sebastian pocketed his phone.

He closed his eyes and counted to ten. *He* had been the one who'd set up this operation from prison. Not Ross. Yeah, Ross had fronted it, but it was Sebastian's brains that came up with the idea.

Once he had the money from this shipment of drugs, everything was going to change. It would be a pleasure to bring Phillip Ross down. But killing the person who busted him and sent him to prison would be even better.

Still seething, he climbed out of the gray Corolla. Sebastian missed his Range Rover that had been confiscated the night Hart was shot. Another mark against her.

He unlocked the door and entered the rustic cabin. After the last few days, he needed a good workout, but he would have to settle for exercises he could do without equipment, which was nothing new. If there'd been a gym in this one-stoplight town, he would have risked going to it. At least he'd brought a mat that he could practice karate moves on.

He hadn't let his time in prison go to waste, making himself do push-ups and squats in his cell, even filling a trash bag with water and lifting it. Sebastian had also made friends with an incarcerated martial arts expert. Learning how to defend himself had come in handy, but it wasn't the only thing he'd learned from him. Or the most important.

He'd learned to quiet his mind and take advantage of the natural forces that shaped the order of events. In the past he'd tried to control the outcome, taking hurried preemptive actions that often resulted in failure. Victory came to those who waited and struck at exactly the right time.

Sebastian gripped the portable pull-up bar he'd attached to the hallway door and knocked off a hundred body lifts. Being patient didn't mean sitting by and doing nothing.

Tonight he would plant a tracker on her vehicle so he wouldn't be caught off guard again. With the tracker and listening devices in her house, he would know her every move.

It wasn't that he disapproved of Ross's plan to make her look like a dirty cop. It just wasn't enough after she'd sent him to prison. He would still get his payback, but like a slow, torturous death, in due time. When it came, Jenna Hart would welcome death.

However, he needed to be more careful, or the hours he spent planning would be for nothing. He hadn't known about the man who arrived right after he knocked Hart unconscious with a karate chop to a pressure point located at the base of her skull.

Judging from his dress and the gun strapped to his waist, the friend was a cop, but not one from around Pearl Springs—he knew what every law enforcement officer in Russell County looked like.

He wasn't FBI—he didn't have that look. Must be state. Regardless, the man was a new wrinkle and complicated things. From everything Sebastian had gleaned about Jenna Hart, she wasn't in a relationship. If she was and the cop stuck too close to her, it would mean taking him out as well.

Sebastian mulled the problem over in his mind. If the man was a TBI agent, that upped the risk. He'd driven past her house, and the only vehicle in the drive had been Hart's, so he wasn't with her 24/7. All Sebastian had to do was to be patient. He would get the opportunity he wanted.

And he was an expert at making murder look like an accident.

17

Jenna could kick herself for letting Max catch her in the bedroom checking on the data drive. Now she had to explain what she was doing in the spare bedroom with a screwdriver.

She sighed. "We'll talk about it on the way."

The look he gave Jenna said they would indeed discuss it. "I'll meet you outside," she said.

She waited until the door closed behind him before she returned the tiny data drive she'd taken out of the wall socket, then she pressed tape across the plate so she'd know if anyone disturbed it.

Max was probably waiting on her at her SUV, and Jenna hurried to catch up with him. She entered the kitchen and gasped. Max was kneeling on one knee at her back door, examining her deadbolt. "You scared me. I thought you were outside."

"I was checking your deadbolts." He stood. "You ready?"

Jenna nodded and tried to decide just how much she was going to share as they walked to her SUV. It wasn't that she didn't want to tell him—she needed to tell someone. If the intruder had killed her today, no one would even know to look for the drive that had the blurry photos showing Phillip and Sebastian together.

Her mind buzzed. If ever an honest man lived, it was Max. He said he'd always had her back, but he'd been out of her life for several years now. She couldn't turn on trust like it was a light switch. At least not until she had some answers. Jenna just didn't know what the questions were.

"Let's use my truck—I'm more familiar with it." Max opened the passenger door, and she climbed in. Once they were on the road, she took a deep breath and released it.

"You okay?" he asked.

She nodded. "Why *didn't* you call after you left Chattanooga? You kissed me and then walked out the door and ghosted me."

Max had been tapping the steering wheel, and he stilled. Then like her, he drew in a deep breath and slowly let it out. "I know, and like I told you yesterday, I'm really sorry about that."

"Words are easy." Especially for someone like Max, who could charm robbery suspects into confessing.

He took his gaze off the road for a second and turned his head toward her. "Truth?"

She nodded.

He returned his gaze to the road. "I was in a bad place when I left Chattanooga. Shannon had done a number on me . . ." He tapped the steering wheel again. "Time to man up," he said and sat up straighter. "I really have no excuse for the way I hurt you."

Quiet settled between them. He broke it first. "Are you open to letting me make amends?"

Jenna took her time answering. He seemed truly sorry, but his silence had hurt. "We'll see. It really hurt when I didn't hear from you after I was shot. I thought maybe you believed the rumors."

"I never heard them." Neither of them spoke for a couple of miles, then Max said, "For the record, I don't understand why you were relegated to a desk job after the psychologist released you. You were too good of a cop for that."

Jenna looked up, surprised by the concern in his voice. Maybe he wasn't part of the good-ol'-boy network. "Apparently you're the only one who feels that way."

"You're wrong about that," he said. "I'll grant you there are a few who resent women on the police force, and some of them are in authority, but they are the same ones reaching retirement age. I promise, more than one detective respected you when I was on the force there."

"Then why didn't they speak up when Billingsley let it be known I'd never work an investigation again? I wasn't the only cop who'd suffered PTSD after getting shot, and they returned to work once the psychologist released them."

"I don't know . . ." Then he quietly added, "I would've spoken up if I'd been there."

The anger Jenna had held against him dissolved. She rested her head against the seat as peace washed over her. She and Max had always been tight while they worked together, and she'd missed it.

"You want to know what I regret?" she said softly.

"What?"

"That I let them run me off. But they had me second-guessing myself, and when a cop loses their confidence, they're no good to anyone."

"Is it getting better since you've come to Russell County?"

"Definitely. Alex is great to work for—I think I was her first hire. Why do you ask?"

He hesitated. "I worried you might be experiencing PTSD from the shooting."

"Alex told you?" He nodded, and she turned and watched the passing trees out the window. Max didn't push, just let her be while she gathered her thoughts.

"Other than occasional nightmares, the PTSD is gone—I haven't fainted at the sight of blood since the psychologist released me. And I did not have PTSD back at the house," she said quietly. "I heard an intruder. When you saw me in the bedroom, I was making sure he hadn't found the data drive I hid."

"Okay. What's on it?"

"Photos I took of Phillip and Rick Sebastian the night I was shot."

"The gang leader?"

Jenna nodded. It felt so good to talk to Max about this.

"You didn't turn them over to Billingsley?"

She shook her head. "Billingsley and I were like mixing vinegar and baking soda. Even when you and I worked together in robbery he had a reputation for not wanting women detectives in the gang unit. That never changed in spite of pressure from higher up."

Max slowed and made a right turn. "I never understood why you joined the gang unit—you knew what Billingsley was like."

"I probably wouldn't have, but after you left, I worked with one of the inner-city churches, and I got close to the kids. That's when I learned just how widespread the gangs were. I kept hearing about this Sebastian who was rumored to be the head of the Scorpions, but he was like a ghost.

"When two of the kids in my group overdosed, I vowed to bring him down. Took me three months to even identify him, but I developed a really good confidential informant. She's the one who told me about Sebastian's coke habit and when he'd be getting a new supply. That's when I arrested him—he had enough of the drug on him to get five years." Jenna wondered if he'd kicked the habit in prison. "If only my camera and phone hadn't been stolen that night, he would've been looking at ten to twenty."

Max tapped the steering wheel as they drove up the mountain. "If your phone and camera were stolen, how—"

"I emailed a few of the photos I took with my phone to myself before everything went south."

"I still don't understand why you didn't turn them over to Billingsley."

"I didn't trust that he wouldn't trash them." Even now, she wasn't sure her former boss and Phillip weren't in cahoots. "And there's a problem with them—they're grainy, and they're not time-stamped. Without the originals on my phone that show when they were taken, there's no way to prove they were taken the night I was shot."

"Wait. Didn't they automatically upload to the cloud?"

She shrugged. "They should've, but whoever stole my phone deleted the photos from everything. If I hadn't emailed them to myself, I wouldn't have anything, such as they are."

He thought a minute. "How about the metadata—"

"I thought of that too, but the metadata is linked to when a person accesses or downloads a photo from their email. Check any of the photos you've received in your emails and you'll see what I mean. I didn't open my emails until just before I got out of the hospital."

"So, if Phillip believes all the evidence was destroyed, why would he be looking for something?"

Jenna bit her bottom lip. "Because I might've hinted to him that I had evidence even though the photos had been deleted from my phone."

"What do you mean?"

"Before I left the hospital, I called Phillip and accused him of being at the school that night. Told him I had evidence putting him there. Not sure what else I said, but evidently enough to let him know I thought he was a dirty cop."

Max winced.

"I know, not the smartest thing I've ever done, but I'd just learned the camera and my phone had been stolen, and I was pretty loopy and not thinking straight. By the time I was released from the hospital, there was a rumor floating around the precinct that I was the dirty cop. That I'd set up the meeting with Sebastian and it went south.

"Of course it was only a rumor, nothing anyone could prove because Sebastian was claiming he wasn't there. So he couldn't very well turn around and say otherwise."

"Didn't you have any backup?"

She shook her head. "It was supposed to be a routine surveillance. I wasn't to engage the subjects. Officer Creasy—don't know if you remember him—"

"I remember him."

Max's tone indicated he didn't particularly like him.

"He was supposed to be parked two streets over. If I observed a drug deal going down, I was to radio him so he could pull the subject over and arrest him. That way my position wouldn't be compromised. Creasy didn't arrive on the scene until after I was shot and Sebastian had disappeared, so he never saw him." She rubbed her shoulder. "I never said anything about Phillip to my supervisor because I didn't think Billingsley would believe me— Phillip had pretty well convinced everyone I was a hysterical woman out for revenge because he broke off our engagement."

"It's hard to fight something like that," Max said.

"You're not kidding, and what I have on the data drive wouldn't hold up in court, but he doesn't know that."

Max was quiet a minute. "You said Sebastian is in prison, but if he got away that night—"

"He was out on bond after I arrested him on the possession of cocaine charge. He probably thought the charges would be dropped after I was shot, but I was well enough to testify in court—he got five years."

"So he couldn't have been the one who broke into your house. Do you think it was Phillip?"

Her face clouded. "I don't know. This isn't the first time someone has broken into my house—it happened before I left Chattanooga.

I never knew who it was, but since Phillip was tight with Sebastian, I figured it was Sebastian or one of the Scorpions. Or maybe even Phillip himself."

Jenna rubbed her temple. Sifting through the memories took a mental toll. She leaned back against the seat and closed her eyes, shifting her thoughts to the break-in. Why couldn't she remember going into the kitchen? Could she have seen the intruder's face?

Max's GPS broke the silence in the truck, telling him to turn onto the road that led to Eagle Ridge. When they came to a fork, it directed him to the left.

"Go right," Jenna said, opening her eyes. "For some reason GPS always sends you the long way around here."

He did as she directed and wound around the other side of the mountain. "Who lives on the other road?"

"There are a few rental cabins. Mark Lassiter lives almost to the top . . . and Mae Richmond and her granddaughter, Dani. I figure Mark and Dani will be the next to announce a wedding."

It wasn't long before they came to the spot where Slater's Hummer had plunged off the road.

"I don't know which is worse," Max said. "This being an accident or someone having it in for the man."

Jenna had been thinking the same thing. "Murder times two is always worse."

"You're right. And now this Paul Nelson. If these are linked, what if the murderer isn't done?"

That's what Jenna was afraid of. "What could the two men have done for someone to hate them this much? It's bad enough killing Slater, but why kill his wife as well?"

Max slowed as they came to Slater's drive. "Maybe we'll get the answer to that at his house."

18

D ylan and Taylor are here," Jenna said, nodding at the Ford
Interceptor identical to her own. Her phone rang, and she
glanced at the screen. "It's Alex."

Max parked beside the Interceptor. "I'll see you inside."

She nodded and punched the answer button. "Hart."

"How do you feel?"

Surely her boss hadn't called just to check on her. "A little off-
balance, but nothing major."

"Good. Have you remembered what happened?"

Jenna shook her head even though Alex couldn't see her.

"Nothing other than what I heard. I didn't see anyone." She
rubbed her neck, and winced when her fingers found a tender spot
at the base of her skull on the right side. Why was her neck sore?

"Are you certain you didn't faint?"

At this point Jenna wasn't certain of anything. "I don't think so."

Alex was quiet for a minute, then she said, "Wayne reported
no one on your road saw anything unusual this morning."

Jenna wasn't surprised her neighbors hadn't seen anything—
whoever broke into her house was too smart to let someone see
them. And that meant there was no way to prove anyone had
even been in her house and attacked her.

"If it's the burglary ring, maybe the photos Dylan pulled from the last victim's security cameras will help identify the burglars."

She hoped so. Even though the intruders wore ski masks, someone might recognize a mannerism or their posture.

"And you might think about getting security cameras."

"Believe me, I will." Jenna hadn't figured on burglars hitting a Russell County deputy's house. She looked over to Max, who had exited the car and was heading toward the house. "We're at the Slaters', and once we finish, Max and I are going to process my house."

"Sounds good."

She disconnected, blew a strand of hair away from her face, and automatically reached to pull her hair up in a ponytail as she climbed out of the SUV.

Max had made it just inside the living room when she caught up with him and relayed what Alex had shared.

"I know you were hoping for a different outcome," he said.

"Yeah." She pulled on a pair of nitrile gloves. "Let's see what we can find here."

Max pulled on a pair of gloves as well. Taylor was working in the kitchen, and Dylan sat at a desk in the main living room examining papers. He looked up. "Big house. One bedroom downstairs and four upstairs."

Jenna surveyed the area. The main floor was an open concept plan with the kitchen, dining room, and great room in one shared space. It was like a fancy magazine spread, the kind where nothing was out of place, unlike her lived-in house. "Don't suppose you've found anything."

"I wish," Dylan replied.

"Bedroom down that hall?" She pointed to her left.

"Yes, and Katherine's office, which I've already processed."

"I'll do the bedroom."

"Where do you want me to start?" Max asked.

Taylor closed the pantry door and turned toward them. "Anywhere you want."

"Then I'll take an upstairs bedroom," Max said.

Jenna walked down the hall to the bedroom. Like the great room, it was magazine perfect, and probably a guest room with the main one upstairs. She went through the dresser and chest, checked under the mattress, and searched the few clothes hanging in the closet. Nada.

Thinking of her situation, she checked for any false plates on the receptacles and light switches. Nothing there, either. Jenna was wasting her time here.

A few minutes later, she climbed the stairs to the second floor. Max was in what looked like the main bedroom. "Find anything?"

He shook his head. "It looks like this might be the wife's bedroom—I don't see anything that would belong to a man."

"I'll check the next one." Jenna entered the room down the hall, and the first thing she noticed was the scent of a woodsy cologne. It was bound to be Joe Slater's bedroom. She scanned the room that held normal bedroom furniture except for the old-fashioned rolltop desk that looked out of place.

Maybe it was an heirloom . . . or maybe Slater liked to use his bedroom as a combination office. If the latter was the case, why? With a house the size of this one, he could've had a whole office in one of the rooms. The desk looked like a good starting place.

Jenna raised the rolltop and blinked. She'd figured Katherine was the meticulous organizer, but she didn't have anything on her husband. The top of the desk was completely clean—no papers scattered, and there wasn't even a stray pencil on it.

Voices on the landing drew her attention. She walked to the door and looked out just as Joe Slater's sister, Emma, topped the stairs and paused to catch her breath.

"Those stairs get me every time." She took another deep breath. "They said you were up here."

"Did you need something?" Jenna was surprised Dylan had allowed her in.

Emma worked her mouth and blinked as she looked away.

Way to go, Jenna. You've made the woman cry. "I'm sorry. I didn't mean to sound abrupt, but—"

"It's all right. The funeral home called . . ." She swallowed hard. "Clothes . . . I came after clothes."

That made her feel even worse. "Have they released . . ." Why couldn't she ever say the right thing? "Sure. You want to get Joe's first?"

"Please. The man downstairs—I forget what his name is—said you needed to look through whatever I take."

"I do, but that won't take but a minute."

"Jenna?" Max called as she stepped aside to allow Emma into her brother's bedroom.

"Emma came after clothes for the funeral." She turned to the sister who had stopped at the door. "This is Max Anderson from the Tennessee Bureau of Investigation."

"Of course." Now she looked even more confused. "But why TBI—"

"I'm here on another case and just helping out with this," Max said. "Good to meet you, just wish it were under better circumstances, and I better get back to what I was doing."

Emma smiled her acknowledgment. "Guess I better do the same. I'll get Joe's clothes and then pick up Katherine's. I won't be but a few minutes." Emma disappeared into the walk-in closet.

She was true to her word and emerged shortly with a dark navy suit and light blue shirt. She laid them on the bed then picked out a tie and socks and shoes. "Don't know why they want these articles since no one will see them," she muttered.

Jenna looked up from the desk where she'd been looking through the cubbyholes. "I've often thought that." She returned some stamps to the spot where she'd found them. "Is the desk an heirloom?"

Emma laughed. "No, but you would've thought it was from the row they had over it when he wanted it in his bedroom. Katherine was fit to be tied. She'd set up an office on the main floor and couldn't understand why it couldn't go down there." She shook her head. "My sister-in-law had definite ideas on decorating."

"I can see that—the house is beautiful." Jenna stood and walked to the bed, where the clothes were. There was nothing in any of the pockets, and she told Emma she was free to take them.

"Thanks. I'll just grab Katherine's and get out of your hair. Do I bring them for you to check?"

"Max is processing her room. He'll check them," Jenna replied. "When is the funeral?"

"Friday, but I wanted to get this behind me. The medical examiner in Chattanooga indicated their bodies would be released Thursday." She closed her eyes briefly. "There's just me—they didn't have any children—so I didn't see any reason to wait once their bodies are released."

"I totally understand. Again, I'm sorry."

Emma started for the door and stopped. "Will you be through with the house today?"

"Hopefully."

After Emma left for Katherine's room, Jenna turned back to the desk that Joe Slater had insisted stay in his bedroom. What did he want to keep an eye on? Maybe she'd find an answer in one of the drawers. She started with the top drawer. Stationery and files were color-coded. Jenna was vaguely aware of Emma thanking Max and then thumping down the stairs as she thumbed through the files.

Financial statements. Insurance papers. Health records. Jenna opened another drawer. Notepads. Another drawer revealed ledgers. Still nothing to warrant secrecy. She pulled on another drawer. Locked. Bingo. Maybe. She looked in the cubbyholes for a key. No luck.

"Hey, Max," she called out. "Do you have a set of lockpicks?" Jenna didn't expect him to have any, but . . .

A minute later, he stepped into the room. "What?"

"Lockpicks—do you have a set?"

"I thought that's what you said, but why?"

"This drawer is locked, and I don't see a key."

A slow grin spread across his face. "As a matter of fact, I do have a set in the truck."

"Why does that not surprise me?" She matched his grin. "What else do you have? A secret decoder ring . . . shoes with a phone . . . thermal camera?"

"If I told you—"

"Yeah, yeah. Just get the lockpicks."

He laughed. "Be right back."

A few minutes later he returned with a small leather case and shined his phone light on the lock. "This should be a piece of cake."

It didn't take long for him to unlock the drawer and open it. Jenna sighed. Four more ledgers. "They look just like the other ones I found. Why would he lock these up?"

Max picked one up and flipped through it. "Looks legit. Maybe he was hiding money from his wife?"

She pulled on the drawer to take it out, and it caught on something. Jenna bent over and shined her light, trying to see what it might be. "I don't see any reason it won't come out."

Max tugged on the drawer underneath it, then felt along the bottom. "There's something here." He pressed on the bottom of the drawer. "Pull now."

She did, and it released. After taking the ledgers out, they turned the drawer over and discovered a padded envelope taped to the drawer.

"Probably need to get Dylan or Taylor up here to document this," Max said.

She agreed and yelled for them, and soon the two were examining the drawer and taking photos. Once they finished, Dylan peeled the envelope off and drew out a sheet of paper.

"I wasn't expecting that," Max said.

Jenna stared at the words cut from magazines and newspapers—*"You've lined your last pocket"*—a replica of the letter Harrison Carter had received. "Well, this ties Joe Slater to our former mayor, and if we find a similar letter at Paul Nelson's . . ."

"Might not need a letter. Nelson's pockets were cut out," Dylan reminded them.

Jenna stared at the letter. "Maybe the ledgers hold more than we thought."

"Ledgers?" Dylan said.

Jenna pointed to the books she'd laid on the desk. "He had them locked up."

"We'll need a forensic accountant to go through them," the CSI tech said.

"It looks as though there's more to the threatening letter than Carter is admitting," Max said.

19

Max checked his phone as he descended the stairs behind Jenna. When they'd separated to search the house, he contacted an administrator in the prison system and asked him to check on Rick Sebastian's status in prison. He'd hoped to hear something by now.

"Find anything else?" he asked when they joined the CSI team.

Dylan shook his head. "I looked over the journals. You were right—it'll take a forensic accountant to decipher what's in them."

"I'm not an accountant, but my bet is riding on kickbacks Slater and probably Nelson and Harrison Carter received."

In Max's initial interview, Carter had quickly let him know he'd never been involved in any type of illegal activities. It looked like the state senator had lied to him.

"We're going to check the newspaper archives, but I want to find someone who can give us the lowdown on Carter's administration," Jenna said.

"That would be Sheriff Stone or his wife, Judith, but they're in Kentucky with Mark Lassiter," Dylan said. "Next would be Mae Richmond, but she's with them too. But you could call the sheriff. Maybe get them all together on a call."

That was a thought. What he wanted to do was confront Harrison Carter, but that would have to wait until he had a few more facts.

"Wait . . ." Taylor turned to Dylan. "What's the old hermit's name? The one who used to work at city hall?"

Dylan stared down at the floor, then he looked up with a grin. "Mr. Darby. He would know more than anyone in town, but good luck on getting him to talk."

"I remember him," Jenna said. "He used to save mints for me at church. He always seemed to like me."

"You must be the only person in town he liked," Taylor said.

Max jotted down the name just as his stomach growled and the other three turned and looked at him.

He palmed his hands toward them. "Hey, I didn't eat breakfast this morning."

"Neither did I." Jenna checked her watch. "It's not two yet—Pete's Diner is still serving lunch. It would be a good place to go over the security details."

He caught himself before he said "It's a date." "Sounds good." He glanced at Dylan and Taylor. "You two coming?"

They both shook their heads. "We need to finish up here, and then go to Jenna's house, and then to Paul Nelson's," Taylor said. "And his insurance office."

"I don't think there's anything to find at my house," Jenna said. "Besides, I told Alex that Max and I would do it."

Dylan raised his eyebrows. "If you're sure."

"Yeah. You two are slammed."

Max looked at her. "And if you're ready . . ."

Jenna nodded, and he ushered her out of the house. She was being so nice to him, he almost wanted to ask who she was and what she did with Jenna. "Lunch first and then your house?"

"Sounds good, but first, let's look around the yard. It won't take long. I don't really know Joe and Katherine Slater except what I saw in the house, and yards can tell you a whole lot about a person."

He followed her as she walked around the house and turned toward a flower garden at the back.

"It's beautiful here," Jenna said softly. She swept her hand toward the garden. "The roses were probably Katherine's . . . evidently she loved flowers. Maybe her husband helped her."

Roses of every color from yellow and orange to blue and lavender to different shades of red. "Reminds me of a box of crayons."

"I wouldn't have described it that way . . . more like a rainbow."

"Or a rainbow . . ."

She turned toward him, her eyes twinkling. Then she sobered.

"The Slaters were real people who loved and lived and now they're dead." She fisted her hands. "I want to get who did this."

"We will."

His heart thudded against his ribs as she hooked a strand of silky black hair behind her ear. He'd somehow forgotten the way her long eyelashes framed those October-sky-blue eyes, and the way she didn't bother to hide the few freckles sprinkled across her nose.

Liar.

It wasn't that he'd forgotten, but after what happened with Shannon, he hadn't wanted to experience that misery again. Sure, it'd been the drugs talking when she'd hurled bitter accusations at him, but he'd let her words get to him. Words like, if he'd been man enough, she wouldn't have turned to drugs. And the guilt that he hadn't recognized her drug use until it was too late was overwhelming.

It had been a dark time until a pastor friend reminded him that what happened to Shannon wasn't Max's fault, and what she thought about him didn't matter—it was how God saw him. That friend and working with a kid he'd arrested turned Max around.

He checked his phone again as they walked to his truck. Nothing. He pocketed the phone and opened the passenger door. "Still feeling okay?"

"I'm good, and eating will make me even better."

When they reached the road, Jenna said, "Can I see that photo of the letter Carter received? I want to compare it to the one Slater received."

"Sure." Max pulled up his pictures and tapped on the letter. "Here."

He handed her his phone and then pulled onto the road.

Jenna laid both phones side by side in her lap. "The letters look identical. Have you been able to trace the origin of the clippings used in Carter's?"

"The lab is working on it."

"The letter isn't exactly a threat," she said. "Crazy, yes, but I imagine most politicians get letters like this all the time."

She used her fingers to enlarge the photo. "Don't get me wrong, I totally understand with these two deaths connected to him, TBI would get involved now, but what made them pay attention to this in the first place?"

Max hadn't realized just how much he'd missed her quick mind and the way she always saw past the surface in their cases. He couldn't stop the grin that spread across his face.

"What?"

"Nothing. I wondered the same thing, but he'd had that near accident where someone tried to run him off the road. Add having friends in high places, and you can understand why I'm making sure nothing happens Saturday . . . or the next big rally, wherever it is. We don't want another Gabby Giffords."

While running for reelection to Congress, Gabby Giffords had suffered a brain injury in an assassination attempt.

"It's a bad state of affairs when a candidate has to worry about getting shot," she said. "But then it's nothing new."

Max kept his focus on the curvy road. At the four-way stop he pocketed his phone then turned toward town.

"I suppose using words clipped from print is to keep you from analyzing his handwriting," she said.

He agreed.

She repeated the message. "'You've lined your last pocket.' The sender is obviously alluding to the three men receiving kickbacks."

"And he's avenging their wrongdoing. But why now? Why not when they were in office?"

20

From his vantage point, he observed the vehicles parked in the Slater drive. Would they find the letter? It didn't matter. Nothing would stop his next move.

Movement in the backyard had him grabbing the binoculars and zooming in on the figures. Jenna Hart and the guy he'd seen at the accident scene yesterday. Today he was more casual in a short-sleeve polo shirt and khakis instead of the white dress shirt and dark slacks.

He focused on Hart. Just his luck that the deputy had found Paul Nelson's body last night. Or maybe it wasn't so bad—might make Harrison Carter sweat a little.

Yeah, he liked that idea. What he didn't like was Jenna Hart being the lead detective—he'd heard someone say that in town this morning. He frowned. The girl was like a bulldog when it came to something she wanted. And she would want to solve this crime.

He lowered the binoculars. If she got too close, he'd just have to take her out, just like Slater and Nelson . . . and eventually Carter.

21

J enna was surprised at how quickly she and Max slipped into their old roles and brainstormed what they needed to do. While they'd waited for their food, he shared the email from his logistics team approving the location of law enforcement personnel.

She checked her watch, not believing they'd been sitting in the booth an hour and a half going over the security measures while they ate.

"Then you agree," Jenna said, looking up from the notes she'd made on her iPad. "We need ten officers on duty Founders Day?"

Max nodded. "City and county are providing two on the platform along with two of Carter's private security, four officers out front, and four more in the crowd. Plus Carter's other two security guys."

She'd missed these sessions. Jenna scooped up the last bite of peach cobbler in the small bowl and grinned. "That was good."

He smiled back. "I see you haven't lost your love of sweets."

"Yeah. Probably never will." She glanced at her notes again and grunted. "This is going to be like herding cats."

"Herding cats?"

Jenna winced. "I cannot believe I said that. I am becoming my grandmother!"

Max turned his head, obviously trying not to laugh. He was

probably recalling the times she'd talked about her grandmother's use of folk sayings.

"If that's the worst thing that ever happens to you . . ."

Jenna ducked her head. He was right—she could do a lot worse than be like the grandmother who helped raise her.

"How is Eva?"

"Sassy as ever." Max had met her grandmother a few times at the family picnics the department liked to put on to foster family support and encouragement for officers.

Big mistake—Granna decided Max was the best thing since sliced bread and a perfect match for her. It hadn't mattered that Max was Jenna's boss, or that she and Phillip were becoming an item—her grandmother had thought that was a mistake from the get-go. Even now, Granna asked about Max at least a couple of times a month, in spite of Jenna telling her she hadn't seen him since he became a TBI agent. "She asks about you sometimes."

Talk about an understatement.

"Tell her I said hello, and that I'll try and see her while I'm in town."

"She would like that." Except it wasn't happening. If it did, Granna's comments would start weekly.

Her face warmed under his intense gaze. Not to mention her heart pounding like she'd run a marathon.

"Don't believe I've heard 'herding cats' in a while, but it certainly fits," he said, grinning.

"I once used it a lot, dealing with Levi and his friends."

"Who's Levi?"

"He's the only good thing that came out of what happened in Chattanooga."

"Oh?"

She nodded. "He's eight. His dad was killed the same night I was shot in that drug deal that went south. His mom had taken off with a boyfriend, and he lived with his grandmother in the apartments behind James A. Henry. I helped out with the mentoring program at the apartment community center while I was recovering. That's when I used the 'herding cats' phrase."

"So how is he doing now?"

"Better. I set him up with a Big Brother, but I still try to get to Chattanooga and see him occasionally. His grandmother has serious health problems, and I've brought him to Pearl Springs for the weekend a couple of times, to give her a break. I'm planning to get him again this weekend."

Max opened his mouth and quickly closed it.

She narrowed her eyes. "What were you going to say?"

"This weekend?"

Jenna groaned. What was she even thinking? Even if the murders got solved, she would be working on the security for Carter. "Right. Not this weekend, but soon."

"I hope you don't overload yourself. Stress can sometimes trigger PTSD."

"I'm fine. No more problems, other than a healthy dose of caution—which is a good thing to have as a deputy."

"Then it's probably good for you to invest yourself in the kid. Except—what would you do if he was here and you were called out to an emergency? Your grandmother is getting up in years."

"Granna loves having Levi around. She'd fill in for me. Besides, it's only for a weekend every now and then, not even once a month," she said, keeping her voice from sounding defensive.

But one thing he'd said had hit a nerve. Her grandmother was eighty, and an eight-year-old boy might be more than she could handle. "And I'll make sure it's a weekend I don't work when I bring Levi here."

The look he gave her said they both knew her job didn't work that way. He held up his hand. "Wait—I shouldn't have said anything, it's just . . . kids take a lot of time."

"And you know this how?"

22

For once it felt good to put Max on the defensive. Jenna waited for his explanation.

Max shifted his gaze toward the door, then back to her. "I've been doing the same thing with a kid in Nashville."

She leaned back in the booth and eyed him. "I can't believe you were giving me grief when you're doing the same thing."

"It's different—Cody is a teenager."

"And what does that have to do with the price of eggs in Russia?"

He dropped his head. "You're right. Consider me properly chastised for meddling in your business."

"Thank you very much." Then she chuckled. "I can't believe you've gotten involved in mentoring a kid—they make you break out in hives."

"I was surprised myself."

"How and when did this happen?"

He picked up the toothpick that had held his sandwich together and chewed on it. "A couple of months after I moved to Nashville, I arrested this thirteen-year-old boy. Cody Reynolds. He'd broken into a tobacco shop as part of a gang initiation, but I saw something in him. He didn't really want to be in the gang.

"Like Levi, the dad was nonexistent but he does have a mother—a single mom who works two jobs to keep a roof over their head. She doesn't have a lot of time for him. I talked the judge into releasing him on the condition he meet with me two days a week. Sometimes he spends the weekend at my place—my parents are crazy about him."

Her anger at him melted. "He was looking for a family."

Max nodded. "Then last winter, I got the flu that turned into pneumonia, and after a stay in the hospital—"

"You were in the hospital?" She hadn't heard about that. "I'm sorry. If I'd known—"

He waved her off. "It turned out fine. I was only out of commission for a few weeks, but when Cody found out what happened, he showed up at the house and helped me out. It changed him—knowing he was helping me changed his whole attitude."

She looked at him. "He's what? Eighteen now?"

"Seventeen. Going into his senior year of high school. He's the quarterback of the football team. Got a 3.5 GPA. If he can bring that up a little, I think he'll get a scholarship to UT—he wants to be a coach and help kids like him."

Jenna's heart swelled. "Helping him is something to be proud of, Max."

He shook his head. "It's helped me as much as it has him."

"I know what you mean. I feel the same way with Levi when I do get a chance to spend time with him."

He chewed on the toothpick. "Are you still riding horses?"

"I am. In fact, I usually ride four or five times a week." Jenna grinned at him. "It's that downtime you were talking about."

He had the grace to blush. "So, you finally got yourself a horse?"

Evidently Max had paid attention when she'd occasionally shared in the office about riding and wanting to buy a horse. "I have an eight-year-old thoroughbred. Ace."

"Good for you. Does Levi ride?"

"A little. Ace is too much for him, but the owner of the barn where I board him has a pinto that he lets Levi ride the few times he's been here."

He raised his eyebrows. "He's not afraid?"

"That kid isn't afraid of anything. Up until now I've only let him sit on Patches while I lead. Of course, that's after he brushes and feeds her . . . and cleans out her stall."

"I'm glad you're letting him know he's not getting a free ride."

"There's no such thing. It's important that he understands that taking responsibility for a horse is part of riding." She grinned. "He'll be happy the next time he comes—he gets to ride the pony at a walk all by himself around the ring."

"Sounds like you're making a difference in someone's life too."

"I hope so. His mother . . ." Jenna shook her head. "The grandmother thinks she's dead since they haven't heard from her in almost a year—probably overdosed."

"That's sad. I'm glad he has you and the Big Brother you set him up with." Max's phone rang, and he glanced at the screen. "Oh, good, it's a call I've been waiting for. I'll be right back."

While he was gone, Jenna stacked the plates they'd shoved aside and didn't notice the diner owner approach.

"I'll get those," Ethel said. "I would've gotten them earlier, but you two looked like you didn't want to be disturbed."

"You were right." Jenna tilted her head. "What can you tell me about Harrison Carter?"

"Other than I didn't much care for him? He was . . . oh, goodness, I don't know where to start."

Ethel snapped her fingers and then pointed to an older gentleman sitting in a corner booth. "Mr. Darby can tell you more than I can. That's him sitting right over there."

Mr. Darby was the one Taylor and Dylan had mentioned earlier. She looked up at Ethel. "Are you talking about our local hermit?"

"He wasn't always a hermit—he used to be friendly as all get out."

"Thanks." It was worth a shot. She stood and approached the booth. He didn't seem to notice Jenna, or he was simply ignoring her.

"Mr. Darby?"

He flinched when she called his name. He turned toward her with a frown. "Yes?"

She could tell by the puzzled expression that he was trying to place her.

"Jenna Hart," she said. "You used to give me mints at church."

He looked her up and down. "Little Jenna?"

"Yep, except I'm all grown up. I guess you're retired now."

He nodded.

"You worked at city hall, right?" She already knew he did, but it seemed like a good opening.

He nodded again.

Not very talkative, but Jenna couldn't say she hadn't been warned. "You were there when Harrison Carter first became mayor, right?"

She didn't think the man could get any more still, but now he just froze, except for his gaze that darted to the door.

"That was a long time ago."

She strained to hear him. "But you worked there back when he was mayor, and Joe Slater and Paul Nelson were councilmen?"

"Why are you asking me about them?"

If her father knew about the wreck, she figured Mr. Darby would have heard about it as well. "I'm sure you've heard that Joe Slater drove off the side of Eagle Ridge and—"

"What?" He swallowed hard.

So he hadn't heard. She explained what had happened.

His bushy brows lowered in a frown. "You say both of them died?"

"I'm afraid so . . . and Paul Nelson's body was found last night."

His eyes bulged, and the old man licked his lips. "Wasn't nothing like a heart attack, was it?"

"No, I'm afraid Mr. Nelson was shot."

"And the Slaters?"

"They weren't shot, but we're not certain it was an accident."

Mr. Darby leaned against the back of the booth, his face pasty.

Jenna hadn't expected the news to hit the man so hard. "I'm sorry. I shouldn't have dropped this on you like that—I really thought you would've heard the news. Are you all right?"

He leaned forward and grabbed his glass of water, gulping it. When he set the glass back on the table, he muttered something under his breath that Jenna didn't catch. Then he looked up at her. "Are you sure it wasn't an accident?"

"We're not sure of anything at this point, except three people are dead. Is there anything you can tell me about the people involved?"

"No. I don't know anything that could help you."

He'd answered a little too fast. "You're certain you don't know someone who would want these three people dead."

"Don't have a clue." He grabbed his ball cap and set it on his head. "I gotta get home."

"Mr. Darby, if you know anything that would help us with these deaths, you need to tell me."

When he looked up, his demeanor had changed. The shock had faded and his guileless blue eyes held hers. "I don't know what's going on around here, and I like it like that. It's why I hardly ever come to town. Haven't seen the Slaters or Paul Nelson in years, so I have no idea what happened."

She took a card from her pocket and held it out. "If you remember or hear anything, give me a call."

Darby looked at the card like it was a snake, and she laid it on the table.

"Don't expect I'll hear anything." He slid out of the booth and stood. "Good day to you."

Jenna's baloney meter was going off loud and clear. "Keep my card, anyway. Who knows? Something may come to you."

"No need." He left her card on the table and walked out the door, passing Max as he came back in.

She picked up her card and returned to their table.

Max nodded toward the door. "Who was that?"

"Mr. Darby."

"The janitor at city hall?" Max seemed to have something on his mind.

"One and the same, and before you ask, he wouldn't tell me anything. Although he did seem shocked about the Slaters and Paul Nelson."

"Okay."

There was definitely something on his mind. Jenna waited for him to spit it out, and when he didn't, she said, "What's bothering you?"

"Let's wait until we head to your house." He grabbed her check, and she frowned.

"Hey, we're going Dutch."

"Not today."

She narrowed her eyes at him, and he held up his hands. "Can't an old friend buy you lunch?"

"On the condition I buy next time."

"Gotcha."

"I'll be outside."

Max was quiet as they drove out of town. She knew better than to push—he'd talk when he was ready, and he didn't get ready until they pulled into her drive.

"Can I come in?" he asked.

Her spidey sense tingled. Something was wrong. "If you're about to tell me some bad news, I need a cup of coffee. How about you?"

"Good idea." He followed her inside.

"Kitchen is back here . . . oh, wait, you've already been in my kitchen today." She couldn't stop rattling off and busied her hands making coffee. Use a pod or make a whole pot? Her coffeemaker did both. She settled on a pot. "Strong?" she asked over her shoulder.

"Just regular."

It seemed to take forever for the coffee to brew, but finally she handed him a cup. "Sugar or cream?"

"Black is fine."

"You want to drink it outside on my patio—it's not in the sun?"

He nodded, and they headed out to the patio.

"This is nice," Max said, looking out at her view of the mountains, and she nodded, waiting for him to tell her whatever the call had been about.

Finally he sighed.

"That phone call . . ." He sat opposite her and raised his gaze to meet hers.

A shiver ran down her back.

"It was from a friend who works in the prison system."

"Okay . . . and?"

"When was the last time you checked on Rick Sebastian?"

"What's to check? He's at Pikeville—"

"Sebastian isn't at Pikeville." He leaned forward. "He was released a month ago."

23

W hat?" Jenna couldn't believe what Max had just said.

Why hadn't she been notified that he'd been released? Rick Sebastian had stood in the Hamilton County courthouse after his conviction and threatened to kill her once he got out. Granted, he'd only stared straight at her and mouthed the words "You're dead." She'd reported it but didn't think anyone believed her.

"How could they release him? He was supposed to serve at least half his five-year sentence, and it hasn't been that long yet."

"Overcrowding in prisons. Evidently, he's been a model prisoner, and they needed room for what they deem 'more dangerous criminals.'"

"At least tell me he's on parole."

Max shook his head. "Walked out a free man."

How was this possible? Jenna frowned and rubbed the scar in the soft part of her shoulder where the bullet entered. If the drug dealer followed through on the threats he'd made to kill her, would he then be considered dangerous? Like being the boss of the Scorpions wasn't enough?

Alleged boss. That's what the DA had said when Jenna had not been able to tie him to any crime other than possession of two hundred grams of cocaine. A crime that should have sent him to prison for five years.

"I'm sorry to spring this on you like this," he said. "But I didn't want you blindsided."

"Thank you for that." She fought the tears that stung her eyes and wrapped her hands around the coffee mug.

Max leaned forward. "You can't get them all, Jenna."

"He needs to be off the streets." She set the mug down hard. "The Scorpions—it's the worst gang in Chattanooga. And he got away with shooting me."

Max opened his mouth and Jenna held up her hand. "The investigation into the shooting was closed by the time I got out of the hospital, and I know the investigators concluded that the dead gang member at the scene fired the bullet that hit me, but they were wrong. Rick Sebastian was at John A. Henry that night, and he shot me."

"Were you wearing a vest?"

"Always." She touched her shoulder. "The bullet came in at an angle through the arm opening. Rarely ever happens."

"I just wish you'd showed the photos you have to Billingsley."

"He would have shot them down. He'd already warned me not to accuse Phillip of something I couldn't prove." She stood. "I'll let you see them for yourself."

She collected the jump drive and her computer and returned to the kitchen. Once the grainy images appeared, she turned the computer where Max could see them. "See? It's impossible to tell where the photos were taken—the school isn't evident—or when they were taken. Phillip could argue the photos had been taken months before. And Sebastian is little more than a shadowy figure. I know it's him, but would anyone else? Probably not."

Max turned to her. "I understand why you might be hesitant to show these to anyone. How about the kid you saved? What did he remember?"

"Not much. He was focused on his dad. He and his grand-mother were new to the apartments, so neither of them recognized any of the players." She cocked her head. "You know how sometimes everything comes together like clockwork? Well, that night was just the opposite—if anything could go wrong, it did.

"I have to focus on the good. They didn't all walk. At least I put some of the gang members away. And Sebastian served time. But it should've been longer, especially after he threatened me, not once but twice."

Max hesitated. "I hope you consider me your friend, and if I ask questions, it's not because I don't believe you. I just need more information. You say he threatened you. That should've been enough to charge him."

Her shoulders sagged. "No one heard him but me, and no DA would touch it—it would've been a he-said-she-said situation."

"Tell me what happened," he said gently.

Sebastian's words echoed in her head, and she swallowed down the bile that rose up in her throat. "The first time was after I came back to work . . . I was working the desk Captain Billingsley assigned me, and it was just before Sebastian's trial for the cocaine bust. He was still out on bond, and another detective in the Unit had brought him in for questioning in the death of a rival gang member, which nothing came of, by the way. I'm telling you, Sebastian is like Teflon—nothing sticks to him.

"I happened to be on the elevator when he and the detective escorting him to the lobby got on. The elevator was crowded and noisy. He managed to lean in close and say, 'The next time you won't survive.'"

"Too bad no one else heard him."

"Yeah. I barely heard him." She shrugged. "Like I said, it was noisy."

"You said he threatened you twice?"

Jenna nodded. "The second time was in the courtroom after

he was convicted, and he only mouthed the words 'You're dead.' Evidently no one saw him do it other than me."

Max reached for her hands and gave a gentle squeeze, stilling the frantic pace of her heart. When he'd been head of the robbery division, he'd always been there for her, for all of his detectives, unlike her boss in the gang unit.

She and Max had always connected. How she'd missed that. Jenna hadn't connected with anyone on that level at the Russell County Sheriff's Office except Alex . . . and maybe Wayne.

She looked up at him. "Tell me something?"

"If I can."

She probably shouldn't even ask, but it had bugged her for over five years. "I understand why you went to the TBI—I even thought about applying—but why did you leave Chattanooga? The Bureau has an office there."

"It was time to leave," he said after a long pause. "And you need to call Alex and let her know about Sebastian."

Max had never been one to lay his cards on the table, and this was no exception. "Do you think it's possible he was the one who broke into my house this morning?"

He hesitated, and her body tensed, remembering he wasn't completely in agreement with her that someone had broken in.

"It crossed my mind," he finally said.

"Surely he wouldn't risk coming to Pearl Springs and doing something stupid like break into my house, would he? He'd have to know he'd be the first suspect, right?"

"Not to mention strangers around here stick out like a neon sign—believe me, I know." Max took their cups to the sink. "I think Sebastian would be too smart for that. He didn't get to be the boss of the Scorpions by making moves like that."

"Alleged boss, according to the DA." She blew out a breath. "And I really don't see him leaving his homies in Chattanooga."

He hesitated. "That's the one thing that worries me—someone

else took over when he went to prison—he may be looking for a place to land. Not that I think it'll be here. Just stay aware of your surroundings, and when I'm here, I'll have your back."

And he would. She'd missed that as well. Not that she didn't have it with her fellow deputies here in Russell County, but it was different with Max. Always had been. "I know."

Max checked his watch. "Call Alex, then we'll get your house dusted for prints."

She took out her phone. "You're right, and the sooner, the better." Before she placed the call, she noticed him eyeing the lock on her back door again. "You keep looking at that lock. Is something wrong with it?"

"No. Did you deadbolt your doors this morning?"

She frowned. "I don't know. I usually do, but I was groggy after last night. I even left my phone at home."

"While you talk to Alex, I'm going to check the perimeter of your house—an intruder could come in through a window, and if one did, there might be footprints."

"Thanks." Jenna called Alex and relayed the information Max had shared about Sebastian.

"I'm sorry, Jenna," Alex said. "I'll call the prison and request his intake photo and then request a mug shot from Chattanooga PD. Tomorrow I'll distribute copies to all the deputies, and they can show them around town. If he's here, someone is bound to have seen him."

"He's a free man," Jenna said. "We can't keep him from showing up here."

"No," Alex said, "but we can keep tabs on him."

"Thanks."

"Anything else?"

"Yeah. I talked to Eric Darby today—he used to be the janitor at city hall when Nelson and Slater were on the city council."

"I know who he is, and he was in town? And he talked to you?"

"Yeah, he was at Pete's Diner," Jenna said. "He seemed really upset about the Slater deaths, and Paul Nelson's too."

"He must have been in shock—that's more talking than I've known him to do with anyone."

"I was kind of surprised too. What happened to him? He used to be so nice to me at church when I was a kid."

"Nobody knows why he holed up in the woods in that little house of his," Alex said. "Maybe if you follow up later at Darby's house, you can get more out of him."

She didn't think so. "Why don't you send Wayne? He's been a deputy for years, and Darby would probably relate better to him."

"No. The old man talked to you—like I said, he hasn't said five words to anyone in town in twenty years—so he must like you. Follow up on it, today if you can, and then take off—after last night, anything on your to-do list can wait until tomorrow."

She checked her watch. Four thirty. She looked up as Max came in through the back door. "Max is still here. Maybe he'll ride with me to Summerlin Ridge."

24

W hat's on Summerlin Ridge?" Max asked when Jenna ended her call.

"Not a what, a who—Mr. Darby, the old man I talked to at Pete's Diner today."

He nodded.

"He wouldn't answer my questions. I definitely get the sense he knows something, though."

"Maybe you need to pass this along to Alex."

"That's what I just did, and she gave it back to me. Alex thinks I can get more out of him than anyone else."

He laughed. "She's probably right—if anyone can get someone to talk, it'd be you."

"She wants me to go today."

He checked his watch. "It's four thirty."

"I know. Want to tag along? Darby's place is about ten miles from here, and it shouldn't take long, but I'm good to go by myself if you have something else you need to do."

He raised an eyebrow. "How about your house? Don't you want to process it first?"

"It's not going anywhere. Besides I don't think we'll find any prints." She gave him a wicked grin. "And I'll let you drive again so your male ego isn't bruised."

He crossed his arms over his chest. "I'll have you to know my ego doesn't bruise that easily—I'm not one of those control freaks who won't let anyone else behind the wheel."

Jenna held up her finger. "Wait a minute and let me run that through my baloney meter."

He grinned sheepishly. "Seriously, I'll take you if you'll let me camp out at your house tonight so I can help dust for prints."

"We'll see."

He knew what that meant, but evidently she'd forgotten how stubborn he could be too. The problem was, Max wasn't 100 percent certain there'd been an intruder, but if there had been, he wanted to be there for her. "Jenna, the intruder could return."

"So you're going to stay here forever?"

"Of course not, but . . ." He lifted his hands in surrender. Not that he wouldn't give it another shot later. "You win."

"Glad that's settled," Jenna said. "Oh, Alex is requesting photos of Sebastian from the prison and Chatt PD. She's going to distribute them in the morning."

"Good deal."

She called the 911 office and got Darby's address, and he put it in his GPS. "You'll tell me if it tries to take me the long way, right?"

"Absolutely."

The ten miles took them half an hour on the narrow, crooked roads. "What do you do if you meet someone?" he asked as they rounded yet another narrow curve.

Jenna chuckled. "Pray. Especially that they aren't drinking . . . or texting."

Max had never spent any time in Russell County and had no idea it was so picturesque. Once or twice he slowed just to admire the mountains when they came to the occasional break in the trees. Layers and layers of mountains stretched as far as the eye could see. He risked a glance at Jenna. "Why did you ever leave here?"

"I went to Chattanooga for college," she said. "And that's where I was born."

"So how did you end up here?"

"My dad was raised here, but he moved to Chattanooga after he married my mom. When she died, he came back home. He thought about returning to Chattanooga when I was twelve, but then his dad died in an accident and Granna needed help—she was in the accident with my grandfather. He also stayed to fight the dam and reservoir that took the family farm. At least that's what Granna told me. Dad never tells me anything."

"He raised you?"

"With Granna's and Sam's help. And don't forget to go by and see her."

"I won't. So, when you finished college, you became a cop. Was it something you always wanted to be?"

"Not really. I took a criminal justice class and that hooked me. Then the Chattanooga Police Department ran a hiring campaign, and I joined up."

Funny how they'd worked together for over a year, but they'd never discussed why she became a cop.

"How about you?" she asked.

He sat a little straighter. "I'm a third-generation cop. My dad and grandfather both were Nashville officers. My grandfather was a patrol cop, and Dad worked his way up to captain."

"Why didn't you become a Nashville policeman?"

"I was afraid of people thinking I got preferential treatment because he was a captain . . . besides, one Maxwell Anderson in Nashville PD is enough."

She turned toward him. "You're a junior?"

Max laughed. "No. They gave me Dad's first name and my grandfather's middle—Maxwell James Anderson." Something

Jenna said raised questions in his mind. "You said your dad was against the dam being built. I'm getting the impression the dam created a lot of controversy."

"That would be understating it. The surveyors were threatened, one was even shot at. But it didn't stop the dam from being built."

"We need to research those years in the newspaper archives."

"*Turn right in 600 feet,*" the GPS intoned.

A weathered mailbox came into view, but with no number on it. Max peered at the dense overgrowth that encroached the road and turned to Jenna. "Do you see a drive?"

"Not yet." She stared at the property. "See if the drive is around the curve."

Max eased the truck down the road.

"There it is." Jenna pointed to a lane barely wide enough for their vehicle. "Something tells me that when we get to the house, I better go to the door. He might not talk to us at all if he sees you."

"You say he wasn't always this way?"

"Not when I was a little girl. He was really kind and friendly." She rubbed the back of her neck. "He used to hunt with my dad and uncle, and I have a memory of them being worried about him becoming a hermit."

Max turned into the gravel drive and braked a hundred feet in. A six-foot gate connected to an equally tall fence blocked them. "He's serious about no one talking to him."

"I thought everyone was exaggerating." Jenna opened her door. "Let me see if I can open it."

He lowered his window as Jenna climbed out of the truck and walked to the wrought-iron gate. "Locked," she called. "I'm going to see how far this fence goes."

Surely not all the way around his property—it'd cost a fortune. Max climbed out of the truck. "I'll go with you."

She opened her mouth to say something but instead nodded. "Suit yourself."

It wasn't long before the metal fence turned to barbed wire. "We can crawl through here."

He reached to hold the top wire up.

"Wait! It may be hot."

Max didn't see any conductors. "How can you tell?"

"Give me a sec." Jenna pulled up a blade of grass and laid it on the wire. She slowly moved the grass over the wire, stopping when her hand was a couple of inches from the wire. She jerked her hand back. "Yep, it's hot, all right, but I think I can scoot under it."

"Hold on a minute." He picked up a dead limb and used it to lift the bottom wire. "Now."

She gave him a thumbs-up. "Good thinking."

Jenna lay on her back and wiggled under the wire. Once she was on the other side, she held it up for him.

"Why do you think he's so paranoid?" Max asked.

"Not a clue. And I don't think anyone in town knows either— it's a great mystery why he became a hermit."

Max eyed the dense woods. "He picked a good place for it."

They worked their way back to the drive. It appeared to be as curvy as the road they had driven to get here.

"How far?"

"Not sure—never been to his house. But it can't be that far." She pointed to power lines. "I doubt the power company would run lines more than a quarter of a mile from the road."

That was encouraging, and after almost ten minutes of walking they rounded a curve and a modest white clapboard house came into view. "Good," Max said. "I was beginning to wonder."

"Why don't you stay here while I approach the house?"

"I don't—"

The unmistakable crack of a rifle dropped them both to the ground.

25

Max's weight was killing Jenna. He'd shoved her to the ground and put his body between her and the shooter. A noble thought if she didn't suffocate. "I can't move."

"You okay?"

"I will be once you let me up." Max rolled away from her, and she breathed again.

Jenna climbed to her knees and retrieved the gun she'd dropped when Max tackled her. Now that the immediate danger was over, she didn't know whether to be glad he'd wanted to protect her or mad that he thought she couldn't protect herself. She decided to go with her first impulse. "Thanks. You have good reflexes. You okay?"

"I'm good. Sorry if I hit you too hard." He glanced toward her. "And I know you think it was completely unnecessary, but I can't help how I react."

"That's why I didn't take your head off." She softened the words with a laugh. "I'm assuming our shooter is Mr. Darby."

"Never assume. Why don't you call out to him?"

"Good idea." She stood, and using a tree as a shield, she yelled, "Mr. Darby . . . it's me, Jenna Hart. We talked at the diner today, and I'd like to talk to you again, ask you some questions about Joe Slater."

"Go away! I ain't got nothing to say."

She turned to Max. "I think that settles the question of who was shooting," she said.

"Yep. Try to reason with him."

"You don't know what I'm going to ask," she yelled. When he didn't respond, she added, "Three people have died and we think you can help us."

More silence. Then . . . . "Told you I don't have anything to say. You might as well leave." Determination resonated in his voice.

"I'm not leaving until you talk to me."

She waited.

"You always were a stubborn little thing." More silence. "All right. You can come to the house, but leave the other officer where he is."

Max shook his head. "That's not a good idea."

"I'll be okay. Mr. Darby won't hurt me." She believed that with all her heart. The man couldn't have changed that much from when she was a kid. "I'll talk him into letting you join us."

She holstered her gun and walked toward the house. "I'm coming in by myself," she yelled.

Even though she didn't think the old man would shoot her, Jenna couldn't help being nervous. Mr. Darby sat on the front porch. He didn't look much like a hermit—she'd always pictured a hermit with tattered overalls and long white hair and beard.

Instead, he was still dressed in his khakis and a plaid shirt. A black dog lay at his feet, at least she thought it was a dog, but her gaze was on the deer rifle across his lap. A chill raced down her back. He could've killed them if he'd wanted.

What made him so paranoid? The question ate at her. She approached the porch and stopped when the huge, shaggy-haired dog stood. A low growl rumbled from his throat. "Afternoon. Does he bite?"

He nodded. "Down, Bear."

Appropriate name. The dog circled and lay at Darby's feet, but he watched Jenna's every move. There'd be no sneaking up on his owner.

She propped her foot against the bottom step. "Any chance you'd put that rifle down?"

"Might've if you'd come alone."

"Max won't hurt you. He's—"

"TBI."

"You knew?"

"Heard some people at the diner talking about you and the TBI agent." He cocked his head to the side. "So what makes you think the Slaters were murdered now—two hours ago you didn't."

"I didn't say they were murdered."

"Didn't have to. Three people are dead and you're here to question me—doesn't take a brain surgeon to figure out it's murder."

That must be why he let her come to the house—he wanted to know how they died. Maybe she could leverage that. "A couple of things. Can Max join us?"

His lips twitched. "I don't suppose you'll tell me anything if he doesn't."

She smiled her answer, and he gave a curt nod. "Hey, Max, come on up."

Darby leaned the rifle against the straight-back chair as Max joined them at the porch. When Bear saw him, the ruff of his neck rose and a low growl rumbled in his throat. "It's okay. At ease," Darby said.

The dog settled back down but stayed wary as she introduced the two men. "And that's Bear." She pointed to the dog.

"Aptly named. Thanks for letting me join you," Max said.

"Don't thank me, thank your partner here—she's beyond stubborn."

Jenna swallowed a smile. "I think of myself as independent."

"Ha!" Max said. "Mr. Darby here has the right word." That

made the old man smile. Max nodded at the dog. "What breed is Bear?"

"Good question. If I had to guess, I'd say some St. Bernard and some Lab, maybe a little Heinz 57." He rubbed the huge dog's head. "Okay, tell me about the Slaters, Paul Nelson too, if you know any more."

Jenna nodded. "Nelson was shot and buried in a shallow grave near where you used to hunt with my dad."

He pressed his lips together in a thin line. "And Slater? You figured out yet the wreck wasn't an accident?"

"Pretty sure you're right—tie-rod came loose on that new vehicle of his and the nut holding it looks tampered with," Max said.

Color drained from the man's face.

"What can you tell us about them?" Jenna asked. "Do you know who would want them dead?"

"Just about anyone who had dealings with them during Harrison Carter's early administration, especially the dam project."

"Was there anyone who was for the dam project?" Max asked.

"Maybe a few people in town who didn't lose their family land. Or those in the valley who had already sold out—they probably didn't care one way or the other."

"I don't understand. I didn't know anyone had sold their property." From what Jenna remembered, most of the people who lived where the dam and reservoir had been created refused to sell—that included her dad's friends she'd talked to last night. The state had condemned their land by eminent domain and seized it.

When Darby didn't respond, Jenna repeated her question.

He looked off in the distance, then brought his attention back to her. "That was probably the wrong choice of words. Your dad knows more about the subject than I do. Just ask him. I've already said more than I should've."

"What do you mean by that?" Max asked. "Has someone threatened you?"

"Nope. Nobody has any cause to threaten me." He checked his watch and stood. "It's about my supper time, so if you'll excuse me."

They had been dismissed. Period. But she wasn't finished. "How about Harrison Carter? What can you tell us about him?"

He chewed on her question, then said, "Like I said, he was mayor when Joe Slater and Paul Nelson were councilmen."

They were going in circles. "Did you like him?" she asked.

Again he was slow on his answer. "Liked him 'bout as well as I like any politician."

The man was infuriating.

"Was he honest?" Max asked.

Darby scratched his jaw. "'Bout as honest as—"

"Any politician," Jenna finished for him. She would fight this battle another day. She stood and fished a card from her pocket. "Thank you for your time, Mr. Darby. If you think of anything that might help with our investigation, would you contact me?"

"Don't think I'll be remembering anything new," he said.

That was exactly what she thought he'd say. She circled her cell phone number. "If you do, you can always reach me at this number. And can I have your phone number? In case I have more questions."

He rattled off his number. "It don't work half the time here, so don't be surprised if I don't answer."

She didn't know whether it didn't work because of reception or if it was his way of saying he wouldn't be answering. Jenna wrote it down anyway.

He stood. "I'll walk down and let you out so you won't have to crawl under the fence."

Now he was going to be nice? She couldn't figure him out, but she had one last question for him. Not that she expected an answer. "Why are you barricaded in like this?"

"Why not? There's a lot of bad people in this world."

26

At the gate, Max stuck out his hand and thanked Darby for unlocking it while Jenna walked on to his truck. "It was good to meet you." He nodded toward the dog that had trailed behind them from the house. "And Bear."

"Bear seems to like you, and he's a good judge of character. But don't tell anyone you stopped by here or that I talked to you."

Max raised his eyebrows. "Why's that?"

"I have a reputation to uphold. People been leaving me alone for twenty years, and I don't want that to change."

Max handed him one of his cards. "I'll be here the rest of the week. Call me if you need anything." He hesitated. "Any particular reason you were in town today?"

"Doctor's appointment. Got a little high blood pressure, and he won't give me a refill on the medicine unless I come see him every six months."

"Take care of yourself. Bear too. And if you remember anything—doesn't matter how small, call me."

The older man rubbed his jaw, and for a second, Max thought he was going to say something, then he gave him a curt nod before turning and walking toward his house with Bear on his heels.

Just as Max opened his truck door, Darby called out to him. "Make sure you have that girl's back."

Max half saluted. "Don't worry, I will."

Once he was in his truck, he watched the old man and dog until they rounded the curve. "Strange fellow."

"I wish you could've known him before he withdrew from society," Jenna said.

"That's what I don't understand. When I think of a hermit, I think of someone who hates being around people. That doesn't exactly fit him—once we broke the ice, he was fairly sociable and seemed more wary than anything else."

She slowly nodded. "And he does come in to town."

"I think he knows a whole lot more than he's telling about Carter." Max had programmed Jenna's address in his GPS and took a right when prompted. "He suggested we talk to your dad . . . are you up for that?"

"Not today. And Alex told me to knock off early and get some rest."

"I can drop you off at your house and talk to him myself."

"No. I'd rather go with you—Dad has a tendency to talk too much sometimes. I would just as soon our suspicions didn't become fodder for the gossips in Russell County," she said.

Max trusted Jenna's intuition, especially since he didn't know her dad.

"Even better would be if we wait until tomorrow and stop by Granna's. She'll tell us more in a casual conversation than my father ever would, and she'll keep it to herself. Besides, if she learns you're in town and you didn't stop by . . ."

"I'd planned on stopping before I leave, but why can't we stop now?"

She chuckled. "This is Tuesday afternoon. She plays bridge with the ladies in her church."

"Then tomorrow it is." He cast a side glance at Jenna. She'd

151

leaned her head against the seat rest and closed her eyes. "You feeling okay?"

"Mm-hmm. Just resting my eyes."

"How about your head? Still hurt?" She'd hit the floor this morning hard enough to raise a bump.

"It's fine. Just missing my sleep from last night."

"When we get to your house, you can nap while I dust for prints."

"We won't find anything. Whoever broke in was too smart to not wear gloves. Just let me relax a minute."

Sometimes he didn't know when to shut up. For the next fifteen minutes, the only sound in the truck was the automated voice of the GPS and Jenna's even breathing. When he slowed to turn in her drive, she sat up and looked around.

"Are we here already?"

"Yep. Feeling better?"

"I am." A text dinged on her phone. She checked it and groaned. "It's from Kirk. Ace got out of his stall, and he won't let Kirk catch him."

"Who's Kirk?"

"Bryan Bishop's grandson. I board my horse at Bryan's barn. This morning I asked the boy if he would feed and water Ace." She looked at him. "You know, until after Saturday. I should've known better."

"Can't the grandfather—"

"No. He's not in the best of health. My horse, my responsibility. There's no need for you to hang around." Jenna thumbed a text and then opened her door. "I'll take care of this. Just have to grab my jeans and a T-shirt."

"Jenna," he said. "Going to the barn is the last thing you need to be doing."

She jerked her head toward him, her eyes blazing.

He cringed and quickly held up his hand. "It's only a suggestion, and probably not a good one . . ."

"Thank you for clarifying." Her lips twitched as the ghost of a smile threatened. "But I'm fine now—honestly, I let you drive to Mr. Darby's because I didn't want to argue with you."

She climbed out of the truck and slammed the door before she jogged to her front door.

He jumped out and hurried after her. "Hold up."

She turned and glared at him. "Why?"

"Your intruder could have returned."

Her mouth formed a small O. "Right . . . I didn't think of that."

"That's why you have me here." He held out his hand. "Key?"

Jenna punched him in the shoulder, but she handed over her key.

The house was just as they'd left it, and to tell the truth, it didn't look as though anyone had searched it. What if she'd had an episode of PTSD earlier today and imagined she'd heard someone inside? And then fainted when she reached the kitchen . . .

"I'll be right back."

When Jenna returned, she'd changed into jeans and a T-shirt.

"My riding boots are in my SUV," Jenna said as she strapped on her service pistol. "I can handle this, so I'll see you in the morning."

He followed her to the front porch. "I know you can, but I'm not staying at the hotel tonight—you said I could stay here."

"No, *you* said you were staying here." She smiled sweetly before she turned and pressed a transparent piece of tape at the top of the door. "Don't know why I didn't think of this earlier."

He hadn't even seen the tape in her hand. If there was an intruder and he returned and entered through the front door, when they came back, the disturbed tape would alert them. "Good thinking. Did you put one on the back door?"

"No. Be right back." She hurried around the side of the house with the tape and returned a few minutes later. "All taken care of."

Max nodded. "When we return, we'll process your house like you told Alex we would."

"*We* return?"

"I'm going with you to the barn."

He could see the wheels in her mind turning. "As long as you understand helping doesn't earn you a spot here tonight."

We'll see about that, Missy. "How about we table that discussion?"

"There's no need to table anything."

"Come on," he coaxed. "I just want to do what any good friend would do."

Jenna blinked rapidly and looked toward the road. She flicked a tear away. "I don't know what's wrong with me. My emotions are on a roller coaster."

"You've had a couple of hard days—three people dead, a possible intruder in your house. Not to mention we were just shot at even though he didn't intend to hurt us—I think a few tears are a normal reaction."

"I don't see you having a come-apart."

He had to tread carefully. "Men aren't nurturers like women. We react differently to situations. And men cry sometimes too—tears aren't a sign of weakness."

"Too bad you weren't my captain in the gang unit."

Max had known her captain. Billingsley had been old school, and a woman working under him would not have had it easy. "I heard the gang unit was being disbanded."

"I heard that too, and I can see why. In the beginning, it was good for the most part, but I always felt my hands were tied, especially after Phillip . . ." She ducked her head.

"Hey. That never should have happened." He lifted her chin, and their gazes collided.

Her tears had deepened the blue in her eyes, and they shone like sapphires. His heart rate skyrocketed. There'd always been a spark between them, one he'd never fanned when he was her supervisor, but he was no longer in that position.

A strand of her silky black hair clung to her cheek, and he brushed it back, hooking the lock behind her ear. Her face was warm as he cupped his hand along her jaw. Maybe he didn't have to be satisfied with just friendship.

His gaze dropped to her full lips. Desire to pull her into his arms squeezed his lungs, but he held back. He might not be her supervisor, but they had a job to do, and it didn't include romance. Maybe when this was over . . .

27

Jenna swallowed hard. Max had been about to kiss her. She didn't know if the pounding in her chest was from dis-appointment or relief that he hadn't. Or maybe she just imagined his intentions.

"This isn't getting your horse caught."

Gruff voice. Stiff shoulders. No, her first impression had been right. He'd almost kissed her. Jenna started to climb into the SUV and hesitated. "You really don't have to go."

He drew in a breath and released it. "I want to. At the precinct, you used to talk about getting a horse, and I'd like to see what you finally chose. But let's take my truck. That way you can rest on the drive over."

Jenna eyed him.

"It's only a suggestion, and it'll give me an opportunity to learn the county better—I don't retain directions as well when I'm a passenger."

True. "Sounds like a good deal for me. Let me grab my boots."

"Good."

She grabbed her riding boots and tossed them in the passenger side before she climbed into his pickup. Max jogged around to the other side, and once she changed into the boots and buckled up, he started the engine and pulled to the end of the drive. "Which way?"

"Left. We have to go through town."

Other than Jenna giving Max directions, it was quiet in the pickup. *Max wants to see Ace.* The thought kept chasing itself and made her excited and nervous at the same time.

It was getting hard to fight the connection that had been arcing between them since yesterday morning.

Nuh-uh. Not going there. Besides, after what happened with Phillip, she'd promised herself she would never get involved with a cop again. A fireman maybe, but not a cop.

But Max was a great guy. Then again, Phillip had been a great guy too. Until he wasn't. And she'd never picked up on the shady part of his character until it was too late.

"Which way?"

His question jerked Jenna from her thoughts. They were approaching a crossroads. "Turn right."

Her phone rang, and she answered. It was her trainer, apologizing for having to cancel their lesson for tomorrow that Jenna had totally blanked on.

"No problem," Jenna said. "See you next week."

Max glanced at her as she disconnected.

"My trainer cancelling our lesson tomorrow. I forgot she was coming."

"You're serious about your riding."

"I am. I found this trainer while I was still in Chattanooga. She's a retired Olympian dressage trainer. But she's not my first trainer—years ago when I was a teenager, Sam was my trainer."

"Sam?"

"My uncle. You'll probably meet him tomorrow at Granna's."

"So you've been riding most of your life?"

"Yep." Thank goodness they were back on a comfortable plane. "You know girls and their horses."

The sign for Bryan Bishop's Red Oak Stables came into view. "We're here. Pull through that gate and park anywhere."

He did as she said and parked near the red barn. "Do you see your horse?"

Jenna anxiously scanned the fenced paddocks for Ace. "Over there." She pointed to the middle paddock. "See the boy with a bucket in hand?"

"The one the horse is ignoring?"

"Ace doesn't want to go in his stall. He needs to work some of his energy off."

"You're not going to—"

She shot him a warning glare.

"Never mind."

"Thank you," she said and removed her service gun. "Since there are usually kids around, I don't normally wear my gun when I'm at the barn."

He nodded and removed his and locked them both in the gun safe under his seat while Jenna climbed out of the truck.

"Nice place," Max said as he joined her. "I grew up on a farm like this."

She shot him a skeptical look. "You don't seem the farm boy type."

It was strange she didn't know that about him, but then most of their conversations had been work related.

"Well, I am. Wouldn't mind having a spread like this someday."

Jenna glanced around the property. Eagle Ridge rose up to the west, a beautiful backdrop for the two-story house, barns, and work-out arenas. On the other side of the barn, horses grazed in two lush pasturelands carved out of the dense woods bordering the property.

"It's a nice place." She pointed to the main barn. "Ace's stall is there. I'll grab his halter."

Max inhaled a deep breath through his nose as they walked to the main barn.

"I never get tired of smelling the scent of hay." Then he laughed. "Unless it was halfway through a hot August day out in the fields when I was throwing those square bales on the trailer behind the hay baler."

She groaned. "I know what you mean."

Her uncle had conscripted her to work in the hay fields every summer, and it was hot, itchy work.

He followed her inside out of the sun.

"I'll be right back."

She hurried to Ace's stall and grabbed his halter. "Be right back."

"You want me to help?"

She dropped her gaze to the ground. "You'll mess up your shoes."

Kirk turned when she entered the paddock. "Miss Jenna, I'm sorry. He got out when I put hay in his stall. When I tried to catch him, he ran in here."

"It's okay."

Ace nickered when he heard her voice. She took the grain bucket from Kirk and rattled it. The horse tossed his head and trotted in the opposite direction.

He wanted to play hard to get. She put her forefinger and thumb to her lips and whistled. Abruptly the horse's demeanor changed, and while he didn't trot over to her, he did walk. At least the months she'd worked getting him to come when she whistled worked. She slipped the halter on. "You've been a bad boy."

He nudged her with his head.

"Don't try to make up now." She patted his sleek black neck.

"How'd you do that?" Kirk asked.

"By whistling . . . and hours of working with him."

She led Ace to the barn with Kirk following. He peeled off at the gate.

"Granddad said I could ride my four-wheeler once Ace was up."

"Go ahead, and thanks for calling."

Max met them at the entrance to the barn.

"Impressive," he said as they walked by.

She blew on her fingers and rubbed her shirt.

"Not that impressive."

Jenna laughed, hooked Ace in the crossties, and grabbed a hoof pick.

Max rubbed his forehead. "Beautiful horse."

"Thank you." She cleaned each hoof and then grabbed a brush and ran it down Ace's sleek ebony neck. The horse nuzzled her hand. "Sorry, no carrot yet."

"What is he, sixteen hands?"

Jenna eyed Max. "You're close. Sixteen-two." Most people didn't typically know horses were measured in hands—four-inch increments—from the ground to the withers at the base of the mane. "How did you know?"

He studied her. "What part of 'I grew up on a place like this' did you not believe?"

What was wrong with her? Max had never given Jenna reason to doubt him. But then neither had Phillip. "Sorry, force of habit."

"So I've noticed," he said quietly.

An uncomfortable silence followed until Ace nudged her with his nose then stamped his foot. "You want exercise, don't you, boy. Just give me a minute."

"You're not riding now, are you? You've had a long day."

"I feel fine, and if I don't work off some of Ace's energy, he'll kick the wall half the night. I won't ride long, just enough to tire him a little."

Max looked as though he wanted to say more, but he turned to the horse instead. "He looks like a warmblood. Hanoverian?"

"No, Dutch Warmblood. He was given to me."

"Really? How did that happen?"

Jenna brushed Ace's neck again. "My uncle was good friends

with the owner, Hank Thomas—they served in the Gulf War together and stayed in touch even though Hank lived in Chattanooga. When he had a stroke, Sam recommended that he let me take over the horse's care, which included riding—this was after I recovered from the shooting. It saved my sanity.

"Unfortunately, Hank never recovered enough to ride again, but sometimes he came out to the barn to watch us work dressage tests. When he died, he stipulated in his will that Ace went to me, and I brought him with me when I came home."

"That was nice of him," Max said. "Is your uncle still a trainer?"

Jenna nodded. "He works at another barn here in Pearl Springs, training young riders."

Max frowned. "Your uncle is a trainer, but you use someone else?"

"It's . . . complicated. Don't get me wrong—Sam's a great trainer. He's worked around dressage and jumping horses most of his life. Even had aspirations of competing in the Olympics."

"It sounds like he didn't. What happened—" He winced. "There I go again, prying into something that's none of my business."

"It's all right." She rubbed Ace's nose. "I'm afraid he let alcohol destroy his chances of competing."

Max nodded sympathetically.

"It hurts to think of what Sam could've been if he'd stayed away from whiskey. And for the record, I did ask him to work with me when I came home, but he said I needed to stay with the trainer I had in Chattanooga. She lives halfway between Pearl Springs and Chattanooga, so it's not a long drive for her."

"What's your end goal?" He grinned at her. "I know you have one."

Max asked hard questions. At one time she'd had aspirations of competing in the Olympics, but that was back when she'd been young and confident. Brash even. And definitely goal oriented. If she set her mind to do something, *fait accompli.*

Done deal. Failure wasn't an option. That's the way she'd been raised.

Jenna hadn't been prepared for her life going off the rails like it had after the shooting. Phillip's betrayal and her superior's support of him had undermined her confidence. Her trust level was a minus ten, and that extended to every aspect of her life, including her riding.

"Right now? It's getting to the next level." Under her trainer, Jenna's confidence was growing, as was Ace's. She stroked his muscled neck just as Max reached to do the same, their hands connecting.

Her world shifted.

28

Until that second she hadn't even noticed how close she stood to Max. The familiar scent of his cologne—the same one he'd worn years ago—teased her. Jenna jerked her thoughts in another direction, anywhere other than on Max. She ran the brush along Ace's back and then each leg.

"Do you take him to shows?"

That was a safe enough subject. "Sometimes. His show name is Ace of Diamonds."

Max rubbed Ace's neck while she retrieved the saddle and bridle from the tack room. "You said your trainer was a retired Olympian rider—I guess you're training for the Grand Prix?"

His question stopped her. "You know more about dressage than you let on."

He laughed. "Not really. My niece is horse crazy, and she rides dressage. Emily is working to qualify for the nationals in Michigan next month."

She put the names together. "Emily Anderson is your niece?"

"You know her?"

"Not so much know her—I see her at shows and always make sure I catch her Grand Prix ride. She and her horse are poetry in motion."

"Thank you . . . but you never said what level you show."

No she hadn't. "Nowhere near Emily's. Ace and I have progressed through second level. My trainer feels we're ready to move on to third, but I don't know. It's much more difficult, and competition and judging are stiffer."

"I never knew that to stop you."

She shrugged. Jenna felt Ace was ready but wasn't so sure about herself. She needed to get over it if she ever wanted to move into what Emily did, the "dancing" part of dressage. That was her ultimate goal now.

"I believe Ace has the ability, but I'm not there yet. The thought of competing against some of the riders in the third level turns my insides to ice water."

Facing the fear of not being good enough and then accumulating points show by show until she advanced to another level had gone a long way in restoring Jenna's confidence. She would advance . . . just not yet.

"So where do you show?"

"Not on the national level like your niece. Mostly local or regional." She turned and said, "You know a lot about horses—do you ride?"

He laughed. "Occasionally, when I have time. And I like a saddle with a horn."

She placed the saddle pad on the horse's back and then the saddle and buckled it before tilting her head toward him. "Yeah, I don't see you in a pair of breeches or a top hat."

Unfortunately, she could easily see him in tight-fitting Wranglers and cowboy boots. She groaned inwardly. Seems the command she'd sent to her brain had been ignored, but she did have a delete button. Jenna immediately erased the image. Unfortunately, it didn't go away.

"Never understood how a rider stays on in that little saddle."

Jenna shrugged. "English saddle is what I've always ridden."

She studied it. "The cantle and pommel are higher in a dressage saddle, so the rider sits a little deeper."

"Yeah, that should make you more secure . . ." Max followed her gaze. "But I still prefer a western saddle with a horn."

"They're great for trail riding," she said. "The Bishops have horses they rent for that, and they provide western saddles . . . if you're interested when this case is over."

"Are you asking me for a date?"

Her heart stalled. "Ah . . ."

"Kidding." He palmed his hands up. "And yes, I'd love to meet you here some Saturday. But are you sure you want to ride today?"

"I'm just going to run through the test we practiced last week with my trainer—it won't take long or too much of my energy, just his. Hopefully."

"If you say so. Mind if I watch?"

Max watching her was the last thing she wanted, but there wasn't a gracious way to say no. He walked beside her as she led Ace out of the barn.

"My folks raise cutting horses on their farm outside of Franklin."

"Is that why you went to Nashville? To be closer to your parents?"

"Partly. They're still in good health, but I didn't get to see them often when I lived in Chattanooga. Now I live just two houses down the road."

So he lived in Franklin. Jenna enjoyed going to shows in the quaint little town on the Harpeth River not far from Nashville. She led Ace to the mounting block and prepared to mount.

"Want me to hold his bridle?"

Jenna shook her head. "He's good."

Ace didn't move while she mounted, and for the next fifteen minutes they warmed up with a variety of exercises from walking to trotting to cantering. She praised him often as they practiced transitions from walking to cantering and then in reverse.

Jenna loved days like this when Ace responded to her commands. It was like being one with the black gelding, and time flew by. Once his transitions satisfied her, she walked him around the ring to cool down before they worked on flying changes.

She glanced toward the woods where she'd seen that flash of light yesterday, half expecting to see it again. She didn't, but the skin on the back of her neck prickled. Was someone out there?

Jenna halted Ace and let him stretch while she scanned the trees. Nothing. No reflection and no movement in the woods. There was no one out there, she told herself, and shook off the feeling. *Focus on the flying leaps.*

"Let's go, boy." She transitioned to a canter, and after fifteen minutes, Jenna leaned over and patted Ace's lathered neck. He was a dream to ride, and it'd been a good workout, but she was more tired than she realized. "Good boy! Let's get you cleaned up."

"You're good," Max said as they approached the fence where he waited. He glanced toward the woods. "But let's get you both inside the barn."

Jenna followed his gaze. She hadn't been able to completely shake the feeling of being watched. "Thanks. One day I hope to be good enough to compete in the higher levels like Emily."

"Looks to me you're ready for that now."

"I wish. Pretty sure Ace is, but I have a lot to learn." Still his praise had her grinning.

The sun dropped behind a cloud, deepening the shadows around them. Ace stared toward the woods on the other side of the arena, his ears pointed forward. He snorted and stepped back. A chill raced down Jenna's back. "What do you see, boy?"

He stamped his foot, and she glanced toward the trees again. "Yesterday I saw a flash of light like the sun reflecting off glass. Me being me, my mind went to binoculars."

"Where?"

She pointed to a spot where the pasture and trees made a V. "It was almost like someone was out there, watching us."

"I didn't see the reflection, but I agree that someone may be out there."

29

Max had learned to never ignore the sixth sense that told him danger lurked nearby. "I felt someone was watching while you were in the arena, but I couldn't identify a threat anywhere." He held Ace's reins with one hand and rested his other hand on his gun. "Come on, boy."

"When did you—" She stared pointedly at his gun.

"My Glock? I went after it while you were working with Ace."

"So I'm not imagining the goose bumps on my neck?"

"No. This ever happen before?"

"Not before this week. The barn has always been my safe place."

Max knew the feeling. He felt the same way at his parents' farm.

Once they were in the hallway, he pointed to a side aisle. "Can we untack there?"

She nodded and led Ace around the corner to another set of crossties. She slipped the bridle off and the halter on, then hooked the crossties. Max helped her unsaddle Ace.

"Do you really think someone is out there?" Jenna asked.

"*Something's* out there—even your horse sensed it."

"It could be a squirrel as far as he's concerned." She'd tried for lighthearted, but her voice trembled.

"Maybe, but there's no sense in taking chances, especially since Sebastian's been—"

An ATV blasted by the barn door, and Ace tried to rear. They both grabbed his halter.

"That was Kirk," Jenna said. "He was probably the one in the woods."

"I'll check and see."

"While you're gone, I'm going to hose Ace down."

Max caught the boy before he hopped off the four-wheeler. "Hey there!"

The boy looked around at him. "Yeah?"

"You Kirk?"

He nodded.

"You spooked a horse."

Kirk shot an uneasy glance toward the barn. "I thought they were all up," he said, his tone defensive.

"Were you in the woods in the last fifteen minutes?"

"Why you want to know?"

"Just curious, that's all." Max drew closer as the boy dismounted the ATV. He pulled his badge from his pocket and showed him.

The boy's eyes saucered. "I ain't done nothin' wrong."

"Not saying you did. Did you just come from the woods?"

"No, I promise—I was going to, but Granddad sent me to the back pasture to find a mare who's about to foal."

His tone told Max he hadn't been happy about it. "Did you find her?"

"Yeah, I knew she was okay. I could've gone to the river," Kirk said. "Wait. Why do you want to know if I was in the woods?"

Max didn't want to alarm the boy since they really didn't know who, if anyone, had been in the woods. "Ace kind of spooked at something there."

"Wasn't me." He started toward the house and stopped. "What's a TBI agent doing here, anyway?"

"Jenna Hart is a friend of mine."

Kirk smiled for the first time. "I'm going to be feeding Ace this week, and sometimes she lets me ride him. She's pretty cool."

"Yeah, she is. You must be a pretty good rider, then."

The boy's chest puffed out. "I am."

Humble too. Max glanced toward the wooded area that was a good half mile away then back at Kirk. "Any chance I could borrow your ATV?"

The boy hesitated. "For how long?"

"Fifteen minutes." Shouldn't take any longer than that to check out the scope of woods. "And I grew up driving one of these, in case you wondered if I can drive one."

"I suppose it's okay. I have a few chores to finish around here, anyway."

"Thanks." Max straddled the four-wheeler that was similar to the one his dad still used. He gave it gas and a few minutes later approached the V-shaped area Jenna had pointed out. After killing the motor and dismounting, he carefully searched for broken branches and trampled grass, signs someone or even an animal had been hanging around.

When he didn't find anything at the edge of the trees, he hiked deeper into the woods. A hundred feet in, he found a path. Max cocked his ear. Sounded like running water, probably a creek. Max wasn't familiar with this part of the state, so he didn't know how large the stream was. If it were shallow enough, whoever had been spying on them could've waded in.

He followed the path to the creek. From where he stood, it appeared too deep for anyone to wade, but it was wide and deep enough for a small craft like a canoe or kayak or even a paddle-board to navigate. Max walked toward the bank.

A branch snapped behind him. He whirled around, and a fist connected with his jaw. Max's head snapped back, and he staggered. He fought to regain his balance, but it'd been years since he'd taken anyone down in a fight, and Max was rusty.

The man, dressed in Levis and a black short-sleeve T-shirt, came at him again. Sunglasses kept Max from seeing his eyes, but it looked as though he had short hair under the ball cap he wore.

Max pivoted away from him. Too late, he saw a flash of silver just before the man slammed a pistol against his head. Max's knees buckled, and he pitched forward, darkness rolling through his brain . . .

"Max! Wake up!"

Jenna's anxious voice barely penetrated the fog in his brain. He struggled to answer, but his voice wouldn't cooperate.

"Max . . . talk to me. What happened?"

"Jenna?" He finally managed to get her name out.

"Thank God you're okay."

He didn't know so much about being okay. Max opened his eyes and tried to sit up, but like his voice, his muscles refused to move.

"What happened?"

"I don't know." He glanced around, but everything was blurry.

"I came as soon as I learned you'd borrowed Kirk's ATV. I found you on the ground. Just be still."

With weakness holding his body captive, there was no way he could do anything but be still. The fog slowly cleared, and Max tried to recall what'd happened. He'd been in the woods . . . heard water flowing . . . and then . . . it all came rushing back. "There was a man here . . . he got the drop on me . . . he must've hit me with the butt of his gun."

"When I found you unconscious, I called Alex. Do I need to call an ambulance too?" Jenna asked.

"No." He wished she hadn't called Alex. But it was protocol. "Help me sit up."

Jenna held out her hand, and Max pulled himself to a sitting position, then braced his back against a tree trunk. His head swam. Maybe not his best idea. "Does Alex know how to get where we are?"

"I told her to find the ATV and then follow the broken branches to the river."

After a few minutes, he lightly pressed his fingers against the side of his head, wincing when he found a tender spot.

"Did you see who it was?"

"Sort of. He wore sunglasses and a ball cap. Bulky guy in jeans and a pullover."

Evidently, he'd been watching them while Jenna worked with Ace. But why? And why attack him?

She took out her phone. "I'm calling 911. If someone hit you in the head, you may have a concussion."

Max held up his hand. "Don't call. I'm not seeing double and I'm not nauseated." He was more embarrassed that the man had gotten the better of him. Max pushed away from the tree he'd been bracing his back against. "I need to stand up."

"Let me help you." She aided Max in climbing to his feet and then steadied him once he was up.

"So, what were you doing before the attack?"

He turned and pointed toward the creek. "I was walking to the bank. It looked like someone or something came up from the creek, and more than once. I was checking it out, except I never got close enough to see."

"It's actually a river—the Blackwater River," Jenna said. "It isn't very big here, but there's a sandbar where the river changed course years ago. It gets wider and deeper before it empties into the Pearl River above the lake." She glanced toward the bank. "The bend is a perfect place to tie up a small boat or canoe and climb up the bank. Maybe the way they got here was what someone didn't want you to see."

"But why were they spying on us in the first place?"

She blew out a breath. "Could it be Rick Sebastian?"

30

E ven as she said it, Jenna wasn't sure Sebastian would risk going back to jail to carry out his vendetta. Besides, how would he have known they were even at the barn?

"It's possible it wasn't about either of us. The path looked worn—as if someone used it regularly. But to what purpose?"

"We busted a meth lab in the county not long ago." Jenna scanned the trees around them, barely aware of the quiet flow of the river in the background. She'd roamed these woods as a kid, tagging along with her uncle on the days he'd worked at the barn training the former owner's horses. It'd been a safe place . . .

"Maybe someone has set up around here and is using the river to transport drugs out."

She nodded. "What do you remember about the attack?"

"Very little." He massaged his temples, and then looked up. "Maybe a sense that someone was behind me . . . when I turned around, he was just there. I should've been more alert." Red crept into his face.

She knew how he felt at being caught off guard.

"How did you find me?"

"Once I found Kirk's ATV, I didn't have any trouble tracking you—you left a pretty solid path to follow."

He glanced toward the riverbank. "Let's see if there's anything around the river that might help us figure this out."

Jenna let Max go first so that if he started to fall, she could catch him. Not that she told him that. His pride was already wounded at getting coldcocked.

Max pointed to a bare spot on the bank that looked like a path down to the river. "I remember now—that's why I was headed this way. See if you can see any footprints."

Jenna kept her gaze glued to the ground. "I see deer prints, and maybe raccoon . . . this must be a watering spot."

When they reached the bank, she could see that's what it obviously was. The bank sloped to the sandbar with all sorts of animal tracks.

"Be careful," she cautioned as Max climbed down on the shelf, then she followed, noticing his shoe prints but no others. She was about to say something when Max pointed to the ground.

"Looks like someone used a branch to sweep the sand," he said.

Jenna scanned the nearby trees overhanging the bank and noticed a birch tree on the edge of the bank with bark missing at the base of the trunk. "I bet he tied his boat or canoe here."

Max examined the tree. "Do people normally travel this river? It doesn't look very deep."

"It's deeper than it looks, but a person would have to use something like a kayak or a canoe to navigate the river here. Most people fish from the bank or set out trotlines," she said. "It's a good place to catch catfish and largemouth bass. As for people canoeing or kayaking on it, this is the first time I've been back here since I returned to Pearl Springs. I don't know about now, but when I was a kid, those were popular activities."

"Jenna! Max! Where are you?"

She looked toward the woods. "Sounds like Alex is here."

Max cupped his hand and yelled, "We're on the river."

They quickly retraced their steps and climbed the bank.

"What are you doing by the river?" Before Jenna could answer, Alex shifted her gaze and pointed at Max. "And I thought you were unconscious."

"He was." Jenna quickly explained what they thought had happened.

Max nodded toward the river. "Someone was here. We found where he covered his tracks and tied up a boat."

"He? You know who it was?"

"No, but Jenna said you busted a meth operation not long ago around here."

"Yeah, in another part of the county," Alex said. "Maybe whoever attacked you was someone looking to hook up with a drug dealer."

Jenna shook her head. "If that was the case, he would've waited until we left."

Alex glanced toward the pasture then the wooded area. "Maybe whoever it was didn't want you to see something, like a boat or a canoe. Did you find anything the CSI team needs to check out?"

Max shook his head. "We searched pretty thoroughly—our guy didn't leave anything behind."

Jenna checked her watch. A little after seven. "Bryan grumbles that his grandson is always exploring the woods around here, either on the ATV or horseback—he could've seen something."

"After what happened today," Max said, "he needs to stay away from here."

Jenna agreed and would tell Bryan so. She rode back to the barn with Alex while Max trailed behind on the ATV. They found Kirk in one of the stalls helping his grandfather with the other horses in the barn. "Evening, Bryan," Jenna said, speaking to the older man.

"Evening. Sorry about Ace getting out of his stall."

She waved off his apology. "It's happened to me."

"Did you find Mr. Maxwell?" the boy asked.

"She did," Max said, coming up behind them. "Thanks for letting me use your ATV. And you're welcome to call me Max."

"Why were you gone so long? You said it'd only be for fifteen minutes."

"Kirk! You know better than to talk to your elders that way."

"It's okay," Max said.

"No, it's not."

"Sorry, Granddad," Kirk said.

He wasn't, but Jenna wasn't going to call him on it.

Alex gave Jenna a wry grin then held out her hand, first to the grandfather, then to Kirk. "I don't think we've met. Alex Stone, Russell County's chief deputy."

"Heard you were running for the office next year," Bryan Bishop said.

"Thinking about it." She turned to Kirk. "Have you noticed anyone strange hanging around the woods?"

"You mean like weird, or somebody I don't know?"

"How about both?"

Kirk's shoulders lifted in a shrug. "Not really."

Max leaned forward. "The ones you haven't *really* seen—are they people you know or strangers?"

"Strangers—I mean, uh . . ." The boy stared at his boots.

"Boy, if you've seen anyone in the woods, I want you to tell these officers right now. Unless you want me to take the keys to that ATV for the rest of the month."

Kirk gulped. "Uh . . . sometimes people tie up their canoes at the river and walk through the woods to the Armstrong place."

"That's the farm next to us," Bryan explained. "Belonged to William Armstrong. His heirs sold it after William died, and the buyer rents the house out. The ones renting it now have been there six months at least. I never see 'em."

"Do you know who bought it?" Max asked.

"Afraid not. None of William's kids live in Russell County, so I haven't talked to them."

Alex turned to Kirk. "Did you see what's going on over there?"

This time the boy's shrug was bigger. "I don't know. I don't mess around there."

"Why's that?" Jenna asked.

"I rode my ATV too close to their barn one time, and they yelled at me."

"Why haven't you told me about this?" his grandfather asked.

"I don't hardly never see them."

Hardly ever, Jenna mentally corrected. "But you have seen them. What do they look like?"

Kirk tilted his head and looked up toward the barn rafters. "Some of them have big arms with tattoos on them. And one of them has a real creepy smile."

"One of them smiled at you?" Jenna frowned. "You were that close to him?"

"Yeah. He wasn't big like the others . . . he had muscles, just wasn't as tall. I thought he was going to yell at me, but he didn't. Asked me what my name was and told me to be careful in the woods. That's when he smiled, real creepy like." Kirk shuddered. "I haven't seen him down there again."

Bryan pinned his grandson with a stern gaze. "See to it that you keep away from the river." When Kirk didn't respond, the grandfather raised his eyebrows. "You hear me, boy?"

He studied the floor. "Yes, sir."

"How long ago did this happen?" Jenna asked.

"I dunno . . . maybe two weeks ago. I was riding down to the river on Blackjack—that's my horse—and I didn't see him until he came up the riverbank. We scared each other."

"And you haven't seen him again?"

The boy shook his head. "I mostly just see the ones that yelled at me—they come on Thursday or Friday."

177

Alex took a card from her pocket. "Next time you see someone, would you give me a call?"

Kirk took the card and nodded. "Yeah, okay."

Jenna caught the boy's eye. "You have to promise you'll stay clear of these men, and that you'll stay out of the woods for now."

"But that's where I ride," he protested.

His grandfather crossed his arms. "Don't argue with her."

"Maybe it won't be for long," Jenna said. "Have you fed Ace yet?"

"Not yet—I was about to when he got out."

"Why don't you help me feed him, then?"

"Sure."

She scooped sweet feed out of a barrel and added a supplement to the mix and handed the bucket to Kirk, then she peeled off two flakes of hay and followed him to Ace's stall. What if Sebastian was one of the men the boy had seen? She unlatched Ace's door, tossed the hay in the corner, and then took the feed from Kirk.

Jenna didn't get the sense that he understood the danger of prowling the woods or going to the river or that he wouldn't sneak down there when his grandfather was busy. If one of them attacked Max, they wouldn't think twice about harming Kirk if they thought he'd seen something he shouldn't have.

"Kirk, it's really important that you stay away from the river and the place next door."

"Those men don't scare me none," the boy said.

That was the attitude she was afraid of. Jenna would have to impress on Bryan that he needed to make sure Kirk stayed away from the river and the woods. She couldn't bear the thought of something happening to the boy.

31

Sebastian stood just inside the dense woods joining Jenna's property, listening for tires on the road. Satisfied nothing was coming, he dashed to the back of her house and pulled on nitrile gloves. He didn't know how much time he would have before Hart and the TBI agent returned. Hardly did any good to put a tracker on her vehicle if she didn't use it. He'd have to find a way to put one on the TBI agent's truck.

He jerked the key to Hart's house out of his pocket. Running into the TBI agent was all Ross's fault for insisting that he check on the farm crew. They were his men, the only ones that hadn't defected to Viper—he didn't need to check on them. Then it was just his luck that the agent cut him off before he could reach the paddleboard tethered to a tree on the riverbank.

With the river clear of fallen trees, it was a good way for him to come and go to the farmhouse without being seen. Too much traffic in and out of the farmhouse would draw attention. The only person who'd seen him come on the river was that kid. He hadn't decided what to do about him yet.

When he reached her back door, he ran his gaze around it, stopping when he saw the tape at the top. He would have to re-member to press it back in place when he left. Then he tried to unlock the door, but the key didn't budge. He jiggled it, and on the third try, he felt it release. Once inside, Sebastian examined the key, noticing a small jagged edge that needed filing. He'd fix that before he left.

For now, he wanted to search for the photos—Hart had interrupted him this morning.

Methodically he went through the other rooms, frustrated when there was no sign of any photos of him and Ross. In her office he placed a listening device in the router—he hadn't had time earlier—then booted up her computer and inserted a data drive that would enable him to change the password. Another little trick he'd learned at Pikeville.

Once he was in, he checked the data drives in her desk. No photos. Just recipes and information he had no interest in. When he finished, he backed out, careful to restore everything like he found it. It had been tempting to put a message on the screen, but that would be evidence.

No, he had other ways to let her know he'd been in her house without Hart being able to prove it. In her bedroom, he moved the remote to her TV from the bedside table to the dresser. In the living room, he rearranged the family photos on the mantel, and while he was there, he scraped the key against the rough brick, filing off the jagged edge.

In the kitchen, he tried the key—perfect. He returned the original key to the hook where he'd found it. She'd never even missed it. Then he placed a listening device in the light over her island and stood back. It wasn't visible from the outside.

Then he opened a cabinet and blinked, surprised that Hart wasn't more organized. All sizes of vitamin and pain relief bottles were haphazardly placed on shelves. Then he turned to the pantry. Same thing—he would return later and arrange a surprise for her, but not today—too many changes and someone might start believing her.

Tires crunched on the drive, and his heart almost stopped. Had to be Hart. He eased to the window in the front room and looked out. It was Hart all right. He dashed out of the living room and down the hall. Seconds later he locked the back door behind him and pressed the tape across it before he ran toward the woods. Sebastian couldn't wait to hear her reaction to his changes.

32

A tired quiet settled between them as the sun dropped over the mountain. They'd picked up barbecue in town, and the aroma just about made her stomach growl. Jenna glanced over at Max in the passenger seat and smiled. He hadn't argued with her about driving his pickup.

"Well, I think we've had enough excitement to last awhile."

"More like a lifetime." Max rubbed the back of his neck. "I feel like an idiot."

"Now you know how I felt this morning."

"I wasn't trying to one-up you," he said with a dry laugh. She laughed with him as she turned into her drive and killed the engine. Her gaze slid to the house, and her breath caught in her chest. A man briefly appeared in her window.

Her attacker was back!

Jenna jerked the car door open. She flicked away the strap over her gun and jumped out. Max yelled for her to stop. She ignored him and raced to the steps, her gun drawn.

She glanced at the top of the front door. The tape was undisturbed, but she knew what she'd seen. Her heart pounded against her ribs. Jenna unlocked the door and pushed it open. "Police! Come out with your hands in the air."

Silence. Behind her, Max ran up the steps. "What's going on?"

"I saw someone in the window."

Max nodded. "Left," he said, keeping his voice low.

Jenna nodded. She slipped inside, hugging the wall on the left. Max was close behind her, going to the right.

They both swept their guns from side to side. The room was empty. She glanced at him. "Kitchen," he mouthed.

Silently they moved through the dining room. When they saw that the kitchen was empty, they backtracked to the living room.

"What happened?" Concern darkened Max's brown eyes.

"I saw a man in the front window."

She scanned the living room to see if anything was missing, and her gaze landed on the family photos on the mantel. Granna's photo had been moved . . . at least, she thought it had been.

"You sure? I didn't see anyone and there doesn't appear to be anyone here now." Max holstered his gun.

She bristled at the implication in his voice. "He was here."

"Was the tape disturbed?"

Jenna shook her head, not trusting her voice. She'd seen someone in the window. She knew she had.

"You put tape on the back door, right?"

Without answering, she hurried out the front door and jogged to the back. That tape hadn't been disturbed, either.

"I don't understand. I know I saw someone—a man."

"Can you describe him?"

"I only saw him for a second. He had his back to the window."

They walked to the front of the house. "Could it have been a shadow?" Max asked. "The front of your house faces west, and the sun was against the window . . . that creates shadows sometimes."

A rock settled in her stomach. He didn't believe her.

"I remember when I was a kid, thinking I saw someone in the attic of the house next door to us. Turned out to be an old hat box. Let's go back to the truck and see if—"

"I don't have to recreate the moment. I know what I saw." It was Chattanooga all over again. She jutted her jaw. "He was about your height and had dark hair."

Her face grew hot as Max studied her. That *was* what she saw . . . wasn't it?

"Why don't we look around to see if he left any evidence of being here," he said.

Instead of making her feel better, his words irritated her. He was placating her, like a father soothing a frightened child. She fisted her hands on her hips. "I know what you think. You think I'm unstable . . . just like my old boss in Chattanooga."

"That's not what I think at all, but sometimes our eyes do play tricks on us. Why don't we dust for prints before we eat our barbecue, and you can check to see if anything has been disturbed."

They cleared the house together, dusting for prints in each room. In her bedroom, she stared at the remote on her dresser. Had she put it there? If she had, it would've been yesterday because she hadn't turned the TV on this morning. No matter, she simply couldn't remember. Same thing with items in her living room. The photos on her mantel didn't look quite right, but she couldn't be sure. The frames were all identical. Had her grandmother's photo been on the end or the middle? Same thing for the photos on the other end. Everything looked suspicious once she questioned her memory. At least the tape across the fake receptacle hadn't been disturbed—but that was no guarantee. The tape on the doors hadn't been disturbed either.

An hour later, they found several prints overlaid with smudges, which was what they'd get if the intruder wore latex gloves. Except for a few prints that matched Max's fingerprints, the ones they found all looked the same. She assumed they were hers since she couldn't remember the last time anyone else was in her house but Max and Alex, but her boss hadn't touched anything.

"Have you checked to see if any of your jewelry is missing?" Max asked.

"I'll do it now." In her bedroom, she sorted through what jewelry she had, which wasn't much. Everything seemed to be there, except . . . where was her necklace?

Max stuck his head in the doorway. "Anything missing?"

"I can't find my gold necklace with a cross."

"When was the last time you saw it?"

She tried to remember. "Maybe a couple of weeks ago? I don't wear jewelry often."

"So it could be misplaced rather than missing?"

Jenna shrugged. "That makes more sense than thinking someone stole it and left behind a three-thousand-dollar laptop sitting in plain sight."

"I agree."

In the kitchen, she set plates down for the barbecue along with real knives and forks. "I'm not eating out of a Styrofoam box or using plastic utensils."

But when Jenna sat down, she wasn't hungry and picked at the food.

"You need to eat," Max said.

"I know . . . but I don't have any appetite."

Jenna managed to eat half of her plate, but her thoughts kept returning to the intruder. If someone was here, why didn't they take her laptop in plain view in her office? What if she had imagined the man?

She'd thought the man who attacked Max could've been Sebastian. What if that had planted a subconscious thought that the gang leader was in Russell County? It wasn't a far stretch to believe he could've broken into her house.

Could she really be suffering from PTSD? Right after the shooting, any loud noise could put her in the middle of the battle in Chattanooga, and blood, even just a drop of it, made her faint.

Had her PTSD returned in a different form? She looked up as Max picked up her plate.

"I think we're done for the night," he said. "As soon as I do the dishes, let's ride into town to the hotel so I can get my things. Tomorrow we'll go see your grandmother first thing."

"I'll do the dishes." She ignored his reference to the hotel. "And I think we have a briefing first thing."

"After that, then."

Jenna raised her brows. "Uh, don't be surprised if Granna starts her matchmaking. I, uh, talked quite a bit about you when we worked together." Her heart stuttered as he caught her gaze and held it.

"Would her matchmaking be such a bad thing?"

She hadn't been wrong earlier, thinking he'd wanted to kiss her. Jenna wasn't sure she could handle this version of Max. Sure, she'd fantasized about him right after his fiancée dumped him and before things got serious with Phillip, but Max never indicated he had the same feelings . . . except for that one kiss . . .

What had changed? Before she got up the courage to ask, her cell phone rang. Alex. Jenna answered and put the call on speaker, dreading any more bad news.

"Dylan and Taylor finished processing Joe Slater's house. You want them to come by and dust for prints?"

Jenna released the breath she'd been holding. "Thanks, but Max helped me. We found a few smudges, but nothing else."

She filled her boss in about their interview with Eric Darby. "We feel he knows something, but it's going to take time before he trusts us enough to share."

"I'll let you two work that," Alex said. "I called Harrison Carter to discuss his rally, and he agreed to stop by the Pearl Springs Park in the morning on his way to Chattanooga around ten. I figure you and Max will want to join us for the meeting."

"Absolutely," Max said.

"Yes," Jenna chimed in.

"Good. I'll see you in the morning at the briefing . . . and Jenna, I hope you don't find any more bodies tonight."

"So do I!"

Alex disconnected.

"You ready to ride to the hotel with me to get my things?"

"Max, I'll be fine. What kind of law officer am I if I can't protect myself? It's hard enough being the only female deputy on the force other than Taylor without it looking like you don't trust me to take care of myself."

He opened his mouth, and she held up her hand.

"Please."

"You are one stubborn woman."

"Independent."

Max studied her, then resolutely nodded. "Keep your phone by your bed."

"I will. And I'll walk you to the door and deadbolt it."

He rattled the door once the lock snicked in place. "See," she called. "You can't get in."

"Okay. Call me if you need me."

She agreed and walked to the hall. His lights swept across the living room, and once they were gone, she stared at the window where she'd seen the man.

Had her mind seen something that wasn't there?

33

Max pulled into Jenna's drive at seven thirty Wednesday morning with the scent of cinnamon and sugar teasing him. He climbed out, grabbed the white paper sack, and called her number as he walked to the porch. She answered on the second ring.

"Good morning."

Her voice didn't sound as though she'd been up long.

"To you too. How would you like a warm sticky bun to go with your coffee?" The buns had been Jenna's favorite breakfast pastry when they worked robbery together.

"Mmm. Are you apologizing for something?"

"No, but I am standing at your front door with four just out of the oven."

The door flew open. Jenna was still holding the phone in her hand. "You said the magic words!" Her eyes sparkled and her lips curled in a smile that sent his heart soaring.

"I was hoping. Do you have coffee made?"

Her smile dimmed a little. "Only one cup, but it won't take long to make another."

"Then you can have the buns." He held them out.

"I trust you . . . bring them on to the kitchen." She tilted her head and studied him. "You look tired."

"It was noisy at the hotel last night." Max wasn't about to tell her he'd slept in his truck just in case someone had broken in on her and decided to visit again. He followed her and noted a chair propped under the back door.

"I thought if my intruder returns, he'll have to use the front door and maybe someone will see him."

"Good idea."

A few minutes later Jenna handed him a cup of steaming coffee and sat across from him, twisting the watch on her arm.

"About last night," she said. "First, thank you for not insisting on staying. You don't understand, but after what happened in Chattanooga, if you had stayed, it would've confirmed that you didn't think I can take care of myself."

"I was worried about you, still am."

"Are you worried because someone broke in here or worried that I'm losing it?"

He didn't answer right away, and her eyes narrowed. She leaned forward. "For the record, I saw a man when we pulled into the drive, and he was standing by the window. Whether you believe it or not."

"Jenna, I know you thought you saw someone, but we didn't find any evidence that anyone had been here."

"Do you think I'm having PTSD again?"

It had crossed his mind. Had her mind created an image of a man in the window? He hadn't seen it, and without a shred of evidence suggesting someone had been in the house again—

A text sounded on his phone at the same time hers dinged, and they both glanced at their screens. "Alex," she said.

He nodded and read the text. Carter was arriving earlier than ten and the briefing had been moved up to eight o'clock.

She looked up at him. "We'll have to hustle to make it, but we're not done with this conversation."

He divided the pastries with her and grabbed the cup of coffee. Once he was behind the wheel of his truck, he followed her SUV out of the drive. Could she be having PTSD from the shooting in Chattanooga? Max wasn't certain she'd recovered mentally from that night. He was pretty sure PTSD and the attitude of her supervisor were the reasons she'd taken Alex's offer to be a Russell County deputy and moved back home.

But what if Sebastian was in Russell County? Could Sebastian know she had PTSD? From what Max had heard, the man had a sadistic streak a mile wide. And if he was in cahoots with Phillip Ross . . . Sebastian could be breaking into Jenna's house, searching for the photos she'd taken of Phillip and Sebastian together.

One thing was for certain. They needed to know Sebastian's whereabouts.

34

Jenna slipped into the room with Max right behind her just as Alex started the briefing. They found chairs near the back.

"Good. You made it," Alex said. She directed her attention to Max. "Do you have the report on the castle nut?"

"No," he said, "but she promised it by late this afternoon. I forwarded you an email from the logistics team approving the plan for positioning security at the park, so we need to firm up those assignments."

"I'll send out a schedule later today," Alex said and then went on to discuss the letter found in Joe Slater's desk.

"How about Paul Nelson's place?" Jenna asked. "Was a letter found there?"

"No, but as soon as we finish here, Dylan and Taylor are going to process Nelson's insurance office. Any more questions?"

When there were none, Alex held up two photos. "On to another subject. These are the only photos we have of Rick Sebastian, a notorious gang leader in Chattanooga. One is before prison and the other is from intake when he was incarcerated. Unfortunately, Mr. Sebastian is camera shy, and we have nothing more recent."

Jenna froze and quickly averted her eyes. She'd known Alex planned to circulate the photos, and she thought she was prepared to see them. Evidently not prepared enough. Sweat beaded her face. Scenes of the night she was shot flashed in her mind.

Get a grip! She couldn't lose it in front of Alex and the other deputies. And certainly not Max—he already thought she was having PTSD. She forced her attention back to the chief deputy.

Alex continued. "He was released from prison a month ago. Jenna was part of the team that arrested him for cocaine possession and testified against him at his trial, and after he was found guilty and sentenced, he threatened her life.

"His hair could be any length or he could've shaved his head. I've requested any photos the prison might have on file, but until we hear from them, use the photos you have now. And don't just keep a watch out for him, show these around, see if anyone recognizes him."

Jenna hadn't scanned the documents in her folder, and she pulled them out, forcing herself to examine them. No matter if he had hair or no hair, she would always recognize him from his hard brown eyes and the arrogant smirk on his face. She stared at the photo with longer hair . . . Had that been the man in her window?

"Any chance he could be connected to the murders of Slater and Nelson?" Wayne asked.

"It would be a far stretch to connect him to them," Alex said.

A timer went off on the chief deputy's watch. "That's all for right now. If you come across anyone who's seen Sebastian, call me or Jenna immediately."

She nodded to Max and Jenna. "My office?"

Jenna followed Alex, feeling much like she had when the principal summoned her in high school, which was absurd.

"Sorry to spring the earlier briefing on you," Alex said. She placed the files from the briefing beside her and sat on the corner of her desk. "But Harrison Carter has an appointment in Chattanooga and requested we meet at nine instead of ten—he has agreed to give us thirty minutes."

"Very generous of him," Max said.

"Yeah. The location is still the park since his security people want to check it out."

She turned her attention to Jenna. "Nathan is picking me up in a few minutes, but I wanted to make sure you were okay. You turned kind of pale when I showed Sebastian's photo."

"I'm fine—it reminded me of how slippery he is. I wish we had a photo of him since his release."

Alex glanced down at the photo on top of her files. "Me too. I'd like to get Dani Collins to do a drawing of what he'd look like if he beefed up in prison—a lot of inmates do since they have so much free time. But that will have to wait until she returns with Mark later this week."

A text dinged on Alex's phone. "Nathan's here. Do either of you have any questions?" When they didn't, she said, "See you at the park."

A few minutes later, Jenna followed Max to their vehicles.

"You sure you're okay?" he asked.

"I'm fine." She clenched her jaw. "Everyone acts like I'm this fragile porcelain doll." Jenna squared her shoulders. "See you at the park."

35

Max followed Jenna to the park, and they arrived at the same time as Alex and Nathan. Dave Martin, the park director, soon joined them, but his assistant, Derrick Holliday, was missing. Not surprising since he'd made his feelings about Carter known.

At 9:15, Carter hadn't shown. It wasn't until almost 9:30 before he arrived with his entourage. That was the only word Max could come up with when he saw security vehicles in front of and behind the senate candidate's Cadillac.

Carter emerged from the back seat and smoothed his hand over his hundred-dollar haircut. The man had class—Max had to give him that. His suit fit like it was tailor-made and probably was. Max wagered it cost more than most voters in Tennessee made in a month.

"Good to see you again," Carter said in his radio voice. He shook hands with each of them, and then walked with Martin to the area where he would be speaking.

"He'd probably kiss a baby or two if any were here," Jenna muttered, and Max nudged her.

"Well, it's true," she said.

"Yeah, but you don't want him to hear you." From what Max

had seen, running for election was a business like anything else, and Carter had it down pat. He also had the good looks and confident air to be successful.

Carter was no worse than a lot of other politicians Max had met—a mile wide and an inch deep. He ducked his head and grinned at his grandfather's old saying.

A few minutes later, the former mayor approached them. "So, you think you have the security all arranged?"

Nathan and Alex deferred to Max.

"Yes, sir." Max handed him a copy of what he'd drawn and spent the next fifteen minutes showing Carter and his security team the locations detailed on the map.

"We'll have people positioned at each of the spots marked with an X," he said, wrapping it up. "Are you still good with providing four of your own security people?"

"Yes. I realize this is a small county, and security might not be adequate."

Alex's lips twitched, but before she could respond, Carter turned to her. "Do you have any suspects in Paul Nelson's murder?"

She lifted her chin. "Not yet, but I'm sure we'll have a break in the case soon."

The look Carter gave her said he believed otherwise. "Are you utilizing the TBI for the Founders Day event to the full extent? I can get a couple more agents assigned if you need them."

Max was certain the director would love to hear that.

"Thank you for your offer," Nathan said, "but I think with your people added, we're good."

Carter checked his watch and looked up. "Do you know when Joe and Katherine Slater's funerals are?"

"I heard they're planning for Friday," Nathan said.

"I'll be returning for it," Carter said.

Nathan nodded. "Sorry to leave you guys, but I have a meeting with our auditor. I'll see you at the funeral, Senator."

"And I have a meeting too. Thank you for meeting with us," Alex said.

Carter turned to Max and Jenna. "If there's nothing else, I'll be on my way."

"Before you go," Max said, "Deputy Hart and I would like a word with you."

Irritation flashed in Carter's face. "Now?"

"Now. We have three murders to solve, and we need to ask you a few questions."

"About?"

"The years you served as mayor while Joe Slater and Paul Nelson were on the city council," Jenna said.

"That will take more than a few minutes, and I don't have that kind of time—I have an eleven o'clock meeting with the campaign volunteers in Chattanooga."

"This shouldn't take long," Max said. "Would you like to sit at one of the picnic tables?"

Carter glanced at the concrete structures that looked as though they needed a good scrubbing. "I'll stand."

Max took out the notepad where he'd jotted a few questions. "First, have you received any more threatening letters?"

"No. I thought someone was tailing me a few days ago, but if they were, that's all they were doing. They didn't try to run me off the road again, but that could've been because of my security detail."

"Good." Max looked down at his notes. "Can you think of any reason Joe Slater would receive the same letter you received?"

Carter blanched. "Good heavens, no!" He paced in front of them. "It's obvious whoever sent the letters is mentally disturbed. You have to catch him before he has a total breakdown—people like that are the ones who take out their frustrations on innocent people."

Max scanned his notes again. "Based on the recent murders

and your connection to the victims, we're focusing on the years you were mayor and Joe Slater and Paul Nelson were on the city council. Can you tell me some of the problems you encountered during those years?"

Carter shook his head. "We don't have enough time to go into all the problems—it's a way of life for mayors and city council members. Nothing you do suits everyone."

"Let me put it another way. Were there any problems that resulted in threats or lawsuits?"

"We live in a litigious society. Someone was always suing over some silly thing. Or going ballistic."

"Like?" Jenna probed.

Carter rubbed his forehead. "Probably the maddest anyone ever got was over a zoning ordinance. Milton Bledsoe threatened to shoot anyone on sight if they tried to stop him from building an auto repair shop on his property."

"Was that Junior's dad?" Jenna asked.

"Junior," Carter muttered. "Who names their son that? But yeah, you have the right family. Milton wanted to build his son a garage so he'd stay in Pearl Springs."

"Did he? Build the shop?"

"Sure. Neither I nor anyone else on the city council had a problem with it. The problem was with Milton and that son. They got it in their heads that the city was going to pass an ordinance to keep them from building, and the son made a big deal about it."

Max jotted the name down. "How about the dam—any problems with getting it built?"

Carter tapped his head with his palm. "I can't believe that wasn't the first thing that popped into my mind. The people who lived in the valley where the reservoir was built are a bunch of backwoods hillbillies."

Beside him, Jenna stiffened. Her expression reminded him of a cornered mama bear.

36

For the life of her, Jenna didn't understand how Harrison Carter had made it as far in politics as he had. Evidently he showed the voters a different personality than he was showing to them.

"You might want to be careful who you call backwoods hillbillies," she said, keeping her voice even. "They do vote, you know, and it would be a shame if you didn't carry your home county."

Color rose in Carter's face. "Sorry. Didn't mean to step on anyone's toes, but those people almost cost us the dam."

"Would that have been such a terrible thing?" She fisted her hands on her hips. "I sure don't see that it's served the purpose you said the community needed it for—we have no new industry."

"That's about to change. It's the whole purpose of having this political rally at the Founders Day picnic. That's when I'll announce a new industry locating in Pearl Springs that will provide two hundred new jobs. But please keep it under your hat. The deal won't be finalized until sometime later this week. I'd hate for something to mess up the deal."

She'd heard Carter planned to make some kind of announcement at the picnic, but she hadn't imagined it would be this. It took the starch out of her sails, as Granna would say. "I hope it pans out," she said stiffly.

"It will. Now, if there's nothing else, I really need to get on the road."

"I'll call you if we run into any more questions that need answering," Max said. "Or I can hold them until the funeral."

Carter nodded his agreement. He turned and strode to his car, stopping to use a handkerchief to wipe the tops of his shoes off before he got in the back seat.

"He'll probably be our next senator," Max muttered.

"Not by my vote." She folded her arms across her chest. "He doesn't respect the voters."

"At least he gave us one lead. Do you know where we can find Milton Bledsoe?"

Jenna nodded. "Pearl Springs cemetery."

"You're kidding."

"I wish. But maybe Junior can give us some insight." Jenna's phone rang, and she glanced at the screen. "My grandmother. Let me make sure nothing is wrong." She answered the phone. "Granna, is everything okay?"

"No."

Her heart leaped in her throat. "What's wrong? Is it your heart?"

"My heart's fine, it's my feelings that are hurt."

"What?"

Her grandmother chuckled. "I heard Max Anderson was in town and he hasn't been by to see me."

"Oh." She glanced over at Max and grinned. "I think we can remedy that." Jenna checked the time. Ten thirty. "Are you up for us dropping by for a few minutes?"

"Right now?"

"Yes."

"I don't have any tea cakes baked, but it serves him right."

"See you in about fifteen minutes." Jenna disconnected and grinned again when he questioned her with his eyes. "Granna's feelings are hurt you haven't been to see her. I hope it's okay that I told her we'd come by there."

"Maybe she can fill us in on Harrison Carter and the dam project."

"That's what I was thinking," she said. "And there's no need to drive both vehicles. We'll go right by the sheriff's office and can leave one of them in the parking lot."

They agreed to leave hers, and he picked her up a few minutes later.

"Where does she live?"

"About a mile past my house." As they approached her house, she said, "Do you mind stopping by my place so I can make sure no one's been there so far this morning?"

"That's a good idea."

They made a quick stop, and Jenna stared at the front window just as the sun ducked behind a cloud. There wasn't even a shadow reflected today.

Her palms sweated as she approached the front door with Max beside her. It was still deadbolted, and she relaxed a little. Inside everything looked normal, and the tape on the plate hadn't been disturbed.

"Thanks for humoring me."

"No problem."

A few minutes later, she glanced toward the window again as Max backed out of the drive. The sun popped out, and rays reflected off the window, creating a lifelike shadow. While it didn't resemble the man she saw late yesterday, once again she wondered if it was possible her mind had been playing tricks on her.

37

Max didn't miss the doubt in Jenna's face as she stared at her house.

While it was still possible that she'd fainted when she returned for her phone, he was rethinking that after what happened to him near the river yesterday. Maybe someone *had* been there yesterday morning and returned in the late afternoon and then slipped out of the house before they reached it. But how?

While he hadn't tried to pick her locks, Max knew it was possible. On the other hand, if there'd been no one in the window, would Max be feeding her paranoia by providing a plausible scenario?

What if he'd misinterpreted her expression, and she was thinking about something else altogether?

"Which side of the road is your grandmother on?" he asked instead.

"The left."

"I'm looking forward to seeing her again."

"Hold on to that thought," Jenna said wryly.

A few minutes later he pulled in front of a Craftsman-style brick house with purple rhododendron in full bloom across the front. "This looks like the kind of place Eva would have," he said.

"I'll tell her you said so."

Jenna's grandmother met them at the door. She leaned on a cane decorated with more bling than a teenager would use.

"It's about time you came to see me," she said, her voice sounding like someone much younger than the eighty he knew her to be. She hugged him, reminding Max of his grandmother who gave really strong hugs.

"You look good," he said. The house smelled of nutmeg and vanilla. "You could pass for Jamie Lee Curtis's twin."

She chuckled. "Maybe in those Halloween movies."

"No, I saw her in an interview on TV—her hair is cut short like yours."

Eva hugged Jenna. "He's a keeper, even if he does lie."

Max turned to Jenna. "Don't you agree?"

Jenna tilted her head. "I never noticed it before, but you're right. Granna, you do favor the actress."

"Now he's got you doing it." Eva shooed them into the living room. "Find a place to sit. I have tea cakes and a pot of hot coffee. Interested?"

"I thought you said you didn't have any made," Jenna said.

"No, I said I didn't have any tea cakes *baked*. I made some as soon as I heard Max was in town and put the dough in the icebox."

"Is that what you used to send me when Jenna came home for the weekend?"

"You remembered."

"There's no way I could forget them—they reminded me of the ones my grandmother made."

He'd been watching his carbs, but carbs or no carbs, there was no way he could hurt her feelings. Their questions might go down easier if they were sharing food. He chose the leather recliner to sit in.

"You and Max visit," Jenna said. "I'll get the refreshments."

"You know where everything is."

Eva's gaze followed Jenna as she disappeared into the kitchen. "I'm so glad to have that girl back home."

She settled across from Max on a blue and white floral love seat. A basket of yarn sat on the floor, and it looked as though she'd been knitting when they arrived. "What brings a TBI agent to Pearl Springs?"

That was one thing he'd always liked about Eva. She was direct. "Harrison Carter is having a political rally at the Founders Day picnic, and I'm checking out the security."

Eva Hart looked as though she'd bitten into a sour pickle. "Since when do our taxpayer dollars go to protect crooked politicians?" she muttered.

He'd struck a nerve. "So, you won't be voting for him?"

"Hardly."

Jenna came from the kitchen carrying a tray. "Here we go."

She set the tray on the coffee table and glanced at her grandmother. "Why don't you like him?"

"Mostly because everything bad in this town started while Carter was mayor."

Jenna frowned. "No one has ever mentioned this to me before."

Eva ran her hand over the rhinestones on the cane. "Maybe it's time someone did."

Max sat back. He certainly hadn't expected this. Before he could ask Eva to explain, a door scraped open.

"That's probably Sam," Eva said. "And don't get him started on Harrison Carter."

The kitchen door swung open again, and a man about Max's six-one entered the room. "Hey, Ma. Jenna." He turned to Max and held out his hand. "You must be the TBI agent."

"My uncle, Sam Hart," Jenna said to Max as the two men shook hands.

Sam had the look of someone who liked the outdoors. Max could see the resemblance to Jenna with his coal-black hair, albeit Sam's was sprinkled with gray.

Sam hooked his thumb in the fancy leather belt looped through his Wranglers and leaned back, eyeing Max. "What are you doing here?"

Suspicion laced the older man's voice. Max hadn't been wrong in thinking Sam had seen them pull into Eva's drive and came to investigate.

"Visiting Granna." Jenna sounded irritated.

Max managed a smile. "I met your mother some years ago when I was Jenna's boss at Chattanooga PD."

Sam bristled like Max's childhood dog when someone tried to take his bone away. "You saying you're here in Pearl Springs to see my niece?"

"Not exactly, although it's been a nice bonus."

Sam turned to Jenna. "What's the word on Paul Nelson's murder?"

"Nothing yet." She poured a cup of coffee and handed it to her grandmother, then poured Max one. "We're having coffee and tea cakes. Would you like to join us?"

"Nah. It's not long until lunch." He turned to his mother. "I'll see you later." Sam stopped at the kitchen door. "Now don't be gossiping about everyone after I leave, especially about me."

Once the back door closed, Jenna turned to her grandmother. "Granna, why did you say not to get Sam started on Harrison Carter?"

38

Granna dropped her gaze to the hands in her lap where she rubbed gnarled fingers. Jenna hadn't meant to upset her. "They used to be friends. What happened?" she asked gently.

"I never knew for sure, only that they had a falling-out over the dam project." Granna raised her gaze. "You know how your uncle is."

Unfortunately, Jenna did. Any opinion other than his was wrong.

"It seems like a lot of people were unhappy with Carter and the city council about the dam project," Max said.

Granna nodded. "Just about the whole county."

"Is there anyone who would still be upset, Granna?"

"You mean upset enough to kill Paul Nelson? Probably. The Slaters, not so much."

"What do you mean?"

"I guess it was in their personalities. People liked Joe in spite of some of the things he did, and of course, everyone liked Katherine. Paul got beat in the next election after the dam project went through, but Joe got reelected every four years." Her grandmother lifted her chin and squared her shoulders. "Enough negative talk. I want us to sit here and drink our coffee and enjoy these cookies."

"And I'm sure they're delicious," Max said. "Would you think about the people who were involved with the dam project and see if anyone pops in your mind who might still hold a grudge?"

"I'm not sure that I want to point a finger at anyone—they might turn it back on me since both Sam and Randall were mighty upset about losing the farm."

"Granna, we're not talking about you pointing the finger at anyone. I don't know all the families involved in the dam dispute, and it would help to know who they were."

"I suppose I could do that," she said. "I'll make you a list."

"Good," Max said. "We'll stop by after we talk to Harrison Carter again."

Her grandmother's face turned stony. "I'll tell you this about him. Don't believe anything he tells you. You know the old saying—if his lips are moving, he's lying—that's Harrison."

"Granna, what do you remember about the land where the dam and reservoir are now?"

Her grandmother frowned. "Other than the families involved, not a lot. Your grandfather wasn't one to discuss business matters with me." She stopped and pointed her finger at Jenna. "Don't let that happen when you get married. I didn't know anything about our affairs when he died, and it made his passing so much harder. If it hadn't been for Sam and your dad . . ."

"What about the land," Max prodded gently.

"Yes, the land. Walter inherited it from his father and that's why he didn't want to sell. He grew up on that farm, and it'd been in his family for fifty years before he was born." Then as if banishing bad thoughts away, she smiled and picked up a tea cake. "You still haven't tried these."

Jenna handed Max a cookie then picked one up and bit into

it. Butter and vanilla exploded on her taste buds. No one could make tea cakes like her grandmother.

Max sampled his and grinned. "These are so good."

"I'm glad you like them." The worry lines disappeared from Granna's face. "It's my grandmother's recipe."

They spent the next thirty minutes talking about families, with Max sharing stories about his parents and Granna telling on Jenna and the troubles she got into as a child. Some of the stories even Jenna had forgotten. Stories that made her grandfather and her mother come alive.

"You have a good memory, Eva," he said.

"Too good," Jenna added dryly. "And you could've kept the story about catching me skinny dipping in the pond to yourself—I was only five."

Granna laughed. "Your mother was so upset, thinking you could've drowned."

"I knew how to swim." She sighed. "I have so few memories of her . . . or my grandfather. We need to do this again."

Granna nodded solemnly. "It's hard for me to talk about them." She smiled at Max. "But he's such a good listener that it loosens my tongue."

"It's because you tell good stories." Max stood and gathered the cups and empty plate. "We need to be going."

She took the tray and walked to the kitchen. She'd hoped her grandmother would bring up the wreck that killed Jenna's grandfather, but she hadn't. Maybe they could find details of the accident in old newspapers.

Ten minutes later, they said their goodbyes and reminded her grandmother they would return soon.

"Thanks for listening to her," Jenna said.

"I enjoyed it, but I thought the time was a good bridge builder—she'll be more likely to discuss the past if she considers me a friend."

They hadn't driven a mile before her stomach growled.

Max cocked his head. "It's almost noon. Why don't we grab lunch at Pete's?"

"Sounds good."

After Jenna picked up her SUV, she followed Max to their small downtown area and got lucky when a car backed out of a space right in front of Pete's Diner. Max had to park a block away.

"They're busy," she said when he joined her.

Busy was an understatement, but the diner fell silent and everyone turned toward them when they entered. *Odd.* She questioned Max with her eyes, and he gave her a barely visible shrug.

Jenna scanned the room for a table and found one near the back. Once they were seated, she picked up the menu. "What day is it today?"

"Wednesday."

"Meat loaf and three vegetables day—you'll like it." She tilted her head. "It's been a long week. Does it seem like it ought to be Saturday already?"

"Now that you mention it . . ."

She scanned the menu for which of Pete's homemade vegetables she wanted. They both looked up when Ethel set their water glasses on the table.

"Any word on who killed Paul Nelson?" she asked, her voice rising above the din in the room.

Once again the restaurant got quiet, and before Jenna could answer, someone at the front of the diner said, "And I heard the Slaters' accident was no accident."

39

J enna's heart sank. Diners started talking at once, and she heard "serial killer" mentioned. Junior Bledsoe stood—she hadn't seen him when they arrived but now noticed that he shared a table with the banker, Todd Donelson.

"What I want to know," Junior said, pointing a finger at her, "is who's going to be next? And what you're doing about it."

Max stood as well. The two men were about the same height, but Junior probably had fifty pounds on Max's lean frame, not that Jenna thought Junior would start anything.

Max held up his hand. "There's no serial killer running around Russell County—"

"You don't know that." Junior's hands fisted at his sides. "You come in here with your big-city ways, acting the big shot. Well—"

"Junior," Jenna said quietly. "You're not helping matters. We're investigating the Slater accident, as well as Paul Nelson's death— it's not like TV where everything gets wrapped up in an hour. Why don't you sit down with us and tell us what you know about anyone who might have a grudge against Nelson."

Uncertainty clouded the big man's face, and Todd tugged at Junior's sleeve. "Don't make a scene."

"We could use your help," Max added.

"Yours too, Todd," Jenna said.

Junior gave them a curt nod. While they grabbed their iced teas, Max slid in beside Jenna in the booth. Junior and Todd sat across from them. Both men removed their ball caps, laying them on the seat.

Junior eyed Max suspiciously. "What's he doing here in Pearl Springs, anyway?"

She pressed her knee against Max's leg, hoping he understood she should handle this. "He came Monday to coordinate with Nathan and Alex the security for Harrison Carter's political rally." Jenna leaned forward. "Max was my boss in Chattanooga. He's a good guy."

Junior's expression softened, but he still frowned at them.

Todd nodded. "Why is the TBI involved in Carter's rally?"

"It's a long story, one we're not at liberty to discuss," she replied.

Junior rubbed his jaw with his thumb. "Somebody threatening to kill our illustrious former mayor?"

"Do you know anyone who would want to?" Max asked.

The big man snorted. "Just about anybody he and the city council imposed those silly zoning regulations on . . . and then there's those who were forced to sell the government their land, my dad and your folks included." He raised his eyebrows and looked down at Jenna. "That enough?"

"What are you talking about?"

"Carter about started a war with his rules and regulations in town. And you ought to know what happened with the dam project. Your granddaddy refused the government's offer. He was totally against everyone selling their property and vowed to fight it."

Junior picked up his tea glass and rattled the ice in it before using a spoon to dip out a couple of slivers. He set the glass down. "After he died in that *accident*, Eva didn't have the heart to fight any longer. She turned the fight over to Sam and your dad, and they caved."

Jenna frowned. "The way you said that—you don't think it was an accident?"

Junior shrugged. "I can't say . . . and with three deaths this week of people involved in what was going on back then, I'm not sure I should. You might want to watch your own back."

"What else can you tell us?" Max asked.

"Nothing concrete, just things I observed."

"Like what?" Jenna asked.

"Like your granddaddy and Todd's dad, Earl, dying in 'accidents.'"

She shifted her gaze to Todd. The lanky banker hunched over his glass of tea. "How much land did your family own?"

He picked up his cap and studied the John Deere logo. "Two hundred acres in the valley where the reservoir is now. Land my daddy and granddaddy loved." He looked up. "After my dad died, my grandfather lost heart. He took whatever the state offered—don't know how much, but it was enough to send me to college."

"I'm sorry," Jenna said. "I don't remember the accident that took your dad's life. Do you mind talking about it?"

Todd's melancholy expression hardened. "He supposedly shot himself climbing out of a deer stand, but anyone who knew my dad would never believe that. He was too safety conscious about his guns."

"So, what do you think happened?" Max asked.

"Me?" Todd straightened. "I think he stood in the way of Carter's ambitions. My dad was planning on running against him in the election later that year, and her grandfather was backing him." He lifted an eyebrow. "If I were you and something happened to Harrison, I'd probably be looking at me or Junior as the main suspects."

Looking at the two men across from her, Jenna found it hard to believe either was their killer, but she needed to check their stories out. The sheriff's office should have a file on her grandfather's accident in the archives as well as one on Earl Donelson. Jenna made a mental note to ask Alex about it. "Anyone else we need to know about?"

Junior stared up at the ceiling then returned his gaze to Jenna, his brows raised. "Gordon Marsden's dad. After he died, Gordon ended up selling out instead of fighting like his dad would've wanted."

"How did he die?" she asked.

"He had a stroke 'cause he got so upset at the price the government first offered him for his land. His blood pressure got so high it popped a blood vessel in his head. At least that's what the doctors said—the blood pressure part, anyway."

"Anything else?" Max asked.

Junior ran his finger up and down his glass, making lines in the condensation.

Todd cleared his throat. "It wasn't long after the dam and reservoir project got off the ground that Slater bought his first Cadillac, and he didn't borrow money from the bank to pay for it, at least not from my bank. That was also about the time Paul Nelson started wearing those expensive clothes of his."

Junior laughed. "Don't know if either has anything to do with the dam project, but the timing of Slater's Caddy and Paul's fancy duds always struck me as peculiar, but maybe it was one of those serendipity things."

Max jotted a note on his pad and looked up. "How many families owned land where the dam and reservoir are now?"

"I'd have to stop and think. A whole bunch of folks sold their property to some company before we even knew there was a dam in the works." Junior nodded to Todd. "You'd know more about that."

Todd nodded. "At the time, I thought it was strange that a company would come in here and buy up a bunch of land, but hunt clubs had made a comeback, and that's what the farmers who sold believed the company planned to use the land for."

"Do you know the name of the company?"

Junior shook his head. "If I knew it, I've forgotten it."

"Something to do with the earth . . ." Todd shook his head. "Just don't remember."

Max nodded. "How about the others? How many families held out?"

"About ten or eleven families sued or fought the dam to the end."

"Could you give me their names?" Max held his pen poised, ready to write.

Junior and Todd rattled off seven names, half that Jenna was familiar with.

"I don't remember any of the others." Junior turned to Jenna. "My daddy sold out after your grandfather died, and there wasn't a day that went by that he didn't regret not fighting that dam to his dying day. It ain't served one useful purpose other than a place for people to have fun on the water."

Ethel approached with Jenna's and Max's meals, and Junior checked his watch and stood. "I have cars waiting to be worked on."

Todd stood as well. But they didn't leave until Ethel walked away. Once she was out of earshot, Junior said, "I don't know what caused Slater's car to go off the road, but you might want to check out your granddaddy's accident."

40

idn't you and your dad have a row with the city about building a garage?" Max asked before Junior could walk away. He'd been waiting for an opportunity to ask Junior about Carter's remarks.

"We didn't have a squabble with them—it was the other way around. Dad just told 'em he didn't care what they passed, he was building a garage on the empty lot beside his store. They're the ones who made a big deal out of it, but the garage got built. And nobody made us tear it down."

"He's right," Todd said. "The mayor and city council are the ones who made a fuss."

That wasn't the way Max heard it, and he personally couldn't understand why the city would have a problem—the garage was bound to bring in tax money, and anytime there was a way to keep a hometown boy at home, it was a good thing. Unless it was a power play, and he could see Carter doing something like that. He stood and extended his hand. "Thanks for talking to us."

The three men shook hands and Junior and Todd walked back to their table while Max sat down and put away his notepad and pen. He'd thought about using his tablet to make notes, but considering his "big city ways" might irritate Junior, he opted for old school. He turned to Jenna. "I'd say first on our agenda for this afternoon is to find your grandfather's accident report."

She opened her phone. "I'll text Alex. She'll know where to look."

After Max blessed their meal, they dug into the food. After a few bites, he said, "I don't usually like meat loaf, but this is great."

"Pete claims it's his mama's recipe."

"Well, I'd like to have it."

She chuckled. "What? To give to your mama?"

He gave her the evil eye. "No. For me." They ate in silence for a few minutes, then Max said, "We need to find out what company bought up the property before the dam was built."

"That shouldn't be too hard—should be listed on Russell County's Registrar of Deeds website."

"Yeah, but we'd need the name of the person they bought property from." Max tapped his finger on the phone.

"How about we stop by the courthouse on the way to the office?"

"That's probably the quickest way to find out."

After they finished eating, they walked to the courthouse on the next block and climbed the steps to the main floor. Max searched for the registrar's office. "Do you see it?"

"No, but it could be on the next floor. Let me step into the Circuit Court's office." Jenna disappeared into the nearest office and soon reappeared. "It's upstairs."

Halfway up the steps, Max said, "We could've taken the elevator."

"What? And miss all this exercise? Come on, softy."

The registrar's office was the last room on the right. Max held the door for Jenna then followed her inside.

"May I help you?" An older woman stood behind the counter that divided the room, her eyebrows raised expectantly. Then she smiled. "Jenna Hart, as I live and breathe! I heard you were back."

"Seven months now," Jenna said, eyeing the white-haired clerk.

Then her eyes widened. "Mrs. Croft! I didn't know you were the registrar." She turned to Max. "This is my fifth-grade teacher." She turned back to the registrar. "How long—"

"Oh, ten years now." Her blue eyes twinkled. "I'm so glad you came back to Pearl Springs. Now what can I do for you?"

"We're looking for the name of a company that bought property in the valley before the dam was built," Max said.

"Hmmm . . . That would have been around the 1990s, and I wasn't here then. None of the records prior to 2002 are digitalized. Let me think about that a minute." Then she smiled. "We need to look at the maps. Follow me."

They pushed through the half swinging door and followed her to a room with all sorts of maps rolled up. She pointed to the wall. "That's the current map—we'll compare it to one from the time period you're looking for."

She pulled a map, looked at it, rolled it back up, and picked another. "This is it."

Mrs. Croft unrolled the map and laid it on a table in the middle of the room. "Here's the Pearl River."

She traced her finger along the river, occasionally looking up at the current map. Finally she tapped on an area that corresponded to the lake. "This is where the dam and lake are now."

After writing down the number on it, she walked to bookshelves containing ledgers and ran her fingers over the backs. "Let's try these first."

She pulled out two large red leather-bound books and handed one to Jenna and the other to Max. "I believe you'll find what you're looking for in these pages. If you don't find it, look in the books on either side. Feel free to spread out on the other table."

"Thank you," Jenna called after her as the older woman left them.

Max took his book to the table and opened it. The first deed was in 1997. "What year should we be looking for?"

"'98 or '99."

He flipped over to the middle of the book. The deed was dated March of 1998. This was more like it. Max turned the pages, quickly scanning each for a company name as the landowner on the deed. He hoped Junior was correct and not just assuming a company had bought up the land at a low price and then turned around and sold it to the state.

He was three quarters through the book when he saw a company name. TerraQuest Corporation. Close enough to Todd Donelson's earth reference.

"I found something!"

"I think I have too," Max said. "What's the name on yours?"

"TerraQuest."

Same as his. "I believe we've found the company. What's the date?"

"February 1999. Yours?"

"December '99." He took out his phone and snapped a photo of the deed. "See how many deeds you can find with TerraQuest as property owners and take a photo of each one."

"Do you want me to document any other deeds with the state as the purchaser?"

"That's a good idea."

She nodded, and both set to work documenting the deeds. They found twelve tracts of land that the corporation had sold to the state for the dam, and seven that belonged to individuals.

"Did you notice the difference in what the state paid Terra-Quest compared to the others?" Jenna asked.

"No." Max hadn't taken the time to read the details of the deeds, and he scrolled back through his photos, enlarging one to read the print. There was quite a discrepancy. "I wonder how much TerraQuest paid for the land?"

"There's a reference in the description for previous sale and owner. We'll have to pull more books, but at least we know which deed book to look in."

"That's a silver lining." He high-fived her.

Max scrolled to the description while Jenna did the same on her phone. They both reached to pull the same book.

"That figures," she said. "Maybe the TerraQuest deeds are all together."

They weren't but neither were they that far apart. Max compared the price the corporation had paid for the land with the price the state paid them and whistled. "TerraQuest made a killing."

"And they were paid a whole lot more than anyone else, but why?"

Max didn't like what he was thinking, but crooked appraisers in the past weren't unheard of. Nowadays an appraiser would have to get really creative to pull what appeared to have happened here. He shared his thought with Jenna.

"I wonder how we could find out who the appraiser was?"

"It would be on the transcripts of the eminent domain trials, and those records will be in the Chancery Court office."

"I wonder who owns this TerraQuest?" Jenna said.

"Mrs. Croft might know, particularly if the company has purchased land since she's been registrar."

Max shelved the heavy books, and they went in search of the registrar. She was busy with a man dressed in khakis and a short-sleeve shirt. When they finished their conversation, the man glanced at them, and his eyes widened.

"Jenna Hart? I haven't seen you since you moved into your old place."

She winced. "I'm sorry—I've been so busy." Jenna turned to Max and introduced the two men. "Years ago, Dad gave me the house I'm living in, thinking I'd come back home. I didn't want to sell it, and Mr. Weaver owns a rental management company—he took care of renting it out while I was in Chattanooga." She turned to Weaver. "By the way, thank you for making sure no one damaged anything."

"You say you manage rentals?" Max said. Something nagged at his mind. If Rick Sebastian was in Pearl Springs, he would need a place to stay. When the older man nodded, Max pulled up the photo of Sebastian the county and city officers had been circulating and held out his phone. "Have you rented anything to this person?"

Weaver peered at the phone, then took out a pair of black-rimmed glasses and looked again. He shook his head. "Haven't seen anybody who looks like that."

"Have you been approached by anyone you don't know?"

"All the time. About half my rentals go to people I never see— they contact me by email and provide references and put up a hefty deposit. I do require a photo ID, though." He nodded toward Max's phone. "And none of them look like this guy."

Max figured there was nothing to stop them from providing a fake ID. "How many houses have you rented lately?"

"Lately? Seven or eight."

"Are you in charge of the Armstrong place?" Jenna asked. "Bryan Bishop said the new owners were renting it out."

"I am. Rented it to some people from out of town back in March. They're never late on the rent, either—deposit drops in my bank account right on the dot."

Max took out his notepad. "Do you have a name?"

Weaver briefly shifted his eyes toward the ceiling, then he shook his head. "I'll have to look at my records."

"Bryan's grandson said they scared him."

"That boy is scared of his own shadow," Weaver said. "But I know these are nice people."

His tone said they were insulting him by insinuating he'd rent to anyone who wasn't.

"I'm sure they are," Max said. "Would you mind giving us a list of the names and addresses of non-local people renting property for the last six months?"

"I suppose I could, but you'll have to wait until the morning. I have a doctor's appointment in Chattanooga, and I'm leaving as soon as I get finished here."

"Nine o'clock?" Jenna asked.

"That's when I generally get to my office." He nodded. "See you there tomorrow."

When the door closed behind him, Mrs. Croft asked, "Did you find the deeds you were looking for?"

"We think so. Have you ever heard of TerraQuest Corporation?"

Mrs. Croft tapped her lips with her index finger. "The name rings a bell, but I'm not sure how." She turned to her computer. "Let's see if that name pops up."

The hourglass appeared. "This thing has been so slow all day." She shook the mouse, and a message popped up on the screen. *No files found.*

"That's strange," the registrar said. "Why would a corporation come in and buy that land and then disappear?"

Why indeed? Max intended to find out.

41

Jenna took out her phone, pulled up one of the TerraQuest deeds she'd photographed, and examined it. "Says here the deed was prepared by Cal Pipkin. Maybe we can get information from him."

"I doubt it," Mrs. Croft said. "He died ten years ago."

Jenna wanted to growl. Dead ends everywhere they turned. Literally. "Did anyone take over his office?"

"His grandson, Harold, but he may not have kept Cal's records. His office is across the street."

Jenna turned to Max. "Why don't we check while we're downtown? If we strike out there, Dylan's computer savvy, maybe he can find the company."

They thanked the registrar, and Jenna handed her a business card. "If you remember why the name seems familiar, give me a call."

"I will," the older woman said as they walked out the door.

When Max suggested the elevator, Jenna shook her head. "I don't normally avoid elevators, but this one is old. It creaks and rattles."

They'd reached the second floor when her phone rang. "It's Alex." She answered and said, "You're on speaker and Max is with me."

"Fine. Just wanted to let you know the two photos of Rick Sebastian have been shown to every retail business in town, and no one has seen him."

"How about any of his associates?" she asked. "He could've had one of them break into my house."

"We don't have photos of all his known associates from Chattanooga PD, and no one has seen the ones we do have."

Jenna didn't know if the information should make her feel better or more anxious. "As small as Pearl Springs is, if any of them show up, they'll stick out."

"Right."

"How about the file on the wreck my grandfather had?" Jenna asked.

"I found it." Alex hesitated. "But I would rather discuss it with you in person."

A chill inched down her spine. "How about in thirty minutes? We're on our way to Harold Pipkin's office to check out something."

When Alex agreed, Jenna disconnected the call. "We need to get my grandmother's thoughts on the accident, see how it tallies with the report once we get it."

"I agree, but I have a feeling she won't want to discuss it," Max said. "How about Sam or your dad?"

"I don't know. We can always ask, but let's start with Granna."

He nodded and followed her down the stairs. Once they were outside, the same feeling she'd had earlier returned. Someone was watching her. She could feel it. Jenna scanned the area, and everything seemed normal.

"What is it?" Max said.

"Nothing." She pointed across the street. "That's the attorney's office. Let's go see if he knows anything about his grandfather's clients."

No one sat at the desk inside the law office, and Jenna glanced around at the beige walls and the furniture that, while not worn, looked like it'd been there awhile. "Harold must not have changed anything after his grandfather died."

"Maybe he doesn't have enough business to afford changes," Max said.

"It gives me hope that maybe he hasn't gotten rid of his grandfather's files."

A fiftysomething woman stepped into the room and stopped when she saw them. Jenna blinked. She remembered Trudy Mills from church when she was a teenager, and that she worked for Cal.

"I didn't hear you come in. May I help you?" She did a double take. "Jenna Hart? Is that you?"

"Yes, ma'am."

"I heard you were back in town. It's good to see you."

Jenna made the introductions.

"So you're Harold's secretary?" Jenna said.

"Make that personal assistant, Missy," Trudy said, arching an eyebrow. Then her mouth twitched. "That's a fancy title for secretary, but he insists that I use it. Pays the same."

Jenna swallowed a smile.

"Is Mr. Pipkin in?" Max asked.

Trudy frowned. "Do you have an appointment?"

"No," he said. "But we won't take up much of his time."

"Time is something he has plenty of, but he's not here. He usually takes two hours for lunch and . . ." Trudy glanced at her watch. "He still has fifteen minutes."

"May we wait?" Jenna asked.

"It's a free country. I would offer you coffee, but we're fresh out."

"We don't need any," Max said. "Have you been with the attorney long?"

"He sort of inherited me. As Jenna knows, I worked for his

grandfather, although I think young Mr. Pipkin would like to trade me in for a younger model," she said, giving them an as-if eye roll.

"His grandfather is why we're here," Max said. "Maybe you can help us."

"If it has to do with one of Cal's clients, I'm sure I can."

Interesting. She called the grandfather Cal, but the grandson Mr. Pipkin. Jenna had a feeling they would get more information from her than the lawyer. "It's about a company called Terra-Quest. Cal Pipkin wrote the deeds for land they bought back in the late 1990s. It was located where the reservoir is now."

"I don't remember the name, but if Cal wrote the deeds and recorded them, there should be a file somewhere. Do you know the year?"

Max took out his phone and opened his photo album. "December 16, 1999."

"It'll be in the archives. Give me a sec." She disappeared down the hall and five minutes later returned with a folder. "What do you want to know?"

"Is there any contact information on TerraQuest there?" Jenna asked.

Trudy flipped through the papers. "There's a PO box in Chattanooga listed for Cal to mail the deeds. But that's all. I checked to see if there was a TerraQuest file, but there wasn't."

"Do you have any recollection of these deeds?"

"Cal wrote so many deeds, and that long ago . . ." She shook her head. "I'm sorry."

Jenna's shoulders slumped. Another dead end. She forced a smile to her lips. "Thanks for taking time to talk to us."

"Don't you want to stay and talk to Harold?"

"I doubt he'll know as much as you've already told us," Max said.

"You got that right," she muttered. Then Trudy smiled. "Stop by anytime."

They stepped out into the sunlight, and he walked with her to her SUV. "Well," Jenna said. "That was . . ."

"Interesting," he finished for her. "Let's go see what the accident report says."

She nodded. "If we have time, maybe we can start on the list of landowners who had their property taken by eminent domain."

Jenna had an eerie sense someone was watching her, just like earlier. She turned in a circle, scanning the downtown buildings with vehicles parked out front. A few cars passed by. No one seemed to be paying any attention to them or acting suspiciously. Was she totally losing it?

"Anything wrong?" Max asked.

"Not really . . . it's just I feel someone watching us."

He scanned the same area Jenna had. "Where?"

She shook her head. "I don't see anyone . . . it was just a feeling. It's gone now. Ready?"

Max scanned the area again, slower this time. "I don't see anything."

"I told you it was probably nothing, just my overactive imagination. I'll see you at the sheriff's office."

She opened her door and climbed in. Max probably thought she was suffering from PTSD again. At the sheriff's office, she parked and met him at the entrance.

"I was thinking about TerraQuest while we drove here," she said. "It looks like someone bought up the land knowing the dam was going to be built."

"Or they gambled that it would be. Holliday at the park said Harrison Carter applied for a grant while he was city engineer— somewhere around twenty-eight years ago. We need to find out when it was approved."

"That might be in the newspaper archives, or maybe Granna knows."

"Did you call and check to see if she's up for another visit today?"

"No, but I will." Jenna called her grandmother and confirmed that they could stop by her house in about an hour.

"She's good with it," she said. "Now let's see what that accident report says."

42

Alex was in her office, but before they could ask about the accident report, she said, "I found the file, but I'd like you to sit down before we discuss it."

Jenna gave her a wary glance. "Why?"

"Just sit."

They each took a wingback chair across from her desk and waited. Alex handed each a stapled copy of the report. Max opened his right away, but Jenna hesitated. Alex was acting strangely, and that couldn't be good.

Her boss cleared her throat and said, "The accident was caused by a tie-rod coming loose."

Jenna stared at her boss as blood drained from her face. *A tie-rod . . . just like Joe Slater.*

Her grandfather was murdered? Bands gripped Jenna's chest, making it hard to breathe as panic edged into her brain. *Not now.* She forced herself to breathe, but still the room closed in on her.

Beside her Max murmured something and Alex answered, but the noise in her head drowned out their words.

"Are you all right, Jenna?"

Alex's words jolted her, and she focused on the chief deputy. "I'm fine. Are you sure? About the tie-rod?"

"I called my grandfather to make sure there hadn't been a mistake, and he confirmed it," she said. "Gramps and your grandfather were good friends."

Jenna took a deep breath to clear her head. Had her grandfather been murdered for his land? "Did the sheriff ever consider it might not have been an accident?"

"It was an old farm truck, but he knew your granddaddy would've checked things like that. The sheriff's office didn't have a CSI team then, and Gramps had Junior check it out. He couldn't find any evidence of tampering. Of course now we have better ways of checking that."

Max glanced at Jenna. "Why didn't Junior tell us that at lunch?"

"Good question."

"Have you heard from your CSI on the nut you found?" Alex asked.

"No. I'll call right now." Max took out his phone and stepped out of the room.

"I'm sorry," Alex said. "I know this is a shock."

All Jenna could do was nod. *Granna.* How was she going to take this? She rubbed her forehead. "Can we keep this quiet until I figure out how to tell my grandmother?"

"The part about your grandfather's truck, yes, but I'm afraid most people already know about the tie-rod on Joe's Hummer and are speculating Joe and his wife were murdered. If anyone remembers what caused your grandfather's accident—"

"I think Junior has already put it together." Jenna dropped her gaze to the report. "Anything from the Hamilton County medical examiner?"

"Not yet, but I expect at least a preliminary report by morning."

The door opened and they both turned and looked expectantly as Max entered the room.

"She said the microscope showed tiny scuff marks on the nut

like an open-end wrench would make. And the cotter pin you found on the road did not come from the Hummer. It was much too old." He raised his eyebrows. "But the one you found in the garage did."

"I can't believe the killer used the same method twice," she said.

"It happens more than you'd think," Alex said. "Killers aren't always the brightest bulb in the box. Often they think if something worked the first time, it'll work again."

Max nodded. "Like a case last year. A husband reported his wife died when she fell down their basement steps. When we looked into the husband's history, we found that his first wife died the same way ten years ago. He's awaiting trial now."

"Whoever killed Joe and Katherine Slater figured we'd never put the two accidents together," Jenna said.

"That's a likely scenario." Alex leaned back in her chair. "What do you two have for me?"

She let Max fill Alex in on the information they'd gotten at the registrar's office. When he finished, Alex said, "I'll put Dylan on TerraQuest's trail—if anyone can find them, he can."

Jenna stood. "We stopped by Harold Pipkin's office before we came here." Alex's brows quirked up, questioning. "His grandfather wrote the deeds for the property TerraQuest bought before the dam was proposed."

"It's hard to believe anyone would kill just to purchase land on the off chance the dam would actually be built."

"Unless whoever owns TerraQuest was pretty certain the dam was a done deal, and they were going to reap a profit," Jenna said.

"Still . . ." Alex teepeed her fingers. "How much money do you think we're talking about here?"

"I don't know. I do know on the deeds we checked, the state offered TerraQuest more money for their property than they offered to those who held out, but we didn't check them all." Jenna took out her phone. "I'll do that now."

She brought up each deed and checked the purchase price. *Wait a minute.* "That can't be right."

Max looked up from his phone. "I think you're seeing the same thing I am."

"What are you two talking about?"

Jenna exchanged glances with Max. "You tell her while I double-check something."

She opened her calculator app and entered numbers while Max continued.

"On the ones I checked, the government paid almost three times the price for the land they purchased from TerraQuest as they did from individual landowners."

"You're kidding. Maybe the acreage was different."

Jenna shook her head. "The acreage varied, but in the ones I just calculated, TerraQuest received almost three times as much per acre."

"Okay," Alex said. "We need to find out just who owns Terra-Quest."

"And then locate and talk to the original property owners," Max added. "I think I'll text Harrison Carter to see if he's familiar with the company."

"Wait until we talk to him at the funeral," Jenna said. "I'd like to read his body language when you bring it up."

"You think—"

"I don't think anything, Max," she replied. "Except we shouldn't rule out the possibility he's involved."

"You're right."

Jenna handed Alex a list of people who'd sold to TerraQuest. "Do you know any of these people? We wanted to talk to them."

Alex looked over the list. "Some have died, but I'll get you an address for those who haven't."

"Thanks. Just text it to us." Jenna checked her watch and stood. "Granna is looking for us in twenty minutes."

"What are you expecting to learn from her?" Alex asked.

Max had stood as well. "She started to tell us something about Carter when her son came over and she clammed up."

"Interesting." Alex tapped her fingers together. "She should know—Eva Hart has her finger on the pulse of almost everything going on in Pearl Springs."

Jenna sighed. The problem would be in whether Granna would share what she knew.

43

The Pearl River Reservoir came into view. His hands cramped from gripping the steering wheel so tightly. Hatred boiled up from his chest.

If it hadn't been for the dam and reservoir . . . It was time to finish his plan. Draining the lake and killing Carter were the last two items on his list.

He flipped the sun visor down and turned the white pickup with a Tennessee Department of Environment and Conservation logo adhered to the door onto the access road. The truck eased past the parking lot for visitors and continued on to the chain-link fence blocking access to the dam.

His insides were like a sugar-loaded kid on steroids. What if the guard recognized him? Never mind that he hadn't recognized himself this morning with the fake mustache and gray crew cut wig.

He stopped at the wire gate and grabbed his clipboard while an overweight guard swaggered toward him with a no-trespassing frown on his face.

Relief was swift—it was the new guy. Still, he couldn't stop the fear encroaching his body. Sweat dampened his palms. What if the guard questioned the TDEC logo? At first glance, it looked real, but if the guard looked closely, he was bound to notice it wasn't painted on but a decal with an adhesive backing.

He hadn't come this far to lose it. Pushing aside the fear, he rolled down his window. "Good morning. I—"

"You're not supposed to be on the access road." The guard glowered as if to dare him to say otherwise.

The name on the badge said Tim. "I've been sent to conduct moisture tests. TDEC received a report from the computers monitoring the gallery of an increase in seepage. Nothing to be alarmed about."

The frown barely eased. "I didn't get a notification anyone was coming."

He'd anticipated this. "Really?" He handed him the clipboard with his fake authorization. "My boss was leaving for vacation at noon, and I bet it slipped his mind. His name and number are at the bottom of the page." While the guard scanned the paper, he said, "You're new, right?"

The guard looked up from the paperwork. "How'd you know?"

He had familiarized himself with all the guards who manned the dam. "I usually deal with John, and he said they were supposed to hire someone."

"Yeah, I did orientation under John."

He pointed to the clipboard. "If you have any questions, you can phone my boss . . . although I'm sure he's left for his trip." He waited a beat. "I can give you his cell phone number."

Tim stared at the authorization a few seconds longer. "No need, but I'll have to see your ID."

"Sure." Victory. He fished the fake TDEC credentials from his wallet and handed them to him. After Tim checked the name on the authorization against the ID, he handed both back. "Hold on while I open the gate."

He allowed himself to blow out a breath while the gate swung open.

"I'll be over there in a minute to open the gallery door," Tim called after him.

He parked at the end of the access road, climbed out of the truck, and slipped on a backpack with enough C-4 inside to blow a hole in the dam. While he waited for Tim, he hooked a utility belt around his waist before he donned a silver hard hat and grabbed the telescoping ladder he would need.

Tim was panting when he reached him and briefly eyed the backpack while he caught his breath. "I can't go with you to the gallery," he said as he unlocked the door. "Nobody to man the guardhouse, and besides, the thought of going underground and all that water overhead gives me the creeps."

"Totally understand. John never accompanies me, either. Just leaves me the key so I can lock up when I'm done."

Tim hesitated.

"Just trying to save you a trip," he said with a shrug. He didn't want to worry about Tim coming back before he was finished.

The guard's shoulders relaxed and he handed him the key. "If it's okay for John . . . just don't lose it."

"Gotcha."

A few minutes later, he had the door opened and noted the time, then flashed a light down the dark, spiral staircase. There had to be a light switch somewhere. He shined a light around the walls, locating the switch just inside the door. If it'd been a snake, it would've bit him.

He shuddered. Now was not the time to be thinking of snakes.

He inched down the steps all the while urging himself to move faster—he didn't want Tim coming to check on him. Since the guard had an aversion to being underground, he probably didn't need to worry. Finally he was on the floor of the gallery where he shucked the heavy backpack and removed the C-4.

Pushing aside the thoughts of just how much water and dirt

was above him, he shined his light down the narrow gallery that was barely wide enough to accommodate two people.

High up on the wall, cables that connected to the control room snaked along the wall. He quickly extended the ladder, making sure the rungs locked in place before he climbed it. The cables were just thick enough to prop a cell phone on, perfect for the one he'd modified. He secured the phone to the cables.

He wedged the C-4 between the cables. Once it was secure, he stuck in a detonator and attached a wire to it and then to the phone.

One phone call. He closed his eyes briefly, imagining the hole the explosion would make in the dam. Within hours the lake would drain, and eventually the land would be free to return to its original state.

A quick glance at the phone reception assured him the phone had connected to the cell service that was used to transmit information from the gallery to the control room. Days ago, he'd hacked into the control room database and retrieved the password.

He laughed to himself, the sound muffled. No one would expect him to know how to hack into anything. Just showed how easily people could be fooled.

Even though it was cool in the gallery, sweat formed on his forehead. He wiped his face on his shirt sleeve and then checked his watch. He'd been here thirty minutes. It felt like hours.

He descended the ladder, retracted it, and then backed against the wall and looked up. Someone would have to be searching for the bomb to see it.

His job here was done.

D-day minus 3.

44

Max parked his truck in Jenna's drive and grabbed his laptop before jogging to her SUV. He was worried about her, especially after she'd thought someone was watching them and then zoned out in Alex's office. She needed a break. But getting her to take one was another thing. Maybe a mini-break.

"I googled some of the addresses Alex texted," Max said. He stashed his laptop in the back and climbed into the passenger seat. "And one is not far from the barn where you keep Ace. After we visit Eva, why don't we check out the address and then drop by the barn?"

Jenna turned right out of her drive. "I'd love that. I was trying to figure out a way to check on him, but we have so much to do."

A minute later, he swayed as she turned into Eva's drive. "It's settled then."

They climbed out of the SUV. "I wonder if your uncle will show up."

"I saw his pickup when we passed his house. If he's watching Granna's house, he probably will."

He followed Jenna as she strode to the front door and tapped before opening the door and entering. "We're here, Granna," she called.

"About time," Eva said, coming from the kitchen. "What happened? I was about to give up on you."

"We got tied up with Alex." Jenna hugged her grandmother.

"Come on back. I have carrot cake and a good cup of coffee waiting for you."

"How did you know carrot cake was my favorite cake?" Max asked.

"A little bird probably told me," she said, winking at Jenna.

They followed her into the kitchen. "By the way, Sam said he'd probably stop by too."

They needed to get whatever information Eva had before her son arrived. "You were going to tell us why you thought Harrison Carter had something to do with Paul Nelson's death and maybe Joe's."

She looked up from cutting the cake. "I said I'd think about it. Do we have to jump right into that?"

"It's important," Max said, making his voice softer. "Three people have died, and we have no one with a motive."

"Oh, there's plenty with motive." She gave him a knowing look then plated each of them a large piece of cake and set the servings on the table. "Jenna, would you pour the coffee?"

Once they were all seated, Eva waited expectantly.

"You were saying," Max said.

"Try the cake first."

Was Eva stalling to give Sam time to arrive?

"Granna, you talk while we taste," Jenna said.

Her grandmother sighed. "It's just such a hard thing to talk about. We were all so happy in the valley before that company started trying to buy everyone's property."

"Was that before the mayor and city council proposed the dam?" Jenna asked.

"Yes. Some people sold out, but your granddaddy wasn't about to sell. My Walter told that man who came to the house to get lost and never come back. What he offered was an insult, not that Walter would've sold if it'd been a million dollars. Then three years later the state comes along and tells us we have to sell." Eva stopped and caught her breath, then looked pointedly at Max's cake he hadn't touched. "It's not good?"

"Sorry." He took a bite. "Delicious. Do you know what the initial offer from the state was?"

She shook her head. "It's been so long ago. I couldn't even tell you what they ended up paying us. Sam and Randy handled everything after the accident. They helped me to get moved here." Eva looked around and smiled. "It's the house where I grew up, you know."

"It's good that you could come back home."

Max knew exactly how much the state gave them after the court hearing. He made a mental note to ask Sam about the initial offer, and TerraQuest's offer. While this wasn't stocks, it still smacked of insider trading on someone's part. "Why do you think Harrison Carter could be involved in the death of Paul Nelson and maybe Joe Slater?"

She raised her head, her gaze fiery. "Those three were thick as thieves back then. And until the dam came along, Paul and Joe didn't have a pot to—"

"Granna!"

Eva's face turned crimson. "I don't know what's wrong with me, but every time I get to thinking about that dam reservoir, I want to curse."

"It's all right." Max patted her hand. Maybe they'd better change the subject. He took another bite of cake with his coffee. "This is really good, Eva."

"Thank you." Eva beamed at him. "I love to cook, and Jenna does too."

"Granna, I do not."

"Well, you would if you ever tried it."

"I don't have to." She hugged her grandmother. "I have you. Besides, I cook some, I just don't love it."

"You're a fantastic cook, Eva, and I bet Jenna is too." Like he'd ever find out. He forked another piece of the cake and looked up in time to see Jenna blush.

Once he finished the cake, Max shifted his attention back to Eva. "Okay, back to Harrison Carter. Why do you think he's involved in the deaths of three people?"

Eva pursed her lips. "I said more than I should've. Sam's always saying I need to watch my words." She sighed. "I don't think Carter actually killed them, although I wouldn't put anything past that man. But I think they would still be alive if they hadn't known him. He"— The mudroom door scraped open and stopped Eva in midsentence.

"Anybody home?" Sam called.

She put her finger to her lips and shook her head. "We're in the kitchen. Come have some carrot cake."

Eva's too-bright voice was a dead giveaway they'd been discussing something Sam probably didn't want her to.

"Want some coffee?" Jenna asked when her uncle entered the kitchen. This afternoon he'd added a John Deere cap to his outfit and was chewing on a toothpick.

"I'll get it. You two sure are coming around a lot," he said as he poured his coffee.

Max saw no need to answer him. He had a few questions he'd like to ask Sam out of his mother's hearing, but he didn't want to be obvious about it. "I understand you have coon dogs?"

Sam eyed him with suspicion and gave him a curt nod. "You?"

"Actually, not yet, but my brother does—he's been trying to get me to coon hunt with him. He has some fine Treeing Walkers."

From Sam's expression, Max had gone up on the man's respect meter. "Who's your brother?"

"Lewis Anderson. Lives up near Franklin."

"I've heard of him, and you're right, he breeds good Walkers, almost as good as my Treeing Tennessee Brindles."

"You raise Brindles?" Max pumped excitement in his voice. "My brother mentioned adding them to his brood stock." He gave Sam a wicked grin. "Got one for sale? Maybe just once I can get ahead of him."

"Maybe. I don't sell my dogs to just anyone. They're working dogs, and I put in a lot of sweat training them. I gotta know the buyer will work 'em and not buy a dog just to one-up his brother."

Max took his coffee cup and dessert plate to the sink and ran water over them.

"Nothing wrong with a healthy rivalry between brothers, but that's not why I'd buy a dog." This was the perfect opening to talk one-on-one. "Do you have time to talk to me about your dogs?"

"I always have time to talk dogs."

"Good, but I'm sure the ladies aren't interested. Why don't we step outside?"

"Sounds good to me."

Max caught Jenna's eye. "I won't be long."

"I don't know about that," she said. "When Sam starts talking about his dogs, he doesn't know when to stop. But it'll give me time to visit with Granna."

Without Sam's interference—Max was pretty sure that's what she was thinking. He followed the older man through the mudroom to the outside.

"Got one of my Brindle pups in the back of the truck if you want to see him."

"I'd like that."

"Wouldn't have figured a city slicker like you to be interested in coon hunting."

Max bristled at the label. "First of all, I don't live in the city, and second, I grew up mucking stables and digging packed manure out of horse hooves."

"Couldn't tell it now."

Max didn't know whether to be offended or say thank you. Before he could respond either way, the air filled with a clamor of yelps from the back of Sam's pickup.

"Quiet." Sam's command wasn't loud, but it held authority.

Two of the dogs stopped immediately, but the third continued to bark. Sam grabbed a leash and opened the barker's cage. "Still training him. He's just a pup yet. Quiet, Watson."

He snapped the leash on the dog's collar and allowed him out of the cage. Watson danced in circles around Sam's feet until he told him to sit. Dutifully the dog settled at his owner's feet for about ten seconds and then he pranced again.

"Like I said, he's still in training."

The dog's short coat was mostly brown with muted black stripes and a white diamond on his chest. Expressive amber eyes seemed to take everything in.

"He's beautiful," Max said. "When will he be fully trained?"

"Another couple of months." Sam petted the dog's head. "Taking him out for a training run with these other two tomorrow night . . . if you want to come. There'll be several other hunters with us—some of them I figure you want to talk to—they're all former landowners who lost their land to the dam and reservoir."

So Sam knew what they were investigating. What kind of cat-and-mouse game was he playing? "Okay if Jenna comes?"

This time Sam hesitated, then he gave a slow nod. "Just tell her not to find any more bodies."

"Believe me, I don't think that's on her agenda." Max eyed Jenna's uncle. "Who do you think killed Paul Nelson?"

"It depends on what the motive is. Paul had a wandering eye when it came to the ladies, and it didn't matter whether they were married or not. Some husbands might not take too kindly to that.

"On the other hand, he also was involved in a project that took land that families had owned for generations. Anyone in those families could've killed him, me and Randy included."

"Did you?"

Sam sat on the tailgate. "Nope. And Randy didn't either."

His voice hadn't wavered, and his body language indicated he was telling the truth. Watson placed a paw on Max's knee, and he knelt beside the dog and ran his hand over his back and sides. "Good muscle tone. How much you asking for him?"

"He's not for sale, at least not yet. Just thought you might want to take a look at him for the future."

"How much when he is ready?"

"Twenty-five."

"Hundred?"

"You don't think I meant twenty-five dollars, do you?"

"Of course not." Max ran the prices his brother got for his young dogs through his mind. Comparable. He pulled a card from his wallet and handed it to Jenna's uncle. "Call me when you're ready to sell."

Sam stuck the card in a wallet bulging with other cards. "Sure," he said and checked his watch. "Tell my mother I'll drop by later this afternoon."

"What time tomorrow night?"

"Ten. Jenna will know where."

Another short night of sleep, but they couldn't miss this opportunity to talk to the ones displaced by the dam and reservoir in a relaxed setting.

45

W e're doing what?" Jenna braked at the end of her grandmother's drive and stared at Max.

"Your uncle invited me—us—to join him and his buddies on a dog training session tomorrow night."

"How . . ." She looked to see if somehow Max had sprouted two heads—that was the only way she knew he could've elicited an invitation from Sam like that. "How in the world did that come about?"

Jenna pulled out of the drive and followed the GPS directions as he related the conversation about Sam knowing Max's brother who was a dog trainer and Max showing an interest in one of her uncle's dogs. It made sense in a convoluted way. "Good. It'll save us some time running down some of the landowners, and with Sam's invitation, they'll come nearer accepting you."

"My thoughts exactly. And Sam said neither he nor your dad killed Paul Nelson."

"You asked him that and he answered?"

"Yes and yes. Seemed to be telling the truth."

Jenna turned the words over in her mind, amazed her uncle hadn't blown up. "Are you really interested in Sam's dog?"

"Actually, I am. My brother has been trying to get me involved since I moved back home—it's a hobby that would give us an opportunity to spend time together," he said. "Oh, and I sort of let Sam think my brother and I have a rivalry."

"Gotcha," Jenna said with a laugh. "How is Lewis?"

"Good. Between training his dogs and his job and my job, I don't see much of him—it's one reason he wants me to hunt with him."

She'd met Lewis when she worked with Max in robbery, and he was one of the most laid-back men she knew. Jenna checked her phone. Alex had sent the address of one of the families Terra-Quest had bought out, and it wasn't too far from the Bishop farm. "Ready to check on Ace and talk to Kirk and his grandfather? See if any more of those rough characters have shown up next door?"

"Sure. I hope the boy has stayed away from the river. I'd hate for him to tangle with the person who attacked me."

"Me too." The memory of finding Max unconscious sent a chill through her. "While we're in that area, we could stop by and see if Eric Darby will give us a little more information."

"That'll be a waste of time. Darby will come to us if he decides to talk. Our time would be better spent researching the news-paper archives."

Max was probably right. Jenna followed the GPS directions, and soon they turned into a drive with a modest, ranch-style house. A tricycle and jungle gym in the side yard indicated a family with small children. "I don't see any vehicles."

"I'll go see if anyone is home and leave a note on the door if they're not."

She watched as he jogged to the house and left a note when no one answered his knock.

"Maybe they'll call when they read the note," he said. "Al-though whoever lives here is probably young—I doubt they can tell us much about TerraQuest."

That's the way it went with investigations. A lot of time spent knocking on doors with zero results. Maybe the Bishops had seen something at the farm next to them. She backed out of the drive and drove to the barn, where they found Kirk at the stables, cleaning bridles. "Miss Jenna! Are you going to ride?"

She tousled the boy's red hair. "I don't have time to ride today. How much do I owe you for taking care of Ace?"

He named a figure that Jenna thought was too low and added twenty dollars to the check she was writing while Max talked to Kirk.

"You been staying away from the river?" he asked.

"Yes, sir. Granddad won't let me go there anymore."

"Good."

Jenna handed him the check, and the boy's eyes grew big. "Thanks, Miss Jenna. You want me to keep doing what I'm doing?"

"If you don't mind. We have a big case we're working on." She glanced toward the woods, then opened her phone and scrolled to the photos of Sebastian. "Before, when you saw people, did any of them look like this person?" She showed him the photos.

Kirk studied one of the pictures. "Can you make it bigger?"

She tapped on the photo so that it filled her screen.

"When I first saw that one"—he pointed at the photo of Sebastian taken during intake at the prison—"I thought he might've been the one who had the creepy grin, but the guy in the picture is too skinny."

"And the creepy guy isn't?"

His eyes widened and he shook his head. "He's got these *huge* muscles."

Jenna turned her phone where she could see the photo, trying to imagine what Sebastian would look like if he'd pumped up. "Is your granddad around?"

"He's putting a new fan up in the hall by Ace's stable."

"Good. I think I'll check on my horse."

"I'll come with you," Max said.

They walked the short distance to the other barn and found Bryan Bishop on a ladder about to hang a fan from the ceiling. "Here," Max said. "Let me help you."

While Max helped hang the fan, Jenna walked to the refrigerator in a small alcove and grabbed a carrot she'd stashed for treats. She loved the smell of the barn, a mixture of hay and grain and horse. She wished she had time to ride this afternoon. The ebony horse stuck his head over the stall door and nickered, and she gave him the carrot.

"How are you, boy?" She smoothed her hand down his neck. "I sure miss riding you, but this case will be over soon."

She turned toward the fan when she felt the air circulating through the hallway. "That feels good," Jenna said when Bryan crawled down from the ladder.

"Wanted to get these up before it turned hot." He turned to Max. "Thank you. Made it a lot easier."

"Glad to help." Max tilted his head. "You didn't happen to find out who owns the place next to you or who's renting it, did you?"

"Afraid not. I have seen Tom Weaver there, and I figure he's seeing after the place."

"He said he was," Jenna said. "We're meeting with him in the morning."

"Okay if we drive down to the edge of woods?" Max asked.

"No problem."

Jenna patted Ace's neck. "Okay, boy. I'll see you later."

The horse nickered, and Max laughed. "I swear, I think he understood what you said."

Jenna grinned at him. "Better believe it."

They walked back to the SUV, and Max opened the gate to the access road to the woods and river. After he closed it, he hopped in the SUV. "Do you think Sebastian rented the place next door?"

"I don't know," Jenna said. "Mr. Weaver didn't recognize the photos, but maybe Sebastian wasn't the one he dealt with. Hopefully tomorrow we can find out."

A shadow raced across the dirt road, sending a shiver through Jenna. What if Sebastian was here, living right next to where she kept her horse?

46

Was it possible Sebastian had rented the place next door? Max hoped they got more information from Weaver in the morning. Regardless, they needed a more recent picture of Sebastian. And if he was in Russell County, could he have somehow gotten into Jenna's house?

But how? Deadbolts that required keyed entry were on both doors, and the windows were all locked. He'd meant to walk around the house to see if anyone had trampled the grass outside any of the windows. He'd do that as soon as they returned to her house.

Jenna glanced toward the Armstrong place. "That's a perfect place to set up and make meth or grow marijuana—we're short on deputies, and people around here tend to mind their own business."

Jenna had a point. He took out his notepad and looked back over the notes he'd taken Tuesday. "Kirk said the men came on Thursday or Friday—maybe to pick up a shipment of drugs?"

"It wouldn't have to be meth," Jenna said. She pulled the SUV close to the edge of the woods and killed the motor. "They could be making pills with heroin and fentanyl. And they could be taking it out in canoes or kayaks to a location on the lake."

"Good point." He climbed out of the SUV and waited for Jenna to join him at the tree line. "We're searching for anything that might look like a path."

"They could go a different way each time."

"True. Maybe we need to walk to the river and see if they tie up their boats at the same place each time."

She agreed with him, and they hiked through the woods to the riverbank. "The best place to tie up a boat is the sandbar."

Ten minutes later they approached the river. "Looks like there's been traffic through here." Max pointed at trampled grass near the bank.

Jenna hopped down to the sandy bar and pointed upriver. "Shoe prints! And a lot of them."

Yes! Max joined her and carefully skirted the prints. "Do you have any of that plaster casting material with you?"

"No, but Dylan and Taylor do. Do you want me to ask Alex to send them here?"

He slapped at a deer fly hovering around his face. "We don't actually have a crime here, so maybe we should just photograph the prints."

"Let me see what they're involved in." Jenna punched in Alex's number, and when she answered, Jenna put the phone on speaker and explained what they wanted.

"You think something is going on at the old Armstrong place?"

Max spoke up. "Yes, possibly drug action, but we don't have anything to base a warrant on. We've taken photos of the shoe prints, but casts would be better—just in case it turns out our suspicions are correct."

"Is there any chance this could be tied to Nelson's and Slater's deaths?"

"That's hard to say," Jenna said. "More likely it'd be tied to Rick Sebastian."

"Good enough. Dylan is busy right now, but I'll send Taylor."

"Good deal," Max said. "We'll see what other information we can gather. Tell Taylor to text when she gets to the woods and one of us will come get her."

"I will. Oh, and Jenna, we got more photos of Sebastian's key players in Chattanooga. I'll send them to you—email or text?"

Jenna turned to Max, her expression questioning.

"Text would be easier to access."

"Got it," Alex said. "You'll get them shortly."

Jenna disconnected. "I'd like to get inside the barn where Kirk said the mean guys scared him," she said.

"Without a warrant, anything we found couldn't be used in court."

"I know, but this is highly suspicious."

"I agree," Max said. "Once we get the photos of Sebastian's allies, we'll show them to Kirk and Bryan Bishop. Maybe they'll recognize one of Sebastian's men in the photos."

Max and Jenna searched the narrow beach until a text popped up on Jenna's phone. "Taylor's here. I'll go get her."

"I'll come with you."

Once Taylor made the casts, they followed her out of the woods, stopping once again at the barn where Jenna downloaded the photos Alex had sent and showed them to Kirk. He couldn't match any of the photos with the men he'd seen at the farm next door. "But there were some new cars over there today."

Max arched an eye at the boy. "I hope you didn't disobey your grandfather and drive your four-wheeler to the property."

"I didn't. I promise," he said, shooting his grandfather a quick glance before shifting back to Max. "But if you take that path, you can see the cars from over by the trees."

"Where?" Jenna asked.

"There's a path on the other side of the house. I can show you."

They followed Kirk to the back side of the house where a narrow path led toward the neighbors'. "Just follow this and it'll take you to the edge of their property."

"Is this how you saw the cars?"

Kirk kicked at a clod of dirt. "They didn't see me, I promise. There're trees you can hide behind."

"Promise you won't do that again," Jenna said. "At least not until the people who are there move."

"But—"

"No buts," Max said. "It could be dangerous."

The boy's shoulders drooped. "Okay. But I could sneak in there."

"Kirk, you have to promise us you won't go near this property again," Jenna said. When he nodded, she said, "I want to hear you say it."

"I promise."

"Good. Now go back to the barn with your grandfather."

They waited until Kirk disappeared inside the barn. Max chuckled. "He'll probably make a good deputy one day."

"Probably—if he doesn't get into trouble before that."

Max led the way to the farmhouse next door as they followed the path until the trees thinned except for a row of cedar trees. Probably the property line. Through the breaks in the trees a plank house came into view. Several cars were parked in the drive, all backed in where they couldn't see the license plate.

"Too bad Tennessee doesn't have a plate on the front," Max muttered.

"I've wished that more than once," Jenna replied.

"Any chance Alex might assign deputies to watch the house on the off chance the occupants might do something that would justify getting a warrant?"

"If the county had enough deputies, she would, but we're stretched thin as it is, especially with Mark Lassiter at the field trials and Alex's latest hire, Hayes Smithfield, at the police academy.

Besides, we don't have a crime—just our intuition that something is wrong."

They watched the house for a good half hour, and nothing moved, not even a grasshopper. Even so, his gut told him something was going on at the old farm place, and it wasn't good.

47

M ax offered to drive, and as they neared town, she said, "The library used to have old copies of our local newspaper on microfilm. Maybe we can access information about what went on during Carter's tenure as mayor."

He checked his watch. "It's almost six. What time do they close?"

"Eight, I believe."

"That will give us two hours."

"I better make sure the library has either copies of newspapers from that time or has them on microfilm."

She looked up the number for the library and punched it in, putting the phone on speaker. When someone answered, she asked to speak to the head librarian. When he came on the line she asked if there were microfilm copies of the weekly newspaper during Harrison Carter's tenure.

"Yes, but I can do you one better," he said. "A couple of years ago, the local computer class at the high school scanned them into a website you can access."

"Great. Can you text me the link?"

While they waited for the link, she said, "We can go straight to my house and do our research. You can take the laptop, and I'll use my desktop."

"I have my laptop—I'll use it."

Once they were at her house, Jenna walked around it with Max looking for signs of disturbance. Not that she expected to find anything. Whoever was breaking into her house was like a ghost.

"It doesn't look as though anyone's been here," he said.

Jenna grunted and checked the tape she'd put across the door. No one had entered through this door and the other one had a chair under it. That didn't stop her from wanting to draw her gun, but Max already thought she was paranoid, so she left it holstered and was glad she had when everything looked as it had before they left.

"My office is back here . . . or we can set up in the kitchen."

"Is it much trouble to use the kitchen? Coffee would be handier."

She laughed. "Sounds good to me."

While they waited for the computers to boot up, she made coffee. "What do you think is going on at the Armstrong place?" she asked as the machine gurgled.

"I didn't see signs of a meth operation. They're probably using the place to counterfeit opioids, possibly using heroin and even fentanyl, which is cheaper and easier to get than oxycodone."

"I agree. Maybe we can discover something when we knock on the door tomorrow morning."

She turned as the desktop screen asked for a password. Jenna typed it in. "I'll search for information on the dam and reservoir."

Max set up his laptop across the table from her. "And I'll search for the weekly papers published during Harrison Carter's years."

Jenna poured them each a mug of coffee then started her search. The kitchen became quiet as they worked. She found several articles, including one that detailed the history of the project with a timeline from applying for the grant to the completion of the dam. She printed it out. "Be right back."

She walked to her office and returned with the printed pages and found Max leaned back in the chair.

"Find anything?"

He held up the notepad he'd been writing on. "Not a lot—there was a lot of opposition to the dam that was built during Carter's twenty years."

Jenna handed him the pages she'd printed. "You need to look at this. It confirms he applied for grant money a few years before he became mayor."

Max scanned the document. "So he would have known that the dam and reservoir would be built before anyone else. Let's say he formed a corporation—TerraQuest—and bought up what land he could."

"That's what I thought when I read the article, but we have no proof he owns TerraQuest."

"Yet." While he scanned it, Jenna checked her watch. Almost eight o'clock? She turned to Max. "Are you hungry?"

He glanced at his watch. "Where'd the time go? But sure . . . want to grab something in town?"

"The only thing open is the pizza place, and I don't think my stomach can take that. Let's see what I have in the refrigerator."

A minute later she opened her refrigerator and frowned. It was kind of bare. "I have eggs and bacon, maybe peppers if they haven't dried up . . . how about an omelet?"

"So you do cook?" His gaze ran over her, reminding her of their near kiss that seemed so long ago now.

Jenna ordered her heart to slow down, but it refused to listen. She gave him a wry smile. "It's, ah . . ." She would've had a quick comeback a second ago. "Uh, cook or starve—Granna won't feed me every day." She reined in her heart. "I make a mean omelet, though."

"I'm game. What can I do to help?"

Get out of the kitchen unless he wanted her to burn their meal. "Write up a plan for tomorrow."

"I can do that, but I can cook as well."

Jenna eyed him. "You live two houses from your mother—you expect me to believe that?"

His smoking brown eyes held a challenge. "Tell you what, you take care of the bacon and *I'll* make the omelet."

She stared at him. The way her insides were shaking, that might not be a bad idea. "You have yourself a deal."

First she poured another cup of coffee—hoping it would clear her head, especially of thoughts about Max. It still took everything in her to keep her fingers from shaking when she placed the bacon on the microwave pan. What was wrong with her? This was Max.

Jenna hadn't figured on them cooking side by side, but since her microwave was over the stove and that's where he was making the omelet, there was little choice. The faint woodsy scent she'd noticed in the truck earlier made noodles of her legs when he reached across her for the spatula.

"You might want to check the bacon," he said, nudging her.

She yanked open the door.

"Ow!" Max said, rubbing his head.

"I'm so sorry—" A tiny trickle of blood ran down his temple . . . suddenly she was in the alley behind James A. Henry School. *No! Not now* . . . But there was no stopping the flashback.

Sebastian held the boy in one hand, a gun in the other. Gunshots rang in her ears . . . the odor of gunpowder.

Jenna's stomach churned, and she couldn't breathe. Mouth too dry to swallow . . . icy tendrils tingled her face.

The next thing Jenna knew she was in Max's arms. He carried her to a chair and settled her in it.

"Are you okay?"

She nodded, her face flaming. It'd been a year since the sight of blood affected her this way.

"Hold on a sec, and I'll get you a wet cloth." Max disappeared down the hall and returned with a damp washcloth. "Put this on your face."

She did what he said, and gradually her stomach settled.

"What happened?"

Jenna avoided looking at his head. "B-blood. Sometimes . . ."

"It makes you faint."

"It only started after the night I was shot, and it doesn't happen every time I see blood—certainly hasn't happened since I returned home. The psychologist the department required me to see after the shooting said it was part of PTSD."

"Are you feeling better?"

"Yes. I thought I was over it." Jenna drew in a breath and blew it out before handing him the cloth. "You might want to use this on your head, and I have a Band-Aid if you need it."

"I think it'll be fine." He pressed the cloth to his head. "It's not bleeding any longer."

Then she gasped. "Did I burn the bacon?"

He shook his head. "It's golden brown. And I didn't burn the omelets. Think you can eat while everything is still warm?"

She'd do almost anything to get his attention off what just happened, and that included choking down food. "Sure—these episodes never last long, but they're terribly embarrassing."

"Nothing to be embarrassed about. See if you can stand okay."

She stood and there was no dizziness. "See, I told you. Let me get a plate for the bacon."

Max moved the computers to the end of the table, and Jenna

willed herself to stay upright while she laid out the plates and cutlery.

She took a bite of Max's omelet. "You really can cook."

"Shannon showed me how to make omelets. They aren't that hard."

"What happened with you two?" Jenna slapped her hand over her mouth. "That was none of my business."

He stared at the cup of coffee he cradled in his hand. Then he looked up. "I don't mind talking about her or the breakup now, and it wasn't all her fault. Being a cop is hard on a relationship. We had a lot of good years, five of them, before . . ." He sighed and looked toward the window.

Being a cop was one reason she'd shied away from relationships after Phillip. The hours were long sometimes, and it was hard to leave the job at the station. "I'm sorry."

"Me too. Shannon was a good cook. Early on, she often made elaborate candlelight dinners—although I never quite saw the point in not seeing what you were eating."

They both laughed.

"But then she broke her leg in a skiing accident. The doctor prescribed oxycodone." He blew out a breath. "Unfortunately, she became addicted. I didn't realize it until one night she overdosed. I called an ambulance and found out when it showed up on a drug screen the ER doctor ordered."

"How in the world did you get that information from the doctor?"

"She'd put me on her HIPAA form because she had no family in Chattanooga. The ER doctor told me—he thought I knew. She finally admitted she was getting them off the street after her doctor refused to continue prescribing it."

"I'm so sorry, both for you and her." Jenna had seen what addiction did in her uncle, only his drug was alcohol.

"I tried to talk to her about getting help." Max shook his head.

"She didn't believe she had a problem, and she eventually broke the engagement."

She remembered when that had happened.

"Is she still doing drugs?"

"Actually, she went into rehab about a year ago. I haven't talked to her, but I hope she's still straight."

It was plain he still cared about her.

48

Sweat drenched Sebastian's shirt, but he continued his push-ups. How had Jenna Hart and the TBI agent figured out he'd rented the farmhouse next to the horse barn? He'd like to take them both out, but killing two law enforcement officers would bring the FBI in on the case. And that was too much heat. He wasn't going back to prison.

His biceps trembled. Twenty more push-ups and he would quit. It wasn't getting his mind off the problem, anyway.

He'd told Ross renting a place adjacent to where Hart kept her horse was a stupid move. The cop had rented the place anyway. Said it was perfect for their setup.

Sebastian agreed it ticked all the requirements—out of the way and a space to store the heroin and fentanyl as well as a place to make the pills . . . there'd even been a place for a small grow room. But he'd known the owner of the farm next door would be curious about the new tenants who weren't very neighborly, and what better person to discuss his concerns with than a deputy who came every day?

He finished his last twenty push-ups and grabbed a towel. His cell phone rang and he checked the ID. Ross. "Yeah?" he answered.

"Your text—tell me you didn't give the word to move the operation."

"Okay, I won't tell you."

"Moving right now is stupid."

"No. Stupid is renting a house right next to where Hart keeps her horse. She and that TBI agent know we're there. I've already given the order to move out, so find us a new place to carry on the pill-making operation. One that isn't close to anything Hart is connected to."

"Rescind the order—the buyer is expecting a shipment Sunday morning, and we only have half of what he paid for. If we move, we can't make the deadline."

That was another thing Sebastian didn't like—taking money from someone like their buyer without having the goods. "If you hadn't demanded the money up front, we wouldn't have this problem."

"Deal with it. How do you know they've discovered what we're doing? Jenna isn't that smart."

Pain pierced his forehead right above his right eyebrow. "Because I planted listening devices in her house and heard them talking about it." Ross didn't need to know they only suspected something was going on at the place. The man was so obsessed with the Hart woman, he didn't think straight. "You underestimate her. Find us another place. I would except I don't know the area like you do, and the sheriff and police chief are circulating my photo to everyone in town."

"You don't look anything like your earlier photos." Ross fell silent. "That was the perfect setup, and finding another place for the plants won't be easy."

"I told the men to leave the plants." Sebastian had already marked the marijuana plants off as a loss.

"You gotta be kidding."

"Nope. It's not like we're in the cannabis business." He scanned the small living room. If they pushed the furniture against the walls . . . "You take care of finding us a new setup. We'll use my living room to pack the capsules until we finish this order. The men should be about done packing up—I'll tell them to bring the supplies here."

"Do we really have to abandon the plants?"

"Hart and the TBI agent are going to the farm first thing in the morning—we don't have time to move everything. I told you growing marijuana was a bad idea, anyway."

"You're wrong. Do you have any idea what good cannabis brings?"

Sebastian wanted to laugh.

"Do something to distract Jenna," Ross said. "She's the one driving this investigation."

"Don't worry about it. I will."

49

The actual breakup had been a little worse than he'd described it. Max shook the bad memories off.

Jenna stood. "I don't know about you, but I could use another cup of coffee."

"So can I." She was so different from Shannon. When this case was over, he hoped they had an opportunity to explore their feelings for one another.

She poured them both a cup. "You want to sit on my patio and look at the stars? Might help us to take a break."

"Sounds good."

They took their cups to Jenna's round glass-topped table where they'd sat earlier. He set his cup on the table and waited for her to sit down, then took the chair next to her. In the distance an owl hooted and another answered. Closer to them were the high-pitched notes of tree frogs. "It's nice out here."

"I know." She looked up. "The sky is like a velvet blanket covered in diamonds."

"I didn't know you had a poetic bone in your body."

"There's nothing poetic about that." She tilted her head again. "'If you're ever distressed, cast your eyes to the summer sky, when the stars are strung across the velvety night. And when a shooting star streaks through the blackness, turning night into day . . . make a wish and think of me. And make your life spectacular.' That's poetic."

"Robin Williams," Max said. "From the movie *Jack*."

"Get out of here!" She gave him a sideways look. "That movie was made when we were kids."

"I know. I've watched every one of his movies. *Dead Poets Society* is my favorite."

"Mine too," she said. "My English teacher in high school gave us bonus points if we watched it and wrote a report." Jenna rocked back in her chair. "I like to sit out here before I go to bed at night, especially when I'm having a week like this one."

"It's been a bad one," he said. "And it's only Wednesday." Getting put on security detail for a senate candidate who received a threatening letter. Three murders, being attacked . . . Yeah, it'd been a bad week. "Maybe not the worst week of my life, but it ranks right up there."

"Really?" She turned and looked at him. "You've had a week worse than this? What happened?"

It wasn't a time he liked to dwell on. "Officer-related shooting, and I was the officer and the victim was a sixteen-year-old robbery suspect—it was before you joined us. He pulled a gun when I tried to arrest him . . . it didn't end well. How about you? I don't figure this is your worst week ever, either."

Max knew of two events in Jenna's life that would fit in a worst-week category. He was curious which one she'd choose.

Jenna was quiet for a minute. "It was summer, and a Saturday. My sixth birthday." Her voice had a faraway sound to it as she continued.

"I woke up early, and I knew no one would be up for a while. And I knew I couldn't lay there that long—my mom had promised me a pony for my birthday, and she never broke her promises . . ."

"You don't have to tell me." It wasn't one of the stories Max expected her to tell. He wasn't sure he wanted to hear the story's unhappy ending.

Jenna continued like she hadn't heard him. "While I waited for everyone to wake up, I thought up names, and I must've gone off to sleep because someone yelling 'I can't do it anymore!' woke me up."

"What was it they couldn't do?" Max asked.

"I didn't know at the time. My dad kept saying, 'Ivy, please, keep your voice down. You don't want Jenna to hear you.'"

"I thought they were talking about my pony and Mom wanted to surprise me. Then the back door slammed so hard the windows rattled. I crept into the kitchen . . ."

Jenna swiped her cheek with the back of her hand, and Max wished he'd never asked the question. After a minute, she took a deep breath. "Daddy sat at the kitchen table with a bottle of whiskey in front of him. When I asked where my mom was, he didn't answer me, just uncapped the whiskey and drank straight from the bottle. It was the last time I ever saw him drink . . .

"I ran outside, thinking she'd gotten me the pony, but the yard was empty, just like the driveway where her Honda Civic always sat.

"Later that day Dad told me Mom had died in a car accident. Evidently when she left, she was driving too fast, missed a curve, and slammed into a huge oak tree."

"I'm so sorry."

She looked at Max. "You want to know what my reaction was?" Before he could answer, she continued, "It wasn't pretty and I feel so bad about it now, but I remember thinking, *It isn't fair—Mom promised me a pony, and she broke her promise.*"

She worked her jaw. "You would've thought I would cry because she died, but the only thing that made me cry was when I thought about the pony I never got."

She looked at him. "Do you have any idea how that made me feel as I grew older? I was a terrible human being, and it was probably my fault she died."

"You know it wasn't your fault, and you weren't terrible. You were only six, just a preschooler and wouldn't have understood it was permanent. A six-year-old thinks death—if they're confronted with it—is temporary or reversible, like in the cartoons you probably watched."

"Cartoons . . . really?"

"Don't tell me you didn't watch Wile E. Coyote? How many times did he die and come back?"

"How did you know I watched—"

"Every kid does."

A tiny smile curved her lips up, then she sobered. "How do you happen to know all this?"

He looked up, and the immensity of the sky and stars filled his heart. God had directed him to learn about the subject . . . for such a time as this? He turned to Jenna. "When I started mentoring Cody, I researched how children process death because he'd lost his dad. One of the things I came across was a breakdown by ages, and the information about preschoolers was there."

She stared down at the ground and after a few minutes raised her head. "Thanks for trying to make me feel better." She shook her head. "But I don't know . . ."

Max squeezed Jenna's hand. "Learning your mom was gone was a hard blow for a six-year-old. Sometimes focusing on everything but what really happened is the way we process grief."

Jenna raised her gaze. "Look!"

He looked up as a shooting star streaked across the sky. "Make a wish."

"Okay."

When it disappeared, he said, "What'd you wish for?"

"You first."

He wasn't about to tell her his wish. She wasn't ready to hear it, and he wasn't sure he was ready, either. "World peace."

She laughed. "Baloney. Seriously, what did you wish for?"

"More nights like tonight."

"Oh. Really?"

"Yep. Now it's your turn."

"Same thing you wished for."

Did he dare hope that she was telling the truth? "Tell me the best day ever you've had."

She shook her head. "First, you—what were you like as a kid? What did you like to do?"

"I was . . ." He thought a minute. "Normal. Did kid things, played baseball and football, rode my bike, took judo when I was a teenager."

"You can do martial arts?"

"Now? Not so much, but I was pretty good—made it to blue belt before football took over." He tilted his head toward her. "Now, what was your best day?"

"That's easy. It was the day I learned Ace was mine. It was like my birthday and Christmas and winning the lottery all rolled into one."

If he'd been guessing, Max would've guessed it.

"How about you?" she asked. "What's the memory of your best day?"

He leaned back in his chair, mimicking Jenna's position. He'd had a relatively happy childhood. Did he even have a particular happiest day ever? For years he'd pinned his hopes on having a kid, didn't matter whether it was a boy or girl. After his engagement fell apart, he'd given up on that dream. After all, time was passing, and the only woman he had any interest in at all wasn't interested in a relationship. After what happened with her fiancé, he didn't blame her.

"I guess I'm still waiting for that day."

50

Jenna checked her watch. "It's almost ten."

"Yeah, it's getting late."

They both stood.

"After you." Max bowed slightly and held his hand out.

She hesitated. Sitting out here with him, bathed in the moonlight, sharing stories she'd never told anyone, not even Phillip . . . she didn't want the evening to end.

"You don't mind if I walk you to your back door, do you?"

His husky voice sent chills over her and drew her gaze to his dark brown eyes. Eyes she could get lost in. Walking her to the door was not a good idea. She agreed to it anyway. "Not at all."

Max used the flashlight on his phone to illuminate their way, but she stumbled anyway. He caught her before she fell. What was wrong with her? She wasn't the clumsy sort. "I can make it from here."

"I don't know . . . you might stumble again."

She stared at the ground, her feet unwilling to move. He tilted her chin until she was looking into his eyes once more, the intensity searing her heart.

Max traced his finger along her jaw, his touch awakening every nerve in her body. "You are so beautiful. Inside and out."

No one had ever told her that before. She closed her eyes and relished the moment. Jenna sensed him bending down as he cupped her face in his hands. She leaned into him, slipping her arms around his neck.

Max kissed her lips lightly. *No . . . don't stop there.* She pulled his head closer, and he responded with a deeper kiss.

Rockets went off in her head. Jenna lost herself in his kiss. When they broke apart, she had trouble focusing, not to mention breathing . . . Maybe once her heart slowed to normal.

Max rested his forehead on hers. He seemed to be breathing faster as well.

"Wow," he murmured as he gazed into her eyes. "I, ah, didn't—"

She touched his lips with her fingers. "Don't mess it up by apologizing."

"Apologizing wasn't on my mind." He brushed a strand of her hair back and rested his palm on her cheek. "That was amazing."

"I agree." She leaned into his touch.

Her cell phone rang, and they both jumped.

"Ignore it," he said.

She'd like to. "It may be my grandmother—she could need something."

He reluctantly stepped away. "You're right."

Jenna pulled her phone from her back pocket. "Alex. I better answer it."

She slid the answer button. "Hart."

"I hope I haven't called too late," Alex said.

Jenna glanced at Max and smiled. She motioned for him to follow her inside the house, then she locked the door behind them. "You haven't."

"Good. I wanted to let you know Dylan and Taylor worked late tonight and found a letter like the others at Paul Nelson's office."

"Hold on a second. Max is here. Let me put the call on speaker."

Alex repeated what she'd said.

"It's beginning to look like we have a home-grown threat," Jenna said.

"I'm afraid so," Alex replied. "Someone has a grudge against the three men, and he's carried it out against two of them."

"Did you turn Slater's journals over to the forensic accountant in the Inspector General's office?" Max asked.

"I had a deputy hand deliver them to Nashville yesterday afternoon. Problem is, even if it's discovered that Slater had taken some sort of kickback, we need more to tie it to Carter."

"We'll just have to keep digging," Max said.

"Just wanted to let you know," Alex said. "See you in the morning."

Jenna hung up. "Carter and the other two were up to their eyeballs in something illegal when they were in office. I hate knowing that and not having the proof."

"And I'd bet my last cookie it had to do with the dam and reservoir."

"I agree." She sighed. "And the evening was going so nicely."

"Yeah," he said and then looked toward the front door. "Are you sure you don't want me to stay?"

"After that kiss earlier, you probably shouldn't." A kiss that changed everything, at least for her. Where did they go from here?

"Then I better leave so you can get some sleep."

"Yeah." She made no move toward the door. Why did things suddenly seem awkward? Because he was already regretting kissing her?

"Can I kiss you again?"

"You have to ask?" Maybe he wasn't regretting it . . .

He grinned and took her in his arms. "This changes things, as I'm pretty sure you already know."

"It does seem a little awkward."

"Maybe this will help." Max drew her close and gently pressed his lips against hers. When he pulled back, he said, "That was a goodnight kiss."

"I liked the other one better."

"Me too, but if we'd repeated it, it would be hard to leave you."

"You're right. See you in the morning."

"Sure I can't stay?"

"Definitely not."

With a laugh, he kissed her on the cheek. "I'll wait until I hear the deadbolt engage," he said.

She followed him to the back door and locked it after him.

"See you in the morning," he called through the closed door.

Jenna leaned her head against the wood. She never thought she'd feel this way about a man again . . . especially a cop.

51

After Max left, Jenna laid her keys on the island and checked all the doors and windows to make sure they were locked. Then she cleaned up the dishes, her face heating up when she thought of being in Max's arms.

She crawled into bed, making sure her phone was on the night-stand and her service pistol beside her in bed. That should make Max happy. Her thoughts turned to him again, reliving the kiss. Heat spread through her chest at how she welcomed it.

Don't go there. Was she even ready for this? Even if Max wasn't like Phillip, she was pretty sure he wasn't in the market for a wife. *Wife? Where did that come from?* She wasn't in the market for a husband. She turned over to her side. Max's kiss was her last thought before drifting off.

Jenna woke with a start. But why? She flipped over on her back and lay still, her eyelids barely cracked, listening. Light filtered in through her bedroom window from the outside flood lamp. She picked up an unfamiliar smell, then something moved. No, someone.

"I know you're awake."

The raspy whisper sent chills through her. *Pretend to sleep and catch him off guard?* She cracked her eyes open enough to see a man standing at the foot of her bed, clothed in black, his face hidden by a dark hoodie.

She shifted her gaze to the gun in his hand.

In one movement, she rolled out of bed with her gun and fired.

He jumped sideways and yelled. She'd been going for his chest, but she'd missed. He backed away from her, his gun pointed at her. "You shouldn't have done that," he said, keeping his voice at a raspy whisper.

Jenna crouched on the floor, still holding her pistol on him. They were at a stalemate. "What do you want?"

He laughed. "Just wanted to show you I can get to you anytime I want."

Earsplitting pounding came from the front door. She jerked her head toward the door. As soon as she did, he backed out of her room and ran down the hall.

She scrambled up, but by the time she reached her door, the hallway was empty.

The back door slammed. She ran to the kitchen, and pain shot through her foot when she sprawled over the ottoman that hadn't been there when she went to bed.

"Jenna! Let me in!"

Max. She glanced at the closed back door. There was no way she could catch her attacker now. "I'm coming!" she yelled and picked herself up and grabbed her keys before she limped to the front door.

Jenna unlocked the deadbolt and opened the door. Max burst in, his gun drawn.

"I heard a gunshot."

"Someone broke in—he ran out the back door!" She tossed him her keys. "You'll need the key to get out."

Max took off running to the kitchen, and Jenna hobbled behind him. Nothing made sense. She followed him out the door to her patio and peered into the darkness beyond the house. "Max?"

He didn't answer. She used the light on her phone to sweep across the yard and caught a shadowy image coming from the woods. "Max?" she called again.

"It's me. I didn't find anyone," he called back. When Max reached her, he took her in his arms and held her tight. "Are you all right?"

Max asking if she was all right was starting to sound old. "I am. How did you—"

"I never went to the hotel. Not last night or tonight."

"What?"

"I had a bad feeling about leaving you both nights, so I slept in my truck. There was no place for me to park that you wouldn't see me, and I had to park on the road." He stopped to catch his breath. "That's why I didn't see him approach your house."

She gaped at him. He didn't go to the hotel? No wonder he'd looked tired this morning.

"Can we go in?"

"Oh, of course!" What was wrong with her? Like she had to even ask—someone just broke into her house. And she was still processing that Max had slept in his truck to watch over her. That made her want to cry.

"Are you shot? Do I need to call an ambulance?"

Jenna shook her head, unable to say anything without breaking down. She took a deep breath to calm herself. "I'm fine. Whoever broke in may not be, though."

"You're the one who fired?"

"Yeah, but I'm not sure I hit him." Her legs turned to water. "Let's sit down."

"I want to check the rest of the house first."

She flipped on the kitchen light and possessed enough presence of mind to photograph the ottoman before she returned it to the living room.

How had the intruder gotten in? She puzzled on that while she

274

waited for Max. She turned around when he entered the kitchen. "Find any blood?"

He gave her an odd look. "No. You must have missed him."

"I guess the way he yelled made me think I did." Jenna sank into a kitchen chair while Max examined the lock on the back door.

"This doesn't make sense." He turned to her. "The door is deadbolted, and your keys are on this side of the lock. How did he get out?"

She turned and stared at the door. "I don't know, but I heard this door shut—you should have too."

He shook his head. "I didn't hear anything but the gunshot."

"Maybe he went out a window?" Even as she said it, she knew that wasn't the case. She had heard the door slam shut.

"I checked, and all of your windows are locked and none are broken."

A note of doubt rang in his voice. Did he not believe her? "I didn't make up the intruder."

"I didn't say you did, I'm just trying to figure this out."

"He could've picked the lock."

"Why not just use your keys? They were on the counter. And why would he have gone to the trouble of shutting the door? If I were an intruder, I wouldn't be thinking about locking the door behind me."

Quiet filled the kitchen.

"I'm staying here the rest of the night."

"Why? You don't believe me."

"I didn't say that."

"You didn't have to." She leveled her gaze at him. "Why do you even want to stay?"

"To have your back."

That didn't mean he believed her. She started to protest, but one look at his set expression told her it would be a waste of her breath to argue. And down deep she really didn't want him to leave. "You can take the guest bedroom or the sofa in the living room."

"I'll take the sofa."

Jenna figured he'd say that.

"Tell me exactly what happened."

She took a deep breath and related every detail she could remember.

"Did you recognize him, or did he say anything?"

She wanted to tell him it was Sebastian, but she hadn't seen his face and didn't know for sure. "The bedroom was dark, and he wore a hoodie."

"How about his voice?"

"He never spoke above a whisper. Said he could get to me anytime he wanted to."

"That's all he said?"

She closed her eyes, replaying the scene. "He said something when I shot at him, something like 'You shouldn't have done that.'"

"Could it have been Sebastian?"

"I—" There was no way to be sure, but . . . "If it is, he's bulked up—the man in my room was big."

Her face warmed under Max's intense gaze. "Are you sure this wasn't a nightmare?"

She jerked back. "I knew you didn't believe me."

"I believe that *you* believe someone was here, but I haven't found any evidence of an intruder. There's no blood on the floor, and none of your windows look like they've been tampered with, and both doors are deadbolted and require a key to lock or unlock."

Jenna stared down at her hands. Everything he said was true. Was she losing it? Was the man in the window yesterday a shadow and the man in her bedroom a bad dream?

It wouldn't be the first time she'd had nightmares she thought were real.

52

Sebastian gunned the plain-Jane Corolla he'd rented. He'd cut it a little too close at Hart's house, but he hadn't expected the TBI agent to show up. He should've known the agent would hang around.

Sebastian tapped an app on his phone, and the TBI agent's voice filled the little car. He listened and couldn't keep from grinning. Tonight had worked better than he'd dreamed—Anderson didn't believe there'd been an intruder.

His cell phone lit up, and he checked the screen. He'd missed five calls. He answered on the fourth ring, just before it went to voicemail. "Sebastian."

"You were supposed to call five hours ago. I've been trying to get in touch with you."

"I've been busy and had my phone silenced—didn't want it to ring at the wrong time."

"Did you find the photos?"

"No."

Swearing on the other end made him move the phone away from his ear. "Stop worrying. I have to pick my times to get into her house, but if the photos are there, I'll find them."

"You better. I told you I didn't get you out of prison early for nothing. You owe me. One snap of my fingers and you'll be right back in that cell."

Sebastian ground his teeth. So Ross had pulled a few strings for him. He was paying him back in spades.

He forced the anger out of his body. His time would come, but in the meantime, he needed to keep calm and let Ross think he was in charge, because he was right—he could have him sent back anytime.

"This job is worth more than you're paying me. She almost killed me tonight."

"What? How did that happen?"

"I paid her a little visit." He turned onto the road to the cabin he'd rented.

"Did she see you?"

"Yes, she saw me—but I had a hoodie that blocked my face."

"You think she doesn't remember what you look like? She's a cop, trained to notice—"

"You said yourself that no one recognizes me any longer." He was no longer the hundred-and-thirty-five-pound drug dealer who had to use a gun to intimidate.

"I get it, but why didn't you wait until tomorrow while she was at work? Why take the risk?"

"I wanted to let her know who was in charge." Sebastian hadn't thought about her sleeping with a gun in the bed.

"I'm surprised she missed."

He touched his sleeve where the bullet had come very close. "She was off balance."

"Quit messing around and find those photos."

"And if they're not in her house?"

"Kill her."

53

The next morning, Max was up before Jenna and was glad she'd set out the coffee and filters before going to bed. He made coffee and took it to the patio where he could think and plan.

Her house sat on a hill, and from the patio, he had a view of the mountains, where early morning haze rose like smoke from a chimney. No wonder she liked to sit out here. He turned and looked to the east, where a red sun crept over the horizon.

"Red sky at night, sailor's delight. Red sky in morning, sailor's warning." If the old adage his grandfather liked to quote held true, it would probably storm before evening . . . except he feared the storm might not be weather related.

He pulled his attention back to the problem that had him in a bad frame of mind. The problem he'd worried about all night. Had there been an intruder in the house? He wanted to believe Jenna—not that she was in danger from an intruder, but that there had actually been someone here and she hadn't been dreaming. Either way . . . they had a problem.

It was clear Jenna believed a man had been in her bedroom, and she'd fired at him. But Max had found nothing other than a bullet hole in the wooden doorframe.

He'd seen her lock the back door when they came in from the patio and heard the deadbolt snick in place when he left. If she was having PTSD again, he didn't know what to do about it.

Max sipped his now cold coffee and made a face. Should've put it in an insulated cup.

"Good morning."

Max turned around, and his heart kicked into overdrive. Jenna had braided her hair in one long braid, and she was dressed, down to her gun. "Same to you. Were you able to sleep at all?"

She nodded and handed him an insulated mug before she claimed the chair beside him. "Good coffee."

"Thanks. I doubt it's as strong as the stuff that passes for coffee at the sheriff's office."

"It'll do."

Polite conversation.

She looked toward the mountains. "I walked around the house looking for shoe prints."

Her tone was defensive.

"Find anything?" He'd looked before he made coffee.

She shook her head, and neither of them spoke for a minute.

"The man was real last night," Jenna said, her voice firm.

"I didn't say he wasn't."

"You might as well have—you're thinking it."

"Jenna—"

"What's the plan for today, assuming you still want me to work with you?"

"Of course I do." Max took a sip of the coffee to let the air settle between them.

"We have a nine o'clock appointment with Mr. Weaver."

"I know."

They rehashed the security for the Founders Day picnic, and what they planned to ask Weaver.

Jenna finished her coffee and stood. "I put cereal out and there's milk in the refrigerator. I've already eaten and will be in my office looking through the newspaper archives."

"Okay. I'll let you know when I'm ready to leave." He hated polite conversation.

What little they said on the way to town could be put in a thimble. When they arrived at Weaver's office, he was waiting for them.

"Glad you're on time. I have to get out to the Armstrong place ASAP."

Jenna's eyes widened. "Why?"

"Evidently the people renting it moved out."

"What?" Max's heart dropped. "When?"

"Overnight. Bryan Bishop phoned me just before you got here. He saw a van pull out of the drive early this morning. He was curious and walked to the edge of his property to see what was going on. All the cars that had been parked there were gone, and the back door stood wide open."

"He didn't go in, did he?"

"Just the kitchen. Said it was plain they'd moved out. I have to get over there and see if they took any of the furniture."

It was almost like the men knew they were coming. He glanced at Jenna. The look on her face said she was thinking the same thing. "Mind if we go with you?"

"I don't see why not." Weaver grabbed several files. "We can talk about the other rentals while we're there."

Jenna climbed into the driver's side of her SUV while Max jogged around to the passenger side and climbed in. Silence rode with them as they drove to the Armstrong farm.

They were almost to the farm when Jenna broke it. "It's almost like they knew we were coming."

"My thoughts exactly, but how?"

"Could be coincidence. At least we can check everything out— maybe they left something behind."

Twenty minutes later they pulled in the drive, parked behind Weaver, and climbed out. The place certainly looked deserted. Max turned to Weaver. "Did you get a driver's license from the person renting the place?"

"I always get a license." Weaver flipped through the rental file. "Here it is."

Jenna snapped a photo of the license and handed the paper to Max. It was a Tennessee driver's license for one Johnathan Smith with a Chattanooga address. "You want to call it in to DMV?" he asked Jenna.

"On it."

He followed Weaver inside the house. "At least they left it clean," the rental agent said.

Max walked through the house. Clean wasn't quite the right word. More like sanitized. Even the plates on the light switches looked as though they'd been polished, and there wasn't a scrap of paper left behind, not even in the trash cans. He turned as Jenna joined them. "Any results?"

"The license is fake."

"Fake?" Weaver said. "That can't be!"

"Did you check it out?"

"Well . . . no. It looked real enough."

That figured. All Tom Weaver saw was dollar signs.

"Do you have a key to the barn?" Jenna asked. "We'd like to see inside it."

"What are you looking for?" Weaver asked.

Max said, "We don't know, but it's possible the people who rented the property were doing something illegal."

"Can't trust nobody anymore," Weaver muttered and pulled a key ring with several keys on it from his pocket. After sorting through the keys, he pulled one off and handed it to Max. "Do you need me to come with you?"

"No," they both said in unison.

He stiffened. "Just asking."

They stepped outside into the bright sunlight. "Want to walk or drive?"

"Are you kidding?" Her tone had an attitude.

"Just asking," he mimicked in Weaver's high-pitched voice.

At least that got a chuckle out of Jenna.

"You can drive, but I'm walking," she said. "It isn't that far."

He declined, and they approached the barn, both pulling on nitrile gloves. Once Max unlocked the door, he slid it open and they entered the building. Dust motes swam in the rays from a skylight window. He sniffed the air, and a lingering musk odor explained what the men had been doing here.

"They were growing marijuana," Jenna said. "But I don't think they were growing it in this room. Maybe in one of the side rooms?"

"Check it out." He waved his hand in front of his nose. "It smells like some of them were smoking it."

Judging by a couple of bales of hay against one wall, the building was used as a hay barn at one time. Max kicked a shoe box out of his way and eyed a couple of cardboard boxes. Apparently, it was also a place to store junk people didn't know what to do with. He approached the two tables in the middle of the room.

Jenna wandered toward the side of the room. "I'm going to check out this area."

He examined the tables while Jenna walked the length of the room, her gaze examining every square inch. Kirk had said this building was where the "mean guys" had told him to stay away. What were they doing out here? Max picked up one of the cardboard boxes and lifted the flap in the bottom. Was that—

Metal screeched on concrete, raking his ears. He jerked his head up.

"Hey, Max! Come see what I found!"

Urgency in Jenna's voice propelled him to the side room door.

283

A much stronger musk scent hit him when he approached the opening.

Jenna grinned at him. "I think we better call Alex."

He stared at the pots of marijuana and the system of lights, fans, dehumidifiers, and sprinklers. "I do believe you're right." He fished the small clear cap from the box and held it up. "And that's not all they were doing."

Jenna's eyes widened. "You were right. They were filling capsules."

"Probably with heroin or cocaine. Much easier to transport and sell than in bulk."

"No wonder the men ran Kirk off." Jenna shuddered. "He was lucky they didn't kill him."

54

Jenna was waiting outside the barn when her boss arrived with the CSI team and several other deputies.

"The marijuana plants are in an enclosed area inside," Jenna said.

"I can't believe someone was growing marijuana and packing pills right under our noses." Alex scanned the room. "I should have listened to my instincts the first time we talked to Kirk and put a surveillance team on the place."

"You couldn't have known," Max said. "And there have been quite a few 'incidents' this week that had you otherwise occupied."

Jenna stared at the barn. "Do you suppose the murders have anything to do with this operation? Maybe as a distraction to keep us from focusing on it?"

"You could be right. Let's see what you found." Alex pulled on nitrile gloves and followed Jenna.

She opened the doors to the grow room and Max and Alex followed her inside. Her boss whistled. "This operation cost a lot of money, so why didn't they take the plants with them?"

Max scanned the room. "They must have thought we were onto them and didn't think they had time."

"But how? We haven't talked about this place to anyone or what we suspected." Jenna turned to Max. "Have we?"

He shook his head. "It's like someone tipped them off."

Alex walked through the plants. "What's this?"

She knelt and parted the leaves on one of the plants and pulled out something shiny.

When Alex held up a necklace, Jenna pressed her hand to her throat. She stared at the gold cross dangling from Alex's hand. Her cross . . . how did it get here?

No, it couldn't be hers.

Alex turned a questioning gaze at Jenna. "Don't you have a necklace like this?"

"I . . . have a cross on a gold chain, but that can't be mine." Or could it? She hadn't found it when she and Max straightened the house after someone broke in.

Thoughts flashed through her mind, like rapid-fire bullets. Everything that'd happened at her house had been smoke and mirrors, distractions so she wouldn't pay attention to small details, like her necklace not being in the jewelry box. She'd honestly thought she'd misplaced it.

Her face heated. "If that's mine, it was planted here. If I was part of this"—she swept her hand toward the marijuana plants—"I certainly would've steered you away from this building."

"No one said anything about you being part of this," Max said.

"He's right, and I don't believe for a minute you lost this here." Alex stared at the necklace.

Maybe that was true, but it would put a seed of doubt in their minds—not that either one would admit it—and that's what Phillip and Sebastian wanted. And they wouldn't stop with planting the necklace—they wanted her destroyed.

Alex studied the necklace. "Let's say it is yours—why would anyone plant it here?"

"For the same reason Phillip spread the rumors in Chattanooga. Maybe we're looking at the wrong person, and it isn't Sebastian at all, but my ex-fiancé."

"I still don't understand why," Alex repeated.

"Because he'll do anything to discredit me." Jenna couldn't believe the nightmare with Phillip was happening again.

"But why does he want to discredit you?" her boss asked.

"The photos she has, maybe?" Max said.

"What photos?"

Jenna barely heard Max as he explained about the data drive with the photos on it and why she hadn't given them to the authorities. She'd been so shocked at seeing the necklace, she'd blanked.

"The photos aren't conclusive evidence. If he can make it look like I'm a dirty cop, he can convince everyone I'm trying to set him up if I turn the photos over to a DA."

55

While Jenna waited for Max to change for the meeting with her uncle, she flipped through the new photos on her phone of Sebastian's key men that Alex had emailed her. She hadn't seen any of them in town, but that wasn't surprising. It wasn't like they would parade themselves down Main Street.

She rolled her shoulders. It'd been a long day, most of it spent at the Armstrong place . . . or maybe she was just tired since it'd been several nights since she'd had a decent six hours of sleep. Even last night with Max in the house or maybe especially because he was there. He'd moved his things from the hotel and put them in her spare bedroom, although he'd indicated he planned to sleep on the sofa in case someone tried to break in.

Max was the one person she'd always thought would have her back, no matter what. But how could she trust him now when he didn't believe anyone had been in the house? And that he thought she was having a PTSD breakdown? It was plain that's why he was staying at the house. Jenna lifted her chin. Her mind had not fabricated the man in her bedroom. Was it going to take her death to prove it?

She laid her phone on the kitchen table and stared out the darkened window. What was taking Max so long? It hadn't taken Jenna five minutes to change into jeans and a long-sleeve pullover to ward off mosquitos.

They needed to leave soon if they were going to connect with Sam and the men they planned to interview. She reached down and re-laced her high-top boots for whatever snakes might be around.

"Sorry if I kept you waiting," he said, entering the kitchen. "Do we have time for me to make a cup of coffee? That apple pie I had with dinner is making me sleepy."

"I warned you about the carbs." *Ouch. A little harsh, aren't we?* She pushed a smile to her lips to cushion her words. Jenna wished they could go back to the way it was before he didn't believe her about the intruder. But she couldn't unhear his doubt. She checked her watch.

"You do," she said, softening her voice.

"Thanks."

Silence fell between them while he put the pod adapter in the coffeemaker and popped in a pod. Once the coffee finished brewing, he put a lid on his insulated cup and opened the back door for her. Jenna climbed in on the driver's side while Max rode shotgun.

He placed his coffee in the cupholder. "How do we want to handle tonight?"

"I say play it by ear, but remember these guys are highly suspicious of outsiders, even if my uncle did invite you."

"Is your dad coming?"

"I had a text from him saying he'd see me later, so I'm assuming so."

She glanced at her dad's house when they passed, a little surprised his pickup was still in the drive. Maybe Sam had picked him up. A few minutes later she turned into the pasture road to their meeting place and drove to the edge of the woods where pickups were parked. "Looks like they're all here."

Once they joined the others, Sam introduced Max to the men. Jenna breathed easier when Junior Bledsoe responded with a friendly backslap. Todd Donelson was friendly as well, but Gordon Marsden, her father's former coworker, stood off to the side. She didn't see her father, and she caught Sam's eye. "Where's Dad?"

"I don't know. He said he might be late. Something about being tired after finishing his route and catching a nap before he came. He'll find us."

Jenna stifled a yawn. A nap was something she wished she could've caught and hoped they wouldn't be out too late. Sam opened three cages and put tracking collars on two of the dogs.

Before she could ask why he was using two trackers, he said, "I'm using Chief to train Watson, and I want to watch and see if they're staying together."

Jenna never would have thought of that, but then she'd never trained hunting dogs. She smiled as the dogs danced around, barking to be let free, then she frowned and looked toward the road. It wasn't like her dad to miss a training run.

Sam hooked a leash on all three dogs and then handed one off to Max and another to Junior. When they reached their usual release spot, he cut them loose. "Go get 'em, boys!"

The other men did the same with their dogs. Sam sat on a downed tree the wind had toppled and took out his handheld receiver. After a few minutes, he said, "Watson is sticking right with Chief."

Max peered at the receiver. "Think they'll find a raccoon?"

Sam laughed. "They always find one."

The other men agreed. "What we don't want," Gordon Marsden said soberly, "is for Jenna to find another body."

"Hey—I didn't find that one. The dogs did, but don't worry.

Finding another body isn't on the agenda tonight." She picked up a stick and poked it around a tree trunk to make sure no critters were burrowed under the leaves. Then she slapped at a mosquito feasting on her neck.

Sudden bugle-like barking grabbed everyone's attention. "They've already got the scent," her uncle said.

The men listened to the clamor, identifying which bark belonged to which dog. Once the men settled back to wait, Max nodded at her.

He wanted her to take point. Jenna cleared her throat, and they all looked toward her.

"All of you knew the Slaters and Paul Nelson," she said and scanned the group. "Any of you know who might've had it in for them?"

Deadly silence filled the night air. She didn't rush to fill it. A minute passed. Gordon cleared his throat. "Is that why you're here? You think it was one of us who killed Nelson?"

She jerked her head around to Gordon. "What?"

"Why would she think that?" Max asked quietly.

"Well," Todd spoke up, "every one of us thinks the Pearl Springs city council and mayor stole our family land. Me included."

"Same here," Junior said. "I mean, nobody died, but my daddy never was the same after they had to move off the land."

"Losing land that's been in the family for generations does something to a man," Gordon said quietly.

"But you fought the case," Jenna said to Gordon.

"I did, for all the good it did me. By the time I paid my lawyer, I didn't end up with as much as the government offered the first time."

"Why do you say the mayor and city council stole your land?" Max said.

"Because they're the ones who came up with this dam and reservoir idea, and once the land was bought, Slater and Nelson suddenly had money to buy expensive cars and clothes," Sam said, his voice flat.

"How about Carter?" Max asked.

Junior laughed. "He had sense enough not to start spending money. But we all knew he had it."

"Have any of you ever heard of TerraQuest?" Max asked.

"That was the company that bought up a whole lot of our neighbors' land before word got out that there was going to be a dam and reservoir," Gordon said. "I heard they got top dollar from the government for their acreage—more than twice what any of us got."

"Do you know who owns TerraQuest?" Jenna asked.

"I don't," Junior said.

Before anyone else could answer, excited barking captured the men's attention, and they all jumped up, whooping.

"They found one!" Sam chortled. "And according to the tracker, it looked like Watson was the lead. Come on, let's go see how big this raccoon is." He elbowed Max. "Told you he was a good dog!"

Jenna groaned. They'd lost them. There would be no answers now.

56

Jenna caught Max's eye as the men prepared to trek to the tree where the dogs had a raccoon treed.

He joined her. "What's up?"

"I'm worried about my dad—he never misses one of these. If you want to stay, I'm sure Sam will drop you off at the house."

"No, I'm ready." He lowered his voice. "I think we've gotten all the information we're going to get tonight anyway."

"I agree, and thanks." She waited while he told Sam they were leaving, a little amazed at how well Max had fit in with her family and friends. That was rare. Russell County people tended to be standoffish with outsiders.

They used their lanterns to light the way back to the SUV. "Enjoy yourself?" she asked.

"I did. Lewis has been trying to get me to go coon hunting with him for ages, and next time he asks, I think I'll surprise him and go."

"Good. You'll need a dog."

"I don't think so. I'm only planning on one time."

She laughed. "You'll need a dog—coon hunting gets in your blood." Then Jenna sobered. "I don't understand why my dad wasn't here or why he's not answering my texts."

"Let's go find out."

The house was dark when Jenna pulled into her dad's drive. She could barely see Max's frown in the dimly lit SUV. "Do you think he's asleep?"

"He could be—Sam said he was tired when he came in from work." She fished his house key from the console. "I'm still going to check on him."

When they entered the back door, she flipped on the kitchen light and called out. There was no answer. Maybe he'd fallen asleep in the recliner in the den. Except the house had an empty feel to it.

She took a deep breath to calm her roiling stomach. In the hallway, she called once again, then stepped into the den and flipped on the overhead light.

Her hand flew to her throat. "No."

Signs of a struggle were everywhere. A floor lamp had been knocked over, tables were overturned, and the newspaper her dad read every evening was scattered on the floor. She picked up a broken mug—his favorite. She stared at the broken pieces and wanted to cry.

Max got out his phone and made a call.

"Alex Stone." He'd put it on speaker.

"I'm at Randy Hart's house," Max said. "There's been a struggle and it looks like someone took him."

"I'll be there in ten."

Jenna scanned the room. "Why?" she whispered.

"Has to be one of two scenarios," he replied. "Either the person who killed the Slaters and Nelson, or . . ."

The other option drained blood from her face. Jenna reached for something to steady herself with. "Sebastian."

"But why? And how did anyone get in?"

Jenna stared at Max, trying to decipher his words over the roar in her ears.

No! She didn't have time for a panic attack. Jenna filled her lungs with air and forced her attention back to the room, searching for anything that would give her a clue to who took her dad.

She pulled out her phone and snapped pictures while sirens wailed in the distance.

"This is personal," Jenna said quietly. "It has to be Sebastian."

"Not necessarily—it could be related to the Slater and Nelson cases . . . and Alex said Tuesday that a burglary ring had been operating in the county. Maybe the house was dark and they—"

"Burglary rings aren't usually violent—they just want in and out with goods."

"But what if your dad walked in on them?"

He had a point. "I'll keep that in mind, but my money is on Sebastian."

"Alex isn't going to let you work this case—it's your dad we're talking about."

"She can't take me off. It's probably my fault he's been taken." Jenna glared at Max. "I told you Sebastian was here, but you didn't believe me."

"We don't know who took your dad." He looked over his shoulder as the sirens died.

"Alex can't stop me from investigating this," Jenna said stubbornly.

"You know that's not a good idea."

"What's not a good idea?" Alex had come in through the front door. Dylan and Taylor trailed her. "And which room was he taken from?"

"I'll show them," Max said and led the way to the den.

"You can't take me off this case," Jenna said. "We're already shorthanded with Mark in Kentucky and Hayes Smithfield at the training academy."

Her boss studied Jenna like she was a grasshopper pinned to a board in science class.

Jenna forced herself not to look away. "You need me, and I'll go crazy just sitting around waiting."

Alex nodded. "Mark will be back at work Saturday. You can stay on the case until then."

Tension released in Jenna's shoulders. "Thank you."

Alex took out a notebook. "Don't thank me—it's against my better judgment, but you're right about us being shorthanded."

Max returned to the kitchen, and Alex shifted her attention to him. "Can you help us out on this?"

He nodded. "The kidnapping very well could be related to the case that brought me down here."

"Harrison Carter? How do you think it's related?"

"I think the other three deaths this week are connected to the letter Carter received, which I believe is related to the eminent domain cases from the dam and reservoir. Jenna's family was a part of that, plus, her dad delivers the mail—maybe he saw something."

"That what you think?" Alex asked Jenna.

She shook her head. "I think it's more likely that Rick Sebastian is here in Russell County, and he kidnapped my dad to get back at me."

Sebastian wasn't the only one with a vendetta against her. What if her ex-fiancé was involved as well? Maybe he wanted to trade her dad for whatever evidence she had against him.

"What's on your agenda tomorrow?" Alex asked.

"Checking out the names and addresses of people who sold to TerraQuest," Max said. "And the funeral for the Slaters. Has anyone said when Paul Nelson's funeral will be—we need to go to that one as well."

"His body hasn't been released—it'll probably be Monday at the earliest."

"I want to interview Eric Darby again," Jenna added. "I think he knows something he isn't telling. Maybe my dad's kidnapping will be the thing that loosens his tongue."

Alex scribbled something in her notepad and looked up. "Go ahead and interview the people on your list, and see if you can get any information out of Darby. I'll personally run the investigation into your dad's disappearance."

"Thanks." Jenna crossed her arms. "But I want an active part in it."

Alex pressed her lips together. Jenna had probably stepped over the line. "Talk to the people who know your dad the best— Sam, your grandmother . . . his friends."

That was better than giving her busy work. If Sebastian had been using the Armstrong place to move drugs, maybe he had her dad stashed wherever they'd moved. And the location could be one of the addresses Tom Weaver gave them of rentals in the last month. "I'll check out Tom Weaver's rentals for the past few months. Sebastian could be staying in one of them."

Alex hesitated, then she nodded.

"What time is the funeral?" Jenna asked.

"Three."

They should make that easy unless something broke with her dad's kidnapping.

57

Friday morning Sebastian let himself into Jenna Hart's house through the kitchen door. This morning he had plenty of time—he'd overheard the deputy and the TBI cop talking about their schedule for today. Besides, the app would alert him if they got within a mile of him.

But first things first. Sebastian opened the cabinet door where he'd seen her over-the-counter pain relievers. He fingered the box of headache powders . . . it'd be so easy to replace the powder with heroin . . . maybe a little extra fentanyl . . . The thought made him laugh. No. He wanted Jenna Hart to know who killed her.

Instead, he quickly grouped the pill bottles accordingly, vitamins on one side and pain meds on the other, including the powders. Then he turned to the pantry and grouped the cans according to size and content. That should be a nice little surprise for her.

Now for the photos that Phillip Ross insisted were here. He methodically searched each room, leaving no space untouched, even her dresser. He spied a small box and lifted the top.

Not photos but her business cards. With her cell phone number on it, and he pocketed it. That would come in handy very soon. Tonight, in fact.

Sebastian moved to the second bedroom and repeated the process. Nada. This was a waste of time. There were no photos anywhere in this house.

The app buzzed. Sebastian jerked out his phone and swore. Hart and the TBI agent were a mile away. They weren't supposed to be anywhere near the house. He hurried to the kitchen, let himself out, and pressed the tape back in place before he jogged to the wooded area. His car was parked on a farm road a mile away.

Sebastian wished he'd installed a camera—he'd love to see her face when she opened the cabinet door. As soon as he reached his car, he would listen in, then tomorrow he would break in one last time and remove the bugs.

It was time to stop toying with the mouse and end the game. Tonight was the *pièce de résistance*.

299

58

Jenna pulled into her grandmother's drive, and Max checked his watch. "It's only 7:30. Are you certain Eva is up?"

"Yes. I've already talked to her once, but I want to make sure she's okay."

The aroma of cinnamon rolls reached them when her grandmother opened the door dressed in her blue robe and house slippers. "Has there been any word?"

"Not yet," Jenna said as they stepped inside the house. She hugged her grandmother. "How are you?"

"Praying. And baking."

That's what Jenna expected her to say. "We'll find him."

"I know. God has this—it didn't take him by surprise."

Jenna wished her faith was as strong as her grandmother's. But this was her dad. And she'd seen the worst people were capable of, especially someone like Sebastian . . . or Phillip.

"When did you see him last?"

"He stopped by here on his way home from the post office. Said he was going to take a nap before he drove to the woods."

That's what Sam had told her last night both before and after they knew he was missing.

"Come on to the kitchen," Granna said. "Have you two eaten? I have rolls and coffee."

"I don't want anything," Jenna said as she and Max followed. Putting food or coffee in her roiling stomach was more than she could do.

"How about you, Max?"

"I'll take a cup of coffee."

She sat at the table and picked at her cuticles while Granna poured Max's coffee. Then she set a roll in front of him. "And one for you, Missy. You need to keep your strength up."

Jenna palmed her hands. "I'm sorry, Granna, I can't."

The back door scraped open and they all turned toward it as Sam entered the room.

"Have you found him yet?"

"No." Jenna blinked back tears.

"Have you remembered anything that might help us?" Max asked.

Sam flattened his lips. "No. Yesterday was like every other day—Randy stopped by the house, said he was going home to take a nap first, then he'd come to the woods. Said he'd call us if he couldn't find us. But he never showed. And I didn't see anyone at his house when I left."

Jenna rubbed her hands on her pants. They needed to be doing something more productive, like checking out Tom Weaver's recent rentals. She stood. "I'm ready if you are."

Max nodded. "If either of you hear anything, call us."

By midmorning Friday, Jenna's neck muscles were tight enough to break as she pulled away from one of Weaver's rentals—another dead end. A tension headache threatened, but at least they'd checked off two of the addresses Tom Weaver had given them of recent rentals, this one and another, both families with small children.

They'd also phone interviewed three heirs of the families who'd sold their land to TerraQuest, including the one where Max had left a note for them to call. For what good it'd done them—not one of the families they'd talked to knew anything about the company.

The next address would take them five miles past her house. Jenna felt in the console for ibuprofen and found an empty bottle. She glanced toward Max. "Do you mind if we stop by my house on the way to the next place?"

"Headache?"

"How did you know?" She rubbed her temple.

"That." He pointed to her action. "And I've noticed you massaging your neck."

Jenna dropped her hand. "I guess tossing and turning instead of sleeping has caught up with me."

"I'm good with stopping, and then I'll drive if you'd like."

She nodded, and ten minutes later, Jenna turned into her drive. She checked the front door while Max checked the back.

"Tape was fine on the back door," he said when he returned.

"Here too. Shouldn't be any surprises waiting on us," she said, pointing toward the tape still in place.

"Right."

Pain shot through her right temple. She closed her eye and pressed her fingers to her cheekbone. If she didn't take something fast, she was in for a full-blown tension headache. As soon as she had the door opened, she hurried through to the kitchen, filled a glass of water, and opened her cabinet to grab the ibuprofen.

Jenna froze.

"What is it?"

Before she could stop herself, she blurted, "Sebastian has been here—he rearranged my bottles."

Max joined her. "Are you sure—"

"Of course I'm sure. I've been meaning to organize my cabinets, but I haven't had time. Besides, I would know if I'd done this!" She pointed to the neatly arranged bottles. "If you don't believe me, look at my pantry."

Jenna flung open the pantry door and stared at the neat rows of canned goods, the boxes of cereal lined up together. A chill raced up her spine. Jenna turned to Max. "You've seen my cabinets—they look nothing like this!"

He shook his head. "You've always had the cereal and the coffee on the counter, waiting for me."

That's right, she had.

"What if Sebastian found the photos." Jenna whirled around. "I'll be right back."

"I'll check the windows." Max followed her down the hall.

"I'll check the ones in this bedroom." Jenna quickly knelt beside the false receptacle. The tape was still intact.

The pounding in her chest eased only slightly, and she examined the windows. Both locked down tight. She walked back to the kitchen.

Max returned a few minutes later. "All the windows I checked are locked, and I'm assuming the ones in the bedroom—"

"They're locked."

It didn't make sense. Everything was locked up tight—how had someone gotten in and lined up the medicine in her cabinet and rearranged what was in her pantry?

"Did you examine the back door?"

"No."

Max walked to the back door and tried to open it. "If someone was here, how did they get in?"

"I don't know," she said.

"Does anyone else have a key?"

"Granna does." Hope fluttered in her chest. "She'd do something like this—but not today, not with Dad missing."

"Call and make sure—she may have needed something to take her mind off what's happened."

That had to be the answer. Jenna jerked her phone out and punched in her grandmother's number. "Hey, Granna," she said when her grandmother answered. "Have you been to my house today?"

"No, dear. I haven't left the house since you were here. Why do you ask?"

Jenna gripped the phone. "No reason . . . I just thought maybe you'd straightened up my cabinets."

"No, I've been right here, baking a pound cake for the meal after the funeral. I just took it from the oven."

Jenna braced herself with the table. "Thanks, Granna. If I have any news about Dad, I'll call you. Otherwise, we'll see you at the funeral." She disconnected. "I guess you could tell that Granna hasn't been here."

"I'll dust for prints."

Max didn't believe anyone had been here. Oh, he said the right words, all right. It was his tone that said he was humoring her.

"No need," she said, brushing him off. "Whoever did this would've worn gloves. Are you ready to go to the next place?"

"Aren't you going to take something for your headache?"

"I forgot."

Her hand froze as she reached for the bottle of ibuprofen. He'd handled her bottles. What if he'd switched the pills out with heroin—no, the ibuprofen were caplets. They would be safe.

She wasn't letting whoever did this control her. She grabbed the bottle, uncapped it, and swallowed two pills with a gulp of water. "I'm ready."

Max followed her out the front door and waited while she placed a new piece of tape at the top. When they reached her SUV, he cleared his throat. "We need to talk about the elephant in the room."

"I don't see that there's anything to talk about. I think someone has been in my house and you don't."

"I would if there was some sort of proof."

She waved her hand toward the house. "The cabinets aren't proof enough for you? I've *never* organized my cabinets like that. The more I think about it, something about the intruder's voice makes me believe it was Sebastian in my room."

"But—"

"I don't know how he's getting into the house. Maybe he picks the lock. We both know that's possible."

"Yes," Max said slowly. "But how does he get *out* of the house? It takes time to pick a lock. And why would he close the door when he left? That would take even more time."

"I don't know how he does it, but he's getting in my house someway." She caught his gaze and held it. "I didn't rearrange my cabinets—I'm not crazy."

"Jenna, I don't think you're crazy."

"You couldn't prove it by me." She turned and opened the driver's door. A sudden rush of tears had her blinking furiously.

"Somehow I always thought you'd have my back," she said, her voice breaking.

The next thing Jenna knew, he'd turned her around and pulled her into his arms. "I'm sorry . . . it's just that I'm worried. You've been through so much the last few years. Getting shot, Phillip, changing jobs, and now your dad—with your history, it's enough to trigger PTSD . . ."

Jenna felt him take a deep breath.

"But, I do believe you," he said softly. "If you know someone was in your house, then we'll find out how he's getting in."

That's when the dam broke. He held her close, rubbing her back as she cried. Finally she pulled away. "I'm so sorry—"

"Don't apologize. It's only a shirt."

"At least I don't wear makeup," she said, taking the handkerchief he gave her to blot her eyes. "And we need to get back to figuring out who has my dad. And who TerraQuest belongs to."

"For today, forget TerraQuest—your dad and what's going on here is our top priority." He was quiet as he thought. "You said your grandmother has a key. Maybe she made an extra one and someone took it. Who else has a key?"

"Just my dad . . . oh, wait—I have a spare hanging inside the cabinet over the stove."

"Is it still there?"

"We can check." They returned to the house, and she opened the cabinet door. The three keys she kept there—one for Granna's house, her dad's, and her spare—were all there and hanging in their normal places.

"So much for that theory," Jenna said. "And we need to table this and check out the rest of Tom Weaver's rentals."

Max agreed with her, and they returned to her SUV. "Why don't I drive and you navigate?"

"Good idea." She climbed into the passenger side and booted up her GPS. "We need to stay on this road for two miles, then turn to the right."

They'd passed her grandmother's house when Max said, "I can't get your intruder off my mind and how he has access to your house. It doesn't make sense, unless . . ."

Jenna turned to him. "Unless what?"

"Unless he took the key that first morning and had a spare made. That would explain how the deadbolt was always locked after he left. Where would he go to get a key made?"

Jenna tapped her fingers on the armrest. "The key I had made for Dad and Granna came from Walmart, but the hardware store duplicates them as well."

"Let's call them."

Jenna called Walmart first and learned the store's key duplicator had been down for two weeks, waiting on a part to repair it. The local hardware store had made a few keys but didn't remember making one for a stranger.

"That was a strikeout," Jenna said.

"Where's the next closest Walmart?" he asked.

She named a town thirty miles away. "Then there's Chatta-nooga . . ."

"Call and ask Alex if she can get someone to check out the other stores in a thirty-mile radius of Pearl Springs and have them show Sebastian's photo."

She punched in Alex's number, and the chief deputy agreed with them, promising to check right away.

"Alex will let us know what she learns," Jenna said and pock-eted her phone. "Turn right at the next road."

Max turned at the road she indicated. "I've been thinking about that day I found you unconscious, and I remembered something from when I took judo—there's a way to knock someone out by striking them with a hard karate chop to one of their pressure points . . . like the base of the skull."

She gasped. "That's the spot that was tender!"

He nodded. "Our sensei wouldn't let us practice it, but he showed a video of someone using it. The person who received a karate chop at the base of the skull went down like a sack of potatoes. If it happened to a person and they weren't expecting it, they probably wouldn't know what hit them."

She closed her eyes and released a breath. "So I'm not having PTSD."

"But someone wanted you to think you were—you were set up."

Jenna opened her eyes and turned to him. "The only person who would benefit by people thinking I'd lost it is Phillip."

"He probably has help," Max said.

"Sebastian."

59

None of the cabins had panned out, and Alex hadn't called with any news. Jenna massaged the knots in her neck. The ibuprofen had helped, but not knowing where her father was had her insides tied up in knots. At least Max didn't think she was having PTSD now.

She studied the remaining addresses they had to check out. Was her father being held at one of them? "This address is out by Eric Darby's place. Why don't we check on it then stop by his place and see if he's ready to tell us anything."

Max glanced at his watch. "As long as we don't miss the funeral."

Twenty minutes later, Max pulled off the main road onto a gravel drive and drove a short distance to the house. He put the SUV in park, and they climbed out as a man came out of the house with a box.

"Can I help you?" he asked as they approached.

"I hope so." Jenna showed her badge and then scanned the cabin and yard. "A man went missing last night, and we're checking to see if anyone has seen him."

"You're the first people I've seen today. I'm sure my wife hasn't seen anyone, either."

"Do you mind if we ask her?" Max said.

He shrugged and yelled, "Holley! Can you come out? A deputy sheriff wants to talk to you!"

A thin woman came to the door, questions showing in her face, and they explained what they were looking for. She shook her head. "Nobody's been around here today, but if we see anyone before we leave, we can give you a call."

"Thanks," Jenna said. While she hadn't really expected them to have seen her dad, time was running out.

"Have you seen anything unusual?" Max asked.

The couple exchanged glances. "Well . . ." the husband said. "We've been here a week and there hasn't been much traffic—"

"Until the other night," the wife said, "there's been a whole lot of people up and down the road."

"Really?" Jenna said. "Do you know where they're going?"

The husband shook his head, but the woman hesitated. "I wonder if they're going to that cabin we saw our first day—we were out riding around and saw it."

Max took out his pad. "Where exactly is it?"

The man shrugged. "Maybe a couple miles away—these roads are so curvy, it's hard to tell distance."

Jenna thanked them. "We'll check it out."

They climbed back in the SUV and Max put the gear in reverse. "That sounds like the place we planned to check out next. Put the address in the GPS and see how far it is."

"It's two-point-five miles," she said.

They met two pickups and a car not long after they passed Mr. Darby's drive, and a mile later, the GPS indicated they were arriving at the address.

"Next house on the right," Jenna said.

The small house sat back off the road. "Doesn't look like anyone's home," Max said.

Jenna noted grass near the house that had been pressed down.

Some of it was even kicked up like maybe someone had parked there instead of the drive and then left in a hurry. "I'll make sure."

She hopped out of the SUV and jogged to the front door before he could stop her. It would surprise her if whoever took her dad had him stashed at a place so easy to find him. When no one answered, she trudged back and climbed in the SUV.

"I'm not marking it off the list," she said, her tone brooking no argument.

Max backed out of the drive. "What's the name on the rental agreement?"

"Tony Miller."

"Does it say how many occupants?"

She ran her finger down the paper. "One. Did you notice that someone, or maybe several someone's, had parked on the grass?"

"I did. Call Mr. Weaver and see if you can get any information on this property."

"I'll put it on speaker." The call went straight to voicemail.

"Maybe we can catch him at the funeral," Jenna said.

Something about the place bothered Jenna, but she couldn't put her finger on it. But something else bothered her more. "Why do you think no one has asked for a ransom?"

He didn't answer right away, then Max drew in a breath. "You have to consider—"

"Don't say it!"

"Jenna."

"If my dad were gone, I'd feel it here." She touched her chest above her heart.

"The only thing is . . . sometimes our heart deceives us."

"No." She refused to believe her dad might be dead.

"We're running short of time to make the funeral. Do you think Mr. Darby would open his gate if you called and asked?"

"He may not answer his phone." She put it on speaker after she dialed. Jenna was surprised when the old man answered. "This is Deputy Jenna Hart."

"I know who the number belongs to."

Mr. Darby was in fine form today. "Good. Would you mind opening your gate so we don't have to crawl through the fence?"

A long pause followed, and Jenna checked her phone to make sure she still had a connection.

"I suppose I can do that, but I still don't have anything to say."

"We just want to touch base."

"I'll meet you at the road."

Jenna hung up. Stopping to talk with the old man was probably a waste of time.

"Darby seems like a good guy," Max said. "And I believe he knows something about the connection between Carter and the deaths of the Slaters and Paul Nelson."

True to his word, Eric Darby was waiting for them on the right side of the lane to his house with Bear at his side. Jenna lowered her window. "You want to talk here or the house?"

"Here's fine."

They climbed out of the SUV and Bear trotted to them, sniffing their shoes.

"Hey, Bear," Jenna said softly. She patted the big dog on the head, and he rubbed against her leg.

"Traitor," Eric Darby muttered. "Did you ask your dad about what happened when they bought up the land for the dam?"

She didn't trust herself to speak.

"Her dad is missing."

Jenna shot Max a grateful smile.

The old man stiffened. "What do you mean, he's missing?"

Max explained what had happened, and Darby scratched his head. "Do you think it has to do with what happened to the Slaters and Nelson?"

She frowned. "Why would his disappearance be related to what happened to them?"

"Maybe he saw something—your dad's all over the county in that mail truck," Darby said. "Or maybe he knew something about whoever killed the others back before the dam was built."

Jenna didn't miss the way he suddenly stiffened or the expression on his face that said he wished he could call back the words. "If you're talking about my grandfather and Todd Donelson's dad, their deaths were both ruled accidental, so why did you say they were killed?"

He swallowed hard and shrugged. "I don't know. Seems there might've been some talk—"

"There wasn't." She crossed her arms. "What are you not telling us?"

Darby shifted his gaze toward the road. When he turned back to her, his face had shuttered. "I don't know anything . . . and if people thought otherwise, I might end up dead."

Did he think someone was out to get him because of what he knew? There had to be a way to get him to talk. Jenna shifted toward him. "Why would you say that?"

He toed a stick at the edge of the drive. "Ain't that what generally happens to folk who know too much?"

"Do you know too much?" Jenna asked softly. She tilted her head and studied him. "People never see the janitor. He's like a piece of the furniture. Did you hear something while you worked at city hall?"

"No."

He'd answered too quickly. "Is that why you've hidden out all these years? Out of sight, out of mind?"

He turned toward his house. "I got things to do."

She put her hand on his arm. "Please, Mr. Darby, if you know anything that will help us find the murderer or my dad, tell us."

His shoulders sagged and he stared down at the ground. Then

he shook his head. "If I knew anything that would help you find your daddy, I'd tell you. But I don't."

The finality of his words pierced her heart like an arrow. They were getting nowhere with the case, and there'd been no ransom demand. She pulled on his arm until he was looking at her. "It's killing me, knowing someone has him. I know you still roam the woods around here. If you see or hear anything, call me."

He held her gaze. "I will. I promise."

60

ax backed out of Darby's drive. "He's weakening."

"No. He's scared. He's afraid he'll be the next target, and I don't blame him if he knows that there was something illegal about the dam project. Either Mr. Darby knows something that would identify whoever killed our three victims, or he fears the killer thinks he does." She tapped the armrest. "If we could just get him to tell us what he knows."

Max slammed on the brakes. "We need to talk to Darby again."

He backed up to the gate and blew the horn. "Call and see if you can get him to come back to the gate."

She craned her neck. "No need—I see him coming."

"Come on." He hopped out of the vehicle and jogged to the gate with Jenna on his heels, arriving at the gate the same time as Darby.

"What in tarnation?" the old man growled.

"We need to talk."

"We've been over that. I don't have anything to say." Darby glared defiantly at him.

"I think you do. You overheard something when you worked at city hall that you think will get you killed. That's why you quit and barricaded yourself on your property like a hermit."

"That's crazy."

"Is it, Mr. Darby? If you know something about this case, you need to tell us. We can protect you."

"I can take care of myself. Been doing it for twenty years."

"Yeah, but what about Jenna's dad? What if he was kidnapped by the same person who killed the Slaters and Nelson, and you know something that will help find him?"

The color drained from the older man's face.

"And if the murderer goes after Harrison Carter, and you could stop it . . ." Max wanted to drive home the point, then he softened his voice. "Do you really like living this way, Mr. Darby?"

Indecision warred in the old man's face, then he lifted his chin. "I don't have any choice. And I got things to do."

That said, Darby turned and marched toward his house while Max wanted to beat his head against the steel gate.

"We can't make him talk," Jenna said. "But maybe after he has time to think about what you said, he'll change his mind."

"I'm beginning to think nothing can get him to talk. And if we want to get a back seat row at the funeral where we can observe everyone, we need to move it."

Jenna checked her watch. "You're right. The whole town will be at the funeral and that back row will fill up pretty quick."

It wasn't long before they pulled into the church's parking area that was almost full. Jenna had been right. It looked as though the whole town was here.

They entered through the door facing Main Street, and Max scanned the pews for two spots at the back. There were a couple of places left. He turned to point them out to Jenna, but she was already striding toward them.

Once they were settled, he scanned the mourners, looking for anyone who looked guilty, although Max wasn't quite sure he'd know what that looked like with this group. Statistics showed that

315

killers liked to show up and see the handiwork of their crimes. He doubted this would be any exception.

Harrison Carter was at the front, surrounded by his security detail. "Be right back."

When he reached the senate candidate, he was talking to Slater's sister. Max waited until he stepped away to get Carter's attention. When Carter saw Max, a flash of irritation crossed his face before it morphed into a fake smile.

Carter approached with his hand extended. "Agent Anderson, I had forgotten you would be here."

"With your busy schedule, I thought that might happen and wanted to remind you that Deputy Hart and I would like a few minutes of your time after the funeral."

"Sure thing . . . perhaps the church has a room we can meet in?"

"I'll arrange it, and we'll meet you in the welcome center."

Carter gave him a curt nod and took a slip of paper from his pocket. "If you'll excuse me, I need to go over my eulogy for Joe Slater."

Before Max returned to his seat, he walked to the church office and had no problem setting up a room for their meeting. He followed the receptionist to a room with a large table.

"This is our workroom," she said. "Will it do?"

"It's perfect."

Soft organ music began as Max reentered the sanctuary and walked to his seat at the back of the church, nodding at Carter. The man barely acknowledged him.

Max had the distinct impression Harrison Carter would like nothing better than to skip their meeting.

61

He slipped into the church from a side door. The receiving line reached all the way to the front door. A quick check of his watch confirmed there was no need to get in line—the service would start in ten minutes, and one thing funeral director Harvey Pickford prided himself on was starting a service on time.

There was room on the back pew, and he scanned the rows as he ambled toward the back of the church to see who all was there. Sheriff Stone's granddaughter, the new chief deputy, sat two rows up with the police chief.

When he reached the last row, his mouth turned to cotton. He hadn't noticed that Jenna Hart and that TBI agent were already seated on the pew. It would look odd if he looked for another seat. He swallowed down his fear.

"Excuse me." After plopping down, he nodded to the deputy. "Afternoon."

He had no idea what her response was as he concentrated on slowing his heart rate. A slight noise at the front of the receiving line drew his attention. Harrison Carter was speaking to Slater's sister again. Carter hadn't changed since he left town—he was the only one who counted.

In his mind he heard the explosion his bomb would make and

how everyone's attention would be pulled toward the lake. Then, with everyone looking the other way, he saw himself pointing his rifle at Carter and pulling the trigger.

Organ music swelled in the church, jerking him out of his fantasy. Except it wasn't a fantasy because fantasies didn't come true. And come Founders Day, Harrison Carter would be dead and the reservoir would be drained. The land would be returned to its original purpose.

62

Two caskets sat at the front of the sanctuary, a sad reminder of what had happened Monday. It looked as though the whole town had turned out for the double funeral. Jenna scanned the faces of those who'd come out to pay their respects to Joe Slater and his wife.

Her grandmother sat midway from the front row. Maybe she'd get a chance to speak to her after they finished their interview with Carter. A few women dabbed at their eyes as Harrison Carter expounded about his time with Joe Slater.

Jenna continued to scan the sanctuary, seeking those who'd had their land condemned for the dam and reservoir. Todd Donelson was here, Junior sat with his wife on the left, behind the pall-bearers. She hadn't gotten the impression that either man liked Slater, so she was a little surprised to see them at the funeral . . . unless—

No, she couldn't believe Junior had tampered with Slater's Hummer. He was a mechanic, though—who better to know how to loosen the nut where the tie-rod would fall off? And Donelson wasn't one to get his hands dirty . . .

Gordon Marsden sat on the row behind Junior. Another person she didn't think particularly liked Slater. If her dad were here, he'd probably be sitting with Gordon. Her heart caught. She should be out looking for him. Alex was working hard on the case, but would it be enough?

She itched for the funeral to be over with so they could interview Carter and then check out the three remaining cabin rentals.

A chuckle rippled through the crowd, and Jenna pulled her attention back to the front as Carter made his concluding remarks.

"Time doesn't permit me to tell all the stories I have of Joe and Katherine, and I'm sure you have plenty to tell yourselves. They both will be missed." Carter stepped away from the dais and sat on the front row with Joe's sister.

Jenna should have been paying more attention to what he'd said—she hadn't known the Slaters, and every bit of information she learned about them helped frame a better picture of their lives.

After the funeral, she spoke to her grandmother, then followed Max to the foyer, where they waited for Carter, her patience getting thinner by the minute. By the time he joined them thirty minutes later, her patience had evaporated, especially when he totally ignored her, other than to give her a patronizing smile before focusing on Max. She understood she was only a deputy and Max was TBI, but Carter should at least acknowledge her.

Memories of difficulties in her former life in Chattanooga bombarded her, and she almost missed Max's nod for her to start the questioning. Jenna brushed aside the insecurity that had crawled into her mind. She was good at her job, and Max knew it, and Mr. Senate Candidate was about to find out.

"Thank you for joining us," she said.

Carter's smile slipped. Jenna acknowledged the four bodyguards who had followed them into the room, and then she turned back to Carter. "I don't think you'll be attacked in here, so do we really need your security team? Besides, you may want some of our discussion to remain private."

Briefly Carter's eyes widened, then he gave her a stony glare before turning to the men. "I'll be fine. Just wait in the hallway."

The one who seemed to be in charge crossed his arms. "Are you sure?"

He nodded. "After all, we have Russell County's finest with us."

Jenna forced herself not to react. Carter was used to getting his way, and when he didn't, it wasn't pretty. She exchanged glances with Max, and he flicked his gaze toward the ceiling. Jenna tightened her lips to keep from grinning at his version of eye-rolling.

"Just what do you want to discuss that my security team couldn't hear?"

She turned to Carter. "Several things. Have you received any more threats?"

"Not since I hired the team outside the door."

"Good." Jenna picked up her notepad. "I know your time is valuable, so we'll try to be brief. Let's start with Joe Slater and Paul Nelson. You worked with both—do you know anyone or any reason someone would take them out?"

"I thought Slater's death was due to the accident."

"It's looking more like someone tampered with his vehicle," Jenna said.

Carter turned to Max. "Is that correct?"

Heat flushed through her chest. The man wasn't endearing himself to her. Max's curt nod mollified her somewhat.

Carter paled and stared into space. "Nelson's murder doesn't surprise me, but the Slaters'? No. Everybody liked them, especially Joe. And to kill his wife as well . . ."

"No one comes to mind?" Jenna asked. The man was definitely shocked by the news, or he should win an Oscar.

He shook his head.

"Do you know where Joe got the money to buy that Hummer? Or his wife's Escalade?" Max said.

"Don't know that either . . . unless his wife inherited when her parents died."

"Why did you say you weren't surprised at Nelson's death?" Max asked.

"He was a womanizer, and he was the love 'em and leave 'em type. I'm kind of surprised it didn't happen years ago."

Jenna doodled on her notebook. She hadn't expected Carter to bring that up. "Do you know any of the women he dated?"

"The only women I know about are from years ago—they wouldn't have waited this long to kill him. But, if this town is like it was when I lived here, you can ask Pete's wife down at the diner. Ethel knows everything about everybody."

He was spot-on there. Jenna made a note to talk to Ethel. Carter prepared to stand. "If there's nothing—"

"I have a few more questions," Jenna said.

A pained expression crossed his face. "What are they?"

"First, what do you know about a company by the name of TerraQuest?"

He didn't miss a beat. "Not a thing. Next question."

"Aren't you at all curious about why I mentioned the company?"

"No." He crossed his arms over his chest. "I have a schedule to keep, and I don't have time to dwell on foolish questions."

Max leaned forward. "We think it's an important question."

"Okay. I'll bite. Why did you ask me about a company I know nothing about?"

She nodded at Max to take over the interview. While he didn't seem to like Max, Carter at least respected him more than he did Jenna. She wanted to study his body language, and Jenna couldn't do that and deal with the man.

"I'm surprised you're not familiar with the company," Max said. "TerraQuest bought up a bunch of land in the valley during the early stages of the dam project before the grant was even approved."

If she hadn't been watching closely, Jenna would have missed the tiny twitch in his left eye. The man knew the company—she'd bet her badge on it.

Max flipped back through his notes. "Who applied for the grant to build the dam?"

Carter adjusted his tie. "I did, before I became mayor—that was my job, to find money to fund the city."

"You weren't aware of anyone buying land back before the dam was proposed?"

He raised his right hand. "I have no knowledge of land purchases, not before or after the dam proposal, and I resent the implication of your questions. I have never done anything improper during my public service. Do you have any other questions?"

Granna's voice sounded in her head. *If his lips are moving, he's lying.* But how would they prove it?

Jenna looked over the questions they'd jotted down. "Were you aware several landowners died before the land acquisitions went through?"

Carter sat back in the chair. "Not really. I do remember your grandfather died in an accident about that time, but he's the only one."

Funny he would remember that one unless he meant it as a threat? "You don't remember Earl Donelson dying?"

He frowned and stared down at the table. "Oh yeah. I'd forgotten—hunting accident, right? Shot himself while getting out of a deer stand." Carter stood. "If you don't have any other questions, I would like to get on the road. I have a speaking engagement at the Kiwanis Club in Chattanooga this evening."

Max nodded. "Thank you for your time. We'll see you tomorrow. Are you still arriving around 4:00?"

"Yes. I have a rally in Nashville at noon, and then an interview with one of the Nashville TV stations." Carter paused at the door. "I hope anything said within these walls will stay here."

63

Max looked across the table to Jenna. "That went over like a mud ball."

"Yeah," she replied. "Carter was lying about not knowing about TerraQuest."

"You caught that twitch too," he said. "So, what did we learn other than he wasn't being truthful with us?"

"That he was willing to throw Paul Nelson under the bus if it diverted our attention from him. I know Alex is looking into that aspect of his life."

"So we could be looking at two different cases. Are you ready to check out the rest of those rental places?"

"Definitely. I know where they are—one's not too far from the house."

"I'll meet you at your SUV—let me tell the receptionist we're done with the room."

Jenna pulled to the side door and was waiting when Max came out of the building. He climbed in and fastened his seat belt. "I keep thinking about that house we stopped at," he said as they pulled away from the church. "How the grass was messed up—

definitely more than one vehicle there, and like someone hit the gas really hard and sped out of there."

"Like they knew we were coming?"

They looked at each other. "Pull over so we can check for a tracker."

They climbed out of the vehicle and knelt beside Jenna's SUV, using their phones to shine a light under it.

"I don't see anything," Jenna said.

"I have a bug detector in the toolbox in my truck at your house if we don't find it." He moved down to the rear and felt along the inside of the bumper. His fingers closed over a small box, and he pulled it off.

The tracker was the size of a matchbox with a magnet on one side. He handed it to Jenna.

"I cannot believe I didn't think of this before."

She examined the box. "Do you think Sebastian put it there?"

"Or whoever was in charge at the Armstrong place."

"Or maybe the person who broke in put the tracker on my car when we left it sitting in the drive?"

He nodded. "And possibly a whole lot more, like listening devices."

"What do we do about the tracker?"

"Put it back." He knelt and returned the device where he found it. "That way whoever put it there won't know we've discovered it. We can remove it once we get to your house . . . or even better, change vehicles."

"My gut says we need to go back and check out that cabin on the other side of Mr. Darby."

"I agree, but first we need to check for bugs at your house and leave the tracker there." He opened a family and friends locator app on his phone and added Jenna's number to his group.

"Accept the invitation I just sent you—that way if we get separated we can locate each other."

A text chimed on Jenna's phone, and she clicked a couple of keys. "Done."

When they arrived, Max said, "Once we're in the house, act naturally, and be careful what you say."

"Do you know how hard it is to talk naturally when someone might be listening to every word you say?"

64

Max turned to her. "If there are listening devices in your house, whoever put them there will be expecting you to talk about your dad . . ."

"You're right."

She waited on the porch while Max retrieved the bug detector and swept it around his truck, kneeling once to pull out a small box like the one that had been under her bumper.

He put it back where he found it and jogged to the porch. "That was the only one on the truck. When we leave here, we'll go by the sheriff's office and swap your vehicle."

Jenna grinned. "I like it—that way whoever is tracking us will be following the wrong person."

He adjusted a knob. "I'm turning the sound off so they won't know we're scanning for listening devices. The lights will flash to let us know if the device picks up on one. And while I'm in another part of the house, shut off your computers—they'll cause the device to alert."

"Do you really think someone may have put listening devices in my house?"

"It would explain why the Armstrong place emptied so fast they didn't have time to move the marijuana plants."

Jenna hoped it was a coincidence. Just the thought of someone hearing everything they'd said . . . she couldn't wrap her mind around it.

Once they were inside, Jenna said, "Let me check my email, then I'll make us a cup of coffee before we leave to see Alex."

"Sounds great." Max started with the living room and moved to the bedrooms. By the time he reached her office, she'd shut her computers down. He ran the detector over her framed commendation from the Chattanooga mayor. Nothing. He placed the detector next to a USB charger. Again nothing.

"I'll be glad when the picnic is over," he said and moved to the modem. The device lit up like a Christmas tree. Max gave her a thumbs-up.

Even though Jenna expected Max to find bugs, the reality of being violated swept over her anew. It was all she could do to not throw up. How was she going to carry on a normal conversation when all she wanted to do was find this person—who probably had her father as well—and . . . Arresting him wasn't enough. She wanted to pound him into the ground.

Max tipped her chin toward him. "We'll find him," he mouthed.

She drew in a deep breath and forced lightness into her voice. "I'll go make coffee."

"Make it in to-go cups, and we'll drink it on the way to see Alex. She's waiting for us to finalize the security measures for tomorrow's picnic and political rally," he replied and squeezed her hand.

Come on. Get it together. Jenna pushed her shoulders back and strode to the kitchen. If only there was some way to let her dad know she was looking for him.

She popped a K-cup in the coffeemaker. If the person who took her dad was the one with the listening device, maybe her dad could hear what was being said as well. A song from her childhood popped in her head, and she hummed the first few bars . . . then she softly sang the first words.

"Joshua fought the battle of Jericho. Jer-i-cho—"

"Jer-i-cho . . ." Max sang with her as he entered the kitchen. He swept the kitchen, stopping as the lights flashed like crazy when he passed it by the pendant light over the table. "Great song."

She nodded, handed him the cup of just-brewed coffee, and put a K-cup in for herself. "Dad taught it to me when I was a kid."

Her voice broke, and it wasn't because she was acting. If anything happened to her dad . . .

"You ready?" Max asked.

Jenna waited for her coffee to finish brewing then grabbed it. "I think I've figured out why there's been no ransom note," she said once they were on the road.

"Why?"

"Because Phillip is responsible for Dad being snatched—he has a lot more to lose from my photos than Sebastian. Phillip wants me to be so anxious that I'll give him the photos, no questions asked."

"You could be right."

"And I'll give them to him before I let anything happen to Dad."

Silence hung between them the rest of the drive. Alex's face was grim when they walked into the chief deputy's office. It was even grimmer when they finished explaining what they'd found. Alex pushed a photo across her desk.

"I emailed Sebastian's prison intake photo to Dani Collins and asked her to sketch him with a more muscular build. This is what she came up with."

Jenna studied the drawing. It barely even resembled the man she remembered. "I haven't seen him."

Alex lifted her eyebrows. "Well, the person who duplicates keys at the Walmart in Sharpton has. He identified the person in this drawing as a customer who came into the automotive department Tuesday afternoon and asked him to make a key.

Said he was giving it to his sister. The Walmart guy remembered him because he's a body builder and asked the customer where he worked out, only he never got an answer. The customer mumbled something he didn't catch."

Jenna's muscles tensed. Sharpton was only thirty miles from Pearl Springs.

"He's working with my ex-fiancé, Phillip Ross," she said quietly. How long were they going to make her wait before demanding she give them the photos in exchange for her father's life? Not that she believed they would do what they said, but at least a demand would get everything moving.

"Have you checked out Tom Weaver's list of rentals?" Alex asked.

Max nodded. "We're almost finished. There's one in particular that doesn't fit the rental agreement. It would be the perfect place to hide Jenna's dad . . . I wish we could use thermal imaging."

"Do you have enough for a warrant?"

"Afraid not. Just a hunch—the rental agreement states one person is using the cabin, but it looked as though several cars had been parked there, and they left in a hurry. Probably because the GPS tracker on Jenna's SUV alerted we were headed in their direction."

"Yeah, that's not enough for a warrant. Drive back out there and surveil the cabin. If there's only one vehicle, you can approach and interview the occupants, but if there's more than one vehicle, back off."

She turned to Jenna. "If you do approach, and your dad makes any kind of noise, you can enter the cabin under exigent circumstances since this is a kidnapping case. But I'm not counting on that happening."

Alex walked to a map of the county. "Let's assume this is the place. Give me the cabin's location so I can get around-the-clock surveillance set up."

Max gave her the address, and Alex found it on the map. "It's not far from Eric Darby's place. I'll contact him and see if he'll let us use his property as our base of operation. For now let's assume he will."

Alex quickly laid out a plan of action, pointing out where she would place deputies. "I'll make sure everyone knows their role."

Max nodded. "If we don't gain access to the cabin, once the other deputies are in place, Jenna and I will check out Weaver's remaining rentals this afternoon."

"And we need to trade vehicles with someone," Jenna said.

"Mark Lassiter and my grandparents won't be getting into town until later this evening. His SUV is in the parking area. Use it. Marge has a set of keys for it."

Twenty minutes later Jenna drove past Mr. Darby's drive. "Do you think we should park here and go in on foot or do a drive-by of the cabin?"

"Let's drive by first," Max said. "There may be a side road closer in."

Jenna slowed as they drove past the cabin, and counted four vehicles parked in the drive and on the grass. "Can you see any license plates?"

"A couple," he answered. "I'm writing them down."

Maybe they'd get lucky and one of the vehicles had been reported as stolen. That would give them a perfect reason to storm the cabin.

"I'm texting them to a fellow TBI agent. He agreed to be on standby in case we need him."

They pulled off the road to wait. A few minutes later, a text came back that none of the vehicles had been reported as stolen. "They're checking registrations to see if they belong to any of Sebastian's known associates."

Jenna gripped the steering wheel, her knuckles turning white. "I just don't understand why we can't use thermal imaging."

DEADLY REVENGE

"We can't use it without a warrant, and we have no proof your dad is in there or that Sebastian even rented the cabin. Unfortunately, our gut feeling isn't enough for a warrant."

"But—"

"I want to get Sebastian as much as you do—"

"No, you don't." Her heart jackhammered in her chest. She glared at him. "It's *my* dad he has, and right now I don't care about the law."

"I understand. You think I don't want to bust in there and rescue your dad? The thing is, we have no proof he's even in there. Or that Sebastian is, either."

Jenna closed her eyes against his words. *"God has this, sweetie."* How many times had her daddy said those words? And Granna . . .

She sagged against the seat and pressed her fingertips to her closed eyes. "I just want to get my daddy back."

"I know, and we will—but within the law. We don't want Sebastian to walk free because we violated his right to privacy."

"Why do we have to play by the rules when the bad guys don't?"

"You know why—we're better than them."

Jenna released a pent-up breath. "I know." She sat up straighter. "Sorry for the meltdown."

He squeezed her hand. "If it was my dad, I'd feel the same way. Don't ever forget God's on the side of justice. He has this."

She managed a small chuckle. "Yeah, that's what my daddy always says. So what do we do now?"

"We wait for the surveillance team then we check out the remaining cabins on Weaver's list."

65

Sebastian paced the small kitchen in the cabin. Four of his men were filling the order for Sunday in the living room. Once he had his money from this operation, he'd have enough to set up in Chattanooga again. And this time without Phillip Ross calling the shots.

Phillip had been right. Jenna Hart had evidence against both of them, but why hadn't he been able to find it? He'd searched that house from top to bottom. Didn't matter—after tonight, he would be rid of both problems.

He dialed Ross's number. He answered on the first ring.

"You don't call me—I call you."

"Just thought you might like to be here when I take Jenna Hart down."

"What are you talking about?"

"She's bringing the photos to me."

"How did you—"

"I told you I was smarter than she was. She's waiting for a ransom note, and as soon as it gets dark, she'll get it. Your problem will be over."

"I want to be there. But—"

"My men will have the order completed by tonight. You can take it back with you."

"What if she brings all the Russell County deputies with her?"

"She won't, but if she does, I'll know it."

"You're sure?"

"Guarantee it."

"Okay . . . I'll be there. What time?"

Perfect. And as usual Ross had been predictable. "Why don't you come about nine or even eight and you can help finish the order?"

"You're sure you'll know if she's coming alone?"

"Don't worry about it. I'll know—the cops are too stupid to figure out I put a tracker on her vehicle and microphones in the house."

He pocketed his phone and walked to the bedroom to check on Hart's father. Sleeping like a baby—the medication he put in his drink worked like a charm.

The old man was gritty. Twice he'd tried to escape, which was the reason Sebastian had to sedate him. But now he needed him awake—Jenna Hart would insist on talking to him before she gave in to the ransom demand.

66

don't like it," Max said. After checking the last cabin on the real estate agent's list, they had returned to the sheriff's office and were in the briefing room. "It's too dangerous. And we don't know who's in the cabin."

The registrations returned on the license plates hadn't belonged to any of Sebastian's known associates, but that didn't mean he hadn't recruited new ones.

"It's our only option," Jenna replied. "I'm doing it with or without backup."

"I don't like it either, but I don't see any other options." Alex leaned forward and pointed at the map spread out on the table. "As soon as it's dark, deputies will take their positions." She pointed to a ring of X's on the map.

"Once Sebastian contacts me and sets up the ransom drop, I'll drive to the spot, leave the photos, and you and Alex can arrest him," Jenna said.

Max crossed his arms. "What if he wants you to bring the photos to the cabin?"

"I don't think he will."

"If he does," Alex said, "Jenna will have a microphone she can attach to the outside wall. That way she won't be caught with a wire on her and we'll hear everything that's said. As soon as Jenna says her dad is there, we'll storm the cabin."

Even though he wanted to protest, Max held his peace. If he were in Jenna's place, he'd do the same thing. Didn't mean he had to like it, though.

"Okay, then, we're all set." Alex turned to Jenna. "Sebastian probably won't contact you as long as he thinks you're here, so go home and wait. Try to get some rest."

Max escorted Jenna out of the building and to her SUV. The drive to her house was quiet. "He won't make a move until after dark," Max said before they entered the house.

"I know. I just wish he would call so this would be over."

At 8:30, there was still no call. Max turned to Jenna. "It's nice out. Why don't we eat supper on the patio," he said as she paced the kitchen. Jenna checked her watch, probably for the tenth time in the last thirty minutes.

"Is it that time already?"

"It's past time to eat."

"I'm still not hungry."

"You need to eat." If they ate out on the patio, they could talk freely. "How about a sandwich? I'll make it and bring it out."

"Sure."

He handed her a radio he'd bought earlier in the day to drown out any conversation they had outside. Max had scanned the area around the patio, and found nothing, but the microphones he'd found in the house were the type that could pick up voices a hundred yards away, and playing the radio would mask their voices.

They both believed Sebastian would make a move tonight. Too bad hunches weren't enough for a warrant. Alex had deputies watching the cabin, and so far, Sebastian hadn't shown himself. Either he was inside and staying there or . . . Max didn't want to think of the alternative. In fact, no one had come or gone until an hour ago when the surveillance team had observed a man with a semiautomatic strapped to his waist walking the perimeter of the property. Unfortunately, he didn't match any of the photos they had of Sebastian's men.

Max made ham and cheese on flat wraps and grabbed each of them a Coke. Jenna was staring toward the woods when he set the food on the table.

"What if he's out there, watching?"

"If he is, we've got the wrong hiding place." He didn't believe they had the wrong cabin, and he'd gotten a key from Weaver and a layout of the cabin, including a virtual tour. He'd been studying it just in case something went wrong and he needed to get inside.

She nodded. "I expected him to ask for the photos by now. What will we do if he doesn't call before Carter's event tomorrow at the park?"

"We'll deal with it."

They would only have a skeleton crew for tomorrow's event at the park if Sebastian didn't make his move tonight. If that were the case, Max hoped it was enough.

He prayed before they ate, asking for Jenna's protection.

"Thanks," she said. "I know you're not on board with Alex's plan, but there's no other answer. He'll demand the photos, I know he will."

To say Max wasn't on board was an understatement. He wasn't at all happy with the plan Alex had outlined if the ransom demand came in tonight. He was certain that if Sebastian had her dad, it was because he wanted any evidence Jenna had. He was equally certain that once Sebastian had it, he planned to kill her.

"I'm good with the fact that all the deputies are familiar with the area, and they'll be stationed in the woods surrounding the cabin. What I'm not on board with is *you* taking the photos to Sebastian at the cabin."

"There's no one else. No matter what happens, we'll deal with it."

Jenna was using his own words against him.

He'd never change her mind, either. She was insistent that if Sebastian demanded that she bring the photos, she was doing it if it meant saving her dad.

"Do you have the—"

"For the third time, I have my Sig P938 under my body armor, and the microphone that I'll stick on the post outside the door is in my pocket."

"What if it fails?"

"It won't. But if it does, the one you put under my dashboard will pick up our conversation." She turned and looked at him. "What part of 'God has this' don't you believe?"

He flipped his hands up. "I believe all of it. Just making sure we do our part."

Alex and Max had figured anyone who had sophisticated GPS trackers and listening devices would scan Jenna when she walked in the door. The plan was for her to attach a listening device the size of a quarter to the outside of the house as she entered. It wasn't as good as a wire or a microphone disguised as a pen or button, but Sebastian couldn't discover it by scanning Jenna.

"If things start going south, what's the code phrase?"

"'What makes you think you can get away with this.'"

Even though they had the advantage of discovering the trackers and microphones, sending Jenna into the cabin was too iffy. There had to be another way to get Sebastian.

Her phone buzzed with a text, and they both froze.

"It's from my dad's phone." Jenna read the text aloud.

Bring what you have. Now. Just you. No cops
unless you want a funeral.

Will call once you are on the road with the
destination.

Jenna texted back.

No. Not until I talk to my dad.

A minute later, a call from his number showed up on her phone. "Dad, are you all right?"

"Don't do it," he yelled.

The call ended and Jenna punched the redial button. It went straight to voicemail.

Max immediately called Alex and put the call on speaker. "It has to be Sebastian," he said. "He didn't even name what he wanted. Just that he would give directions once she was on the road."

"It may not be him," Alex replied. "My deputy called a minute ago. Phillip Ross just arrived at the cabin."

67

told you that Phillip was in on it too." Jenna felt in her pocket for the USB drive that had photos of Phillip and Sebastian together.

Max pulled her to him. "After tonight you won't have to worry about either one of them."

She leaned into his embrace, soaking up his strength. Jenna felt his lips moving on her head. He was praying for her. That was where her strength came from. When he finished, she stepped away from him with a sigh. "Time to go."

"I know." Max smoothed her hair back. "Alex deployed the rest of the deputies as soon as we disconnected. The others were already in place."

She nodded and checked her ankle holster again. Not that she would get to keep it—pretty sure Sebastian or Phillip would check her for weapons once they were certain she wasn't wearing a wire.

Maybe they wouldn't find the Sig tucked behind her vest. It wouldn't be easy to get to with the body armor on, but it made her feel better nonetheless.

She raised her gaze to Max again, drinking in his image. "See you on the other side of this."

"Yep." He cupped her face in his hands. "We won't have time for this later."

Max pressed his lips to hers, and she slipped her arms around his neck. When they broke apart, she gave him a shaky smile. "Thank you for having my back."

"Always." He bent and kissed her once more.

She climbed in the front seat of her SUV as he climbed in the back and lay on the floorboard. "I'll repeat the directions he texts me, or if he calls, I'll put it on speaker and you can send the directions to Alex."

Darkness had fallen, and Jenna flipped on her lights before she backed out of her drive. A mile down the road, a text sounded on her phone, and she checked the message. "It's directions but only to get me through town." Evidently instructions would be piecemeal.

"Alex texted that if the route is toward the cabin, she and Nathan will be waiting at the intersection to the road it's on. I'll get out when you stop to turn."

"Good thinking." The GPS would show if her SUV stopped to let him out when she neared the cabin.

The directions in the next text definitely indicated they were taking her to the cabin. At the turn, she stopped just long enough for Max to roll out the back door.

She drove past Eric Darby's and slowed when someone waved her down with a flashlight and then pointed toward the cabin. Thank goodness Max had already gotten out.

Jenna pulled as close to the cabin as she could and got out. The man with the flashlight checked her SUV, then patted her down and found the gun in the ankle holster. "Where's your service pistol?"

"I didn't bring it." She tried to get a look at him, but he wore a hoodie and there wasn't even a moon out.

"Get inside." He pointed the way with his light.

Jenna slowly climbed the steps and stopped at the top by a post. "Why are you stopping?"

"I'm dizzy." She pressed the microphone against the post.

The door opened and Sebastian appeared. "Well. We meet again."

"So we do. Where's Phillip?"

"Oh, he's inside, waiting for you."

She didn't doubt that. Jenna stepped inside the cabin, and another of Sebastian's men ran a scanner over her. Max had been right.

She blinked at the brightness in the room. Once her eyes adjusted, she looked around, her heart almost stopping at the sight of her dad bound in a chair. A gag covered his mouth, but he shook his head.

Jenna turned and gasped when she saw Phillip. Ropes bound him to a chair as well. She shifted a puzzled gaze to Sebastian.

He grinned at her, and now Jenna knew what Kirk meant by the creepy smile.

"Wasn't expecting that, were you?"

68

Max jerked his head toward Alex and Nathan. "What's Sebastian talking about?"

Alex held up her hand. "Maybe she'll tell us."

All three leaned closer to the receiver.

"I'm here. You can turn my dad loose," Jenna was saying.

"Not yet."

"What are you doing . . . That's a jam—"

The receiver emitted nothing but static.

"He's jamming the system. Our phones are useless," Nathan said.

Max pulled out the key he'd gotten from Weaver. "I'm going in the back door."

"Coming with you." Alex checked her Sig.

Max started to argue with Alex but stopped. She was the top law enforcement officer in Russell County. And Alex having his six wasn't a bad idea. "Let's go—there's not much time."

"I'll create a distraction with the guard. Once I get him away from the door, I'll take him down," Nathan said in a tight voice. He drew Alex into a quick embrace.

It was plain he wasn't happy about Alex going, but like Max, he knew there would be no stopping her.

Max and Alex circled around behind the cabin. No outside light—good. They crept to the door, and he silently inserted the key and eased it open.

The door opened a couple of inches and stopped. *Safety lock.* He slipped his hand in and felt the device. An arm and ball, like in a hotel room. *Good.* He'd practiced opening the swing bar latch a few times.

Max jerked the shoelace out of his right shoe. He quickly worked the ends of the string under the top and bottom ball bearing on the arm and pulled the loose ends toward him. Then he worked the looped string on the back side of the knobbed bar and eased the door shut.

"Pray this works," he mouthed to Alex.

Max pulled the two ends of the lace tight and heard the lock swing open. He released the breath he'd been holding. Now, if no one else heard it . . .

Max pointed for Alex to go to the right, and they slipped inside, Max to the left. Both stopped, listening as light filtered in from the hallway.

He recalled the layout of the cabin. There was one way into the kitchen—through a hallway that had bedrooms and a bathroom on one side and the living room on the other. Judging from their voices, they were in the living room.

"Let me get this straight—if I don't kill Phillip, you'll kill my father?" Jenna was saying.

Max's chest tightened. They were out of time.

"Give the cop an A. And I want it up close and personal."

"Jenna," another male said. "Don't do it. I know you—you won't be able to live with yourself if you kill me."

"Don't flatter yourself, Phillip," Jenna said. "And then, Sebastian, you'll shoot me with Phillip's gun."

"Make that an A plus."

Max's heart stuttered.

344

"What's to stop me from shooting you instead of Phillip?" Jenna asked. "Three men aren't enough to stop me from shooting you first."

Okay. They knew how many they were dealing with.

"You'll never get the shot off," Sebastian said.

"Are you willing to risk your life that I won't?"

Alex tapped him on the leg and held up two fingers. He gave her a thumbs-up. That left him Sebastian and one other man.

He visualized the layout of the living room and knew Alex was doing the same. If he were Sebastian, where would he station his men? It wasn't huge—fireplace on one end—probably where either Phillip or Jenna's dad was being guarded. A sofa in the middle of the room. Sitting chairs on either side of a window—

"On the count of three, you'll fire or your dad is dead. One . . . two—"

Max burst into the room. Alex followed and took out one of the men.

Sebastian jerked his head toward him. Her dad rocked his chair, toppling it against Sebastian. The gang leader hit the floor and bounded up, firing.

Jenna fired, hitting Sebastian in the arm, but the bullet didn't seem to faze him.

The other two men raised their guns. Alex and Max fired simultaneously, dropping them both, and Max turned toward Sebastian.

"Watch out!" Jenna screamed.

Pain rocked Max's head as Sebastian's foot connected with his temple. Faster than Max could move, the gang leader whirled around and knocked Jenna's legs out from under her. He leaned over and held his gun to her head.

"It appears we have a standoff." Sebastian nudged her with his gun. "Get up, and you two drop your guns."

Alex dropped hers and Max laid his gun on the table directly in front of him.

Jenna slowly climbed to her feet. "You can't kill us all."

"Yeah," Alex echoed. "The cabin is surrounded with my deputies, and I have a really accurate sharpshooter."

"This deputy and I are walking out the door." He jerked Jenna in front of him. "Tell them to stand down."

"I can't," Alex said. "You jammed the signal."

Indecision crossed his face. "The jammer is on the table. You"—he pointed to Alex—"turn it off and then call off your deputies."

Alex slowly walked to the table. Max locked in on Jenna's eyes and dropped his gaze. He pointed three fingers down before closing two of them.

He prayed she understood.

Max dropped another finger.

When Alex picked up the jammer, he dropped the third finger and grabbed his gun, firing as Jenna dove for the floor.

The front door burst open, and deputies spilled into the room.

69

Jenna leaned into Max, and he wrapped his arm around her waist. Flashing red and white lights from the ambulances strobed the sky. No one died tonight. Phillip was the first one arrested, and Sebastian and his three men were critically wounded, but barring complications, they would live to stand trial.

"Your dad seems okay," Max said.

She shifted her gaze to the ambulance where medics checked her dad. "He's a tough bird."

Max laughed. "I can't believe he managed to topple his chair into Sebastian."

They both turned as Nathan and Alex approached.

"It's been a good night's work," Alex said.

"Yeah," Jenna agreed. "If we can get through the picnic with no one getting hurt, it'll be a good weekend."

They all bumped fists. "Don't do it tonight," Alex said, "but first thing in the morning, write up your report."

"It is morning," Jenna said.

"You know what I mean." Alex smiled. "Tomorrow—excuse

me—today is a big day for us, you two in particular. Why don't you try and get some sleep."

"I won't argue," Max said.

"We'll take Dad home." Jenna glanced toward her dad again. She could have lost him tonight. She breathed a prayer of thanks. "I hope to get him to spend the night at my house."

Alex and Nathan looked askance at her.

"What? You think I can't talk him into it?"

"What do you think?" Alex said with a laugh.

She could try, and she did try, but her dad was adamant that he was sleeping what was left of the night in his own bed. When they reached her house, she turned to Max.

"Why don't you sleep in the spare bedroom? I know it's more comfortable than the sofa."

"I'll take the sofa—it sleeps pretty good."

It was two before Jenna actually made it to bed, and she was asleep almost as soon as her head hit the pillow. Hammering jerked her awake. Was she dreaming? No. The hammering continued. The clock on her dresser showed 5:00 a.m.

She grabbed her gun and eased out of her bedroom. Max stood at the front door. He put his finger to his lips then peered through the peephole.

He blew out a breath and holstered his gun. "Hold on, Mr. Darby!" He turned to Jenna. "Key?"

Jenna holstered her gun and hurried back to her bedroom and grabbed her keys. In the hallway she tossed them to Max. He unlocked the door and swung it open. "What's wrong?"

Darby didn't wait for an invitation and barreled into the house with his dog. "Someone tried to poison Bear."

"Is he all right?" Jenna asked.

"Yeah. I trained him as a pup to not eat anything except what I gave him. About half an hour ago, Bear started barking something fierce. Woke me up, and I knew right then someone was on my property—that's the only time he barks crazy like that."

Darby stopped to get a breath and swayed. He pressed his hand against the wall to steady himself.

"Let's go to the kitchen where we can sit down," Max said.

"Appreciate it."

Jenna reached to take his arm, and the older man pulled away. "I can make it on my own."

Max hid a grin. He was an independent old cuss. They sat around the table, Darby taking the seat Max usually sat at—against the wall where he could see if anyone came through the doors.

Jenna yawned. "Would anyone like coffee?"

"Appreciate it," Darby repeated.

While she made a pot of coffee, Max filled a bowl with water and set it on the floor.

Bear looked up at Darby, and after he nodded, the dog cautiously approached the bowl and looked back at his owner. "Go ahead," he said. "That's why he ain't dead."

Max watched as the dog lapped the water. "Tell us exactly what happened."

"Mind if I wait on the coffee? That'll give me time to straighten out my mind."

His story, his timing. "Sure."

When Jenna handed him a steaming mug, Darby's brow wrinkled. "Your dad . . . have you found him?"

"We have, and he'll be all right."

"Good." His forehead smoothed, then he sipped the brown liquid and nodded. "That's good—tastes almost as good as my perked."

Max locked his fingers on the table and leaned forward. "What happened, Mr. Darby?"

The older man took a deep breath and released it. "Like I said,

Bear was barking, and after he quit, I waited a bit and watched out the window to make sure nobody was there. When I finally walked around the house, I found a pack of ground beef at the side of the house."

He took another sip of coffee and stared into space, the muscle in his jaw working furiously. "The sorry no-goods had put poison in it."

"How do you know?"

Darby looked at Max like he'd lost his mind. "You find a bunch of ground beef on your property with white powder all over it—what are you going to think?"

He hadn't mentioned the white substance. "Did you bring it?"

"It's in my truck."

"Good. I'll have it analyzed." He turned to Jenna. "Unless you have someone local who can run the test."

She shook her head. "TBI would be quicker."

"Be surprised if it isn't rat poison." Darby's jaw clenched as he rubbed Bear's head. "If they'd killed him . . ."

"Why is someone targeting you?"

He dropped his gaze to the coffee mug gripped in his hands. Neither Jenna nor Max spoke, letting the silence weigh on the old man. When he raised his head, tears glistened in his eyes. "I overheard something I shouldn't have."

When he didn't continue, Max said, "What was it?"

Darby cleared his throat. "Slater and Nelson were talking to Carter in the mayor's office. One of them, not sure who, said, 'We have a problem—Donelson says he's coming clean about the dam.'"

Darby turned to Max. "You two probably don't know but Earl Donelson, Todd's father, was on the city council back when this dam project was hatched. His grandfather had a farm in the valley, and Earl was supposed to talk him into selling.

"But the old man refused and he was influencing a whole slew of others. He threatened to take the case to the Supreme Court if he had to. He meant to block the building of the dam."

Max frowned. "Why was that such a big deal—people can't stop a project like that—the state just condemns the land and takes it."

"'Cause Earl was going to testify that the dam wasn't needed."

"I'm sure Carter could bring in experts saying otherwise."

"Mebbe so, but the way they were discussing it, Earl was also going to spill the beans about how Carter and his cronies had bought up a bunch of land in the valley. If the dam didn't go through, they would've lost a passel of money."

Darby sat up straighter and crossed his arms over his chest. "Next thing I know, Earl's dead."

Jenna leaned forward. "But he accidentally shot himself climbing out of a deer stand, right?"

"If you believe that, I got some rocky ground I'll sell you to grow corn on."

"He didn't?" Max said.

"Naw. I heard Harrison Carter say he'd take care of the problem—that he'd heard Earl was going deer hunting that weekend. Next thing I know, I'm going to a funeral for the man."

Max rubbed his thumb around the rim of his mug. It was an interesting story, but he couldn't imagine confronting Carter with it or getting a search warrant to look for proof that it was true. "How does this play into the deaths of the Slaters and Nelson?"

Darby drained the last of his coffee. "Don't suppose I could have another one of these?"

Jenna picked up the mug. Darby locked his gnarled fingers together and massaged the heel of his hand with his thumb while she poured his coffee.

He was stewing. Max could tell, and he left Darby alone. Jenna set the mug in front of him. "I didn't ask if you wanted cream and sugar the first time."

"Black is good." Darby unlocked his hands, and his fingers shook when he picked up the cup, sloshing hot liquid. "Ahh!" He jerked back, almost dropping the cup.

Jenna jumped for the cup while Max grabbed paper towels. "Did you burn yourself?" she asked.

"No . . . at least not bad." He took the paper towel Max offered and dried his hands. "Sorry for being so messy. I'm just jittery."

Max handed him another towel. "That's easy to see. What are you not telling us? Maybe getting that off your chest will ease your nerves."

He hunched over the cup. "I did something a month ago and didn't know it would end up with people dead."

His voice was barely a whisper.

Jenna knelt beside his chair. "What did you do?"

He turned toward her. "It's coming up on the twentieth anniversary of when Earl died, and Todd caught me when I came to town for groceries."

"That was a month ago?" Jenna asked.

He nodded. "That's about the only time I go to town unless I have a doctor's appointment. Anyway, he was asking me what I knew about his dad's death."

Max sipped his coffee, ignoring that it was cold. He didn't want to stop the man once he'd started talking. "Why did he think you knew anything?"

"Todd is smart." Darby sighed. "You see, I quit right after Earl's *accident*, and he'd come to the house off and on over the years, asking what I knew—he didn't believe for a second his dad shot himself."

He gave Jenna a tiny smile. "He'd walk down like you did and crawl under the wire, but I never told him anything."

"Why talk to him this time?"

"I don't know. Maybe it was because he reminded me it'd been twenty years. Maybe I just got tired of carrying the burden of knowing. Maybe it was the whiskey he gave me while we sat in his truck. All the maybes in the world won't change that what I told him sent him over the edge—made a killer out of him."

70

Jenna rose from where she'd been kneeling beside Darby and sat in the chair across from him. "You don't know for sure that Todd Donelson killed the Slaters and Nelson."

Darby's mouth twitched. "Maybe not in the sense that I have proof." He touched his heart. "But I know here."

Just like she would've known if her dad had been dead.

The older man straightened in the chair. "Just like I know Todd's going to try and kill Harrison Carter today at the picnic."

Max checked his watch. "We don't have much time. It's almost six—not quite ten hours before Carter arrives for the rally."

Jenna agreed. "We need a complete workup on Todd Donelson. Like how proficient is he with rifles? That's the only way he could get to him at the picnic."

"And what other talents does he have that we aren't aware of?" Max added.

Bear rose from where he'd been lying at Darby's feet and trotted over to the door. The dog scratched at the wood and gave Darby a plaintive look.

The old man stood. "While you two try and figure this out, I'm going to take Bear out."

"Just don't leave."

"Gotcha."

Max let them out with the key, and Jenna took out her phone. "I'll call Alex. She can get Dylan working on a background check on Donelson."

Alex answered on the second ring. "What's up?"

"Max is here and you're on speaker," Jenna said. "I hope we didn't wake you up, but—"

"I've been up half an hour. What's going on?"

Jenna started at the beginning and repeated the story they'd heard from Eric Darby. Before she'd gone very far, Alex said, "Hold on a second while I grab a notebook and make a few notes."

She had Jenna repeat some of the information, then said, "Go ahead."

Alex stopped her again when she came to the part about the meat left out for Bear. "Bring the meat when you come in today— I'll have one of the deputies run it up to the Tennessee Poison Center in Nashville. I know the administrator, and he'll put a rush on it. Where is Eric Darby and the dog now?"

"He was in my kitchen, but right now he's taken Bear outside."

"Good. Don't let him leave. If what he says is true, Donelson may view Darby as a loose end. And if Harrison Carter thinks Darby knows something that will derail his political career, he might go to great lengths to shut Darby up. What else did he say?"

Jenna finished filling her in on everything Eric Darby had told them, including his opinion that what he told Todd Donelson had sent him over the edge.

"I'll call Dylan and get him started on a background check for Todd." Alex was quiet for a minute, and Jenna heard her tapping on something. "I think Todd Donelson served in the reserves with Sam . . . I'll call him as soon as we hang up."

"How should we handle Harrison Carter?" Max asked. "He'll be here by four."

"We don't have enough to charge him with a crime," Alex said.

"Right now it would be a 'he said, she said' situation. And while Dylan found a link between TerraQuest and Harrison Carter, it's not enough for an arrest."

That didn't surprise Jenna. Shell companies were notorious for hiding the partners involved.

"But it is enough to interest the FBI—agents will be here the first of the week to go over what we've found," Alex said. "They'll nail him."

71

awn hadn't broken when Todd Donelson drove past the park and then turned on Main Street. Two blocks down, he parked his truck behind the bank building he came to every workday, and if everything worked according to plan, in two days he would unlock the doors just like every Monday morning. If not . . . at least he would have avenged his father's death.

He grabbed the backpack with the disassembled AR-15 and slipped it on. D-day.

Thirty minutes later he hung "Closed for Maintenance" signs at the top and bottom of the slide, then stretched a chain across the steps. That should keep any kids from trying to get inside the treehouse.

He stepped over the chain and climbed the steps. Once he shrugged out of the backpack, he laid it on the floor. He soon had "Keep Out" flaps strung across the openings, including the window.

Todd slid the window flap over just enough to see that nothing had been erected to block his view of the platform where Carter would speak. Then he unpacked the AR-15 and assembled it. While he wouldn't be able to see the dam when it blew, he would have a clear shot at the man responsible for building it. And for killing his father.

Then he laid a burner cell phone on the floor beside him. He'd already programmed in the number to the phone that would detonate the bomb.

He checked his watch. Six a.m. Twelve hours before the dam blew.

Now all he had to do was wait.

72

Max glanced toward the area where Harrison Carter had a table set up with campaign material for the Founders Day picnic. The man himself was flanked by his body-guards as he "pressed the flesh" with everyone he encountered. Quite different from the man Max usually saw.

After much back-and-forth discussion, Carter had agreed to wear a lightweight body armor vest under his open-collar blue-checkered shirt. Paired with khakis, he looked polished but casual—the man knew how to woo rural voters.

So far there'd been no sign of Todd Donelson. The two times he'd met Donelson, the man hadn't impressed him as someone who could be dangerous. Max smiled as Jenna approached. Just knowing she was no longer a target lifted his spirits.

He wanted to steal a kiss here and now, but this was neither the time nor place, but once today was over . . . Max intended to see where their relationship might go.

"Any sign of Donelson?" he asked when she reached him.

She shook her head. "I've known Todd Donelson since I was a kid, and it's hard to believe he could kill anyone. What if it isn't even him?"

"He's our best suspect," Max said.

"Just because Mr. Darby told him what he'd overheard doesn't mean Todd Donelson killed the Slaters and Paul Nelson. Junior Bledsoe has a lot of anger directed toward Carter. And he's here."

She pointed across the park where Junior stood talking with Mark Lassiter. Russell County's K-9 dog, Gem, stood at alert beside the deputy. "I haven't had a chance to congratulate them on their win. I'll walk over and talk to Junior while I'm there."

"I'll go with you." Max halfway wished it was Junior—they at least had eyes on him.

"Did you get the text from Alex?" Jenna asked.

"Yeah." Max hadn't been surprised when the chief deputy texted an hour ago that the warrant she'd requested for Donelson's house had been denied. Warrants weren't granted on hunches. But they really needed a piece of his clothing for the K-9 dog to sniff.

"Too bad there wasn't anything at the bank Mark could use," Jenna said.

"The man must be a neat freak."

While the bank's cleaning crew had just finished with Donelson's office when Max and Jenna entered, Max had been certain there would be something in the office they could use. But Donelson hadn't left one article of clothing when he left on Friday.

Junior and Mark turned toward them when they approached.

"Glad you got Randy back," Junior said. "But ornery as he is, I'm surprised they didn't turn him loose the first day."

They all laughed.

"Thanks, and I'm glad that's over." Jenna turned to Mark. "Congrats on Gem winning first in the Fastest Find competition."

He patted Gem on the side. "She was amazing! So focused."

Max turned to Junior. "I'm a little surprised you're still here—Carter speaks pretty soon."

The big man shrugged. "I decided he wasn't keeping me and

my kids from seeing the fireworks after he gets through spinning his version of the truth."

Junior turned and thumbed toward the treehouse. "Don't see why you had to close that, though. My boys love climbing in there."

Max had noticed the treehouse was closed. "Wasn't us—sign says it's closed for maintenance."

"Have either of you seen Todd Donelson?" Jenna asked.

"He's not here, as far as I can tell," Mark said.

"I haven't seen him since we got through blowing up the dams on my property on Thursday. Ain't never seen anybody as good as he is to blow one up—he knows exactly where to put the charge and how much C-4 to use."

Jenna's breath caught. "What are you talking about?"

Junior shot her a puzzled look. "You were there the other night when I asked him to help get rid of a couple of dams those confounded beaver had built."

Max exchanged glances with Jenna.

"I totally forgot it." She jerked out her phone. "He served with Sam in the Gulf War." She punched in numbers, and when Sam answered, Jenna put the phone on speaker. "What was Todd Donelson's job when you two served together?"

"What are you talking about?"

Jenna repeated her question. "We need to know, right now!"

"Demolition expert, but why?"

"I'll explain later." She clicked off the phone. "You heard him."

Max's jaw hardened. "He's going to blow the dam." He turned to Mark. "Is Gem a bomb dog?"

Mark nodded. "She's trained in explosive detection."

"We have to find that bomb," Max said, his voice tight. "They're shooting the fireworks from a boat near the dam—they could all die if he blows it up. Come with me."

Mark gave the command for Gem to come. "We'll be right behind you."

"I'm coming too," Jenna said.

Max shook his head. "I need you to find Donelson. I guarantee he's here at the park somewhere—he'll want to see his handiwork, maybe even use the chaos the bomb will cause to take out Carter."

His heart cinched at the fear in her eyes. Max had felt the same way last night when she entered the cabin. "It's going to be all right."

Jenna hesitated and then nodded. "Be safe."

73

Donelson wiped sweat from his eyes. He hadn't figured on the treehouse being so hot. Once again he parted the flap enough to see through the small opening at the side of the window, and a breeze cooled his face. So far everything looked normal.

He'd had trouble breathing when he saw Mark Lassiter and his dog, but then he reminded himself that without a piece of his clothing, the dog wouldn't find him.

He checked his watch. Carter would be speaking soon. Donelson touched the cell phone, then sighted the podium with his scope, lining the crosshairs in the center.

Ten minutes and the dam would be history.

74

Once Max left, Jenna alerted Alex to what was going on, then she turned to Junior. "You know Donelson—what's he thinking right now? Will he kill Carter?"

"That's a hard one." The big man looked at her and shook his head. "I wouldn't have thought he'd kill Joe and Katherine, or Paul. He must've lost it."

Jenna's cell phone pinged with a text. "Alex found his truck parked behind the bank. So he has to be here somewhere. And she can't get Carter to forgo his speech—he doesn't believe he's in danger."

Junior snorted. "Sounds about like the Harrison Carter I know."

"If Donelson set a bomb, how would he set it off?"

Junior scratched his head. "Funny you ask that. He used dynamite on one of the beaver dams, but the other one, he used C-4 and a cell phone."

So Max probably wasn't dealing with a timer . . . maybe a cell phone to set it off. She scanned the park. Donelson had to be hiding in plain sight. But where? He was a hunter . . . and she wasn't. Jenna liked to hear the dogs run, but that was the extent of her hunting desire. She turned to Junior. "If you were going to shoot Carter, where would you do it from?"

"Somewhere high—that way I'd have a clear line of sight. Maybe a tree or—"

"The treehouse!"

They both spoke at the same time.

Jenna turned and studied the structure. It had a direct line of fire to the stage. What if Donelson had hung the signs?

She started to the treehouse and stopped. If she climbed the steps, he would hear her. Jenna turned to Junior. "I need you to create a diversion to draw Donelson's attention if he's in the treehouse. Can you do that?"

He thought a second, then his lips turned up in a lopsided grin. "You betcha."

While Junior ambled toward the stage, Jenna called Alex and filled her in as she worked her way around to the steps. The small opening where the slide accessed the treehouse had a flap with "Keep Out" on it. The back opening at the top of the steps had the same type of flap.

She glanced toward the stage again. Junior was talking to Wayne, then he hopped up on the stage and grabbed the microphone and a loud screech sounded.

"Is this thing on?" His voice boomed through the speakers. "Yeah, I think it is. Well, I'm gonna sing you a song while we wait for our illustrious former mayor to get through kissing babies."

While everyone's attention was on Wayne and a couple of Carter's bodyguards as they scrambled to stop Junior, Jenna silently climbed the steps.

She reached the top and inched the flap aside. Donelson knelt by the window with his back half turned from her.

A cell phone was in his left hand, and he was punching a button.

75

G em had her front paws against the wall, barking up at the ceiling, but so far Max hadn't been able to see a bomb. He needed more light. "See if you can find a light switch."

The beam from the K-9 officer's flashlight bounced on the wall. "Found it."

A light flickered on, revealing black cables running along the top of the wall. Max aimed the flashlight at the ceiling and followed the black wires.

His heart almost stopped when he saw a patch of white. Then he saw the cell phone. "Found it! Take Gem and get out of here."

"Not leaving you."

"There's no need in both of us staying. I've had some bomb training. You?"

"Only in training Gem on how to detect explosives, not how to disarm them."

"Then go."

"Told you I wasn't leaving."

He admired Mark's courage but questioned his sanity. "You don't happen to have a ladder in your SUV, do you?"

"Sorry."

"I can't reach the bomb." Sweat beaded Max's face. "Is there a bench anywhere?"

"I don't see any. Why don't I get on my hands and knees and you stand on my back."

It would have to do. "Okay."

Seconds later, Max had his shoes off and was balanced on the K-9 deputy's back. The cell phone had a wire attached to it—probably to the ringer. From there a wire ran to a detonator stuck in the C-4. At least it was simple.

But what if it were more complex than it looked? What if Donelson had put in a code in case someone pulled the wire out, triggering the bomb?

The phone rang.

His fingers shook as he gripped the wire.

76

Drop the cell phone!" Jenna yelled as she pulled herself inside the treehouse and held her gun on him.

"Too late. It's already ringing. Third ring and the bomb blows."

"End the call!"

She heard the second ring coming from the phone.

Jenna launched herself at Donelson, knocking the phone from his hand. She scrambled to get it from where it landed on the floor. Donelson grabbed her.

The third ring whirred from the phone.

He turned his head toward the dam.

Feet rang on the steps, and Alex tore the flap from the opening.

"Todd Donelson, you're under arrest."

77

The cell phone rang a second time, and he yanked the wires from the C-4.

Max held his breath.

After the third ring, it stopped. Adrenaline surged through him. They were alive.

He released the breath and pressed his palm against his chest. *Thank you, God.*

He hopped off Mark's back on wobbly legs and sagged against the wall.

"You did it!"

"*We* did it," Max said.

A couple of hours later, he joined Jenna at the park, and they drove to the dam. Darkness had fallen and the fireworks display was going ahead as planned. Max spread two beach towels on the grass, and he sat next to Jenna as she wrapped her arms around her knees.

"I'm glad both ordeals are over," she said.

"Yeah." They were both quiet a minute, then Max said, "I understand Donelson is under suicide watch."

"Yeah. He completely lost it."

"And I missed Harrison Carter's speech. Did he say anything important?"

"He made the announcement that an auto parts manufacturing company was locating in Pearl Springs."

"That'll mean jobs for the area," he said. "So, Carter has done some good."

"But at what price? And if he's elected, how honest is he going to be?"

Max leaned back on his elbow. "He might not get elected. I got a call earlier from the lead FBI investigator who's looking into TerraQuest. The state appraiser involved in the land purchases for the dam and reservoir is asking for a deal—he'll name names in exchange for no prison time. Not sure if the DA will meet those terms, but the very offer indicates there's something there. It might be enough to derail Carter's campaign."

"How about Earl Donelson's and my grandfather's deaths?" Jenna asked.

"Short of Carter confessing, I don't think we can build a case—everyone but the former mayor and Eric Darby are dead, and I'm not sure if the DA can build a case on what Darby overheard. I'm sorry."

"Me too. Even so, you did a good job today, TBI Agent Maxwell Anderson."

"On disarming the bomb or this?" He nodded toward the beach towels they were sitting side by side on.

"Both." She turned and grinned at him. "You're a handy man to have around—always prepared."

He laughed. "I *was* a Boy Scout. But you'll have to thank my niece for the beach towels—she left them in the truck the last time I took her and my nephew water-skiing."

"You water-ski?" Her eyes widened. "I love water-skiing. And rock climbing. And riding horses . . ."

Max held her gaze, his heart beating against his ribs. He'd never felt this way about a woman before. Jenna had totally captured his heart. "I think it's going to be fun learning about each other . . . don't you?"

He held his breath, waiting for her answer.

She leaned close and kissed him lightly on the lips before she pulled away. "It's going to be interesting for sure."

"That was a teasing kiss."

"There're too many people around for a *real* one."

"There's no moon and no one even close by." Max pulled her back into his arms. She slid her arms around his neck as his lips claimed hers, tentatively at first, then his world narrowed to everything but the way she responded.

They broke apart just as a whistle split the air. He looked up at the night sky as an aerial exploded in glowing embers that flickered as they fell back to earth, followed by a rocket exploding in a star pattern.

The fireworks had started.

78

ONE WEEK LATER

Jenna zipped up Alex's creamy white dress. Today Alex was her friend, not her boss. "You look . . ."

"So not like me." Alex smoothed her hands down the knee-length sheath and turned to see the back of the dress.

"Actually I was looking for a better word than amazing, but it fits perfectly."

Alex raised her eyebrows and looked at her in the mirror. "Flattery won't get you a raise."

They both turned as the door to Dani Bennett's bedroom opened and she entered with the bouquet. On her heels were the grandmothers—Judith Stone and Mae Richmond.

Judith handed her granddaughter a veil she'd made and kissed her on the cheek. "You look so beautiful."

"Thank you, but I'd feel better in a pair of jeans. Nathan won't know me."

They all laughed. Jenna scanned the faces in the room. These were her friends. Why hadn't she come home earlier?

Dani handed Alex the bouquet. "Is this what you had in mind?"

The bride took a swift intake of breath and pressed her fingers to her lips.

"It's beautiful and exactly what I wanted." Alex lifted the bouquet to her nose. "It smells heavenly."

Dani had mixed her grandmother's lavender roses with magnolia and gardenia blossoms.

"Dani!" The name came out more of a gasp from Alex. "What do I see on your hand?"

Dani beamed. "I wasn't going to wear it—I don't want to steal any of your day—but I couldn't take it off!"

She held up her hand, and Jenna admired the beautiful emerald-cut diamond on her finger.

"Don't you dare take it off!" Alex said. "What? Where? When did Mark propose? Spill it, girlfriend."

Dani glanced at the grandmothers. "At the trials in Kentucky—those two have known it for a couple of days. We haven't set a date or anything, but I'm thinking early fall."

"I'm so happy for you, and Mark is a lucky man," Jenna said. Dani deserved happiness, especially after what happened in April when their former Pearl Springs pastor tried to kill her.

They all turned when someone knocked on the door. "Is it safe to come in?" a male voice asked.

Alex nodded, and Jenna hurried to let Sheriff Stone in.

"Your husband-to-be is getting a little nervous up on the mountain by himself," he said.

"That's our cue to leave." Judith kissed her granddaughter again. "I'm so happy for you."

Outside Mae's house, two four-wheel-drive golf carts waited to take them to the top of the mountain. The two golf carts had been ferrying the guests up the mountain, and the last trip had taken Nathan and his best man, Mark, as well as the new pastor of Community Fellowship who would be performing the ceremony.

Jenna rode with Dani while the grandmothers accompanied the bride. Jenna sighed. It was a gorgeous day for the ceremony with the late afternoon sun casting a golden hue over the mountain, giving everything a dreamy look. Chairs lined either side of a red carpet, and Jenna waited while two deputies helped Mae and Judith out of the cart and led them to their seats.

Max appeared when Jenna stepped out of the cart. Her heart hiccupped when his gaze swept over her. "You are beautiful," he said and brushed back a strand of her hair the wind had blown across her face before he offered his arm.

A tremor raced through her when he looped his arm in hers. "You're not so bad yourself."

He stood a little taller. "Wasn't sure you'd notice."

How could she not? Even though the wedding was casual, he'd dressed in dark slacks and an open-neck white shirt.

"Mind if I sit with you?" he asked.

"Not at all." Jenna's attention was caught to the front when Wayne lifted a fiddle and began the wedding march. Joining him was Hayes Smithfield on the guitar. She had no idea Wayne could play the fiddle, and play it well, and the same thing for Hayes. They all stood as Sheriff Stone escorted Alex to the front.

"Dearly beloved, we are gathered here to celebrate the union of Alexis Stone and Nathan Landry . . ."

Twenty minutes later, Nathan kissed his bride and the pastor presented the newly married couple. Everyone cheered as they walked to the waiting golf cart with Wayne and Hayes playing "You Make My Dreams."

"Alex and Nathan hope you will join them at Mae's for food and refreshments," the pastor said. "Oh, and ladies, gather around— Alexis is going to toss her bouquet."

Jenna didn't move.

"You're not going?" Max whispered.

"No." She never liked this part of the wedding ceremony. "Been there done this."

Countless times.

"You have to—Alex will be disappointed."

"Let Dani catch it—she's already engaged."

He nudged. "Go."

Jenna supposed she should . . . and joined the other women waiting for Alex to toss her bouquet.

"Okay, ladies," Alex said. "Let's see who's next."

She turned around and tossed the flowers over her shoulder in a high arc.

In slow motion, the bouquet floated down and landed in Jenna's hands as she stretched them out at the last moment.

ACKNOWLEDGMENTS

As we all know, books don't just happen. It takes a collaborative effort, and I have so many to thank.

My friends and family for understanding when I have a deadline and for encouraging me when I hit a wall.

The fine team I have at Revell—my editors, Rachel McRae and Kristin Kornoelje, and proofreader Barbara Curtis. Thank you for making my stories so much better. I'd be lost without you!

To the art, editorial, marketing, and sales team at Revell, especially Brianne Decker and Karen Steele, who have to deal with me directly—thank you for all your hard work. And to the ones behind the scenes, you're awesome!

To Julie Gwinn, thank you for your direction and for working so tirelessly with me and for being my friend.

To Patricia Preston, who helped me brainstorm this story.

To the many contributors at the Crimescenewriter2 group who are so willing to answer my questions, Wes Harris in particular.

To my readers . . . you are awesome! Thank you for reading my stories. Without you, my books wouldn't exist.

As always, to Jesus, who gives me the words.

Patricia Bradley is the author of *Standoff, Obsession, Crosshairs,* and *Deception,* as well as the Memphis Cold Case novels and Logan Point series. Bradley is the winner of an Inspirational Reader's Choice Award, a Selah Award, and a Daphne du Maurier Award; she was a Carol Award finalist; and three of her books were included in anthologies that debuted on the *USA Today* bestseller list. Cofounder of Aiming for Healthy Families, Inc., Bradley is a member of American Christian Fiction Writers and Sisters in Crime. She makes her home in Mississippi. Learn more at www.PTBradley.com.

WANT MORE FROM
PATRICIA BRADLEY?

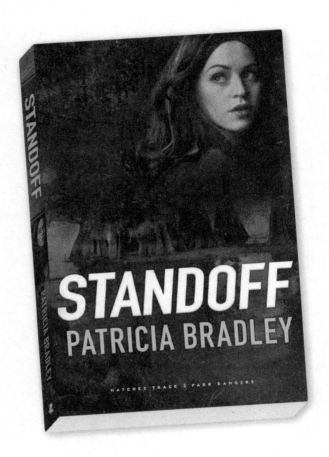

Turn the page to start reading the first book in another thrilling series!

1

Brooke Danvers checked her watch. Her dad had said six and it was almost that. She quickly twisted her hair into a ponytail and then buckled her Sig Sauer to her waist. While she hadn't been sworn in as a law enforcement ranger yet, Mississippi was an open-carry state, and her dad had okayed her wearing it.

She hadn't stopped smiling since he'd asked if she wanted to ride along with him tonight. It didn't even bother her that he'd chosen Sunday night because there wouldn't be many cars out and about.

Brooke glanced toward the flat-brimmed hat that she'd worn all day at Melrose, the almost two-hundred-year-old mansion where she'd led tours. At times it felt as though the August heat and humidity would cook her head. She wouldn't need the hat tonight, though, and left it sitting on her childhood bed.

Returning home after fifteen years while contractors finished the remodel on her water-damaged apartment was proving to be an experience. She'd always heard grown children shouldn't return to the nest, and now she knew why. At her place, she came and went as she pleased without anyone asking questions. But now it was almost like she'd stepped back into her teenage years. Not that she wasn't thankful her parents had offered to let her move into her old room, but it would be good to get back in her own apartment in a couple of weeks. The chimes from the grandfather clock sent her hurrying down the hall to her dad's home office.

It was empty. He'd said he had work to do before they left . . . She quickly walked to her mom's studio.

"Where's Dad?" she asked.

Her mom turned from her easel. "He got a call and left. Said to tell you if you still wanted to do the ride along, text Gary to pick you up."

Disappointment was swift, and Brooke ground her teeth to keep from letting it show.

"He said something about you riding with him tomorrow night."

That brightened her mood slightly. Her phone dinged with a text. Gary, the retiring ranger she was replacing.

Are you riding with me?

She quickly texted him.

Yes. What time?

Give me an hour and I'll pick you up.

She sent him a thumbs-up emoji and hooked her phone on her belt.

"Come see what I'm working on," her mom said.

Brooke edged into the room. It wasn't often she got a chance to see an unfinished work by her mother. The painting was of her very pregnant sister. "Oh, wow," she said. "That's beautiful. She'll love it."

"I hope so. Meghan's feeling kind of . . ."

"Fat? That's what she told me the other day," Brooke said. "I tried to tell her that wasn't true, and maybe this will show her."

"I'm glad you like it. I should have it finished in time to take with the others to Knoxville next month."

The baby's due date was a couple of months away, just after her mom's gallery showing of her work ended. They both turned as the doorbell rang. It couldn't be Gary already, and besides, he would just honk. "I'll get it," Brooke said and hurried to open the front door.

"Jeremy?" she said, her stomach fluttering at the sight of one of Natchez's most eligible bachelors. Had she forgotten a date?

He looked behind him then turned back to Brooke with laughter in his eyes. "I think so."

Heat flushed her face, and it had more to do with the broad shoulders and lean body of the man on her doorstep than the temperature. "I wasn't expecting you. I don't have a lot of time, but do you want to come in?"

"Since it's a little hot and humid out here, coming in would be good," he teased. "And I apologize for dropping by without calling, but I was afraid you'd tell me you were busy."

Brooke steeled herself against the subtle citrus fragrance of his cologne as he walked past her. She'd had exactly two dates with Jeremy Steele and hadn't figured out why he was even interested in her. She was so not his type. The handsome widower tended to lean more toward blondes.

"Hello, Mrs. Danvers," Jeremy said to her mother, who had followed her to the living room.

"How many times have I told you to call me Vivian?"

"I'll try to remember that," he said with a thousand-watt smile.

"Good. A thirtysomething calling me Mrs. Danvers makes me feel old," she replied. "And since I know you didn't come to see me, I'll go back to my painting."

"Good to see you . . . Vivian." Then he turned to Brooke and glanced at her uniform. "Are you working tonight?"

"Sort of," she said. "I was going to ride along with Dad on his patrol, but he cancelled and turned me over to another ranger. Why?"

"I know it's last minute, but I was hoping you'd have time to join me at King's Tavern," he said. "I have a hankering for one of their flatbreads."

Her mouth watered at the thought. Brooke hadn't eaten since lunch, and she could do last minute, at least this time. But the question of why *her* kept bobbing to the surface. Ignoring it, she said, "That sounds good. I'll text Gary to pick me up later."

"Gary?"

She grinned at him, tempted to describe the aging ranger as a hunk but instead settled for the truth. "He's the ranger I'm replacing when he *retires*."

Red crept into Jeremy's face. "Oh, that guy. Are you even sworn in yet?"

"No, that's next week. I talked my dad into letting me get a little early practice." It helped having a father who was the district ranger, even if he wasn't overjoyed about her becoming a law enforcement ranger. Then she looked down. "I need to change first."

"You're fine like you are," he said.

Maybe to him, but she was not about to go on a date wearing a National Park Service uniform and a Sig strapped to her waist. "Give me five minutes."

After Brooke changed into a lavender sundress and slipped into sandals, she gave herself a brief once-over. While the dress showed no cleavage, it accentuated curves the NPS uniform hid. She freed her hair from the ponytail and put the elastic holder in her purse. In this heat, she might have to put it up again.

Brooke checked her makeup. She rarely wore anything other than pink gloss. Thick lashes framed her eyes and the sun had deepened her olive skin to a nice tan. Brooke wasn't sure where she got her darker complexion and hair since her mom and sister, and even her dad, were fair and blond, but she wasn't complaining.

Tonight she wanted something more and added a shimmering gloss to her lips. Then she took a deep breath and slowly blew it out. Didn't do much good with her heart still thudding in her chest.

Why was Jeremy pursuing *her*? The women usually seen on his arm were ones who could mix and mingle with the rich and famous. Women who could further his career. Jeremy was a Mississippi state senator with his sights set on Washington like his daddy, while she was a National Park Service ranger who didn't care one thing about leaving Natchez.

Her heart kicked into high gear. Had the M-word just crossed her thoughts? Impossible. It wasn't only that she wasn't his type, he definitely wasn't hers. She was a simple girl with a simple lifestyle—nothing like the Steeles.

In the 1850s, half the millionaires in the United States lived in Natchez, and the Steeles were among them. A hundred and seventy years later, the family's holdings had increased substantially, not to mention the Steele men had a long history of public service.

Jeremy's dad was the retiring US senator and his son was poised to take his place in the next election. His photo appeared regularly in the *Natchez Democrat*, often with a beautiful woman on his arm. And never the same one.

She sighed. If they lived in England, he would be royalty, and she would be the commoner who ended up with a broken heart.

Brooke chided herself about being melodramatic and hurried to her mom's studio. "Jeremy and I are grabbing something to eat," she said.

Her mom laid her brush down. "What about your ride along?"

"I'll catch up to Gary later," she said.

When she rejoined Jeremy, his eyes widened, and he whistled. "Nice," he said.

Jeremy Steele knew how to make a woman feel special. As they stepped out of the house, she immediately noticed the ten-degree drop in temperature from when Jeremy first arrived and nodded at the thunderheads that had rolled in. "Guess that means we won't leave the top down."

"I think we can make it to the tavern before it starts."

Ten minutes later Jeremy escorted her into King's Tavern, where the original brick walls and dark wooden beams added to the mystique of the inn that had been rumored to have a ghost. The tantalizing aroma of steak drew her gaze to the open grill, but she had her heart set on one of their wood-fired flatbreads.

"Inside or out?" Jeremy asked.

"The backyard, if you don't think it'll rain," she said.

"If it does, we'll simply come in." He gave the waitress their drink order, sweet tea for both of them, and let her know where to find them. They had their choice of picnic tables and chose the one on the hill. Once they were seated, Jeremy reached across, taking her hand. His touch and the intensity in his brown eyes almost took her breath away. "I'm glad you came."

"Me too," Brooke said, trying not to sound breathy. The question worrying around in her head wouldn't wait any longer. "Why me?"

"What do you mean?"

"Why are you interested in dating me? We don't travel in the same circles."

"But we do. We've gone to church together since we were kids."

"And you sit in your family's pew clear across the sanctuary."

His eyes twinkled. "We don't have a family pew."

She laughed. "I'd hate to be the one who sat in your mom's seat some Sunday."

"You're funny," he said. "That's one of the things I like about you."

"But I'm so different from the women you usually date." There. She'd said it.

He lightly stroked the heel of her palm. "That's what I like best. You're real . . . not saying anything bad about anyone I've dated, but honestly, sometimes I think the aura of the Steele name is the attraction. That and Dad's money." Then Jeremy smiled, popping dimples in his cheeks. "But you were never like that. Even in high school you were never afraid to tell it like it was."

Heat infused her cheeks. She'd been accused of that many times, usually by someone who didn't want to hear the truth. "I'm working on not being so blunt," she said. "I hope I never hurt your feelings."

"I won't say never," he said with a wink, "but you never said anything that didn't need saying."

Okay, she'd been rude and hadn't fallen all over him because of who he was . . . Before she could ask *why* again, the waitress approached with their drinks, and Brooke pulled her hand away from Jeremy's, missing his touch immediately. Maybe she should let go of her questions and let their relationship play out.

Once the waitress left with their orders, Jeremy took her hand again. "I've looked a long time for the right person."

His brown eyes held her gaze. He surely didn't mean her. Did he? "What about Molly? I'd hate for her to get attached to me and then we stop seeing each other."

"I don't plan for that to happen. And Molly is already crazy about you."

Brooke couldn't keep from smiling. His six-year-old daughter was a sweetheart.

"How about if we take it slow?" he asked. "Get to know one another?"

"No pressure?"

"No pressure."

Her phone dinged and she glanced at the screen. A text from Gary.

Pick you up in an hour?

Brooke hesitated, torn between wanting to spend more time with Jeremy and getting practical experience on her job. If the text had been from her dad, it wouldn't even be a question—she had so much to learn from him, but Gary, not so much. She'd known him all her life and he'd always been laid-back, never wanting to climb the ladder within the park service. But if her dad thought she should ride with him . . . With a sigh, she looked up from her phone. "Can you have me back to my house in forty-five minutes?"

"Do I want to? Nope," he said. "But I can."

She texted Gary an okay, wishing it was her dad she would be riding with. Then Brooke stared at her phone a second. What had been so important for her dad to stand her up?

DON'T MISS THE REST OF THE
PEARL RIVER SERIES

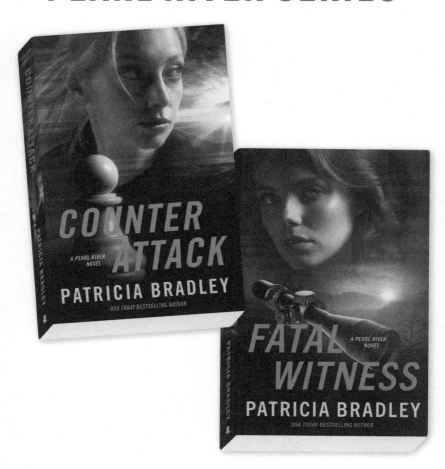

The gripping Pearl River series takes readers deep into the heart of the Cumberland Plateau, where secrets lurk beneath the seemingly tranquil façade.

Revell
a division of Baker Publishing Group
RevellBooks.com

Available wherever books and ebooks are sold.

Find more mystery and romance in the Natchez Trace Park Rangers series

Set in the sultry South, these romantic suspense reads will have you wiping your brow and looking over your shoulder.

"Bradley's novels are ALWAYS page-turners."
—*Booklist*

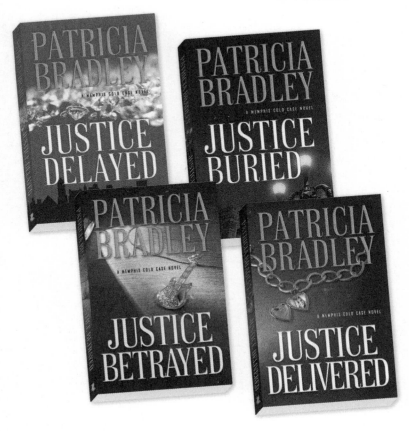

Don't miss the MEMPHIS COLD CASE series from bestselling author PATRICIA BRADLEY.

Meet

Patricia BRADLEY

PTBradley.com

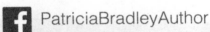

PatriciaBradleyAuthor

PTBradley1

PTBradley1